Grand Guignol Orchestra

4

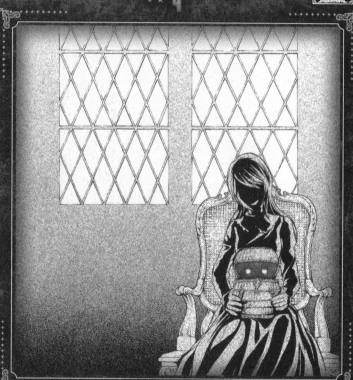

Story and Art by

Kaori Yuki

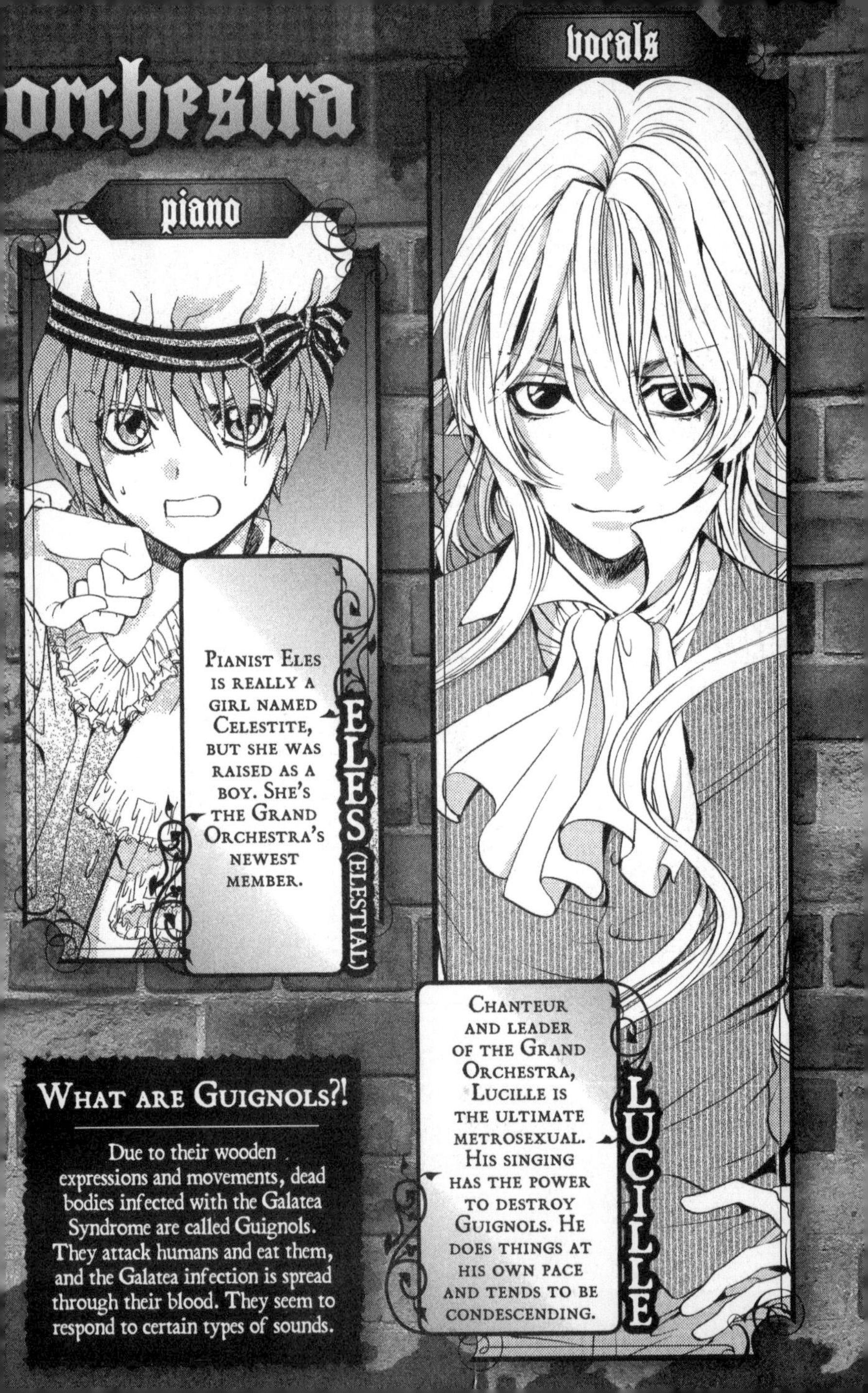
orchestra
vocals
LUCILLE
Chanteur and leader of the Grand Orchestra, Lucille is the ultimate metrosexual. His singing has the power to destroy Guignols. He does things at his own pace and tends to be condescending.
piano
ELES (ELESTIAL)
Pianist Eles is really a girl named Celestite, but she was raised as a boy. She's the Grand Orchestra's newest member.

What are Guignols?!

Due to their wooden expressions and movements, dead bodies infected with the Galatea Syndrome are called Guignols. They attack humans and eat them, and the Galatea infection is spread through their blood. They seem to respond to certain types of sounds.

grand Guignol

MEMBER INTRODUCTIONS

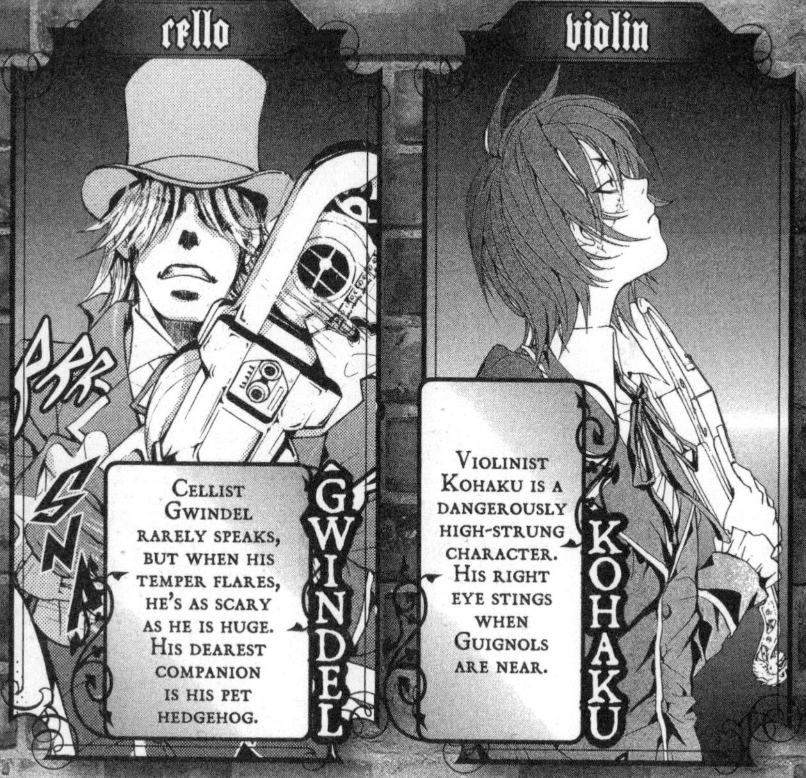

cello
violin
Cellist Gwindel rarely speaks, but when his temper flares, he's as scary as he is huge. His dearest companion is his pet hedgehog.
GWINDEL
Violinist Kohaku is a dangerously high-strung character. His right eye stings when Guignols are near.
KOHAKU

A bizarre plague that gives rise to man-eating zombies known as Guignols has overtaken the world. Lucille and his gang are the "unofficial" Grand Orchestra, willing to perform any piece of music for the right price. Lucille's Black Hymnal contains songs that can perform all sorts of miracles. What awaits this Guignol-hating group of traveling musicians?

grand Guignol orchestra

4

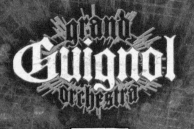

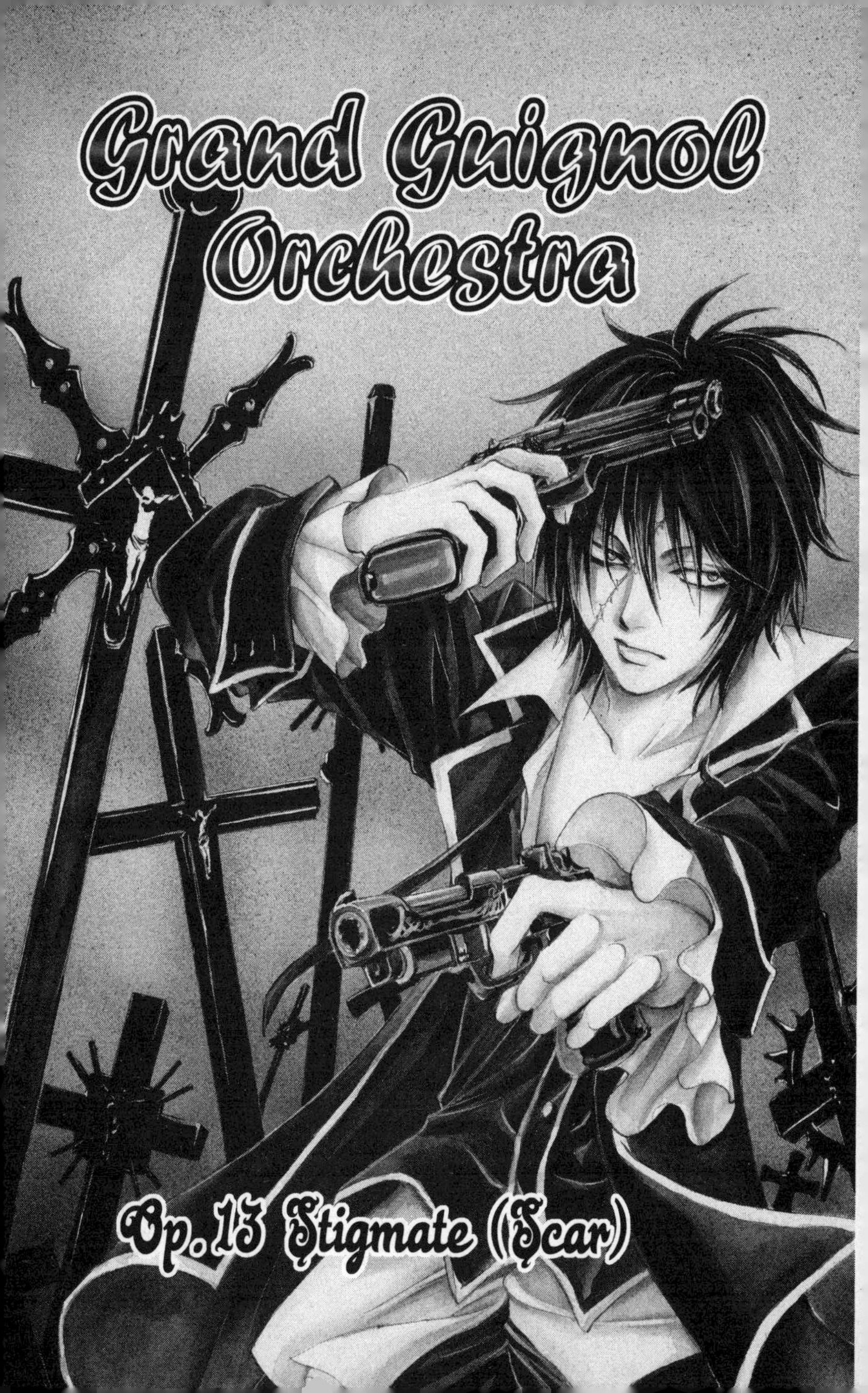
Grand Guignol Orchestra
Op.13 Stigmate (Scar)

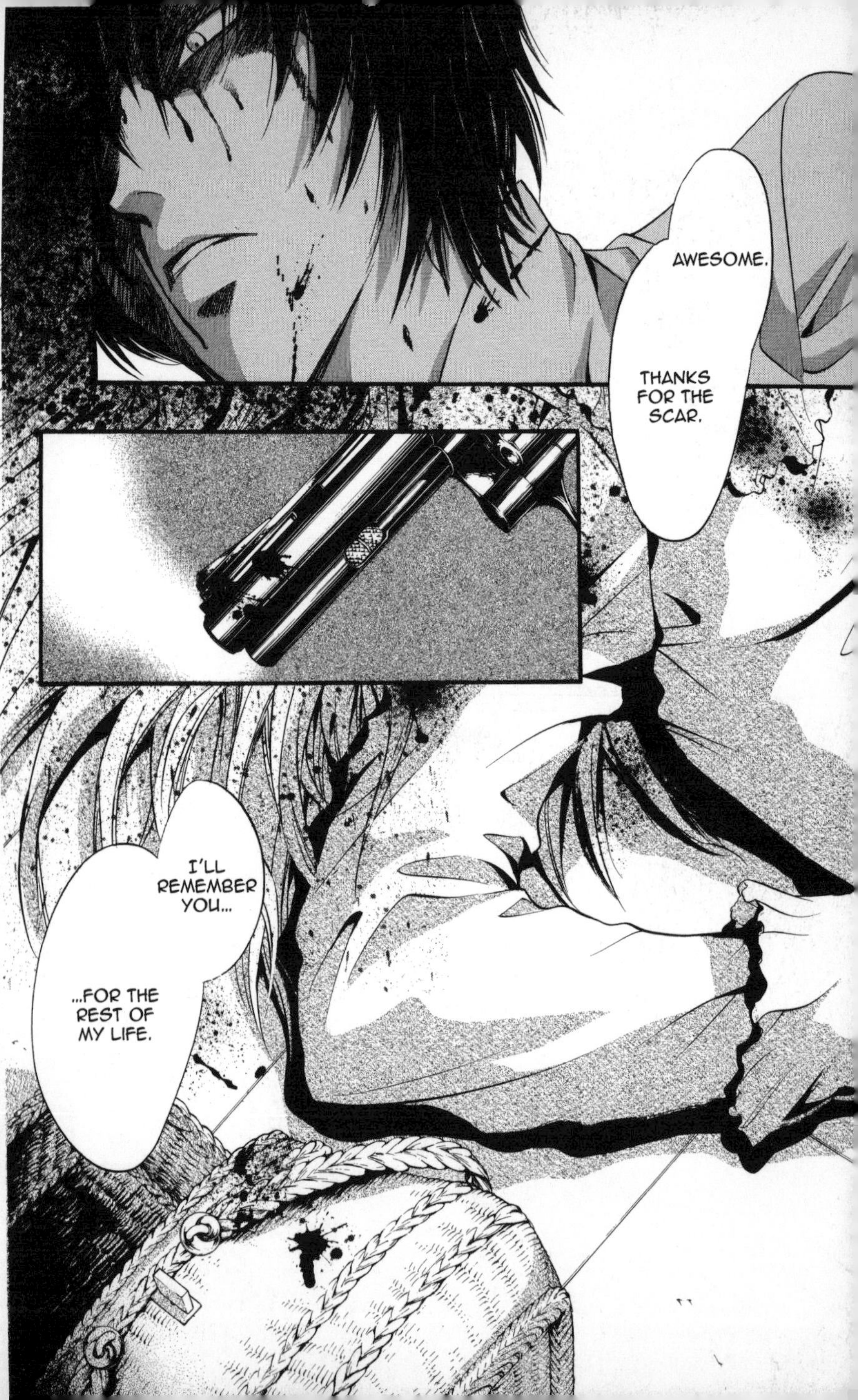
AWESOME.
THANKS FOR THE SCAR.
I'LL REMEMBER YOU...
...FOR THE REST OF MY LIFE.

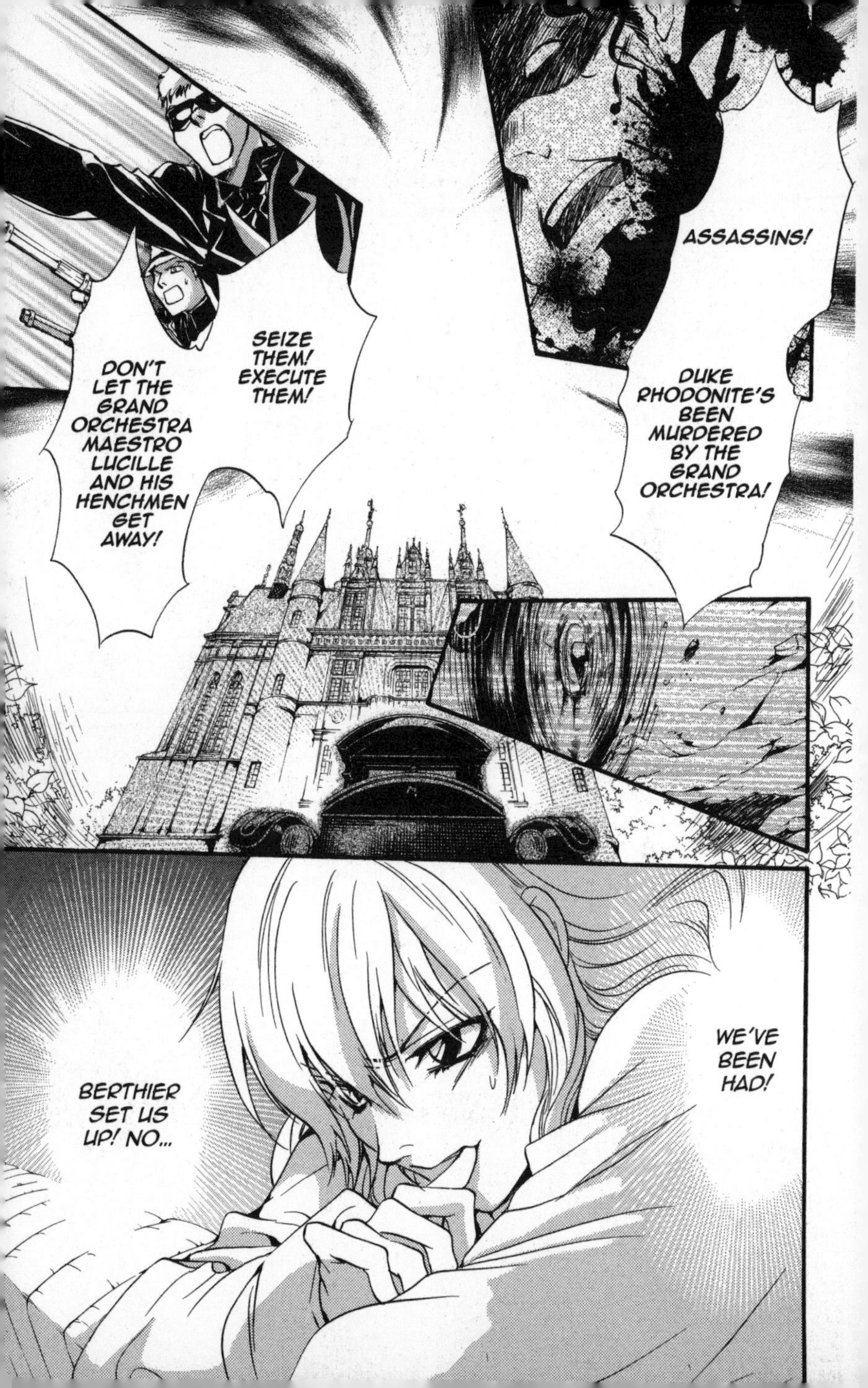
ASSASSINS!
DUKE RHODONITE'S BEEN MURDERED BY THE GRAND ORCHESTRA!
SEIZE THEM! EXECUTE THEM!
DON'T LET THE GRAND ORCHESTRA MAESTRO LUCILLE AND HIS HENCHMEN GET AWAY!
WE'VE BEEN HAD!
BERTHIER SET US UP! NO...

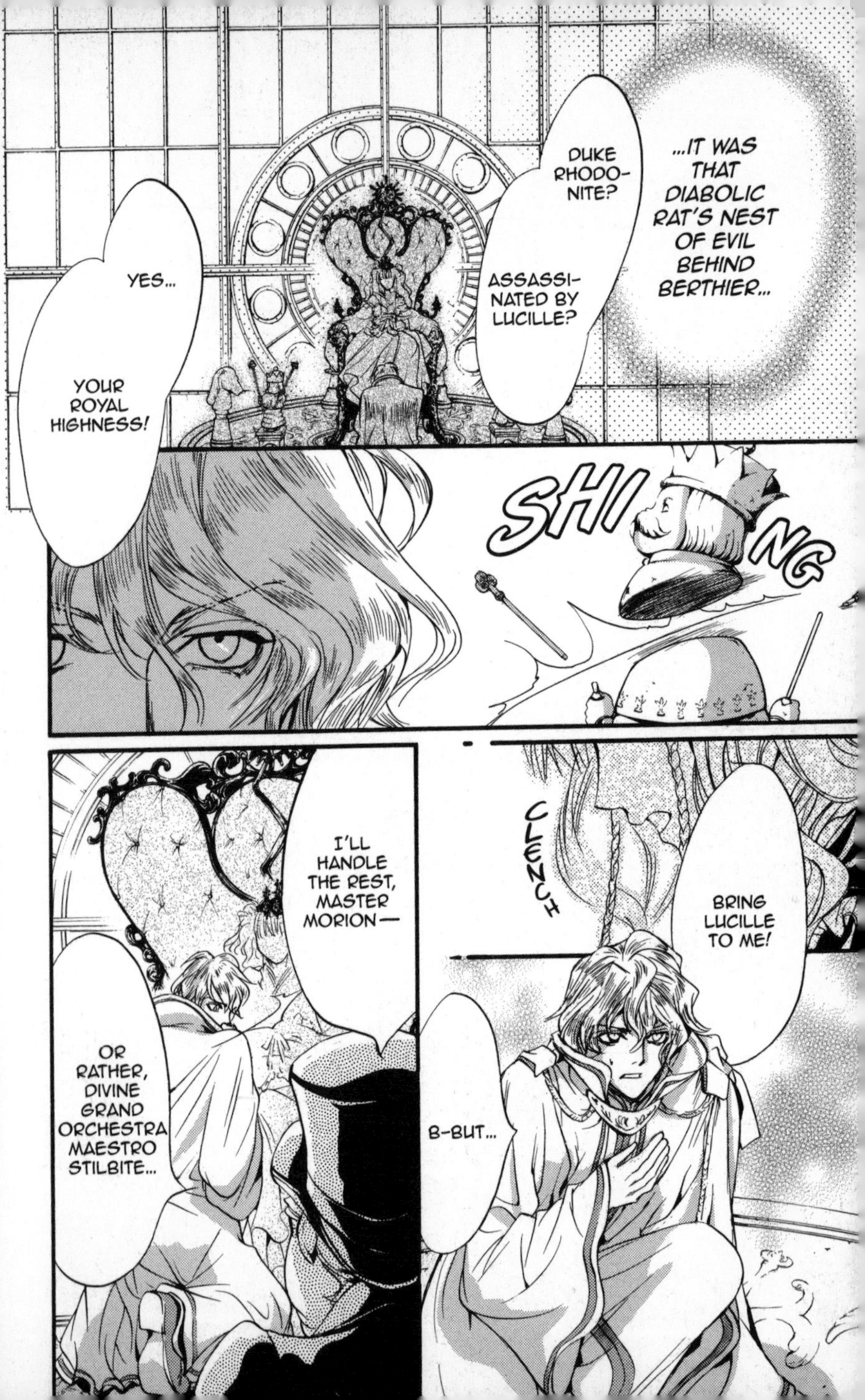
...IT WAS THAT DIABOLIC RAT'S NEST OF EVIL BEHIND BERTHIER...
DUKE RHODONITE?
ASSASSI-NATED BY LUCILLE?
YES...
YOUR ROYAL HIGHNESS!
SHI NG
BRING LUCILLE TO ME!
CLENCH
B-BUT...
I'LL HANDLE THE REST, MASTER MORION—
OR RATHER, DIVINE GRAND ORCHESTRA MAESTRO STILBITE...

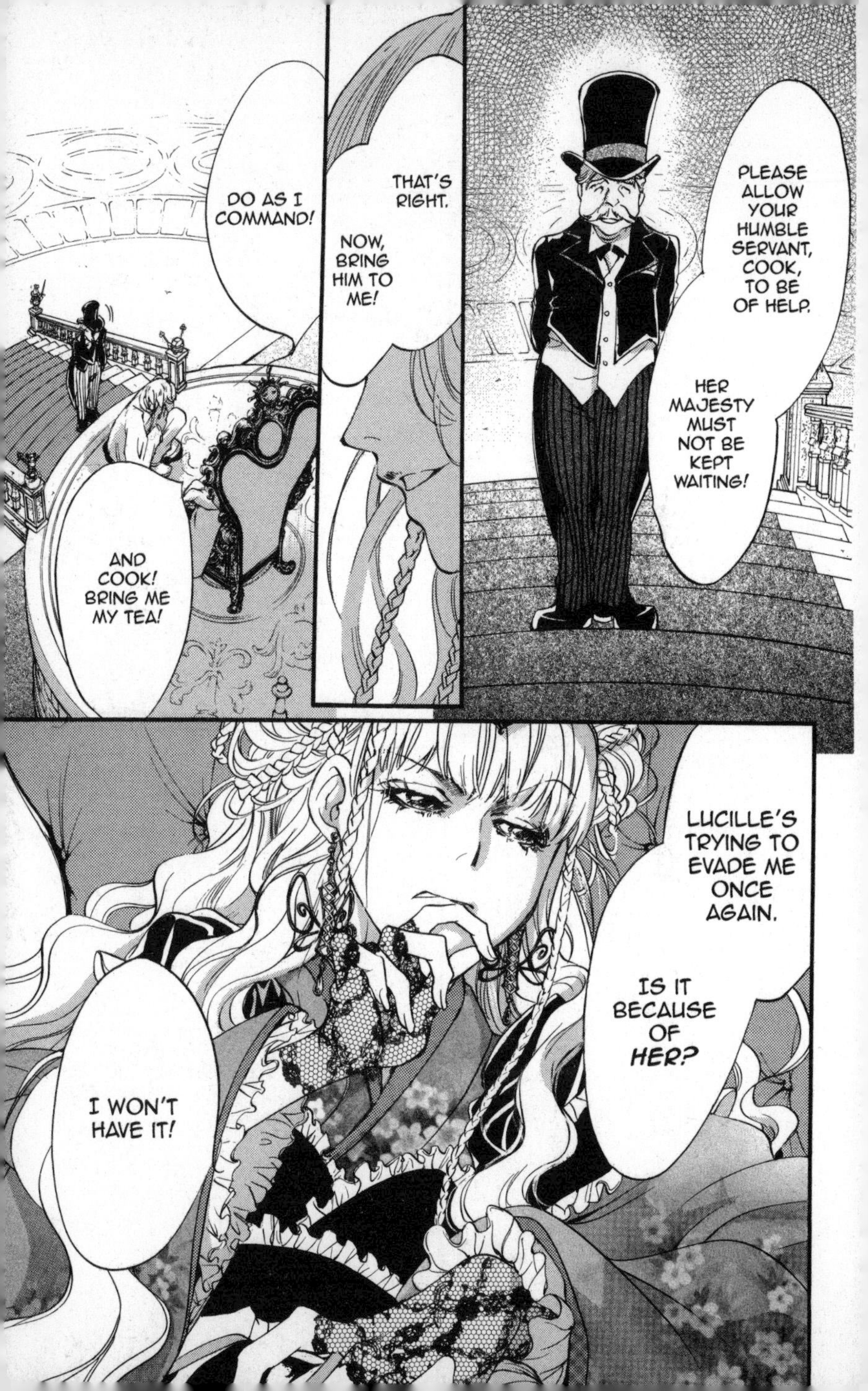
PLEASE ALLOW YOUR HUMBLE SERVANT, COOK, TO BE OF HELP.
HER MAJESTY MUST NOT BE KEPT WAITING!
THAT'S RIGHT.
NOW, BRING HIM TO ME!
DO AS I COMMAND!
AND COOK! BRING ME MY TEA!
LUCILLE'S TRYING TO EVADE ME ONCE AGAIN.
IS IT BECAUSE OF *HER?*
I WON'T HAVE IT!

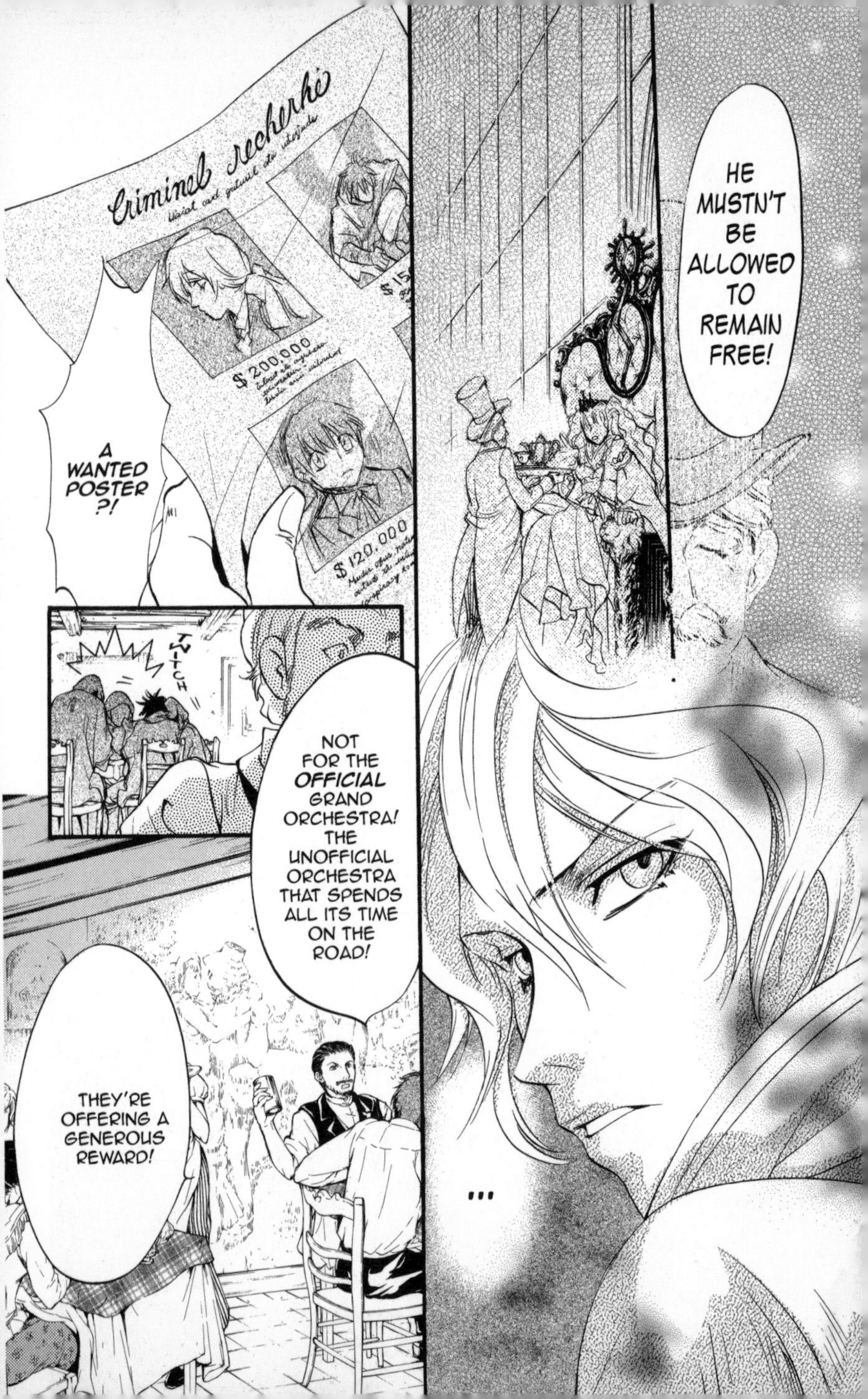
HE MUSTN'T BE ALLOWED TO REMAIN FREE!
...
$ 200,000
$ 120,000
A WANTED POSTER ?!
TWITCH
NOT FOR THE *OFFICIAL* GRAND ORCHESTRA! THE UNOFFICIAL ORCHESTRA THAT SPENDS ALL ITS TIME ON THE ROAD!
THEY'RE OFFERING A GENEROUS REWARD!

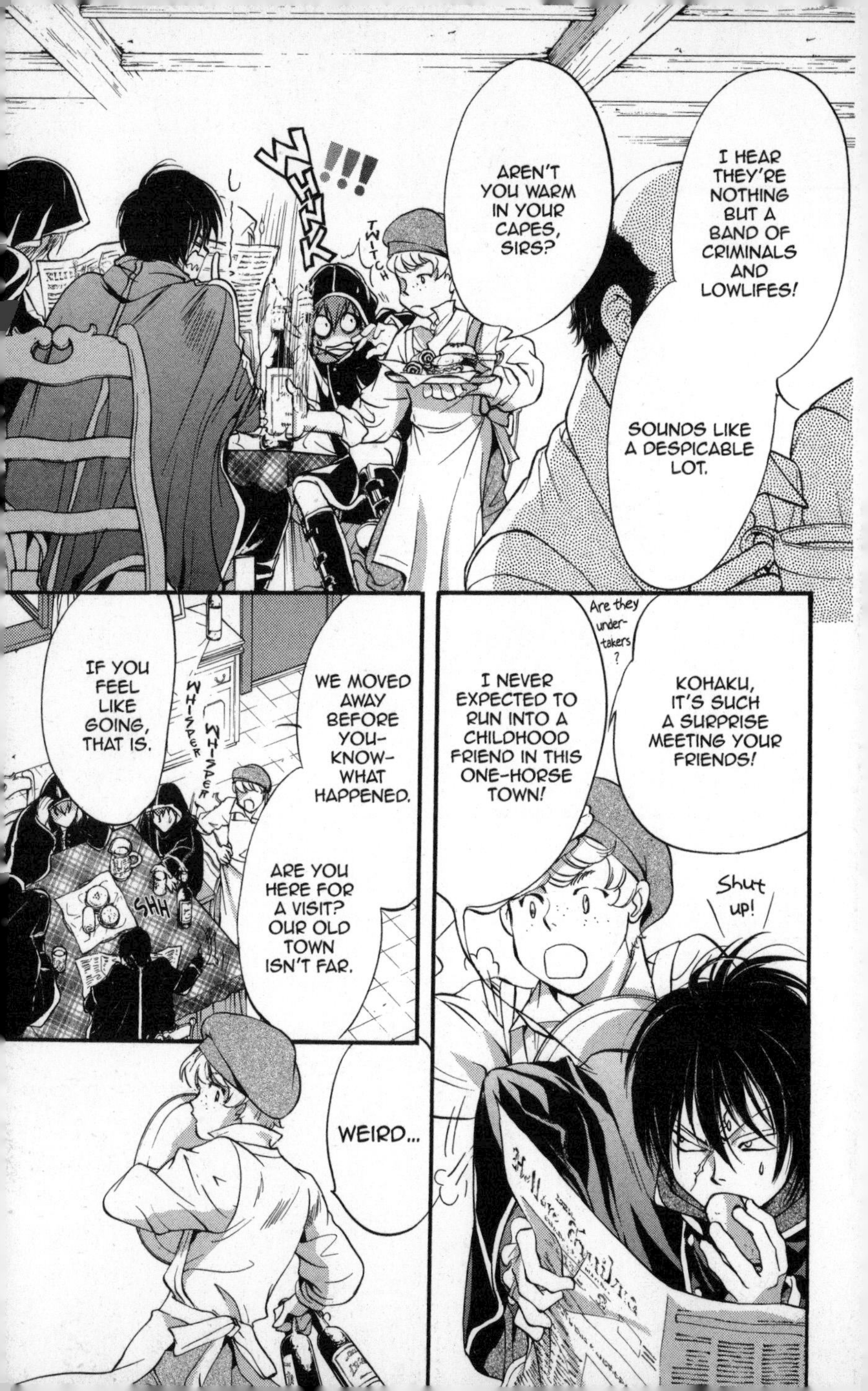
I HEAR THEY'RE NOTHING BUT A BAND OF CRIMINALS AND LOWLIFES!
AREN'T YOU WARM IN YOUR CAPES, SIRS?
TWITCH
SOUNDS LIKE A DESPICABLE LOT.
KOHAKU, IT'S SUCH A SURPRISE MEETING YOUR FRIENDS!
Are they under-takers?
I NEVER EXPECTED TO RUN INTO A CHILDHOOD FRIEND IN THIS ONE-HORSE TOWN!
Shut up!
WE MOVED AWAY BEFORE YOU-KNOW-WHAT HAPPENED.
ARE YOU HERE FOR A VISIT? OUR OLD TOWN ISN'T FAR.
IF YOU FEEL LIKE GOING, THAT IS.
WHISPER
WHISPER
SHH
WEIRD...

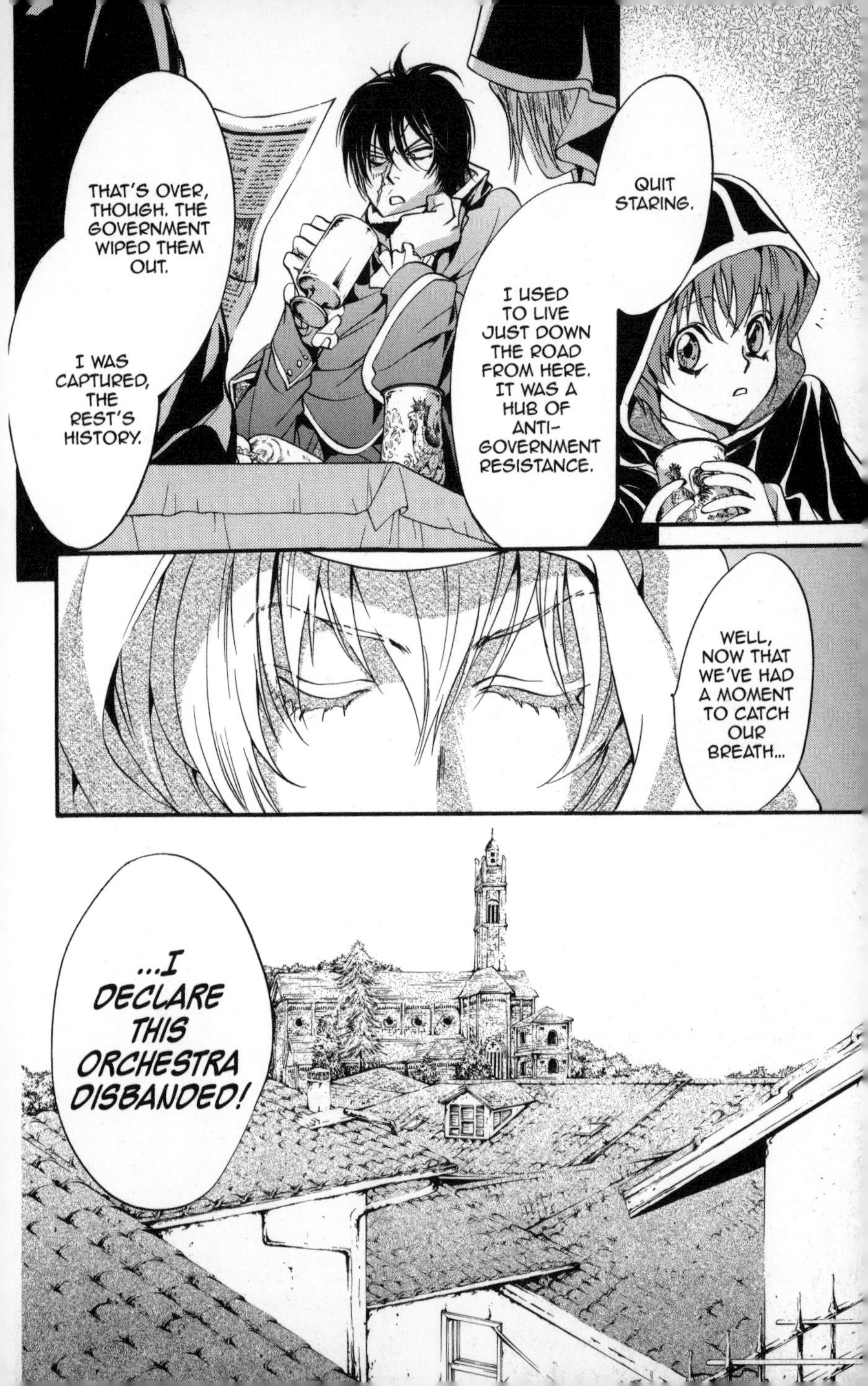
QUIT STARING.
I USED TO LIVE JUST DOWN THE ROAD FROM HERE. IT WAS A HUB OF ANTI-GOVERNMENT RESISTANCE.
THAT'S OVER, THOUGH. THE GOVERNMENT WIPED THEM OUT.
I WAS CAPTURED, THE REST'S HISTORY.
WELL, NOW THAT WE'VE HAD A MOMENT TO CATCH OUR BREATH...
...I DECLARE THIS ORCHESTRA DISBANDED!

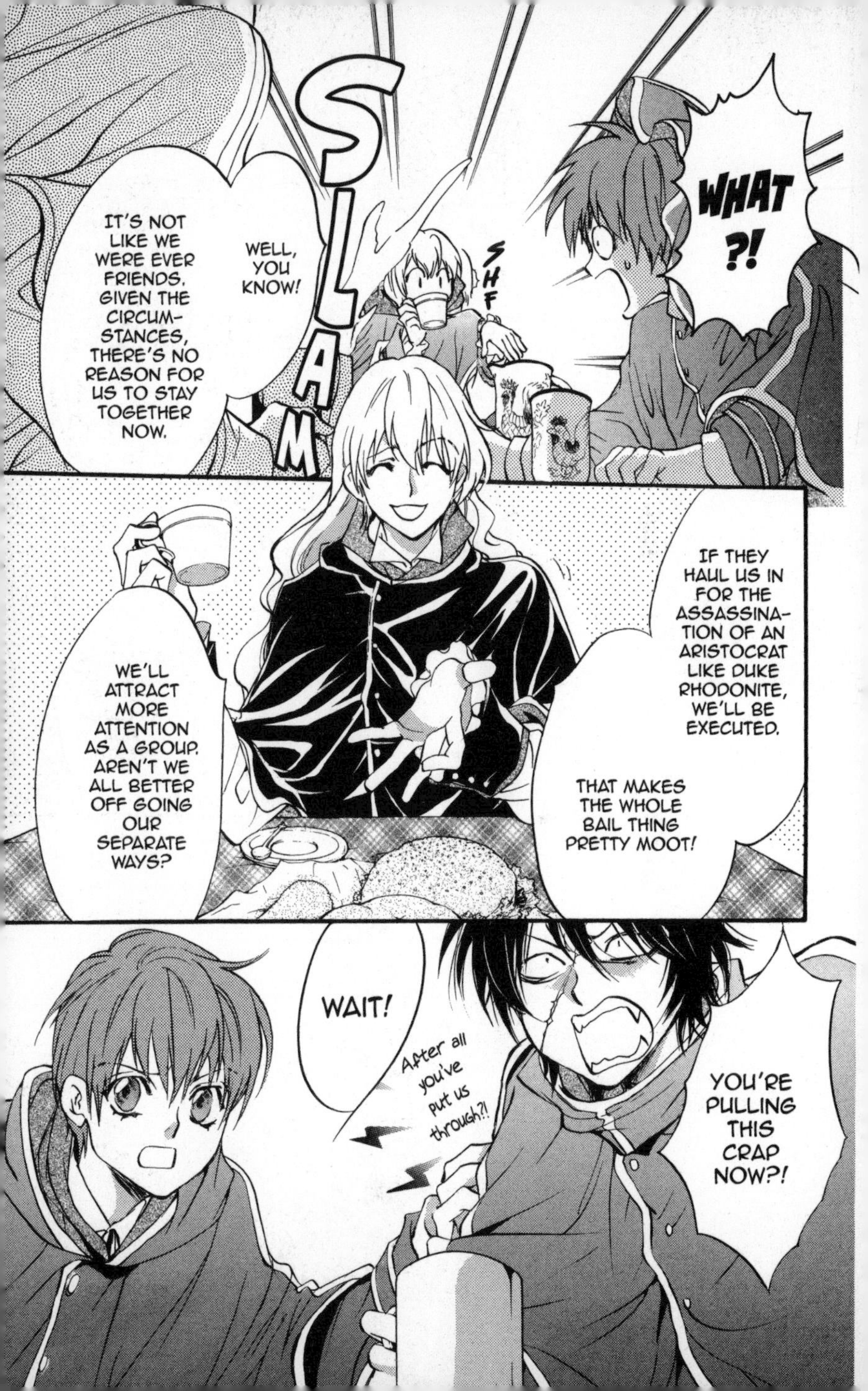
WHAT ?!
SHF
SLAM
WELL, YOU KNOW!
IT'S NOT LIKE WE WERE EVER FRIENDS. GIVEN THE CIRCUM-STANCES, THERE'S NO REASON FOR US TO STAY TOGETHER NOW.
IF THEY HAUL US IN FOR THE ASSASSINA-TION OF AN ARISTOCRAT LIKE DUKE RHODONITE, WE'LL BE EXECUTED.
THAT MAKES THE WHOLE BAIL THING PRETTY MOOT!
WE'LL ATTRACT MORE ATTENTION AS A GROUP. AREN'T WE ALL BETTER OFF GOING OUR SEPARATE WAYS?
YOU'RE PULLING THIS CRAP NOW?!
After all you've put us through?!
WAIT!

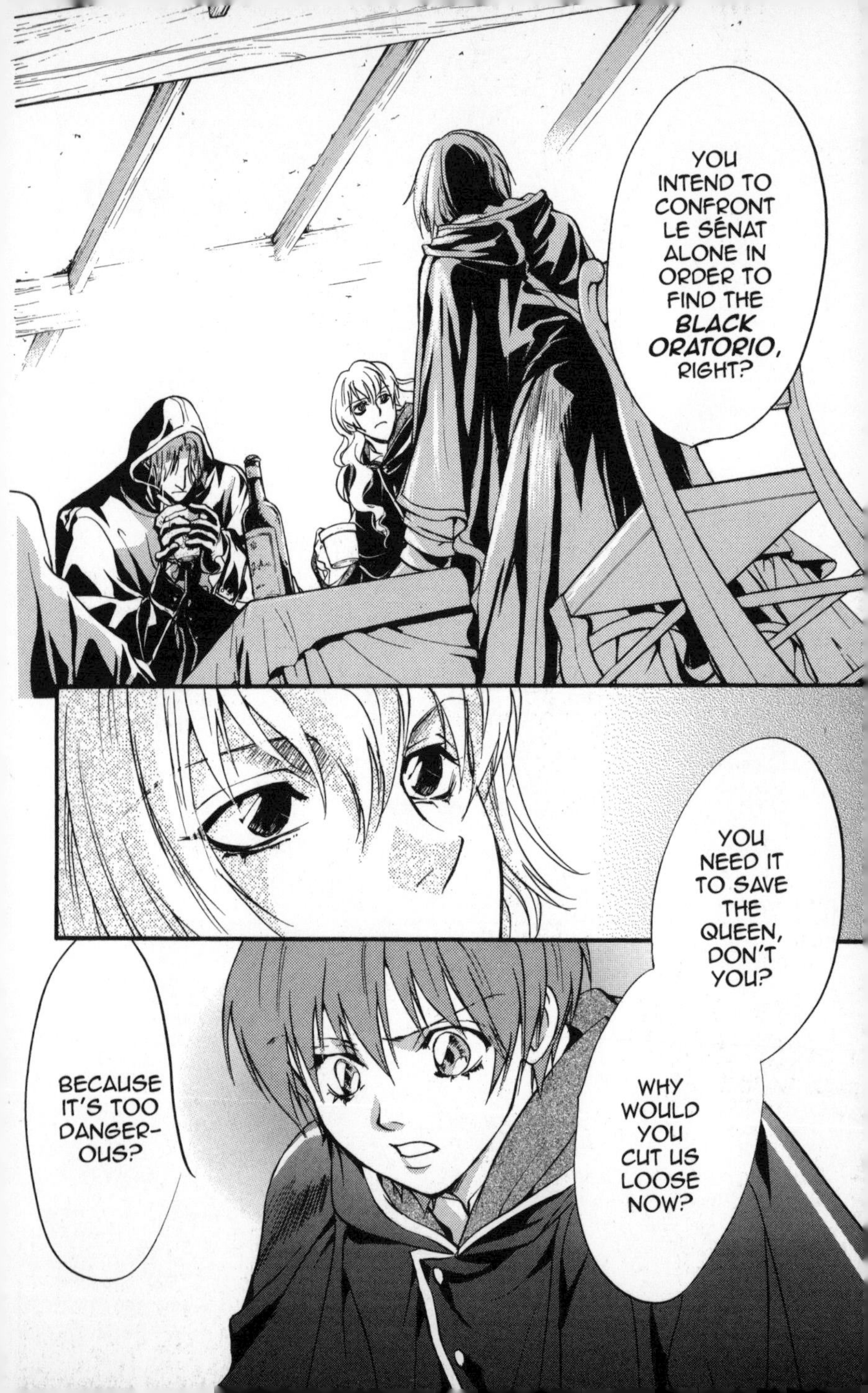
YOU INTEND TO CONFRONT LE SÉNAT ALONE IN ORDER TO FIND THE *BLACK ORATORIO*, RIGHT?
YOU NEED IT TO SAVE THE QUEEN, DON'T YOU?
WHY WOULD YOU CUT US LOOSE NOW?
BECAUSE IT'S TOO DANGER-OUS?

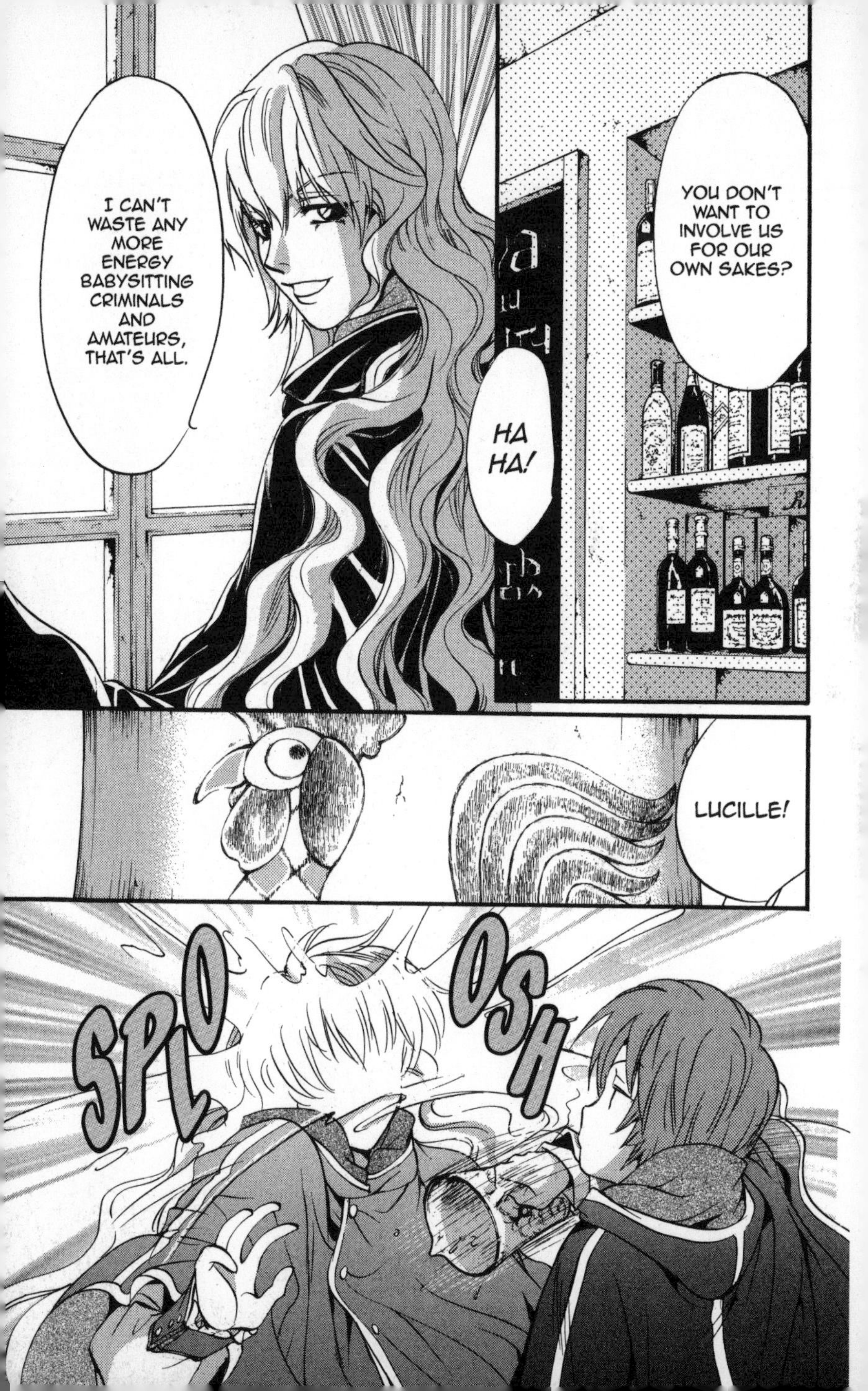
YOU DON'T WANT TO INVOLVE US FOR OUR OWN SAKES?
HA HA!
I CAN'T WASTE ANY MORE ENERGY BABYSITTING CRIMINALS AND AMATEURS, THAT'S ALL.
LUCILLE!
SPLOOSH

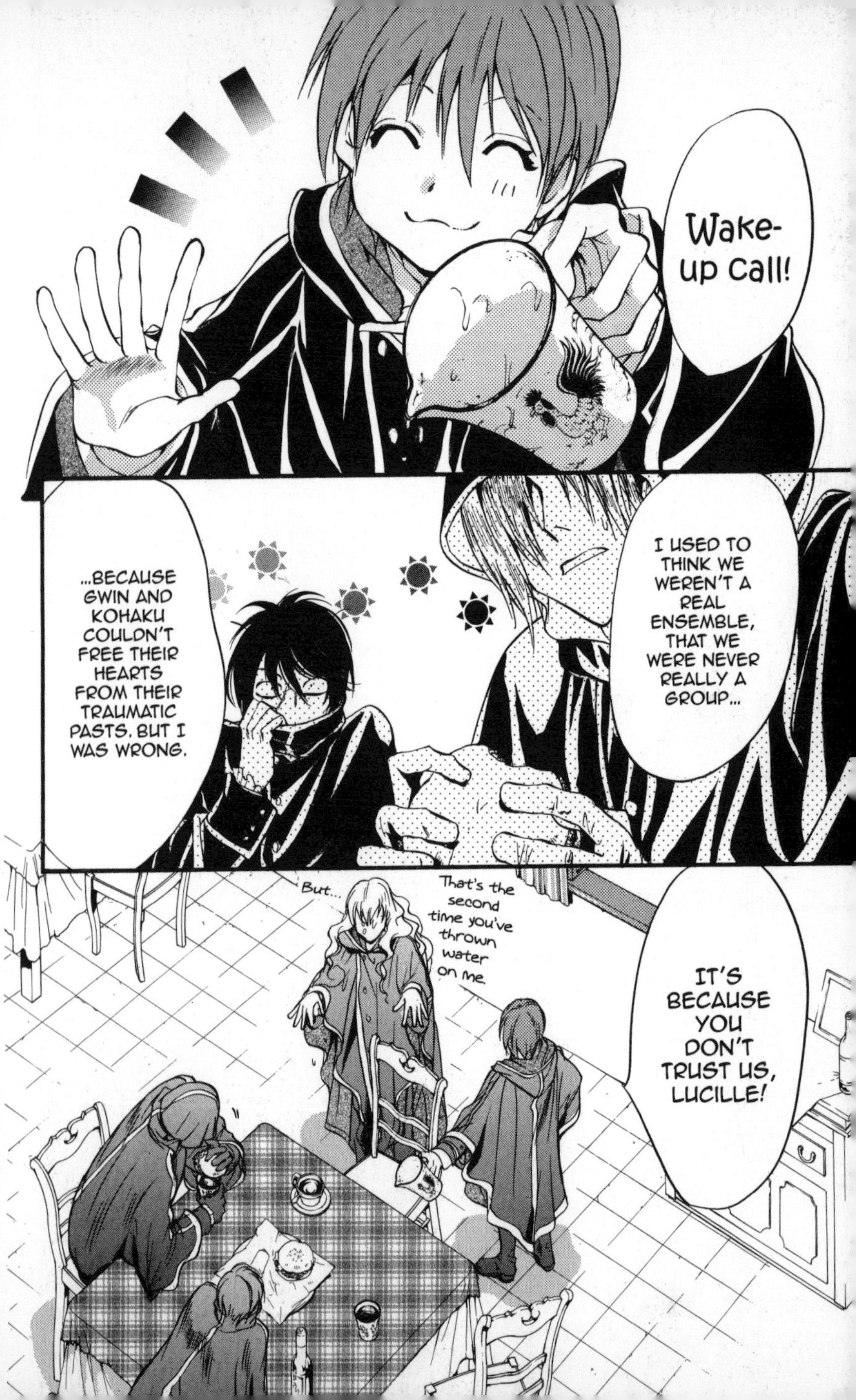
Wake-up call!
I USED TO THINK WE WEREN'T A REAL ENSEMBLE, THAT WE WERE NEVER REALLY A GROUP...
...BECAUSE GWIN AND KOHAKU COULDN'T FREE THEIR HEARTS FROM THEIR TRAUMATIC PASTS. BUT I WAS WRONG.
IT'S BECAUSE YOU DON'T TRUST US, LUCILLE!
That's the second time you've thrown water on me.
But...

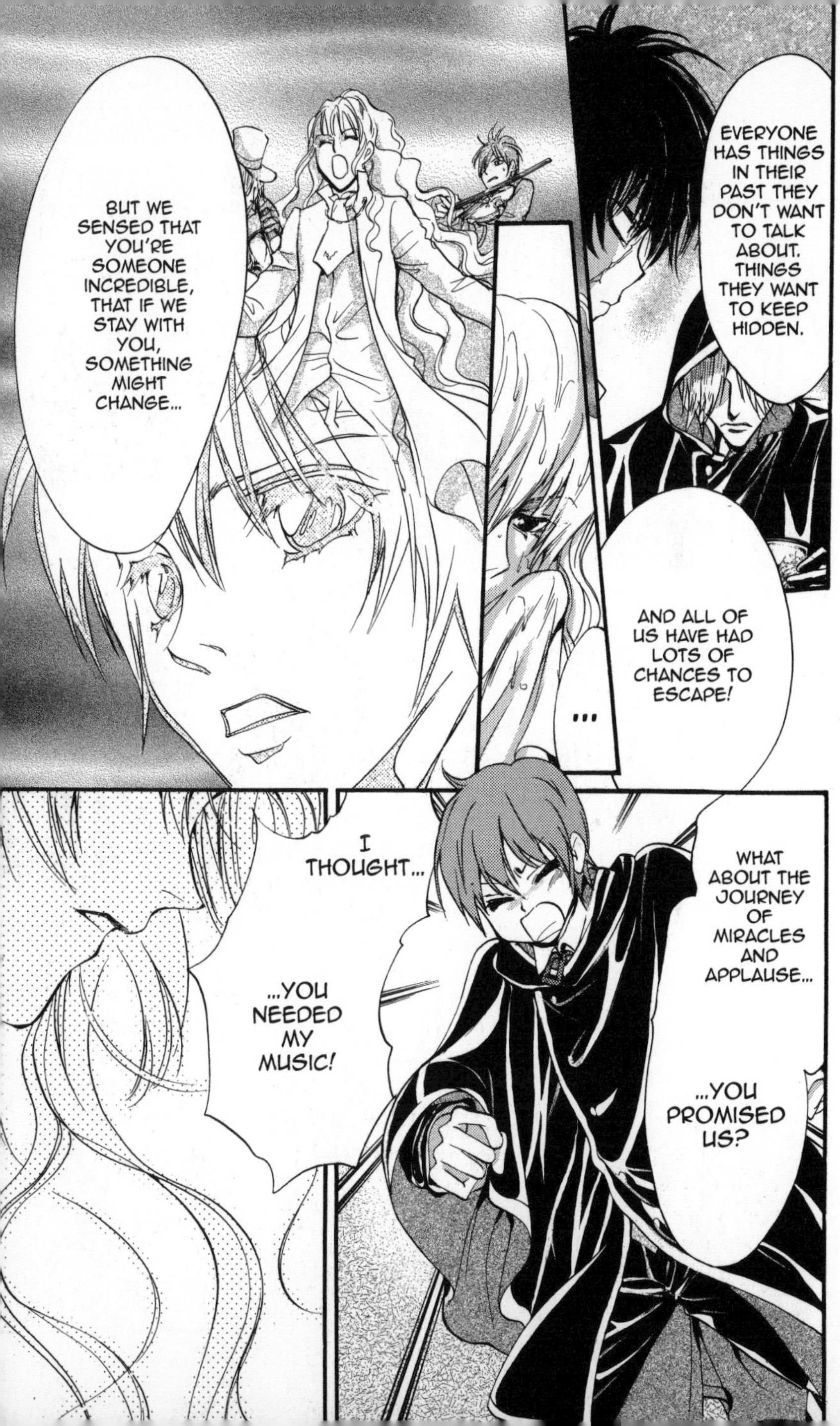
EVERYONE HAS THINGS IN THEIR PAST THEY DON'T WANT TO TALK ABOUT. THINGS THEY WANT TO KEEP HIDDEN.
AND ALL OF US HAVE HAD LOTS OF CHANCES TO ESCAPE!
...
BUT WE SENSED THAT YOU'RE SOMEONE INCREDIBLE, THAT IF WE STAY WITH YOU, SOMETHING MIGHT CHANGE...
WHAT ABOUT THE JOURNEY OF MIRACLES AND APPLAUSE...
...YOU PROMISED US?
I THOUGHT...
...YOU NEEDED MY MUSIC!

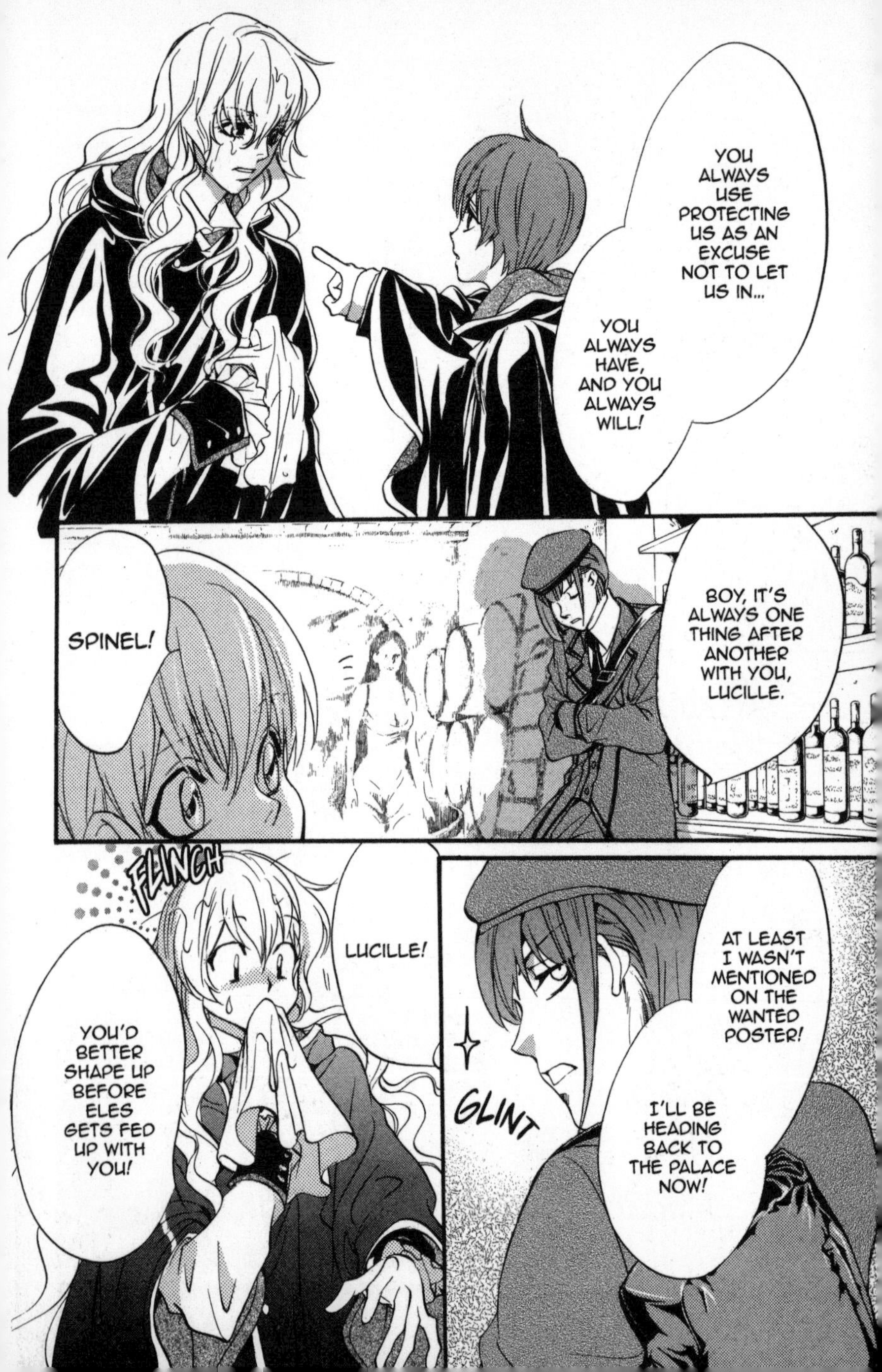
YOU ALWAYS USE PROTECTING US AS AN EXCUSE NOT TO LET US IN...
YOU ALWAYS HAVE, AND YOU ALWAYS WILL!
BOY, IT'S ALWAYS ONE THING AFTER ANOTHER WITH YOU, LUCILLE.
SPINEL!
AT LEAST I WASN'T MENTIONED ON THE WANTED POSTER!
GLINT
I'LL BE HEADING BACK TO THE PALACE NOW!
LUCILLE!
FLINCH
YOU'D BETTER SHAPE UP BEFORE ELES GETS FED UP WITH YOU!

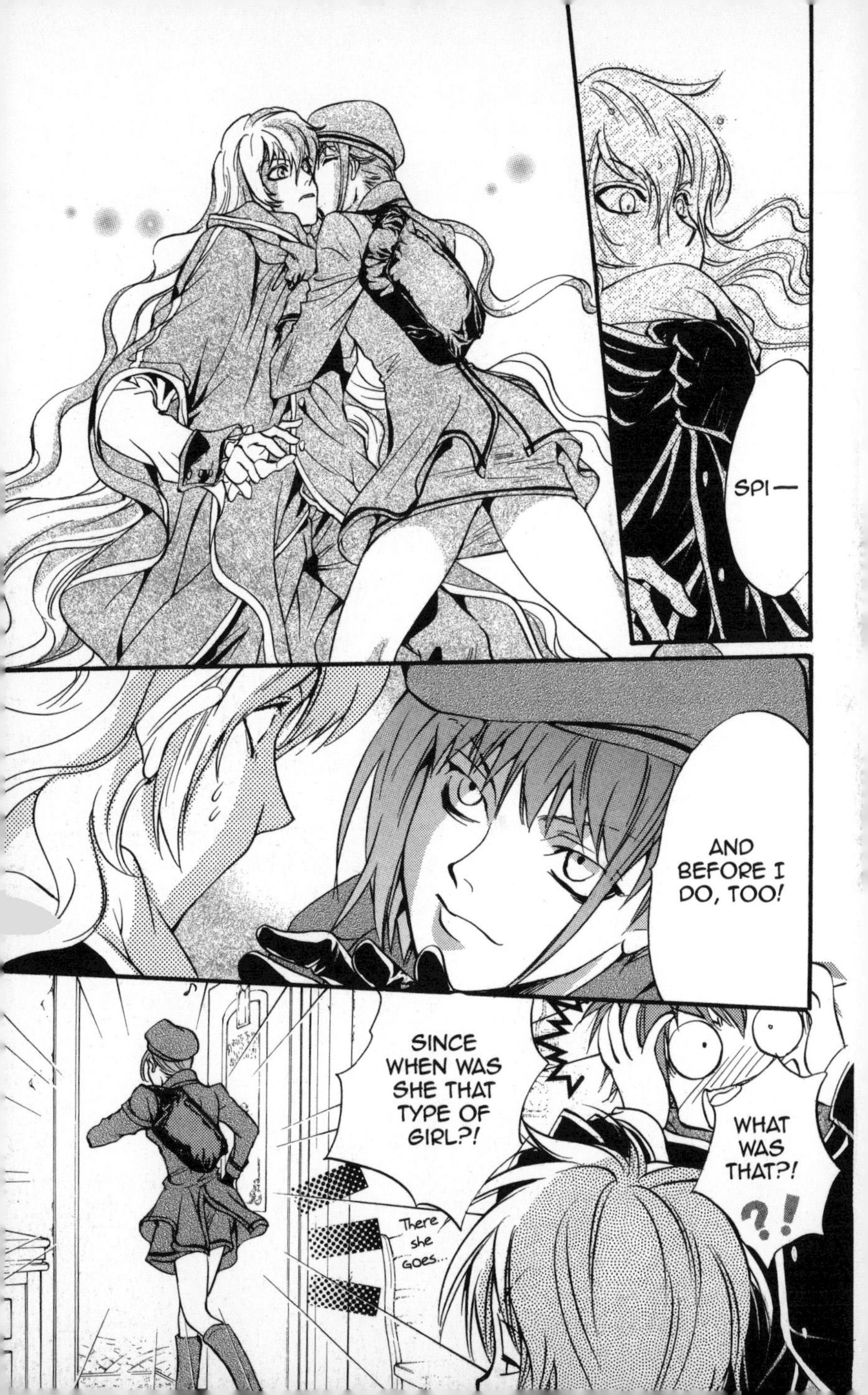
SPI—
AND BEFORE I DO, TOO!
WHAT WAS THAT?!
?!
SINCE WHEN WAS SHE THAT TYPE OF GIRL?!
There she goes...

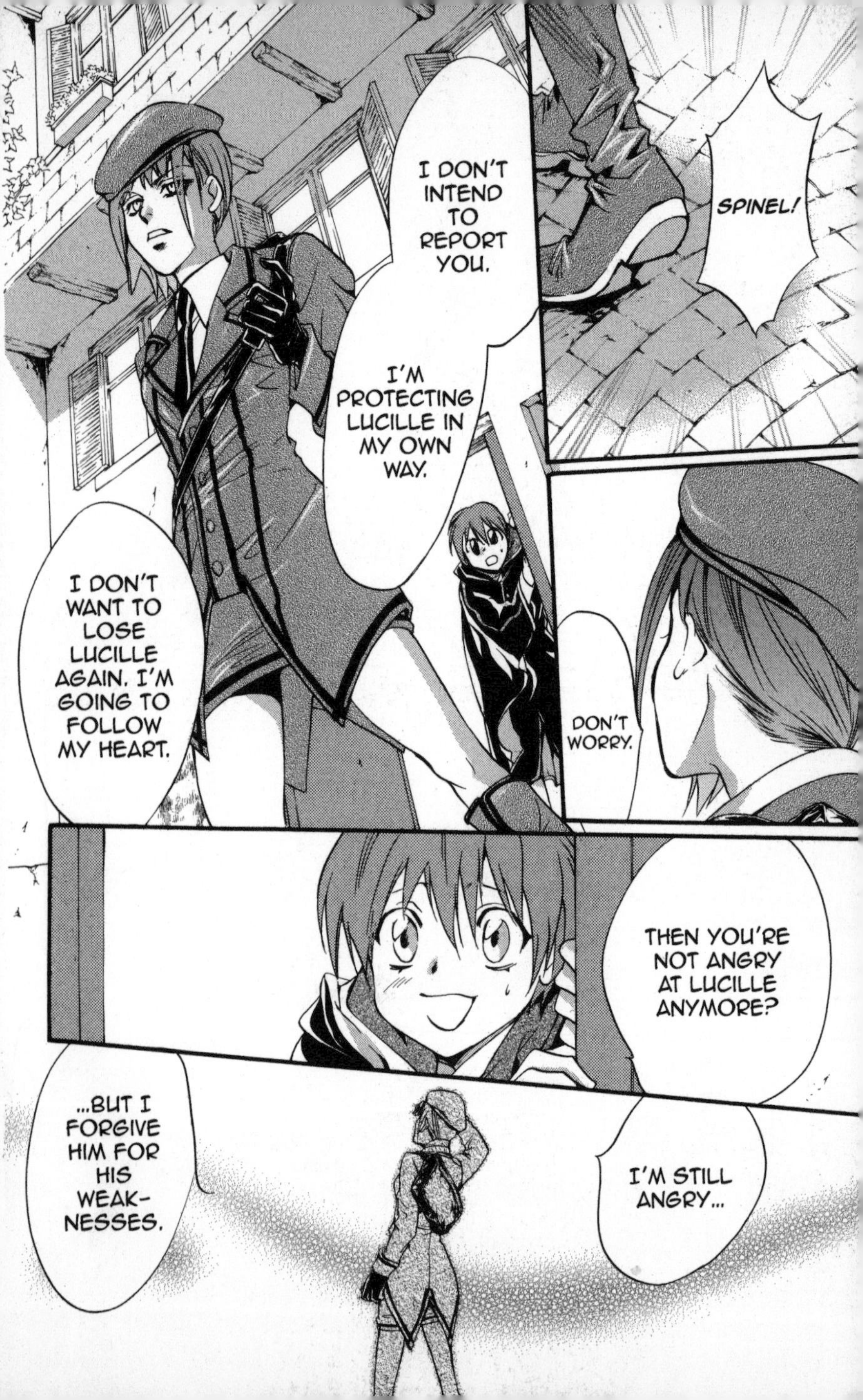
SPINEL!
DON'T WORRY.
I DON'T INTEND TO REPORT YOU.
I'M PROTECTING LUCILLE IN MY OWN WAY.
I DON'T WANT TO LOSE LUCILLE AGAIN. I'M GOING TO FOLLOW MY HEART.
THEN YOU'RE NOT ANGRY AT LUCILLE ANYMORE?
I'M STILL ANGRY...
...BUT I FORGIVE HIM FOR HIS WEAK-NESSES.

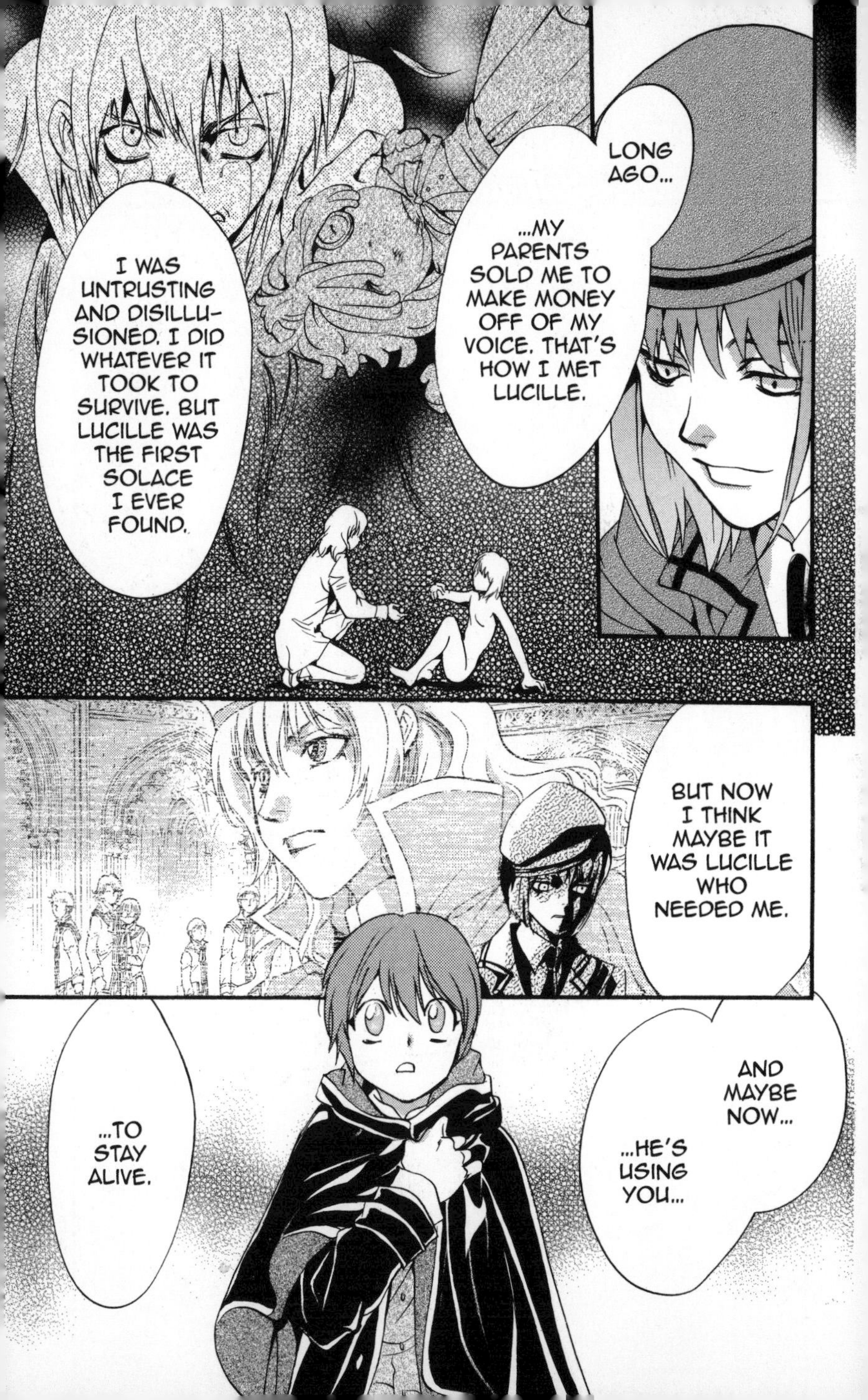
LONG AGO...
...MY PARENTS SOLD ME TO MAKE MONEY OFF OF MY VOICE. THAT'S HOW I MET LUCILLE.
I WAS UNTRUSTING AND DISILLUSIONED. I DID WHATEVER IT TOOK TO SURVIVE. BUT LUCILLE WAS THE FIRST SOLACE I EVER FOUND.
BUT NOW I THINK MAYBE IT WAS LUCILLE WHO NEEDED ME.
AND MAYBE NOW...
...HE'S USING YOU...
...TO STAY ALIVE.

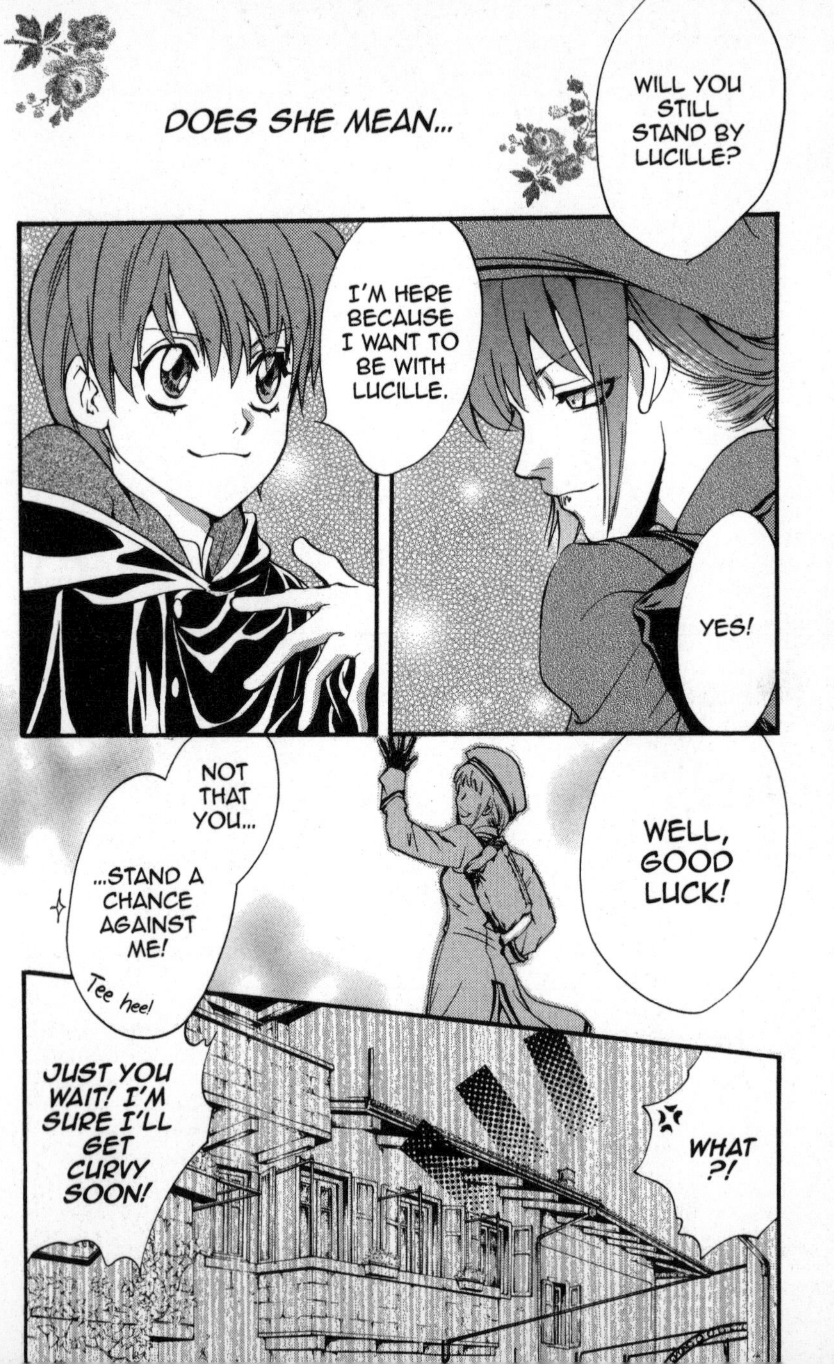
WILL YOU STILL STAND BY LUCILLE?
DOES SHE MEAN...
YES!
I'M HERE BECAUSE I WANT TO BE WITH LUCILLE.
WELL, GOOD LUCK!
NOT THAT YOU...
...STAND A CHANCE AGAINST ME!
Tee hee!
WHAT?!
JUST YOU WAIT! I'M SURE I'LL GET CURVY SOON!

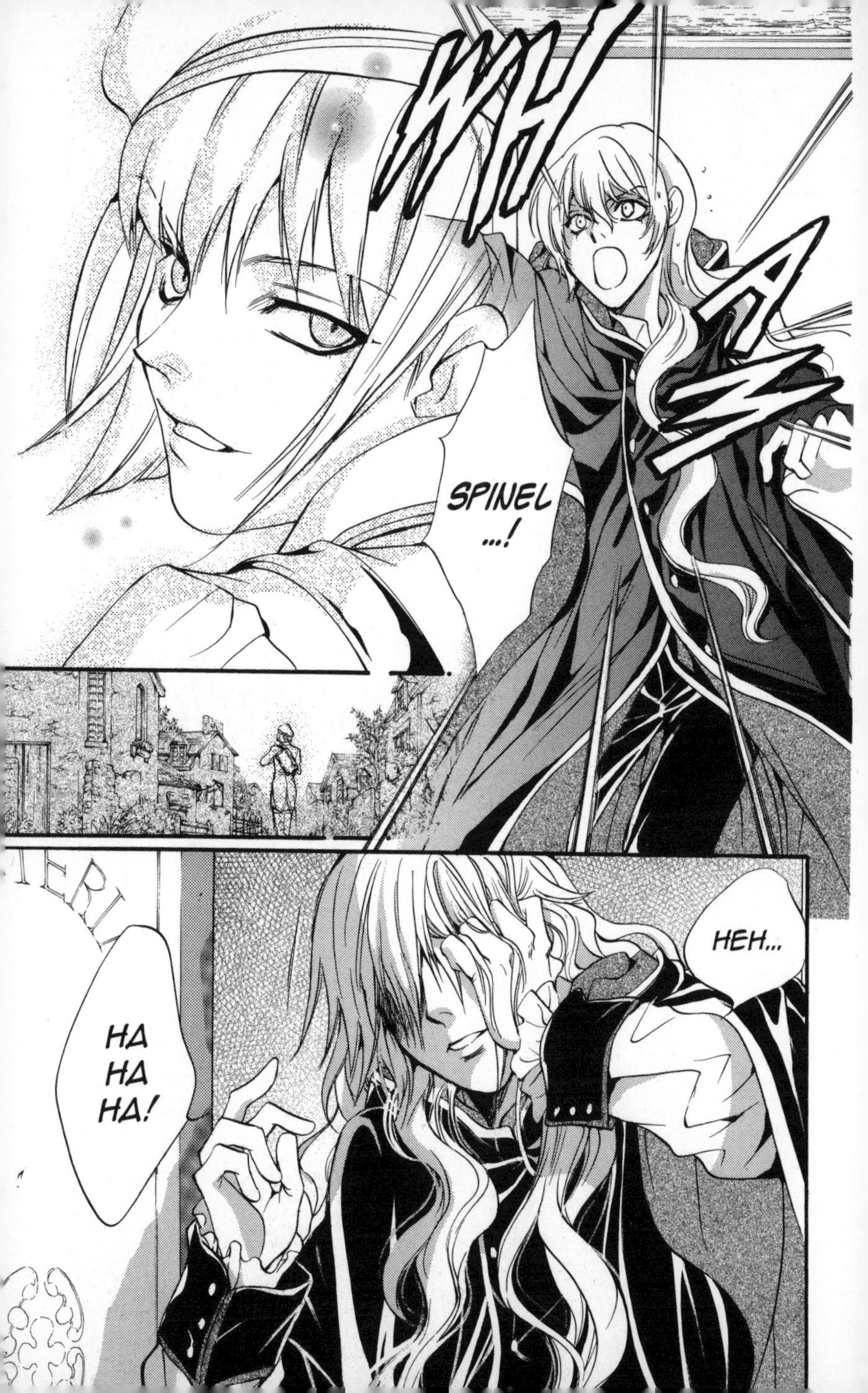
WAH
SPINEL ...!
HEH...
HA HA HA!

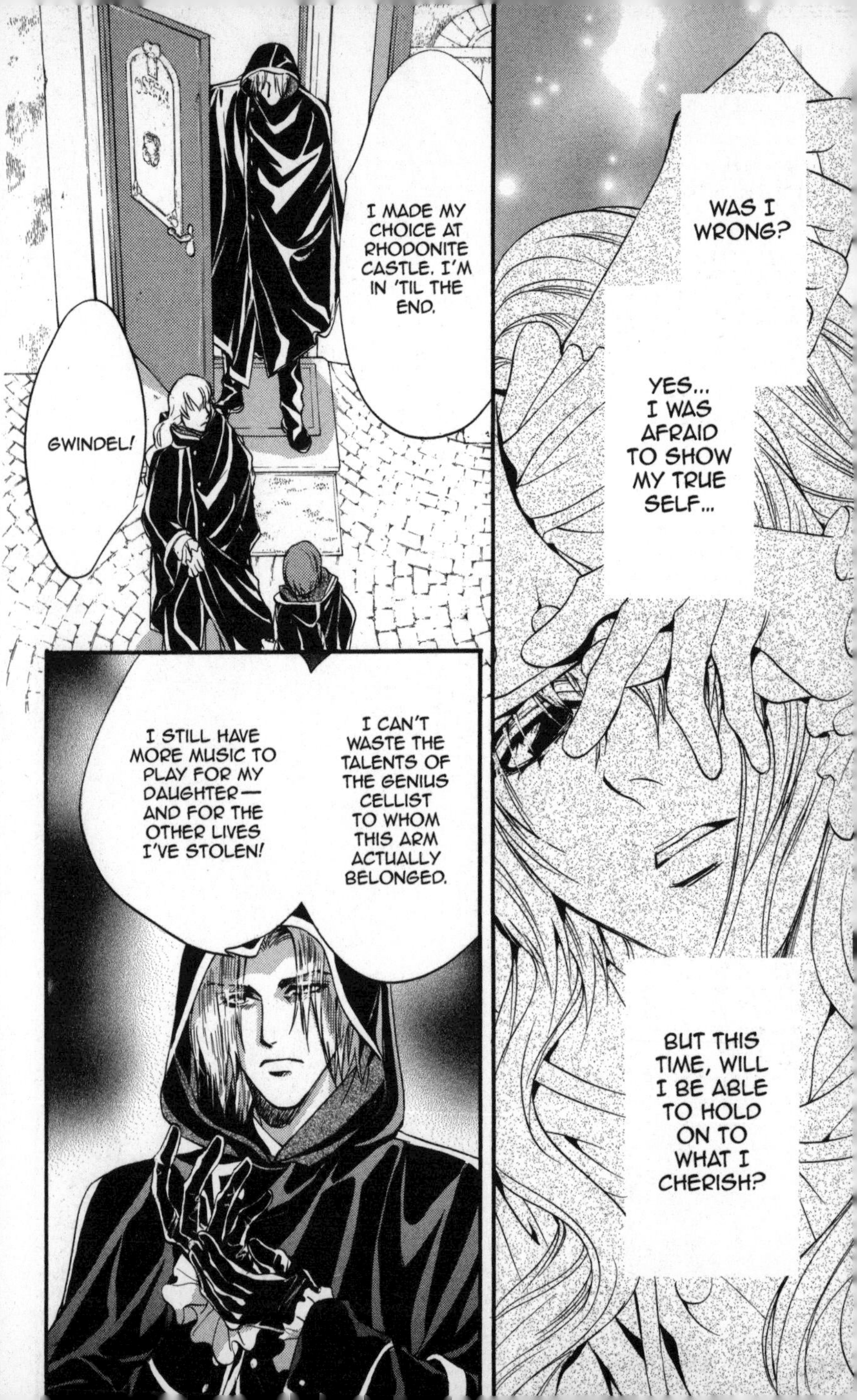
WAS I WRONG?
YES... I WAS AFRAID TO SHOW MY TRUE SELF...
BUT THIS TIME, WILL I BE ABLE TO HOLD ON TO WHAT I CHERISH?
I MADE MY CHOICE AT RHODONITE CASTLE. I'M IN 'TIL THE END.
GWINDEL!
I CAN'T WASTE THE TALENTS OF THE GENIUS CELLIST TO WHOM THIS ARM ACTUALLY BELONGED.
I STILL HAVE MORE MUSIC TO PLAY FOR MY DAUGHTER—AND FOR THE OTHER LIVES I'VE STOLEN!

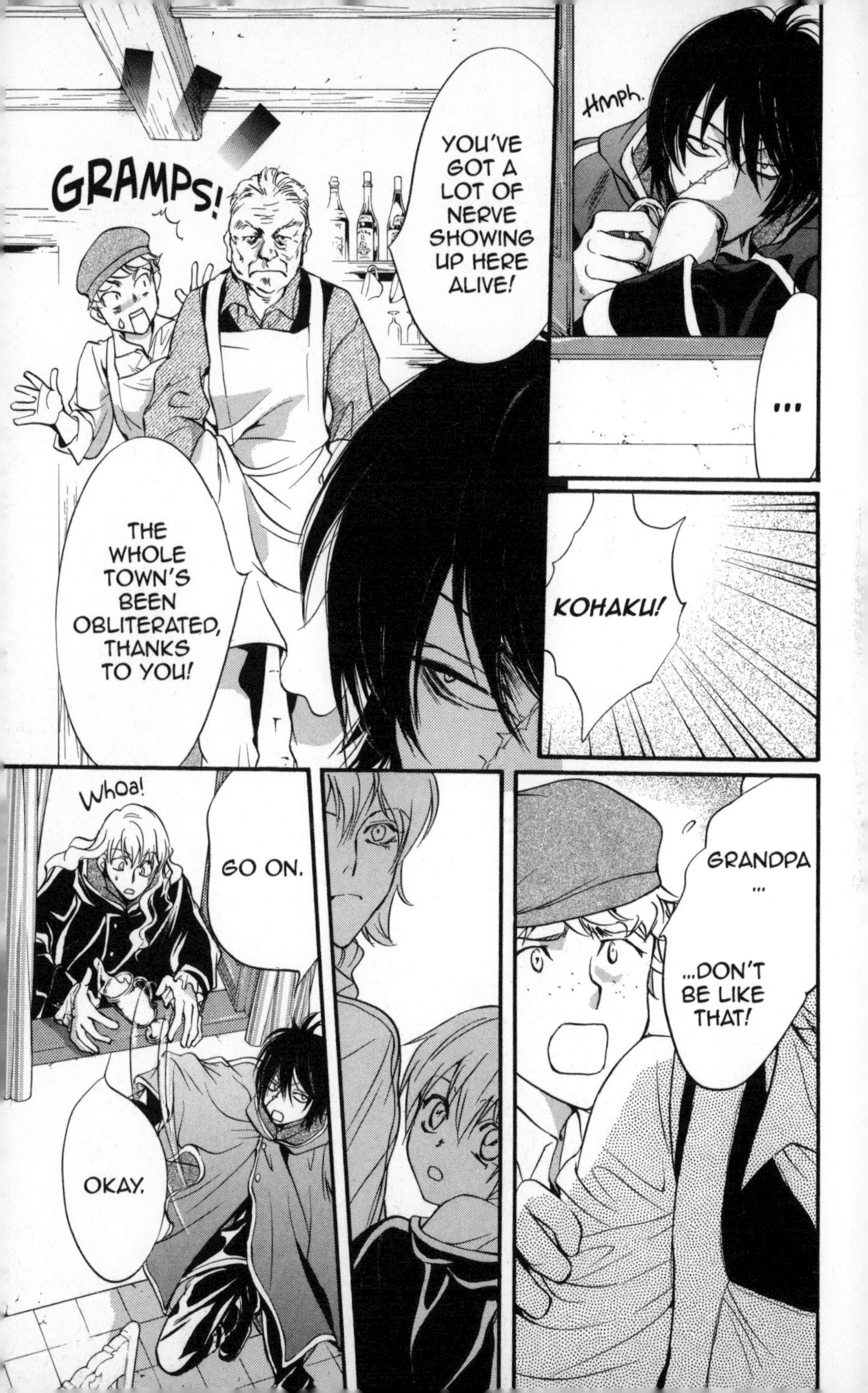
Hmph.
...
KOHAKU!
YOU'VE GOT A LOT OF NERVE SHOWING UP HERE ALIVE!
GRAMPS!
THE WHOLE TOWN'S BEEN OBLITERATED, THANKS TO YOU!
GRANDPA ...
...DON'T BE LIKE THAT!
GO ON.
Whoa!
OKAY.

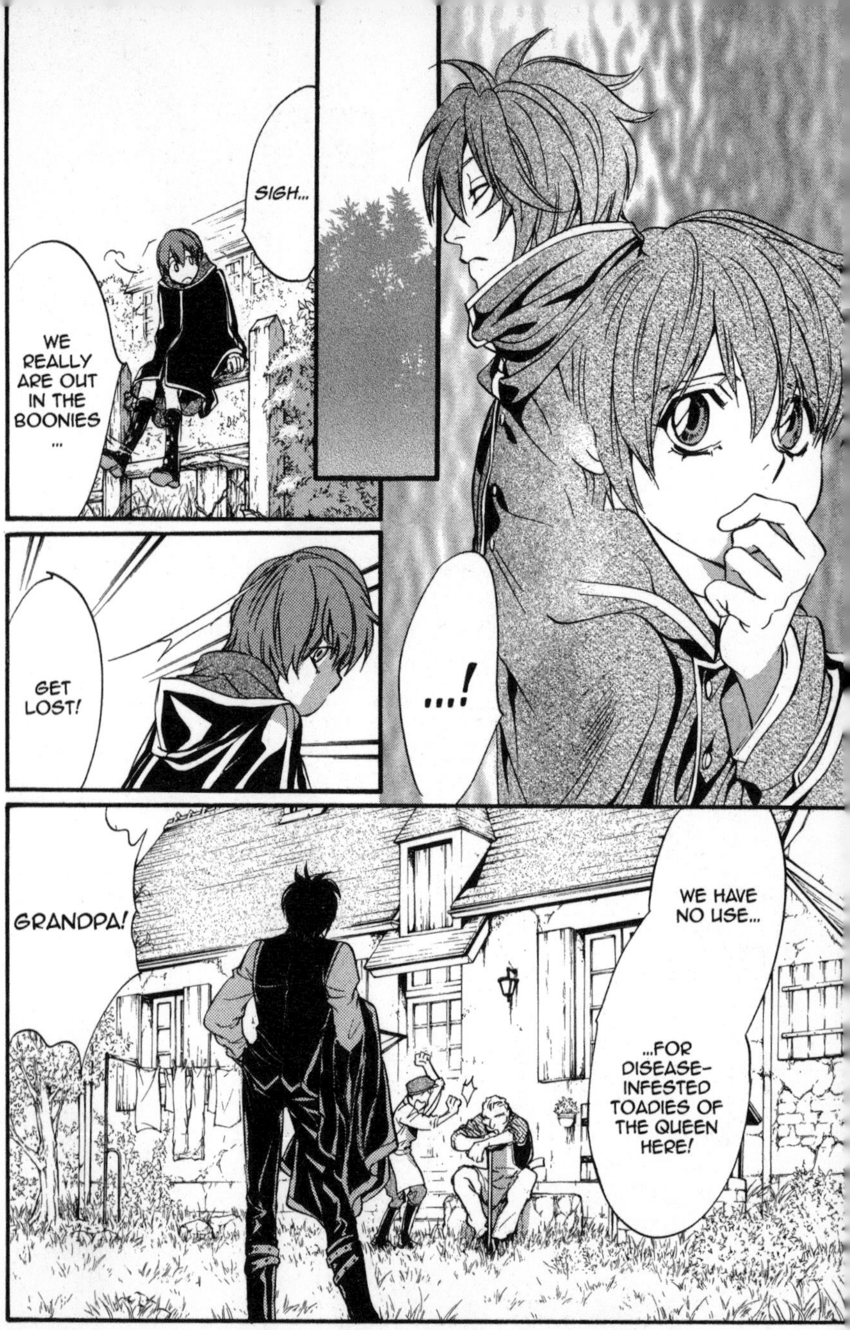
...!
SIGH...
WE REALLY ARE OUT IN THE BOONIES...
GET LOST!
WE HAVE NO USE...
...FOR DISEASE-INFESTED TOADIES OF THE QUEEN HERE!
GRANDPA!

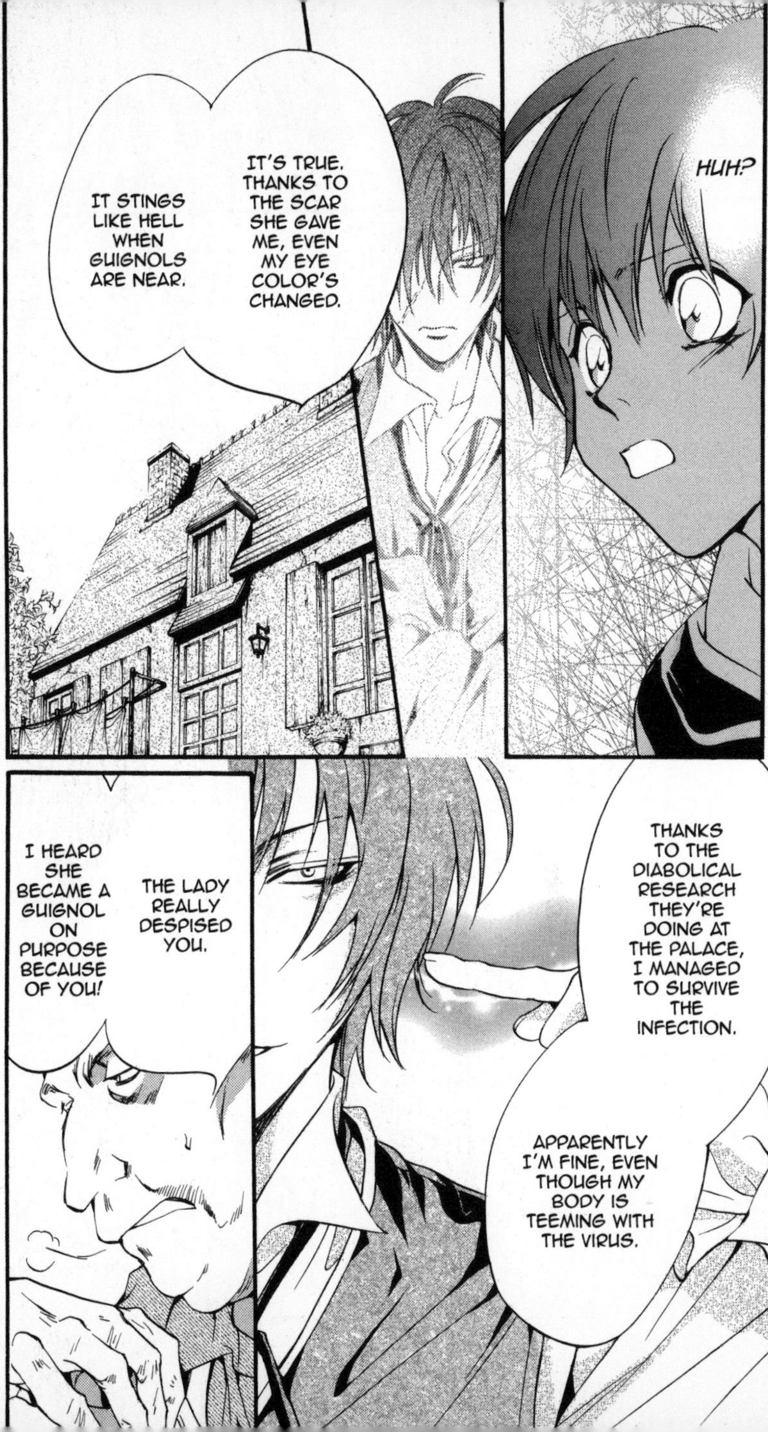
HUH?
IT'S TRUE. THANKS TO THE SCAR SHE GAVE ME, EVEN MY EYE COLOR'S CHANGED.
IT STINGS LIKE HELL WHEN GUIGNOLS ARE NEAR.
THANKS TO THE DIABOLICAL RESEARCH THEY'RE DOING AT THE PALACE, I MANAGED TO SURVIVE THE INFECTION.
APPARENTLY I'M FINE, EVEN THOUGH MY BODY IS TEEMING WITH THE VIRUS.
THE LADY REALLY DESPISED YOU.
I HEARD SHE BECAME A GUIGNOL ON PURPOSE BECAUSE OF YOU!

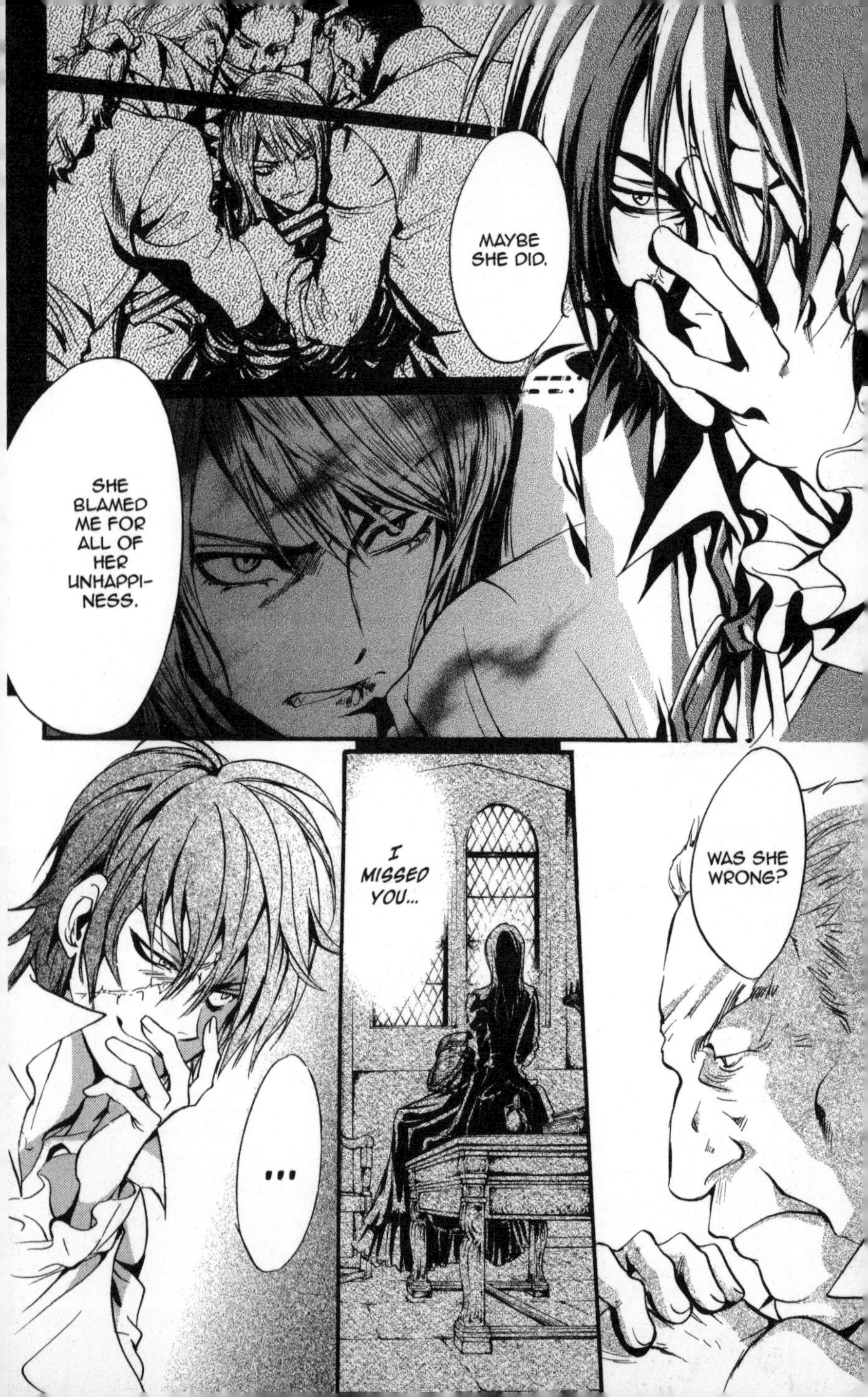
MAYBE SHE DID.
SHE BLAMED ME FOR ALL OF HER UNHAPPI-NESS.
WAS SHE WRONG?
I MISSED YOU...
...

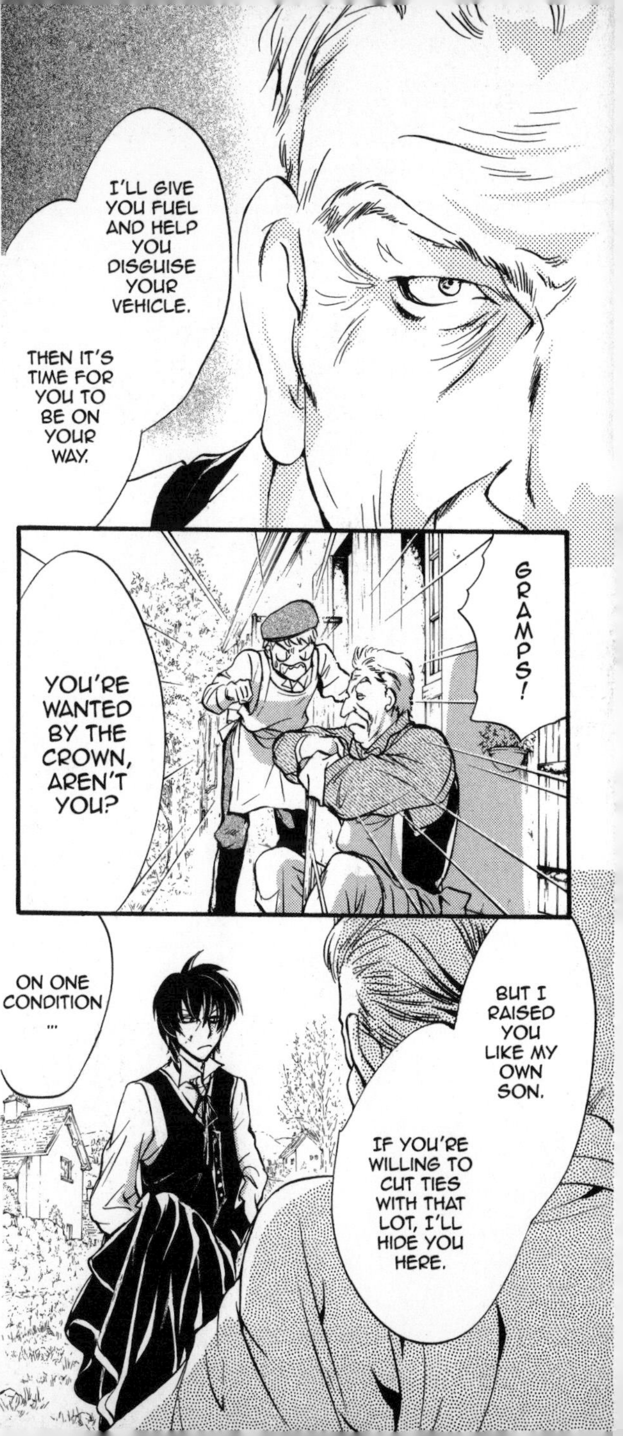
I'LL GIVE YOU FUEL AND HELP YOU DISGUISE YOUR VEHICLE.
THEN IT'S TIME FOR YOU TO BE ON YOUR WAY.
GRAMPS!
YOU'RE WANTED BY THE CROWN, AREN'T YOU?
BUT I RAISED YOU LIKE MY OWN SON.
IF YOU'RE WILLING TO CUT TIES WITH THAT LOT, I'LL HIDE YOU HERE.
ON ONE CONDITION...

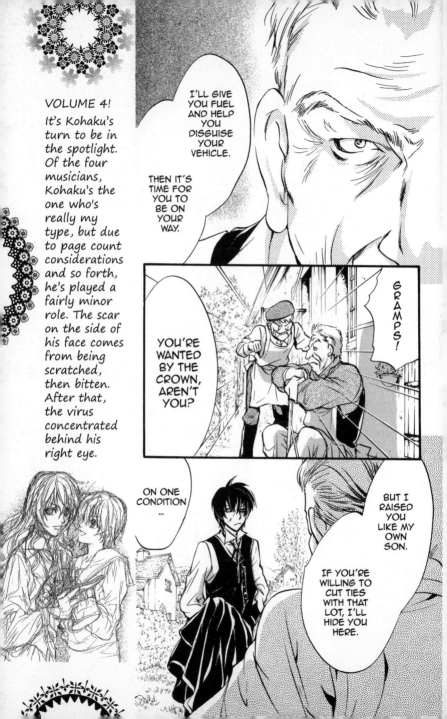

VOLUME 4!

It's Kohaku's turn to be in the spotlight. Of the four musicians, Kohaku's the one who's really my type, but due to page count considerations and so forth, he's played a fairly minor role. The scar on the side of his face comes from being scratched, then bitten. After that, the virus concentrated behind his right eye.

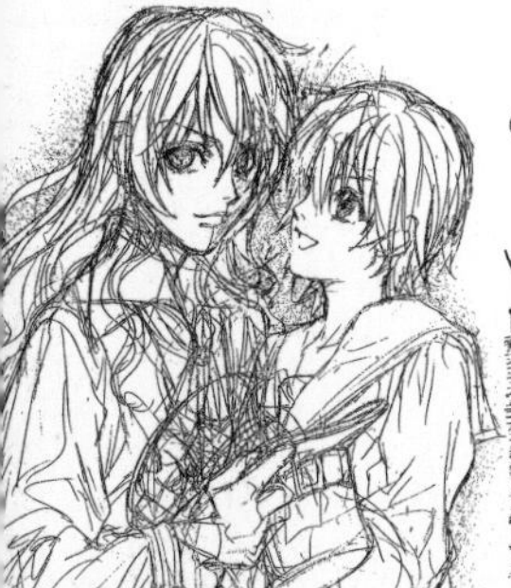

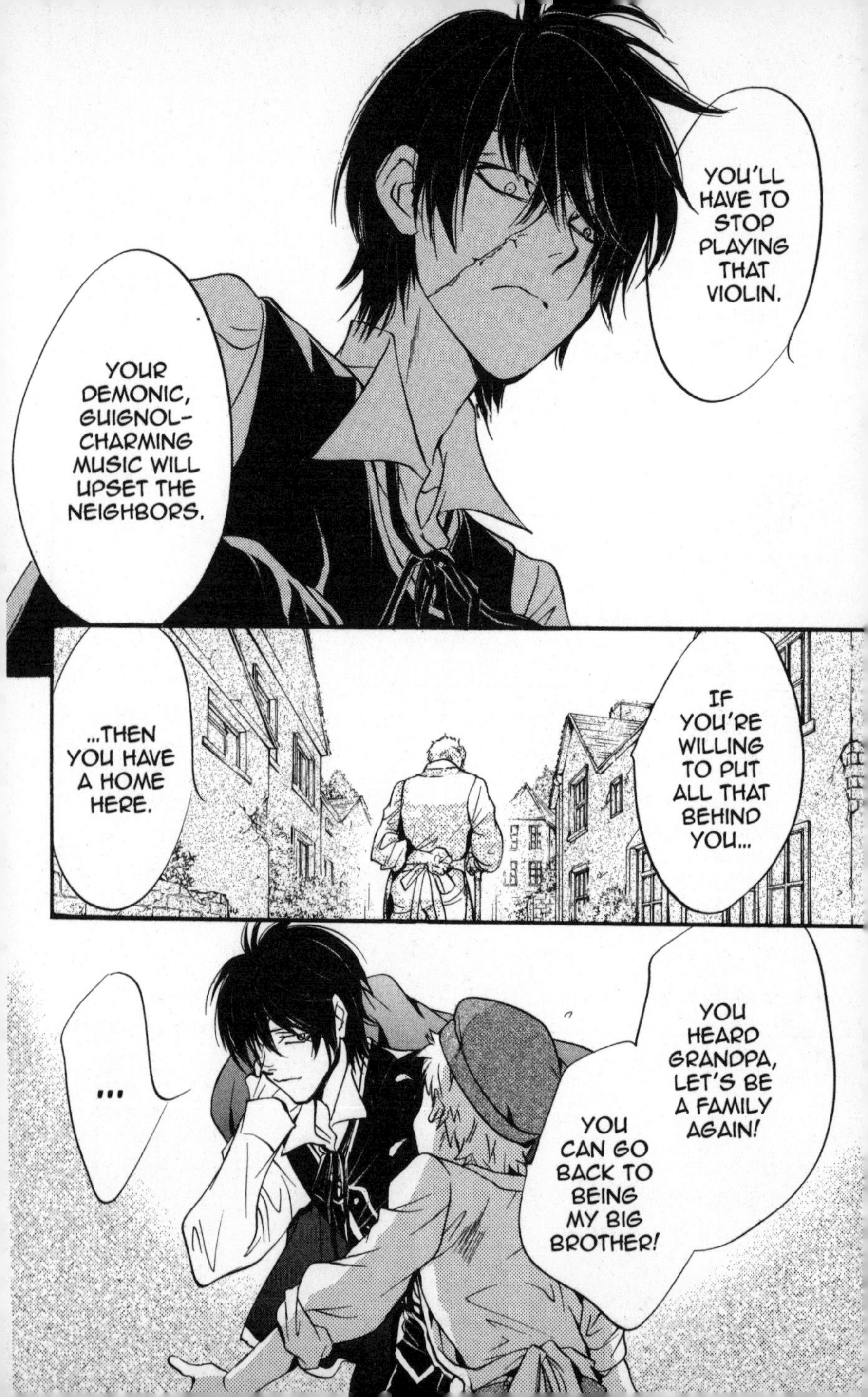
YOU'LL HAVE TO STOP PLAYING THAT VIOLIN.
YOUR DEMONIC, GUIGNOL-CHARMING MUSIC WILL UPSET THE NEIGHBORS.
IF YOU'RE WILLING TO PUT ALL THAT BEHIND YOU...
...THEN YOU HAVE A HOME HERE.
YOU HEARD GRANDPA, LET'S BE A FAMILY AGAIN!
YOU CAN GO BACK TO BEING MY BIG BROTHER!
...

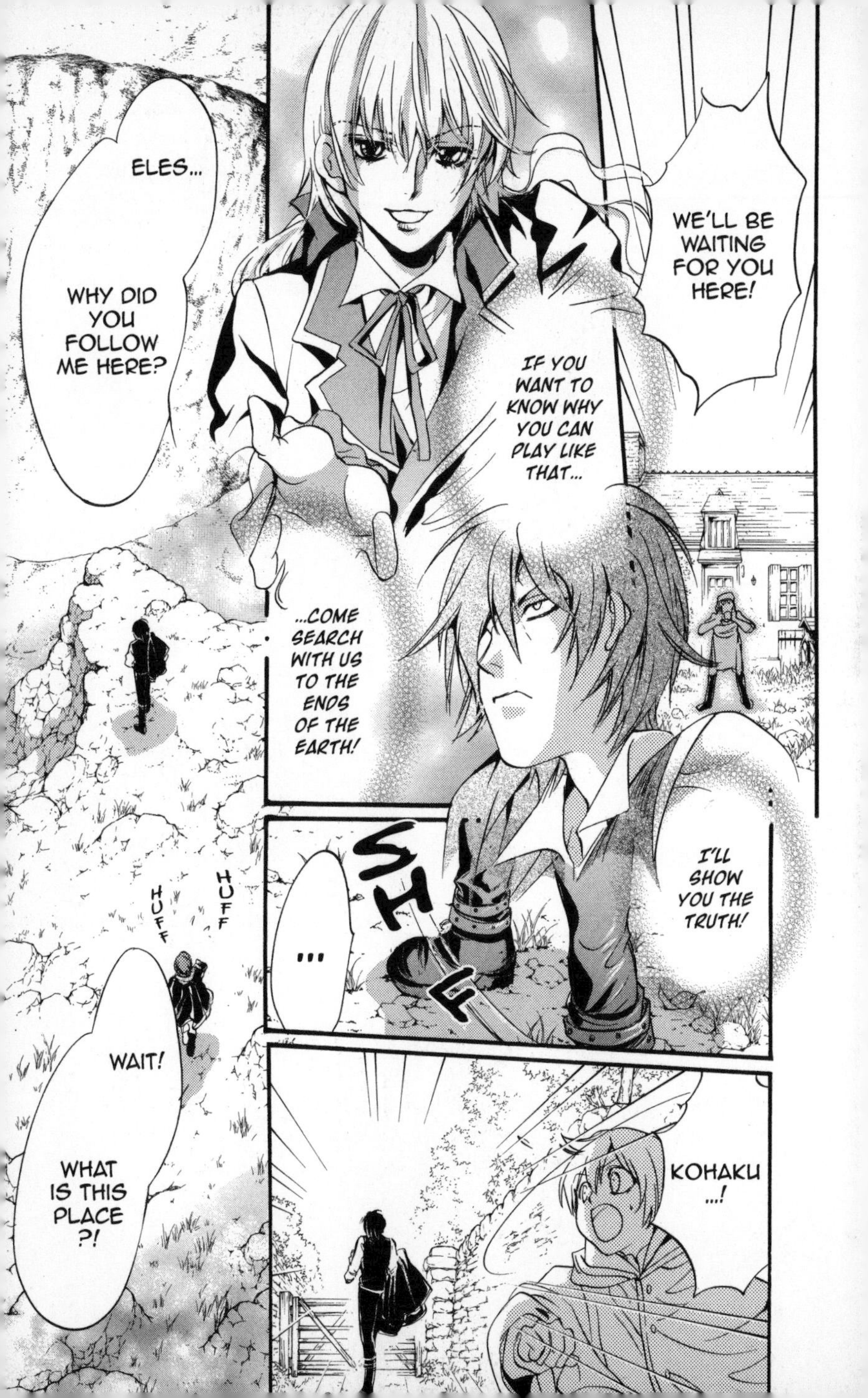
WE'LL BE WAITING FOR YOU HERE!
IF YOU WANT TO KNOW WHY YOU CAN PLAY LIKE THAT...
...COME SEARCH WITH US TO THE ENDS OF THE EARTH!
I'LL SHOW YOU THE TRUTH!
SHFF
...
KOHAKU ...!
ELES...
WHY DID YOU FOLLOW ME HERE?
HUFF
HUFF
WAIT!
WHAT IS THIS PLACE ?!

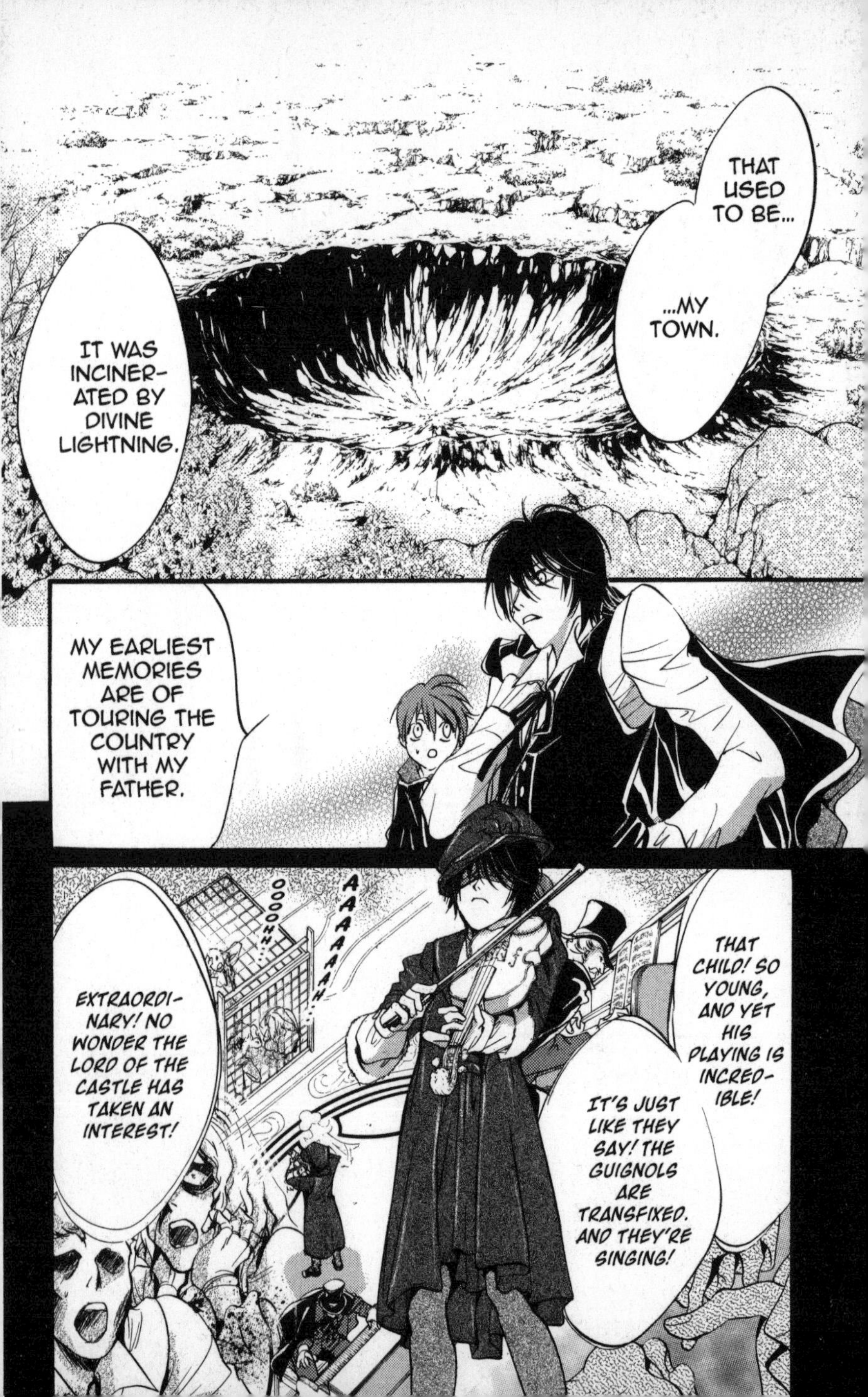
THAT USED TO BE...
...MY TOWN.
IT WAS INCINER-ATED BY DIVINE LIGHTNING.
MY EARLIEST MEMORIES ARE OF TOURING THE COUNTRY WITH MY FATHER.
THAT CHILD! SO YOUNG, AND YET HIS PLAYING IS INCRED-IBLE!
IT'S JUST LIKE THEY SAY! THE GUIGNOLS ARE TRANSFIXED. AND THEY'RE SINGING!
AAAAAAAH
OOOOHH...
EXTRAORDI-NARY! NO WONDER THE LORD OF THE CASTLE HAS TAKEN AN INTEREST!

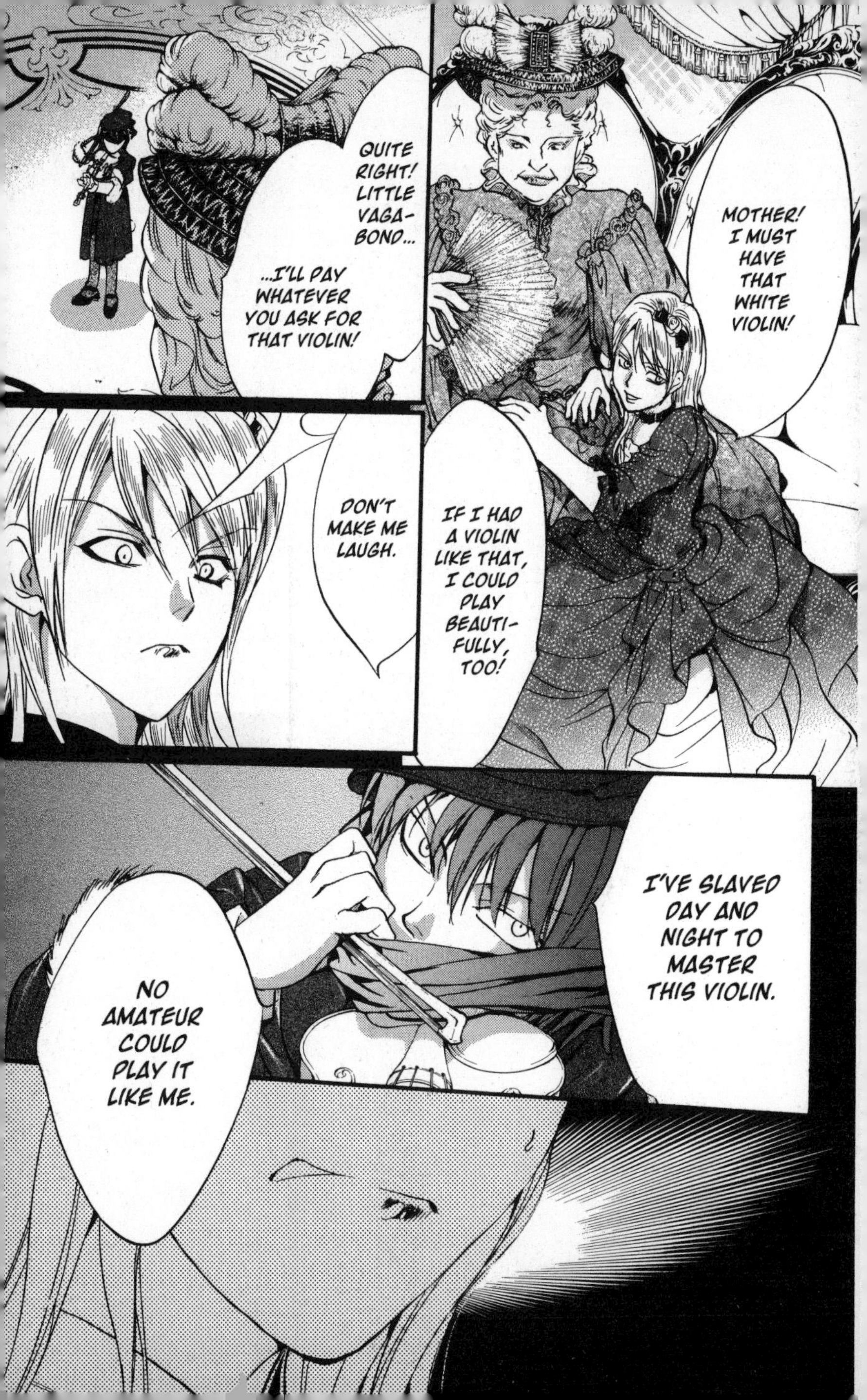
MOTHER! I MUST HAVE THAT WHITE VIOLIN!
IF I HAD A VIOLIN LIKE THAT, I COULD PLAY BEAUTIFULLY, TOO!
QUITE RIGHT! LITTLE VAGABOND...
...I'LL PAY WHATEVER YOU ASK FOR THAT VIOLIN!
DON'T MAKE ME LAUGH.
I'VE SLAVED DAY AND NIGHT TO MASTER THIS VIOLIN.
NO AMATEUR COULD PLAY IT LIKE ME.

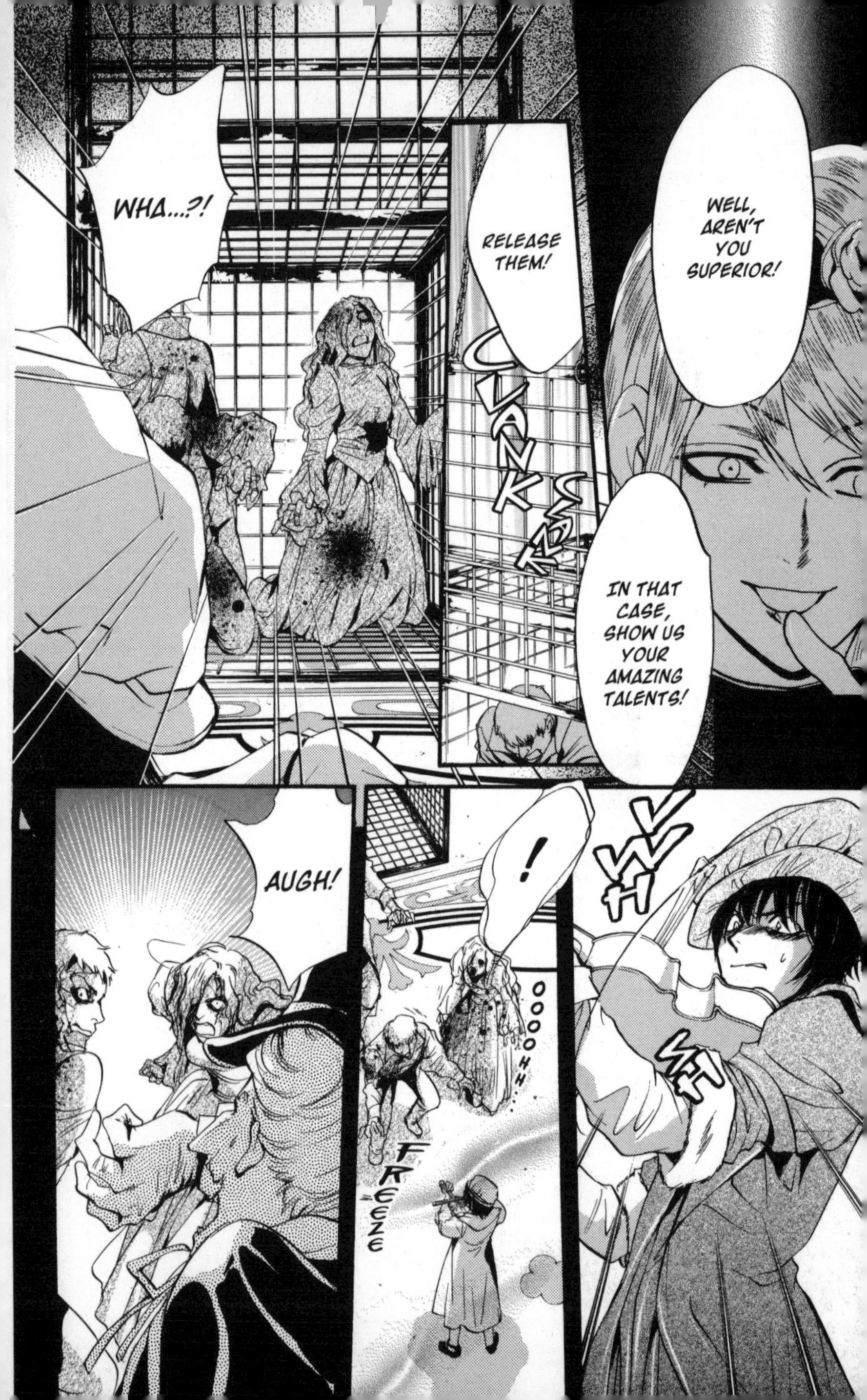
WELL, AREN'T YOU SUPERIOR!
IN THAT CASE, SHOW US YOUR AMAZING TALENTS!
RELEASE THEM!
CLANK
CLANK
WHA...?!
!
OOOOOHH
FREEZE
AUGH!

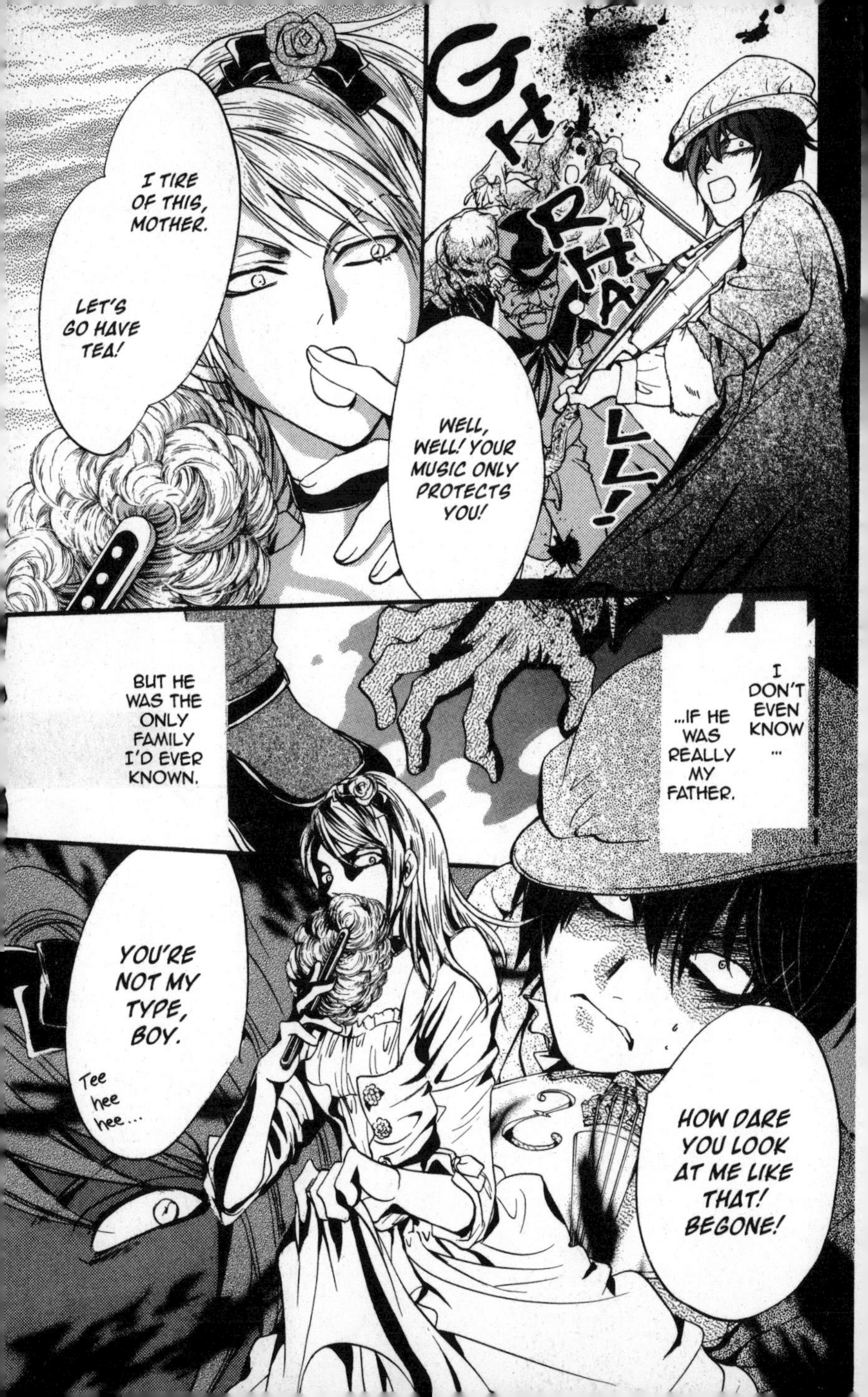
GHRHALL!
WELL, WELL! YOUR MUSIC ONLY PROTECTS YOU!
I TIRE OF THIS, MOTHER.
LET'S GO HAVE TEA!
I DON'T EVEN KNOW...
...IF HE WAS REALLY MY FATHER.
BUT HE WAS THE ONLY FAMILY I'D EVER KNOWN.
HOW DARE YOU LOOK AT ME LIKE THAT! BEGONE!
YOU'RE NOT MY TYPE, BOY.
Tee hee hee...

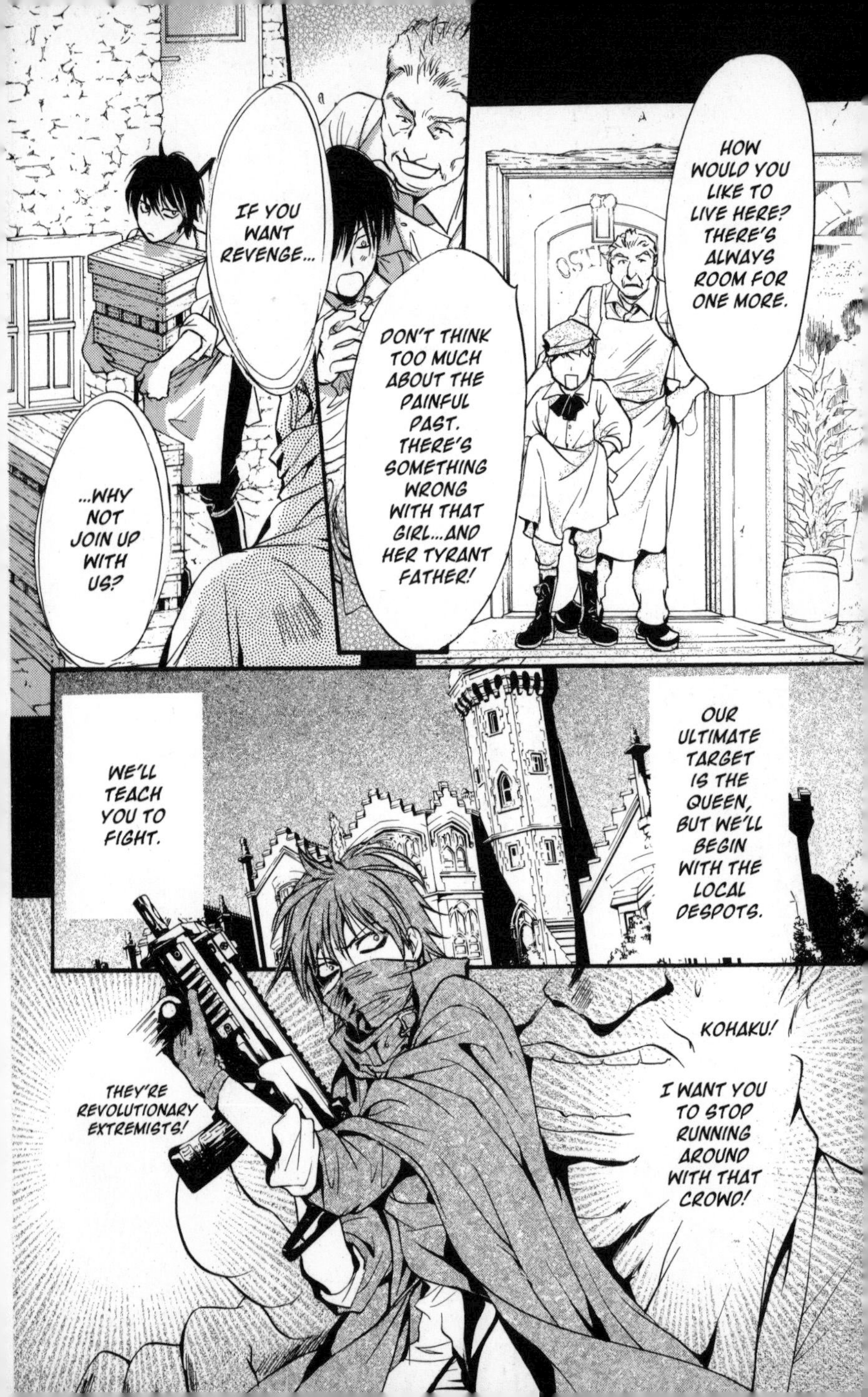
HOW WOULD YOU LIKE TO LIVE HERE? THERE'S ALWAYS ROOM FOR ONE MORE.
DON'T THINK TOO MUCH ABOUT THE PAINFUL PAST. THERE'S SOMETHING WRONG WITH THAT GIRL...AND HER TYRANT FATHER!
IF YOU WANT REVENGE...
...WHY NOT JOIN UP WITH US?
OUR ULTIMATE TARGET IS THE QUEEN, BUT WE'LL BEGIN WITH THE LOCAL DESPOTS.
WE'LL TEACH YOU TO FIGHT.
KOHAKU!
I WANT YOU TO STOP RUNNING AROUND WITH THAT CROWD!
THEY'RE REVOLUTIONARY EXTREMISTS!

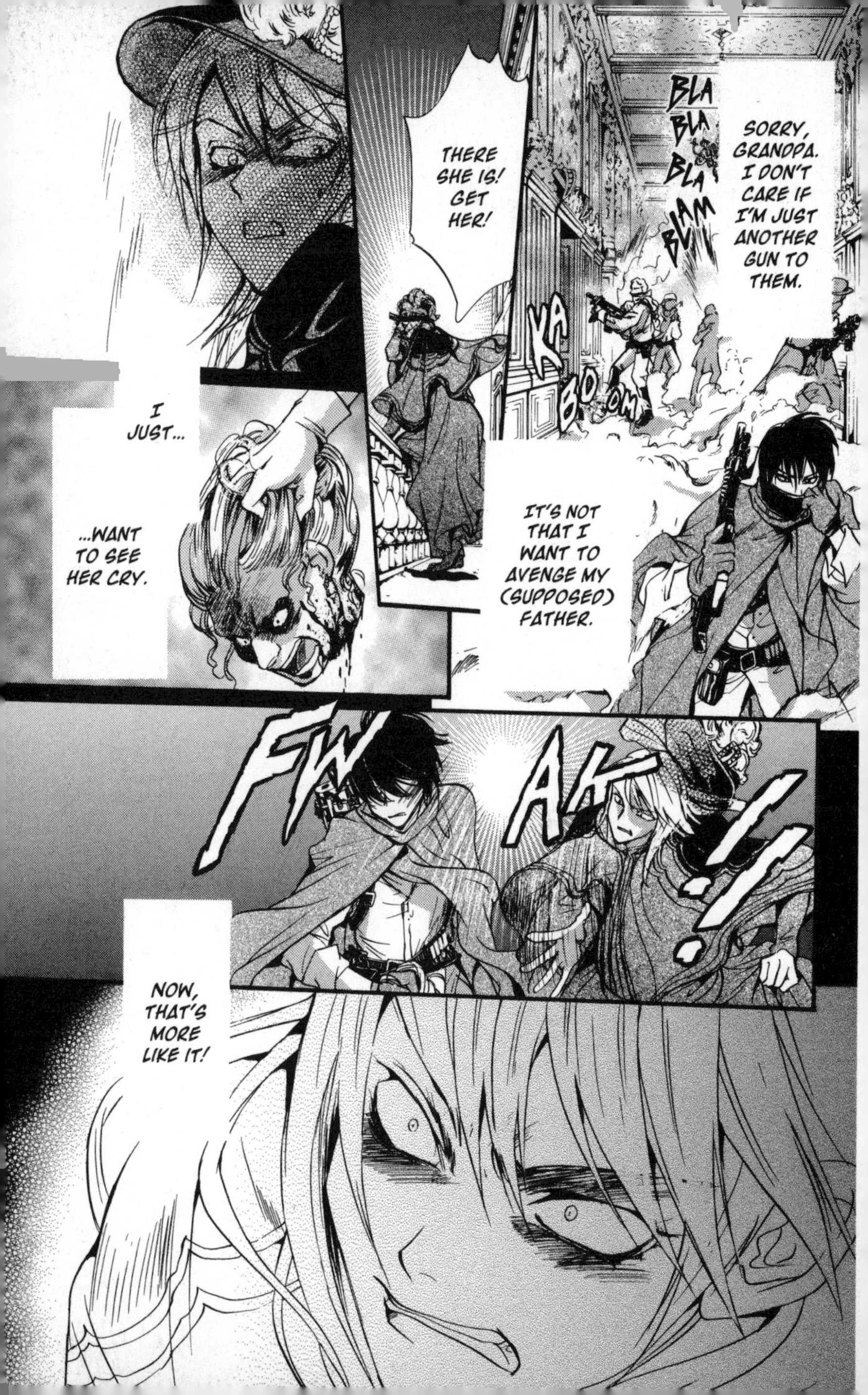
SORRY, GRANDPA. I DON'T CARE IF I'M JUST ANOTHER GUN TO THEM.
BLA BLA BLA BLAM
KA BOOM
THERE SHE IS! GET HER!
IT'S NOT THAT I WANT TO AVENGE MY (SUPPOSED) FATHER.
I JUST...
...WANT TO SEE HER CRY.
FWAK!!
NOW, THAT'S MORE LIKE IT!

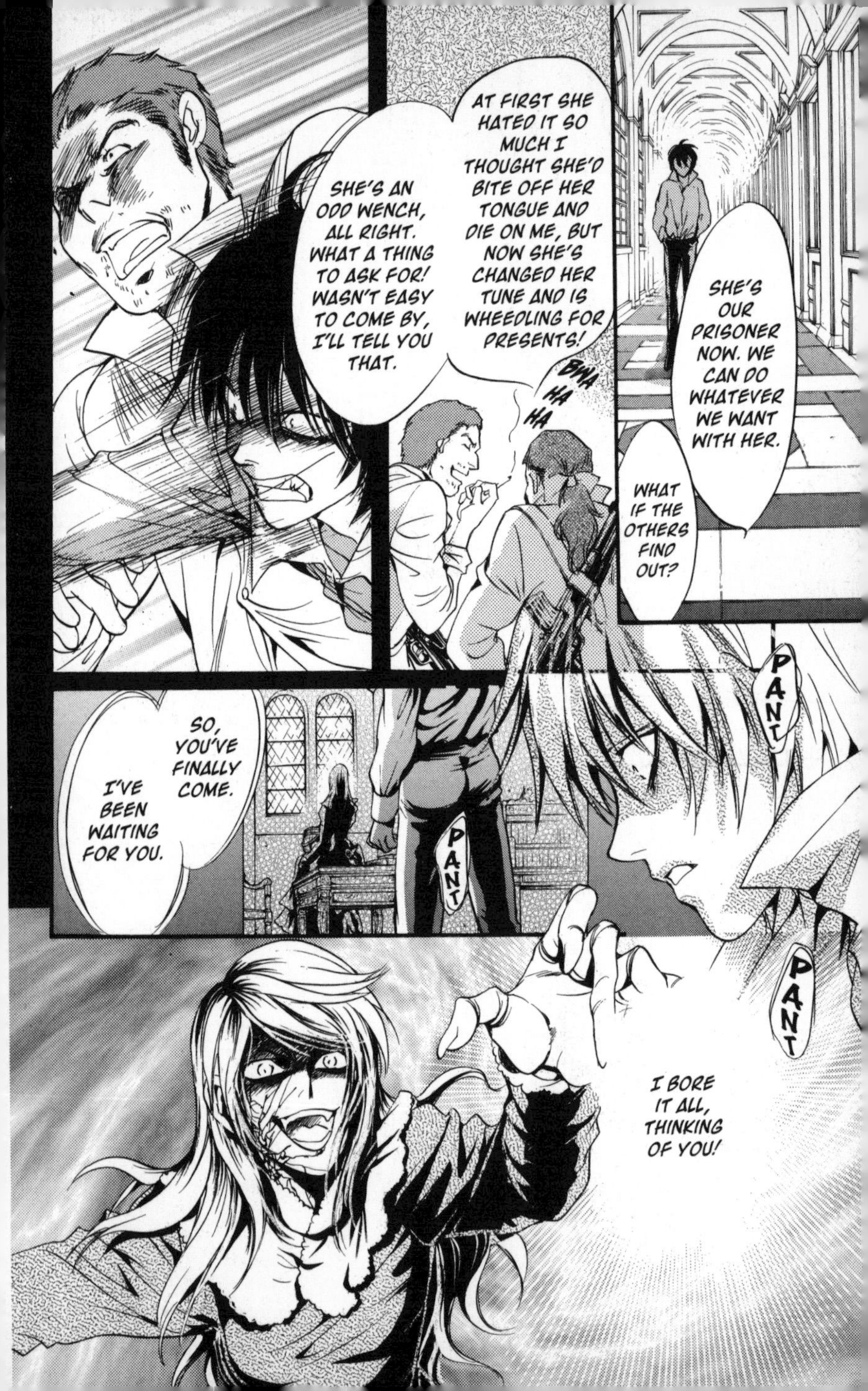
SHE'S OUR PRISONER NOW. WE CAN DO WHATEVER WE WANT WITH HER.
WHAT IF THE OTHERS FIND OUT?
AT FIRST SHE HATED IT SO MUCH I THOUGHT SHE'D BITE OFF HER TONGUE AND DIE ON ME, BUT NOW SHE'S CHANGED HER TUNE AND IS WHEEDLING FOR PRESENTS!
BWA HA HA
SHE'S AN ODD WENCH, ALL RIGHT. WHAT A THING TO ASK FOR! WASN'T EASY TO COME BY, I'LL TELL YOU THAT.
PANT
SO, YOU'VE FINALLY COME.
I'VE BEEN WAITING FOR YOU.
PANT
PANT
I BORE IT ALL, THINKING OF YOU!

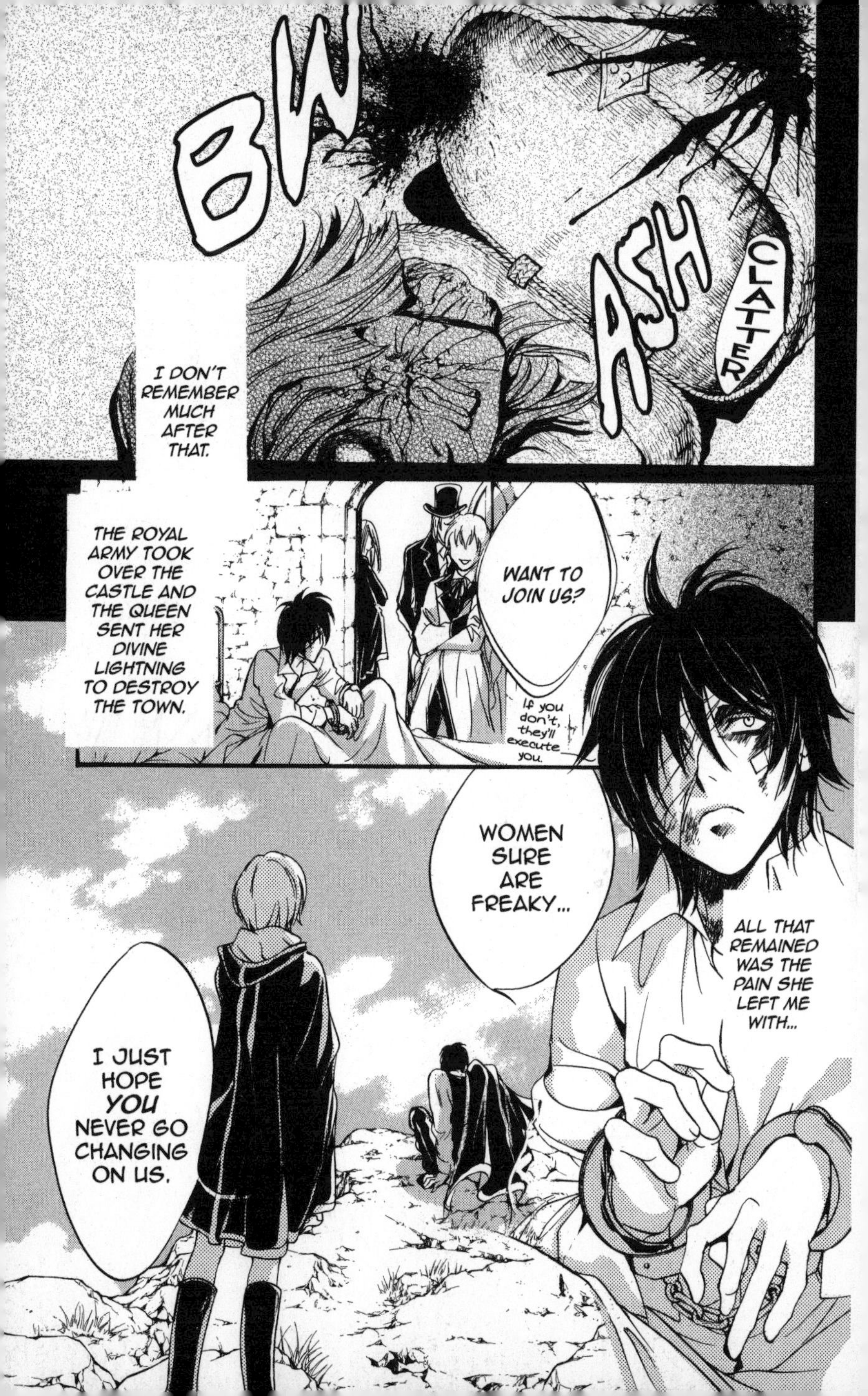
BWASH
CLATTER
I DON'T REMEMBER MUCH AFTER THAT.
WANT TO JOIN US?
If you don't, they'll execute you.
THE ROYAL ARMY TOOK OVER THE CASTLE AND THE QUEEN SENT HER DIVINE LIGHTNING TO DESTROY THE TOWN.
WOMEN SURE ARE FREAKY...
ALL THAT REMAINED WAS THE PAIN SHE LEFT ME WITH...
I JUST HOPE *YOU* NEVER GO CHANGING ON US.

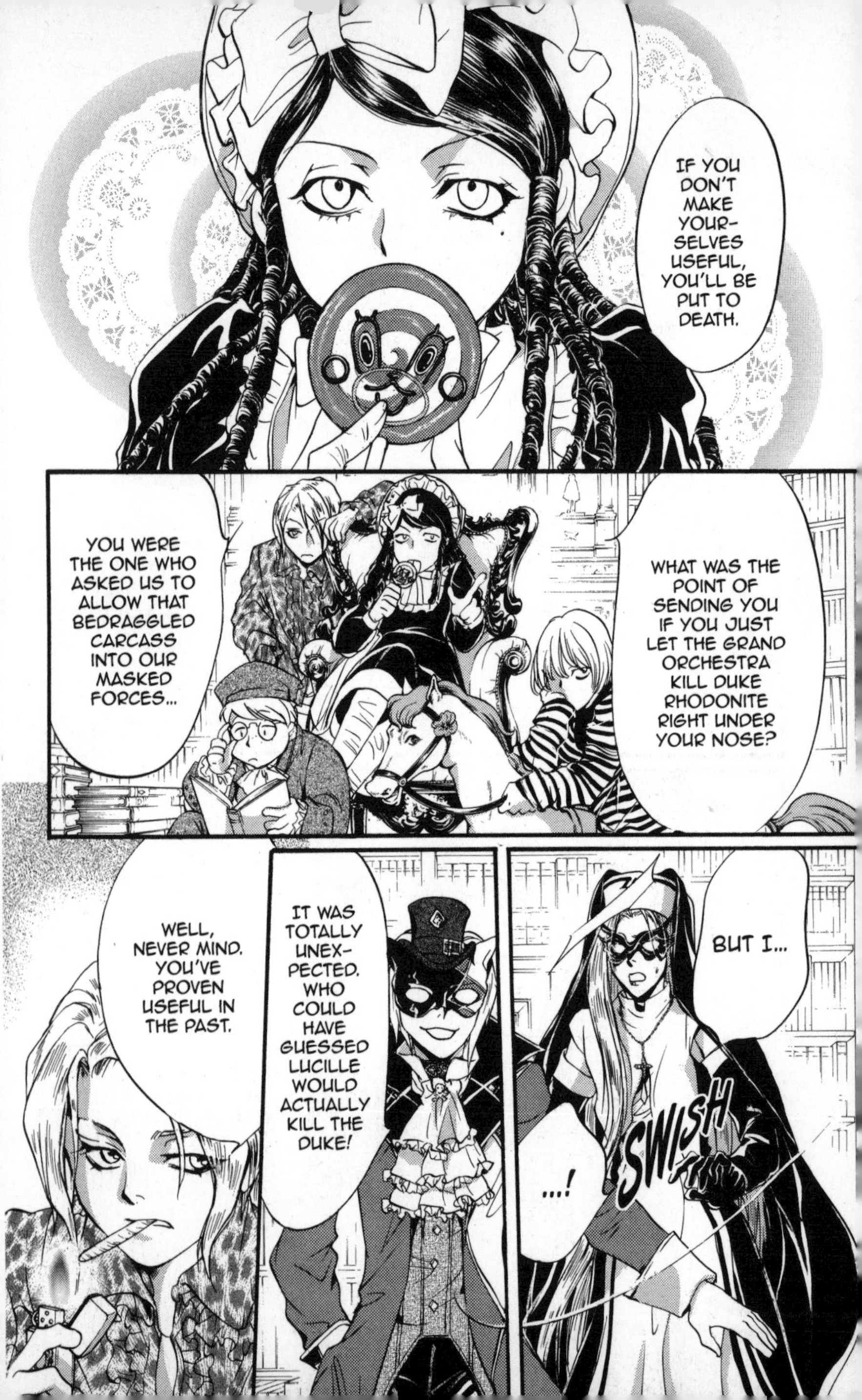

IF YOU DON'T MAKE YOUR-SELVES USEFUL, YOU'LL BE PUT TO DEATH.
WHAT WAS THE POINT OF SENDING YOU IF YOU JUST LET THE GRAND ORCHESTRA KILL DUKE RHODONITE RIGHT UNDER YOUR NOSE?
YOU WERE THE ONE WHO ASKED US TO ALLOW THAT BEDRAGGLED CARCASS INTO OUR MASKED FORCES...
BUT I...
SWISH
...!
IT WAS TOTALLY UNEX-PECTED. WHO COULD HAVE GUESSED LUCILLE WOULD ACTUALLY KILL THE DUKE!
WELL, NEVER MIND. YOU'VE PROVEN USEFUL IN THE PAST.

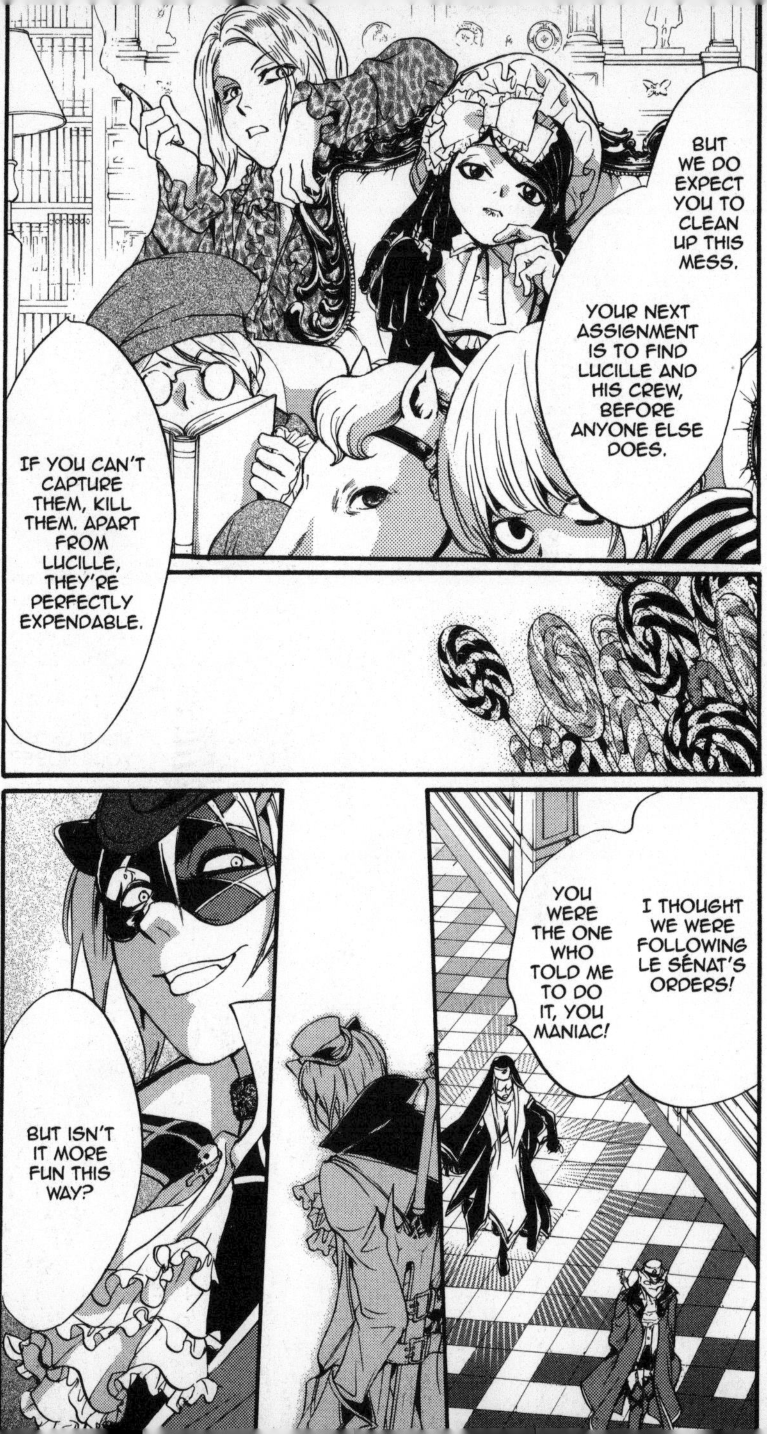
BUT WE DO EXPECT YOU TO CLEAN UP THIS MESS.
YOUR NEXT ASSIGNMENT IS TO FIND LUCILLE AND HIS CREW, BEFORE ANYONE ELSE DOES.
IF YOU CAN'T CAPTURE THEM, KILL THEM. APART FROM LUCILLE, THEY'RE PERFECTLY EXPENDABLE.
I THOUGHT WE WERE FOLLOWING LE SÉNAT'S ORDERS!
YOU WERE THE ONE WHO TOLD ME TO DO IT, YOU MANIAC!
BUT ISN'T IT MORE FUN THIS WAY?

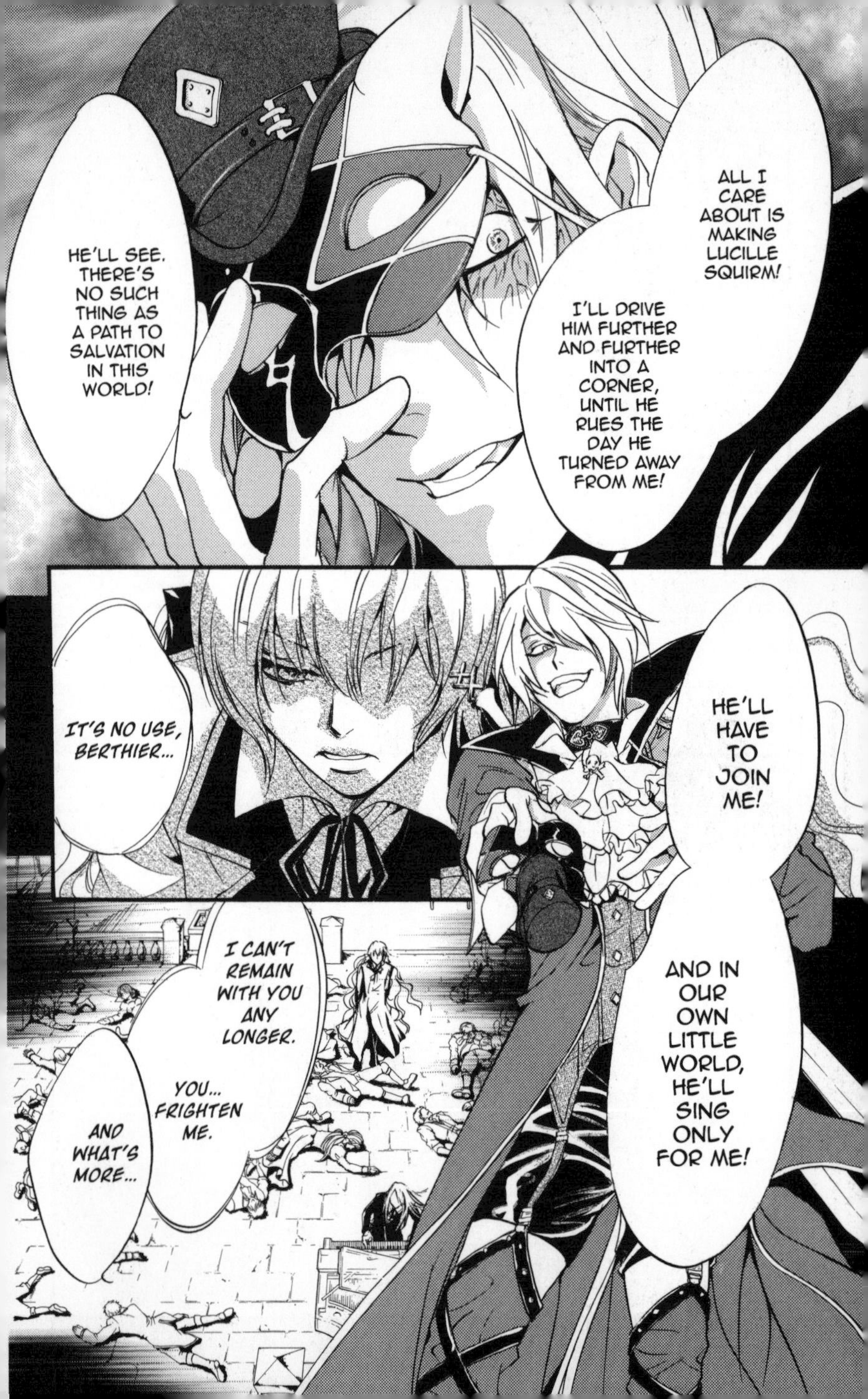
ALL I CARE ABOUT IS MAKING LUCILLE SQUIRM!
I'LL DRIVE HIM FURTHER AND FURTHER INTO A CORNER, UNTIL HE RUES THE DAY HE TURNED AWAY FROM ME!
HE'LL SEE. THERE'S NO SUCH THING AS A PATH TO SALVATION IN THIS WORLD!
HE'LL HAVE TO JOIN ME!
AND IN OUR OWN LITTLE WORLD, HE'LL SING ONLY FOR ME!
IT'S NO USE, BERTHIER...
I CAN'T REMAIN WITH YOU ANY LONGER.
YOU... FRIGHTEN ME.
AND WHAT'S MORE...

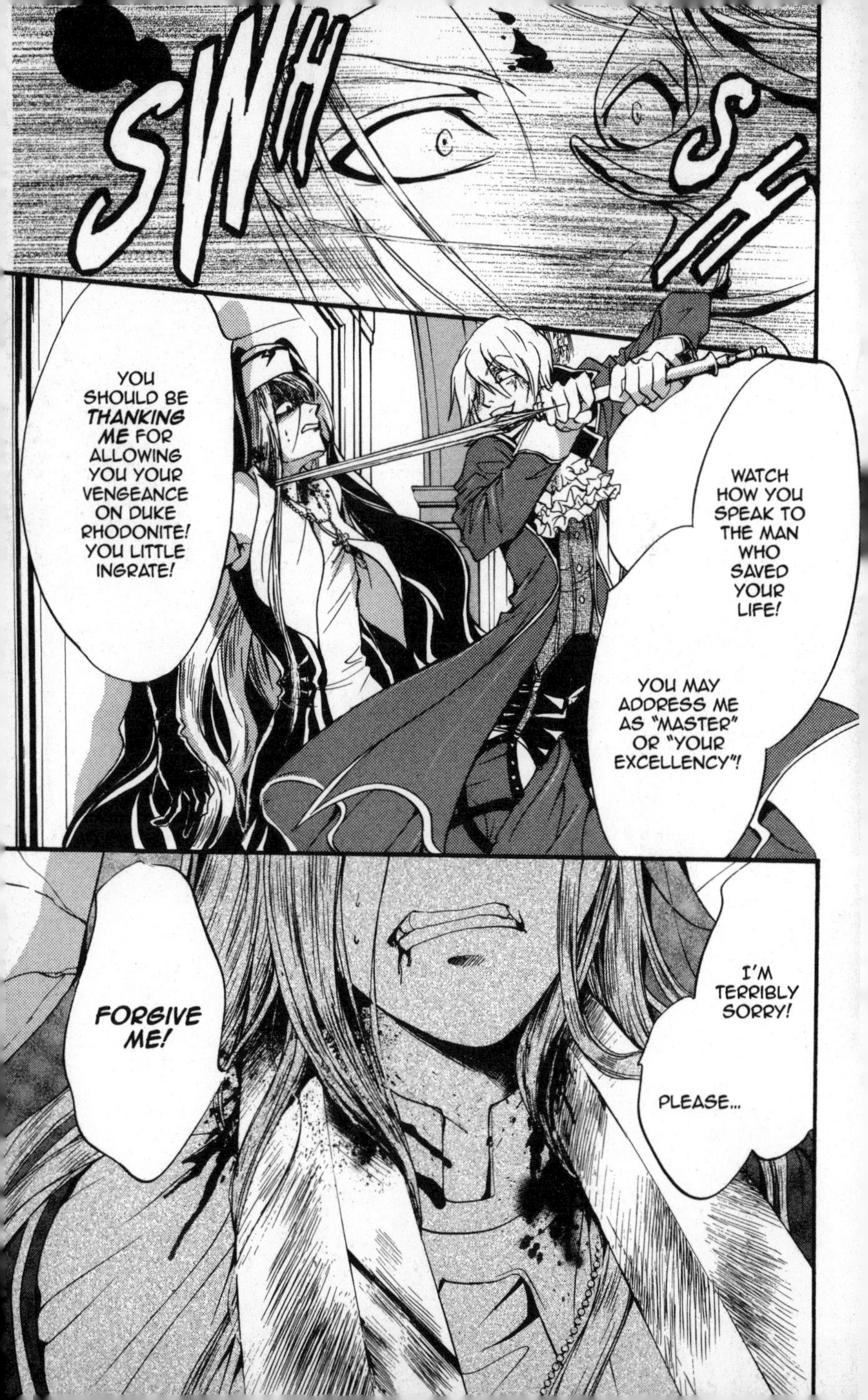
WATCH HOW YOU SPEAK TO THE MAN WHO SAVED YOUR LIFE!
YOU MAY ADDRESS ME AS "MASTER" OR "YOUR EXCELLENCY"!
YOU SHOULD BE *THANKING ME* FOR ALLOWING YOU YOUR VENGEANCE ON DUKE RHODONITE! YOU LITTLE INGRATE!
I'M TERRIBLY SORRY!
PLEASE...
FORGIVE ME!

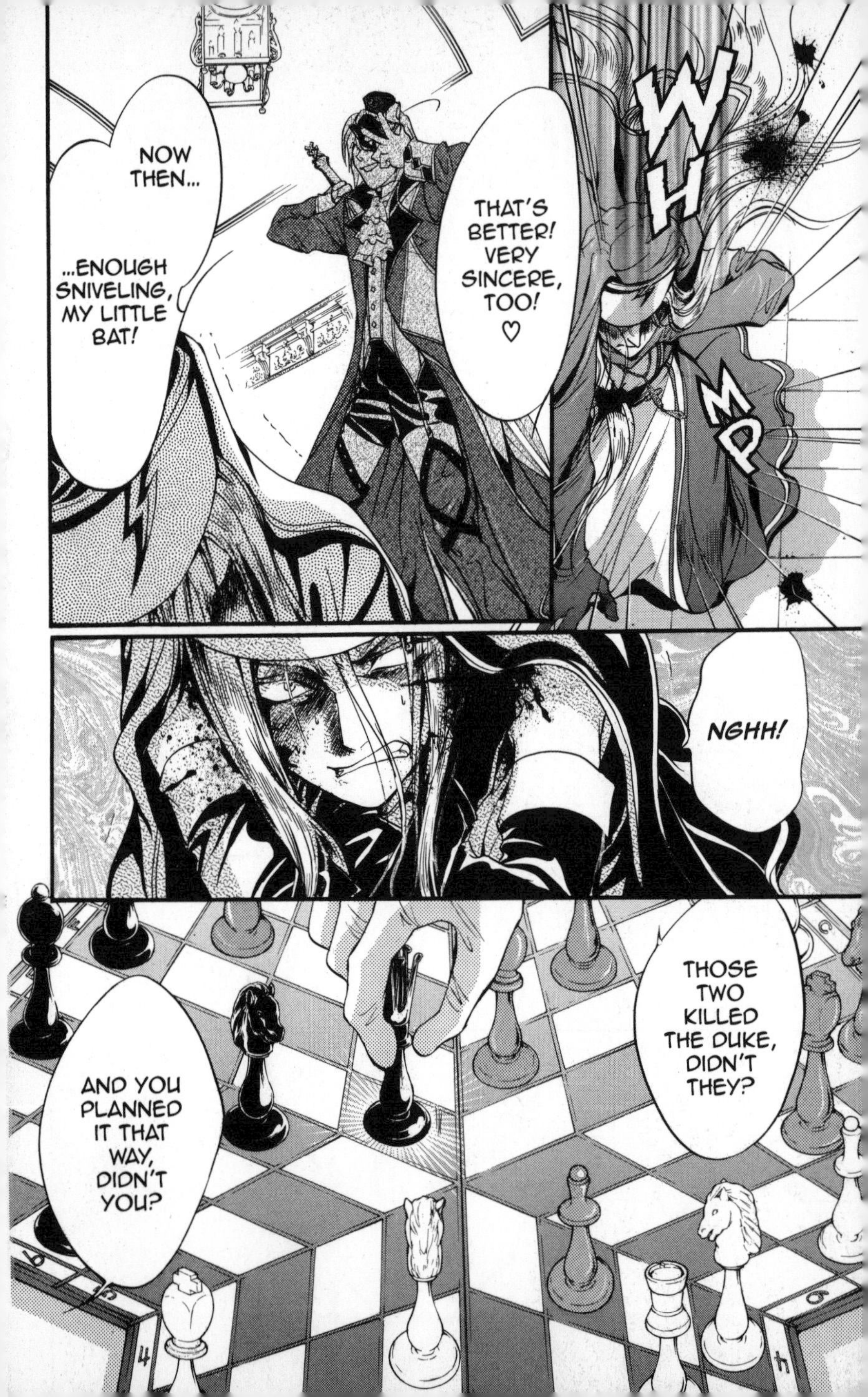
WH
MP
THAT'S BETTER! VERY SINCERE, TOO! ♡
NOW THEN...
...ENOUGH SNIVELING, MY LITTLE BAT!
NGHH!
THOSE TWO KILLED THE DUKE, DIDN'T THEY?
AND YOU PLANNED IT THAT WAY, DIDN'T YOU?

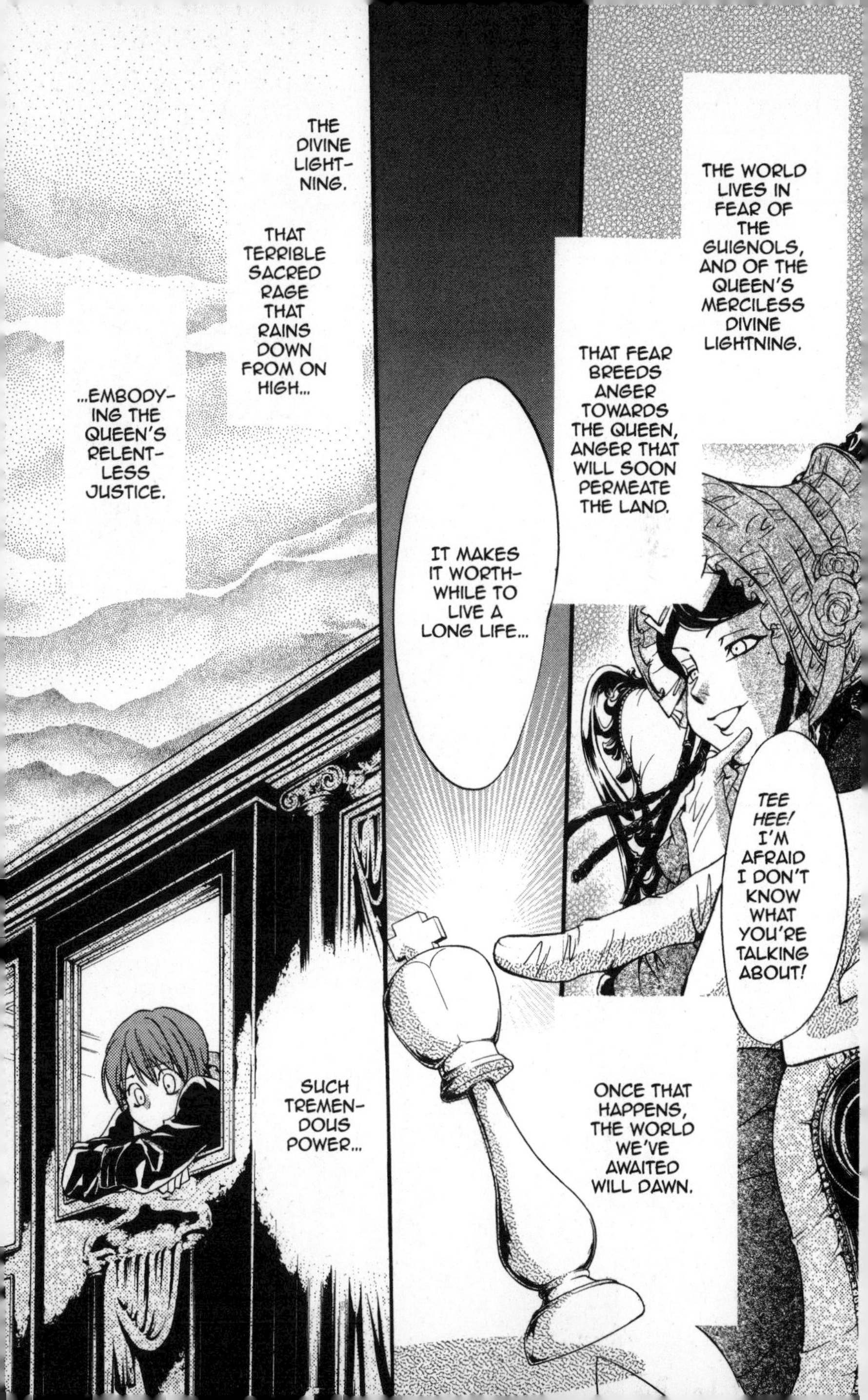
THE WORLD LIVES IN FEAR OF THE GUIGNOLS, AND OF THE QUEEN'S MERCILESS DIVINE LIGHTNING.
THAT FEAR BREEDS ANGER TOWARDS THE QUEEN, ANGER THAT WILL SOON PERMEATE THE LAND.
IT MAKES IT WORTH-WHILE TO LIVE A LONG LIFE...
TEE HEE! I'M AFRAID I DON'T KNOW WHAT YOU'RE TALKING ABOUT!
ONCE THAT HAPPENS, THE WORLD WE'VE AWAITED WILL DAWN.
THE DIVINE LIGHT-NING.
THAT TERRIBLE SACRED RAGE THAT RAINS DOWN FROM ON HIGH...
...EMBODY-ING THE QUEEN'S RELENT-LESS JUSTICE.
SUCH TREMEN-DOUS POWER...

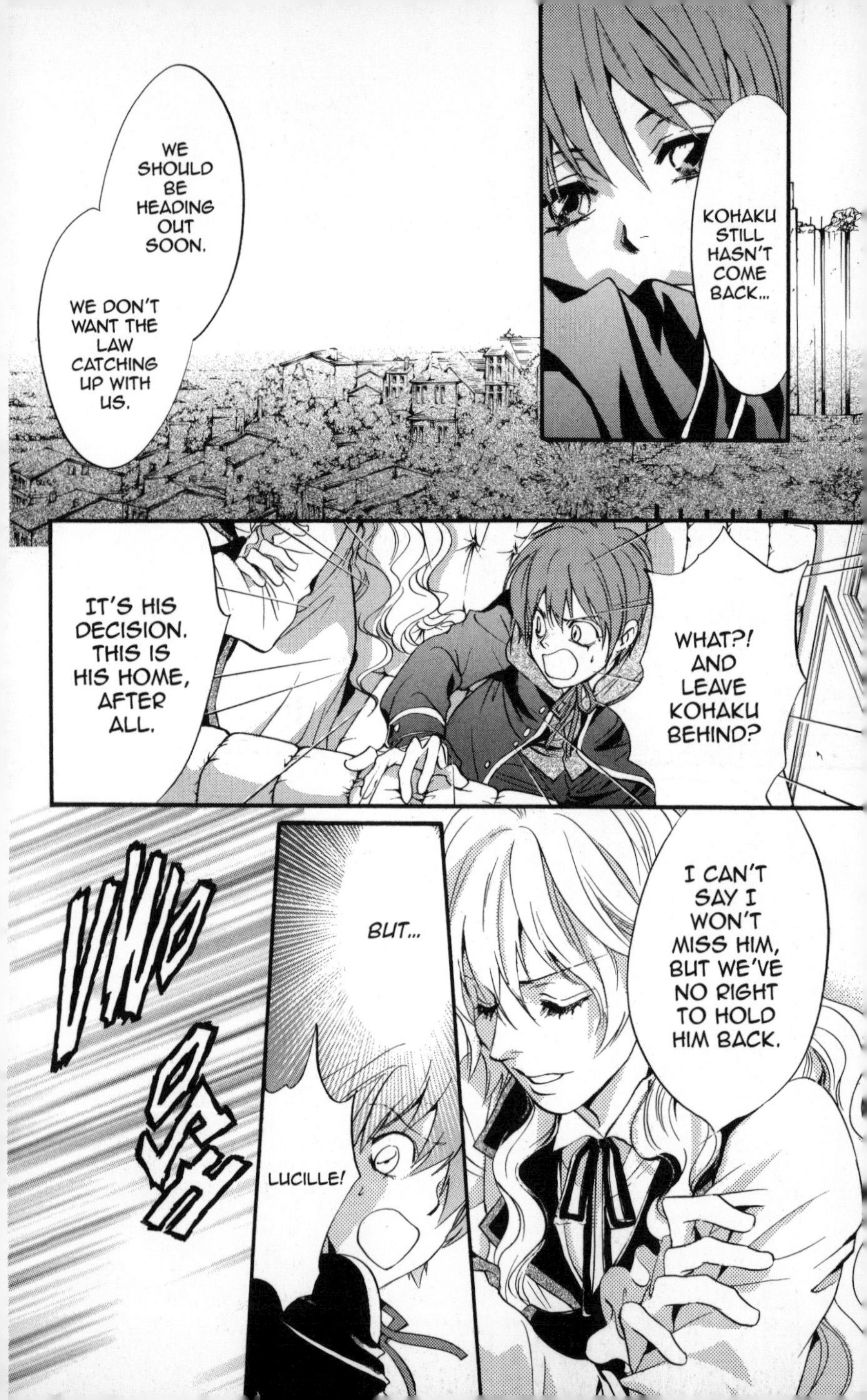
KOHAKU STILL HASN'T COME BACK...
WE SHOULD BE HEADING OUT SOON.
WE DON'T WANT THE LAW CATCHING UP WITH US.
WHAT?! AND LEAVE KOHAKU BEHIND?
IT'S HIS DECISION. THIS IS HIS HOME, AFTER ALL.
I CAN'T SAY I WON'T MISS HIM, BUT WE'VE NO RIGHT TO HOLD HIM BACK.
BUT...
LUCILLE!
WHOOSH

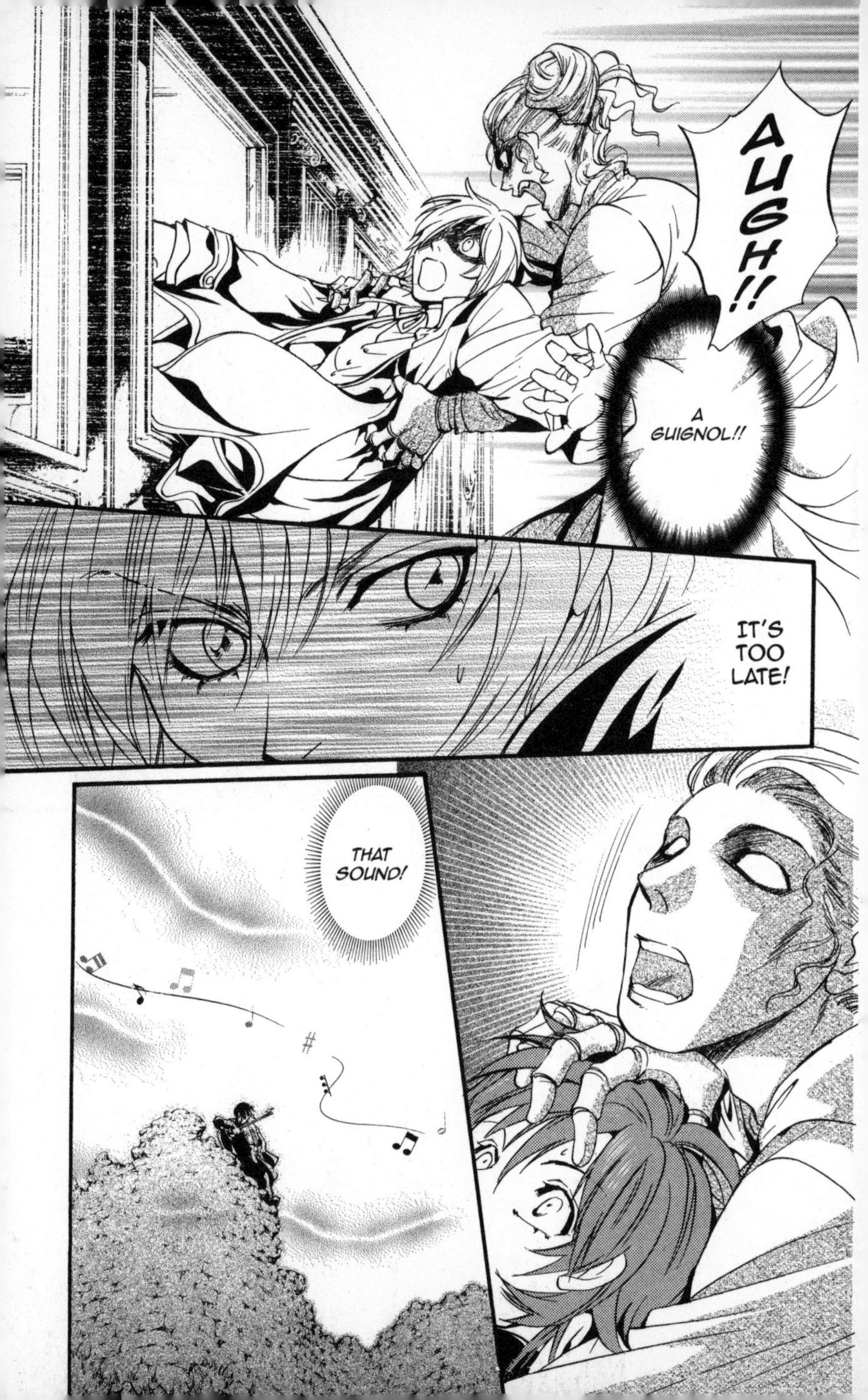
AUGH!!
A GUIGNOL!!
IT'S TOO LATE!
THAT SOUND!

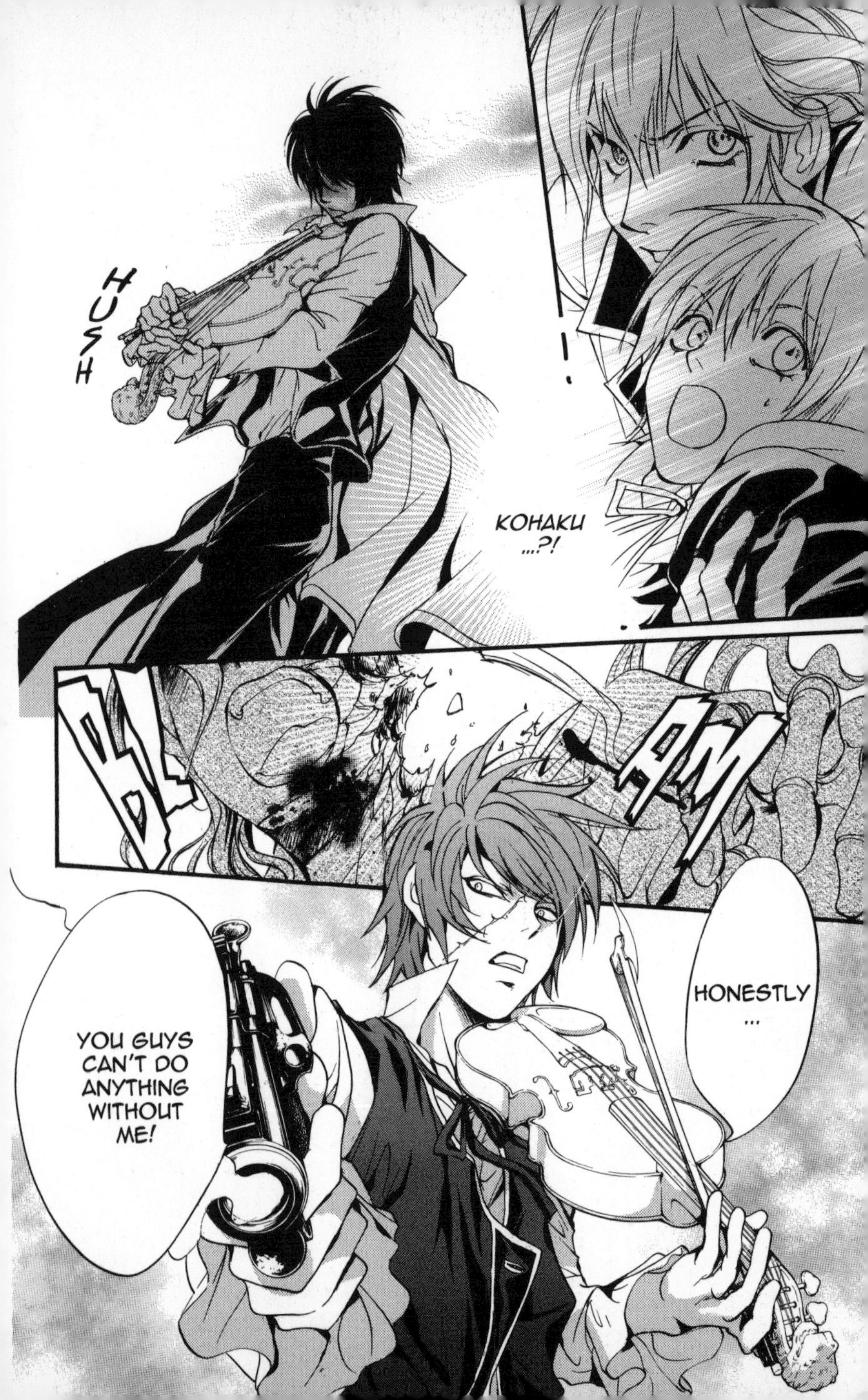
!
KOHAKU ...?!
HUSH
BLAM
HONESTLY ...
YOU GUYS CAN'T DO ANYTHING WITHOUT ME!

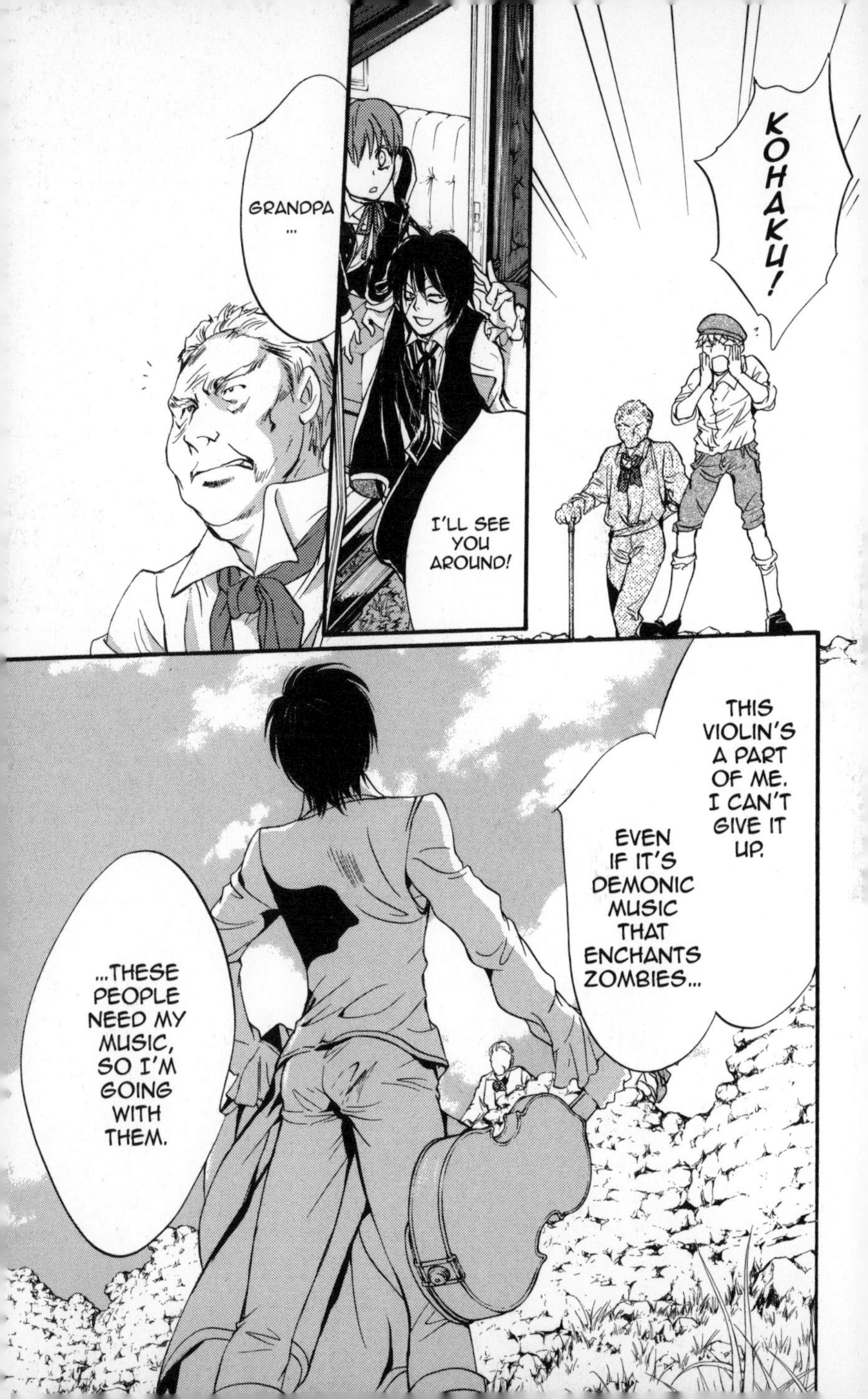
KOHAKU!
I'LL SEE YOU AROUND!
GRANDPA ...
THIS VIOLIN'S A PART OF ME. I CAN'T GIVE IT UP.
EVEN IF IT'S DEMONIC MUSIC THAT ENCHANTS ZOMBIES...
...THESE PEOPLE NEED MY MUSIC, SO I'M GOING WITH THEM.

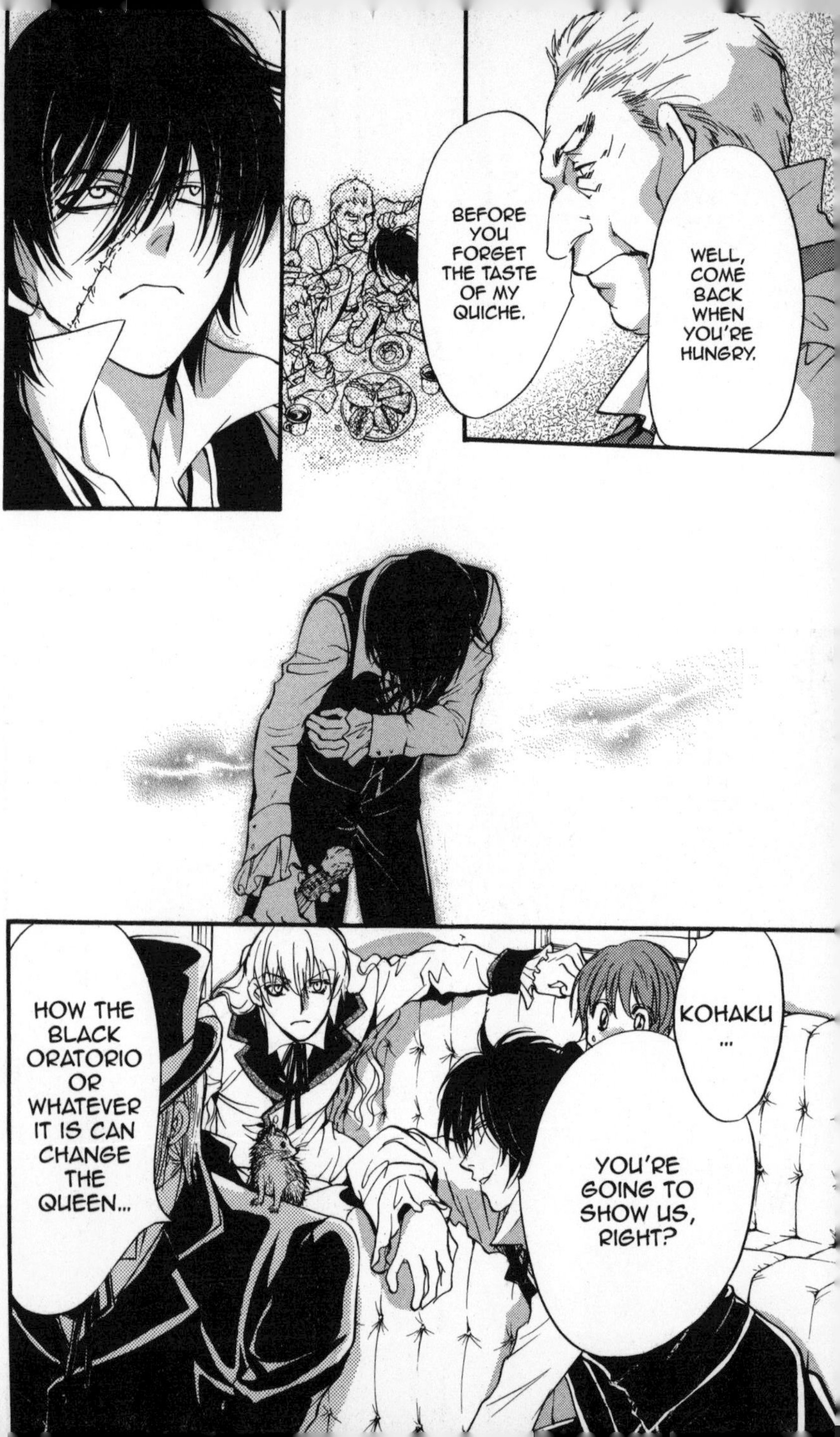
WELL, COME BACK WHEN YOU'RE HUNGRY.
BEFORE YOU FORGET THE TASTE OF MY QUICHE.
KOHAKU ...
YOU'RE GOING TO SHOW US, RIGHT?
HOW THE BLACK ORATORIO OR WHATEVER IT IS CAN CHANGE THE QUEEN...

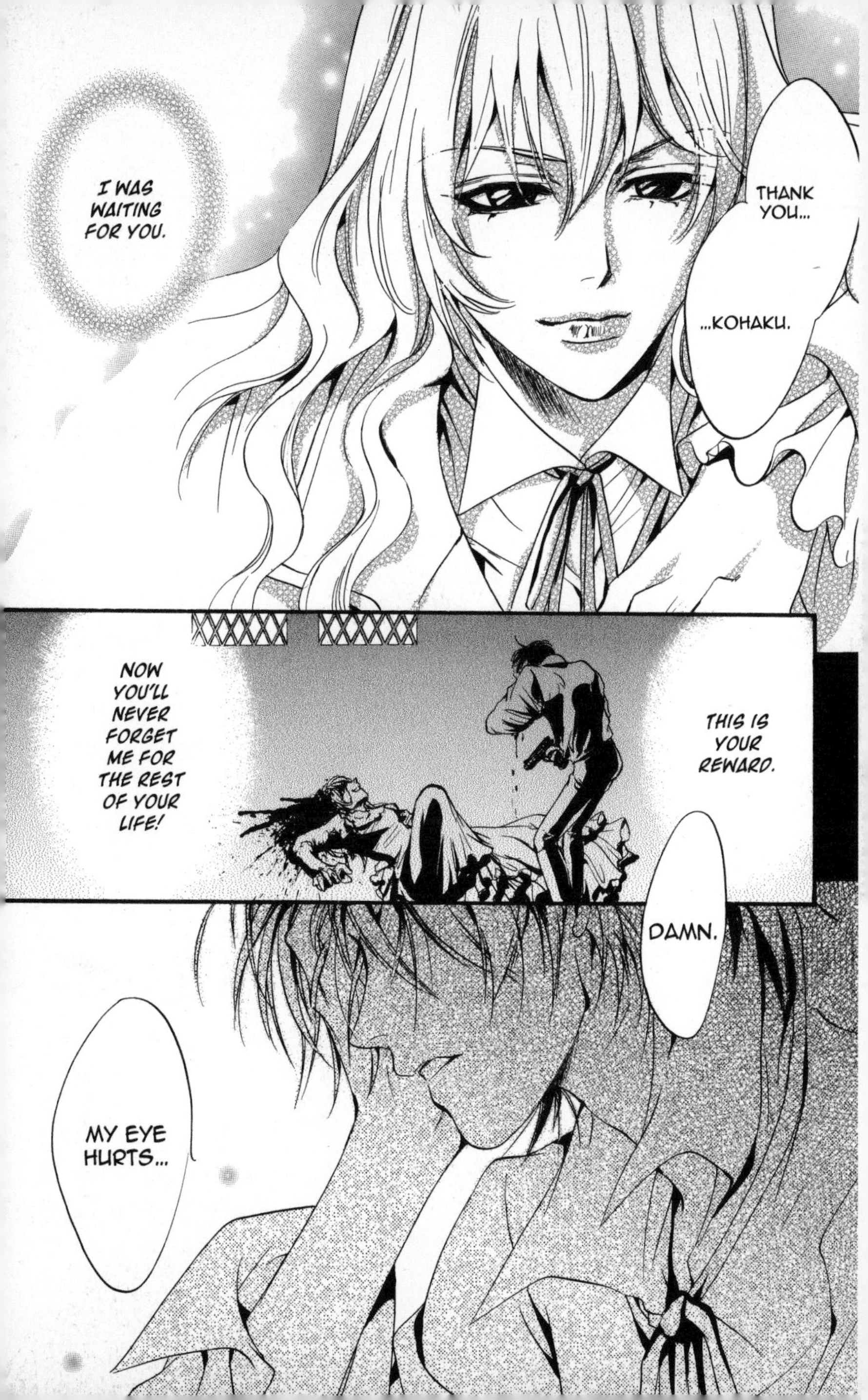
THANK YOU...
...KOHAKU.
I WAS WAITING FOR YOU.
THIS IS YOUR REWARD.
NOW YOU'LL NEVER FORGET ME FOR THE REST OF YOUR LIFE!
DAMN.
MY EYE HURTS...

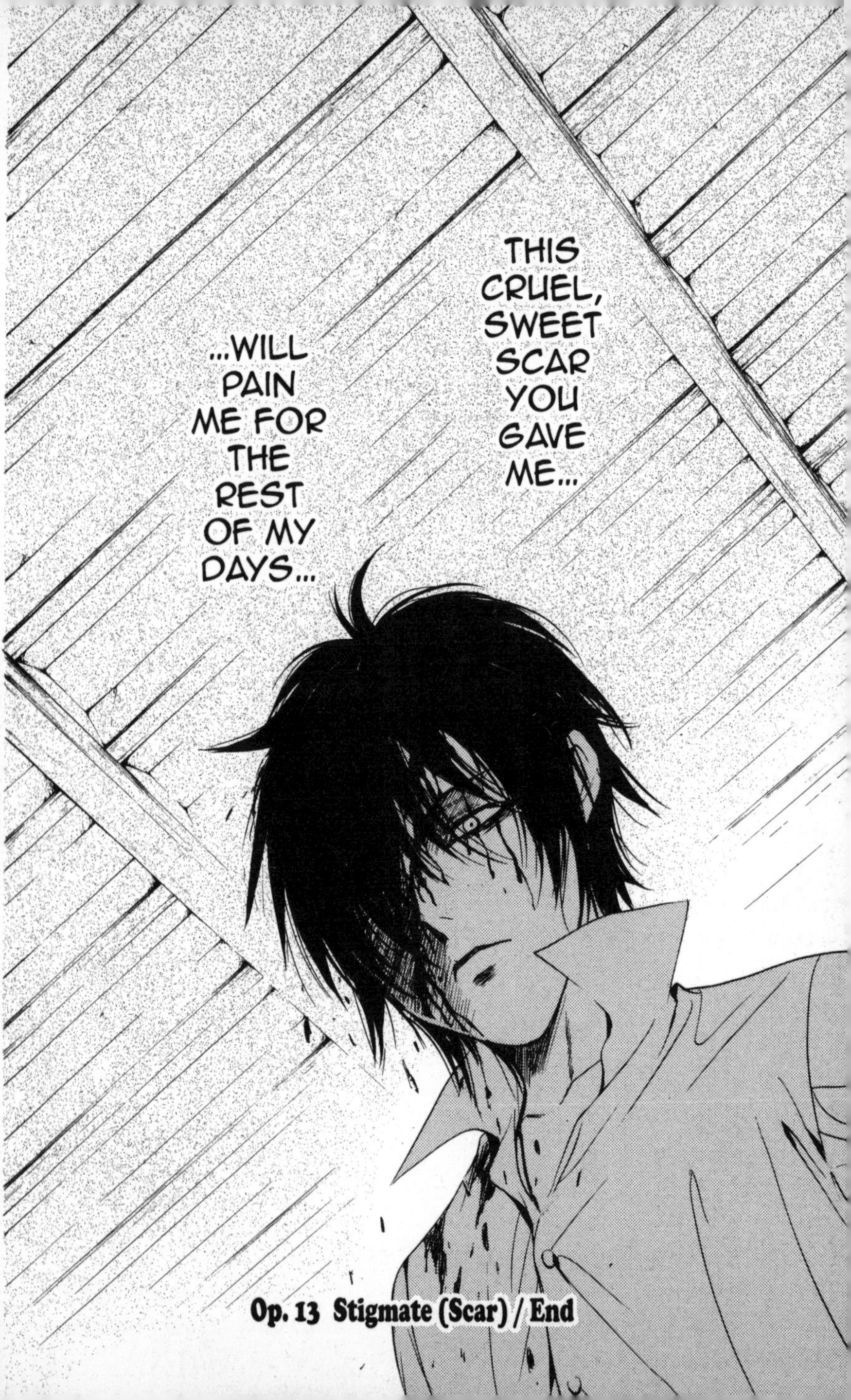
THIS CRUEL, SWEET SCAR YOU GAVE ME...
...WILL PAIN ME FOR THE REST OF MY DAYS...

Op. 13 Stigmate (Scar) / End

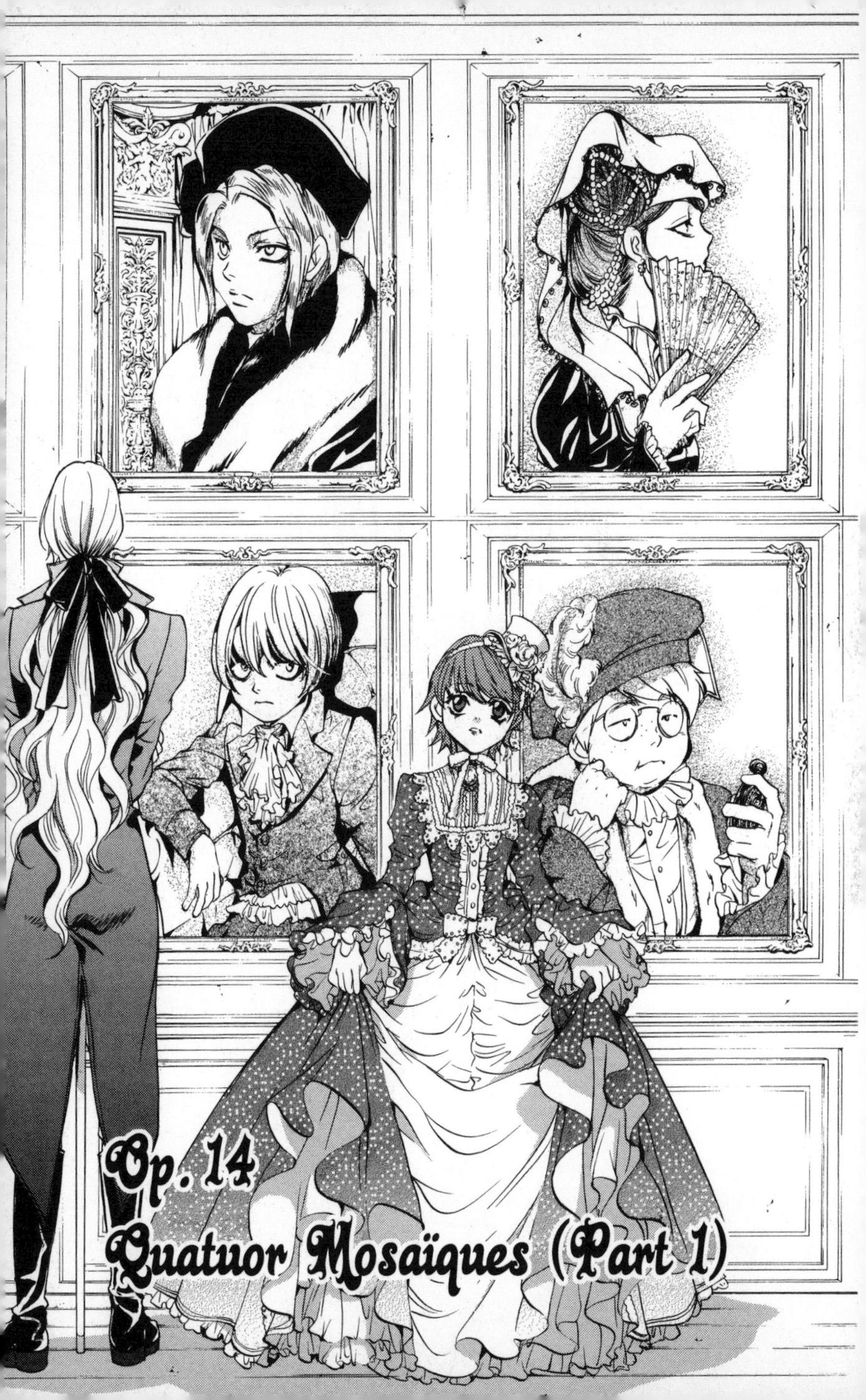
Op. 14
Quatuor Mosaïques (Part 1)

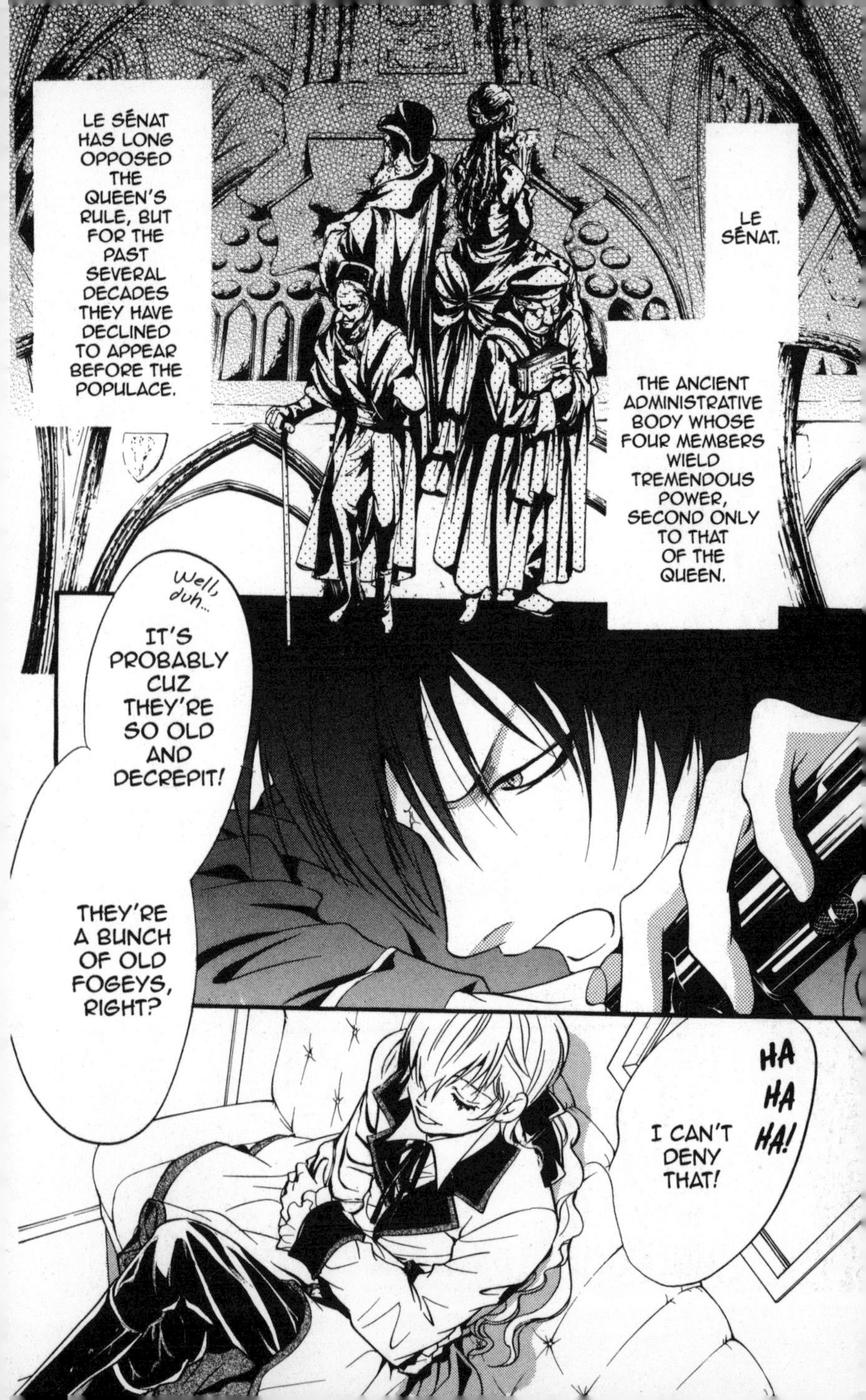
LE SÉNAT.
THE ANCIENT ADMINISTRATIVE BODY WHOSE FOUR MEMBERS WIELD TREMENDOUS POWER, SECOND ONLY TO THAT OF THE QUEEN.
LE SÉNAT HAS LONG OPPOSED THE QUEEN'S RULE, BUT FOR THE PAST SEVERAL DECADES THEY HAVE DECLINED TO APPEAR BEFORE THE POPULACE.
Well, duh...
IT'S PROBABLY CUZ THEY'RE SO OLD AND DECREPIT!
THEY'RE A BUNCH OF OLD FOGEYS, RIGHT?
HA HA HA!
I CAN'T DENY THAT!

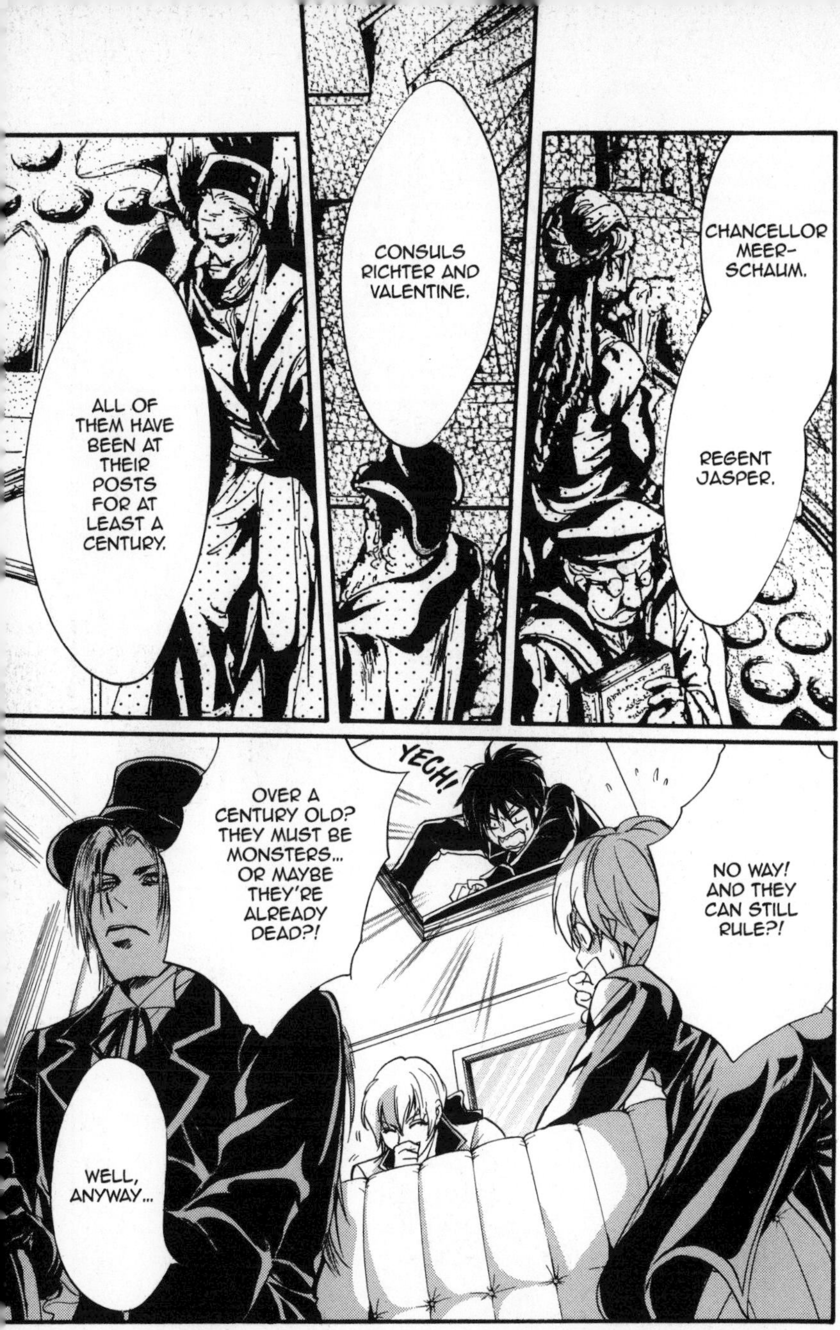
CHANCELLOR MEER-SCHAUM.
REGENT JASPER.
CONSULS RICHTER AND VALENTINE.
ALL OF THEM HAVE BEEN AT THEIR POSTS FOR AT LEAST A CENTURY.
NO WAY! AND THEY CAN STILL RULE?!
YECH!
OVER A CENTURY OLD? THEY MUST BE MONSTERS... OR MAYBE THEY'RE ALREADY DEAD?!
WELL, ANYWAY...

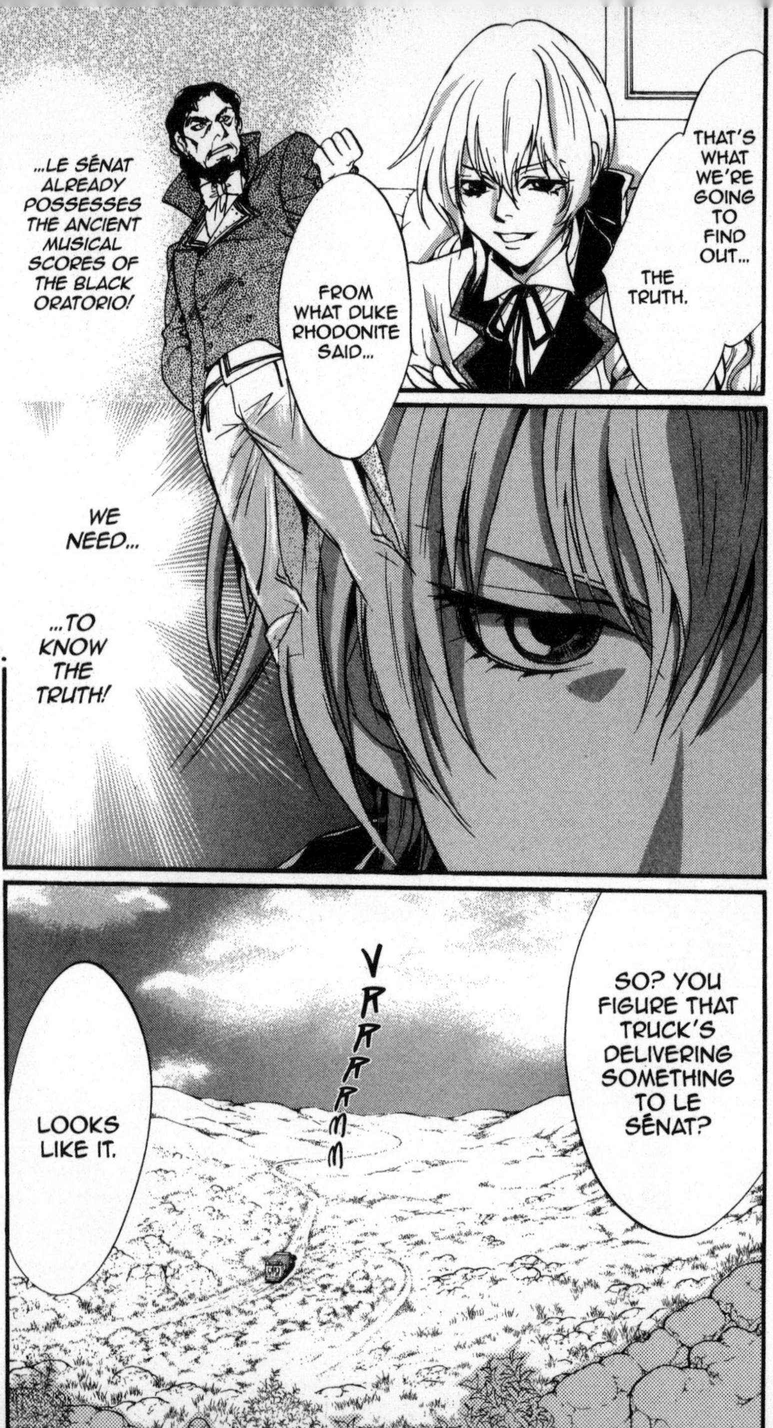
FROM WHAT DUKE RHODONITE SAID...
...LE SÉNAT ALREADY POSSESSES THE ANCIENT MUSICAL SCORES OF THE BLACK ORATORIO!
WE NEED...
...TO KNOW THE TRUTH!
THAT'S WHAT WE'RE GOING TO FIND OUT...
THE TRUTH.
SO? YOU FIGURE THAT TRUCK'S DELIVERING SOMETHING TO LE SÉNAT?
VRRRRRMM
LOOKS LIKE IT.

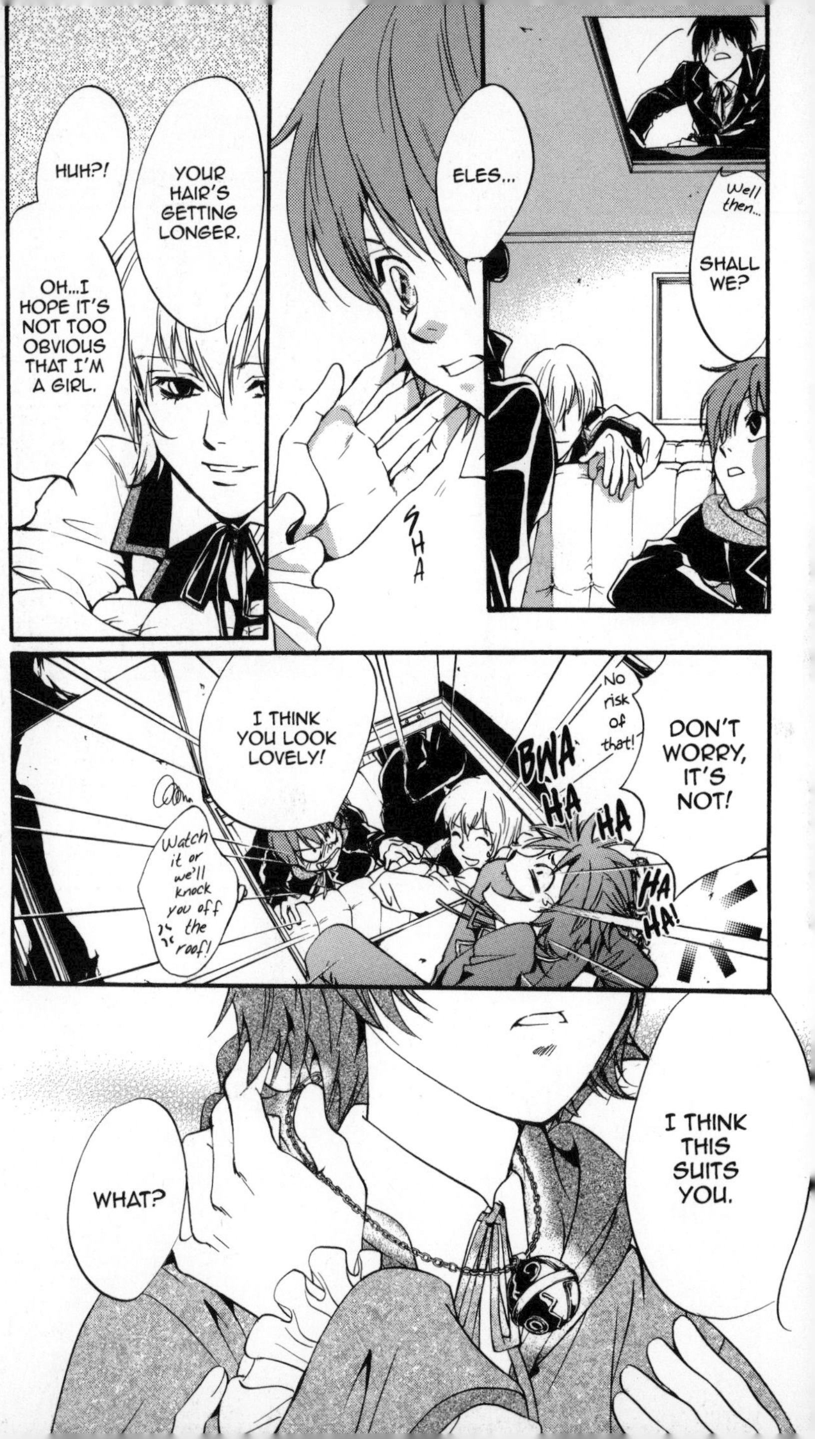
Well then...
SHALL WE?
ELES...
SHA
YOUR HAIR'S GETTING LONGER.
HUH?!
OH...I HOPE IT'S NOT TOO OBVIOUS THAT I'M A GIRL.
DON'T WORRY, IT'S NOT!
No risk of that!
BWA HA HA HA HA!
I THINK YOU LOOK LOVELY!
Watch it or we'll knock you off the roof!
I THINK THIS SUITS YOU.
WHAT?

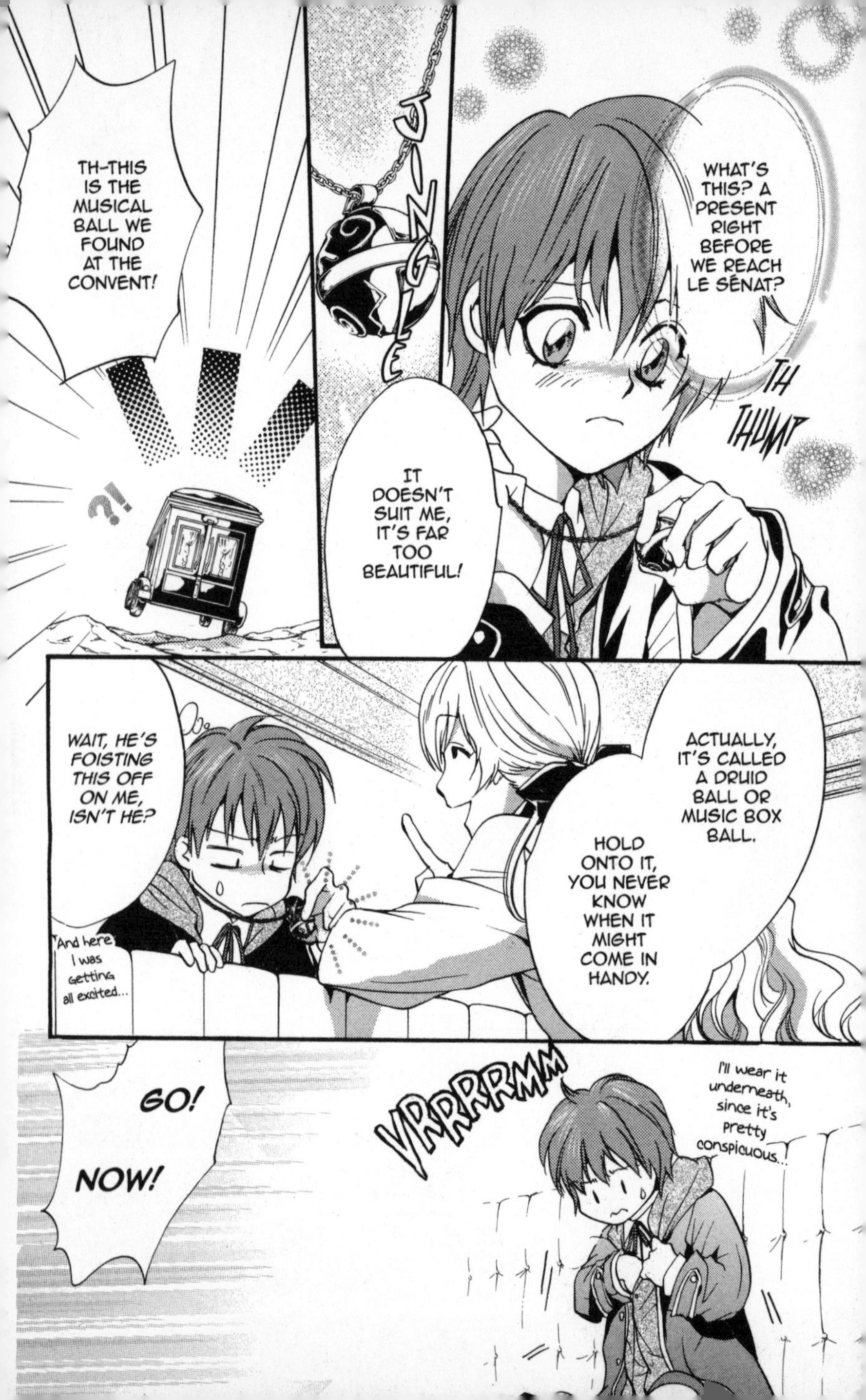
WHAT'S THIS? A PRESENT RIGHT BEFORE WE REACH LE SÉNAT?
TH THUMP
JINGLE
IT DOESN'T SUIT ME, IT'S FAR TOO BEAUTIFUL!
TH-THIS IS THE MUSICAL BALL WE FOUND AT THE CONVENT!
?!
ACTUALLY, IT'S CALLED A DRUID BALL OR MUSIC BOX BALL.
HOLD ONTO IT, YOU NEVER KNOW WHEN IT MIGHT COME IN HANDY.
WAIT, HE'S FOISTING THIS OFF ON ME, ISN'T HE?
And here I was getting all excited...
I'll wear it underneath, since it's pretty conspicuous...
VRRRRMM
GO!
NOW!

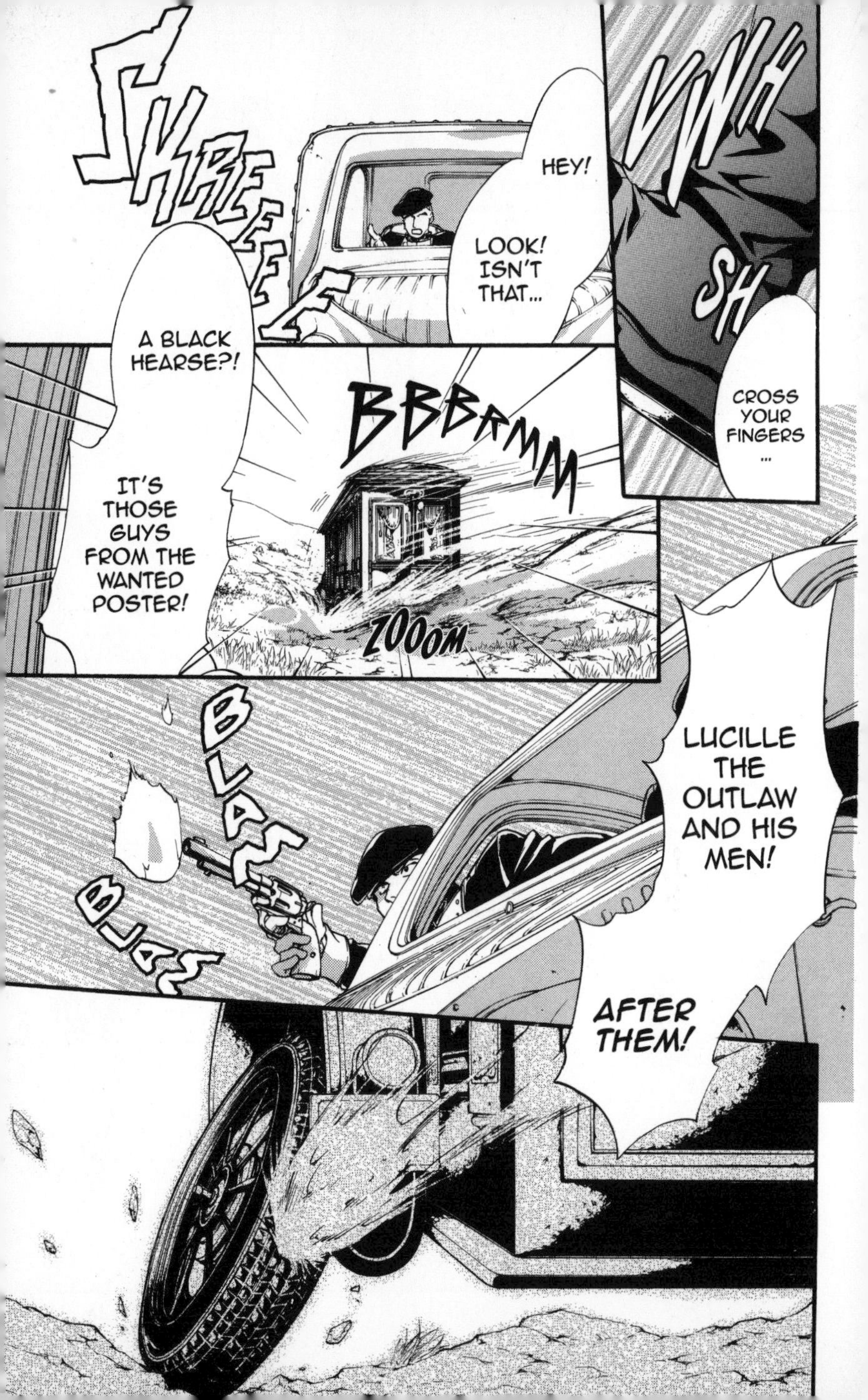
VVNH
SH
CROSS YOUR FINGERS...
SKREEEE
HEY!
LOOK! ISN'T THAT...
A BLACK HEARSE?!
BBBRMMM
ZOOOM
IT'S THOSE GUYS FROM THE WANTED POSTER!
LUCILLE THE OUTLAW AND HIS MEN!
AFTER THEM!
BLAM
BLAM

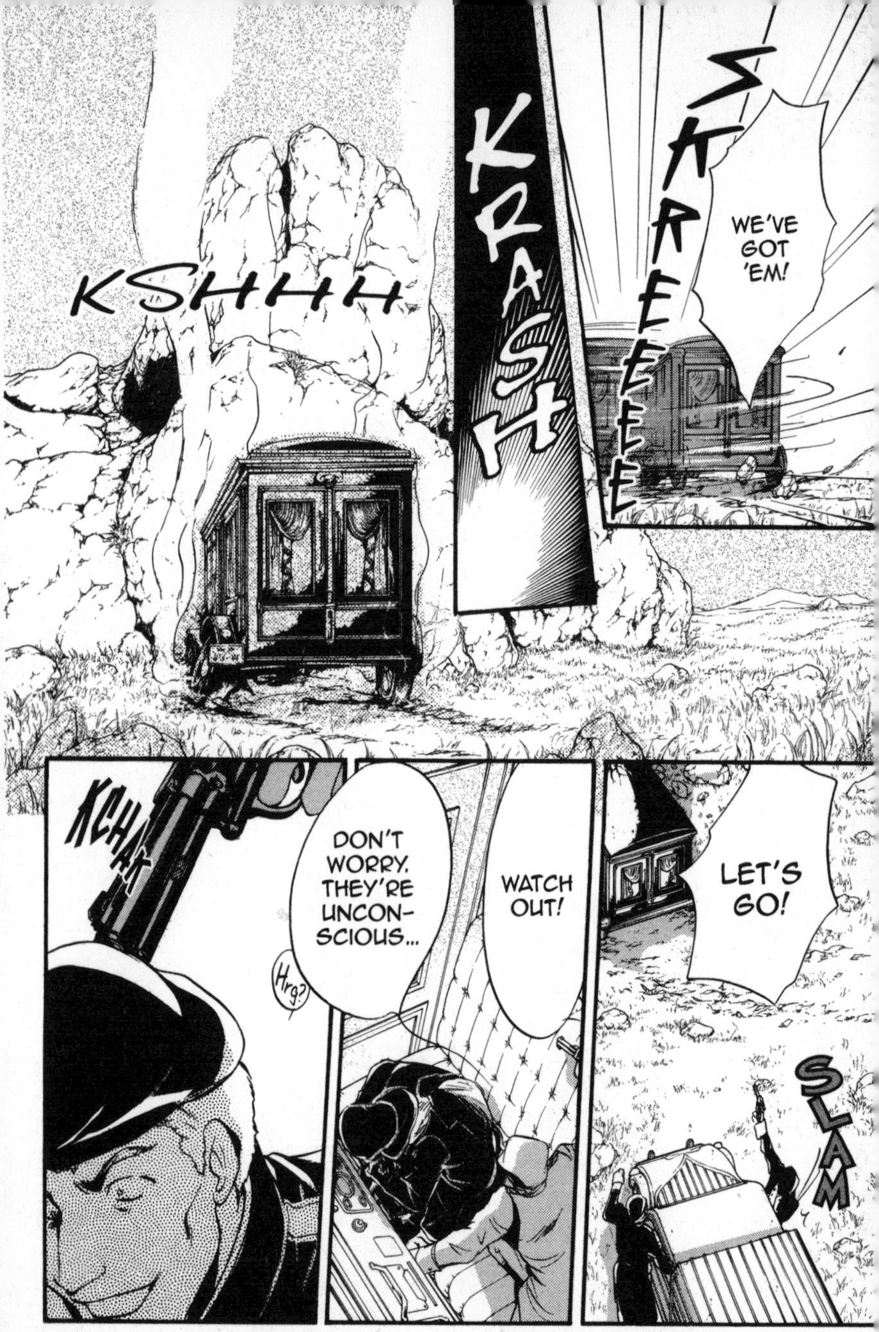
SKREEEEE
WE'VE GOT 'EM!
KRASH
KSHHHH
LET'S GO!
SLAM
WATCH OUT!
DON'T WORRY. THEY'RE UNCON-SCIOUS...
KCHAK
Hrg?

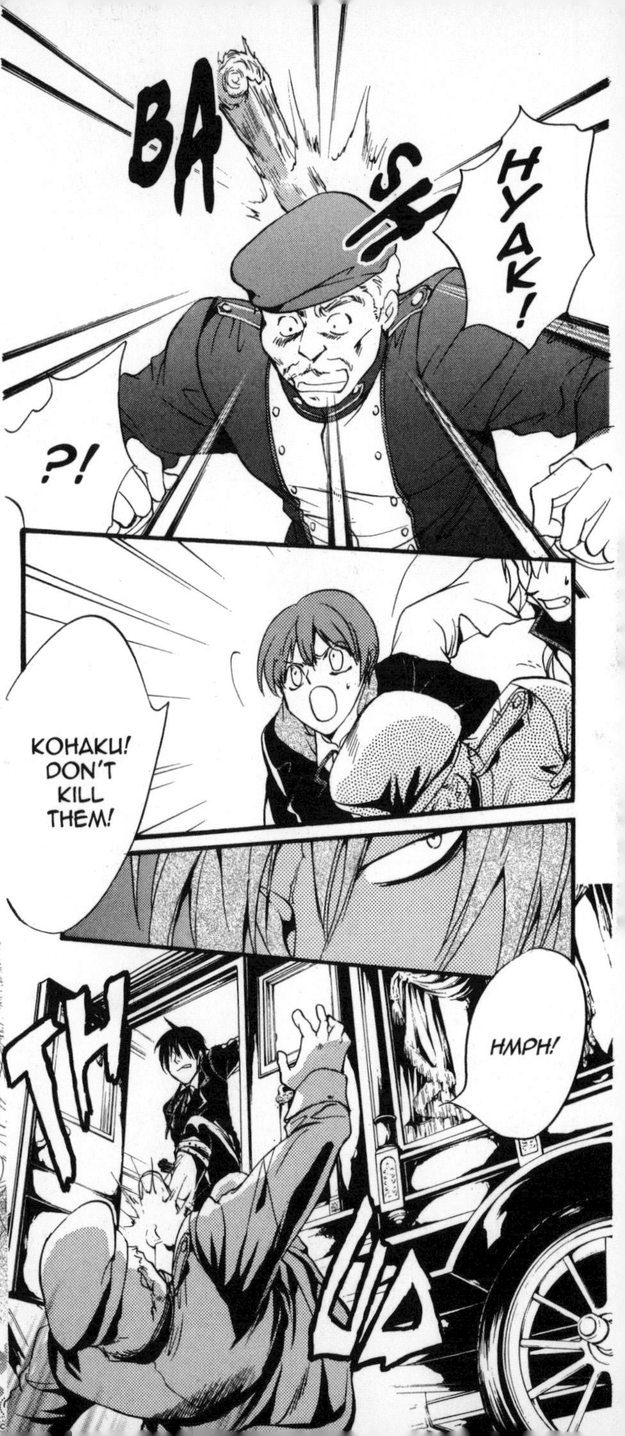
HYAK!
BASH
?!
KOHAKU! DON'T KILL THEM!
HMPH!
TH

I drew the chapter title page with the portraits of Le Sénat and the figures of the four old people for contrast. With four of them, it's been a lot of work making them each distinctive. Also, there are a few distinctive looking members of the Accordeurs—the masked forces commanded by Le Sénat—but I haven't come up with storylines for them.

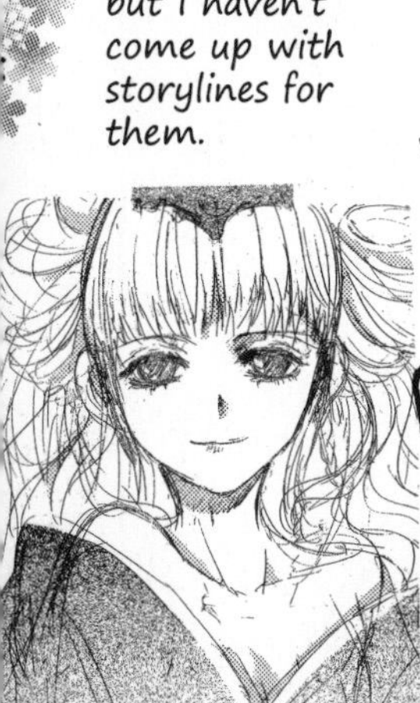

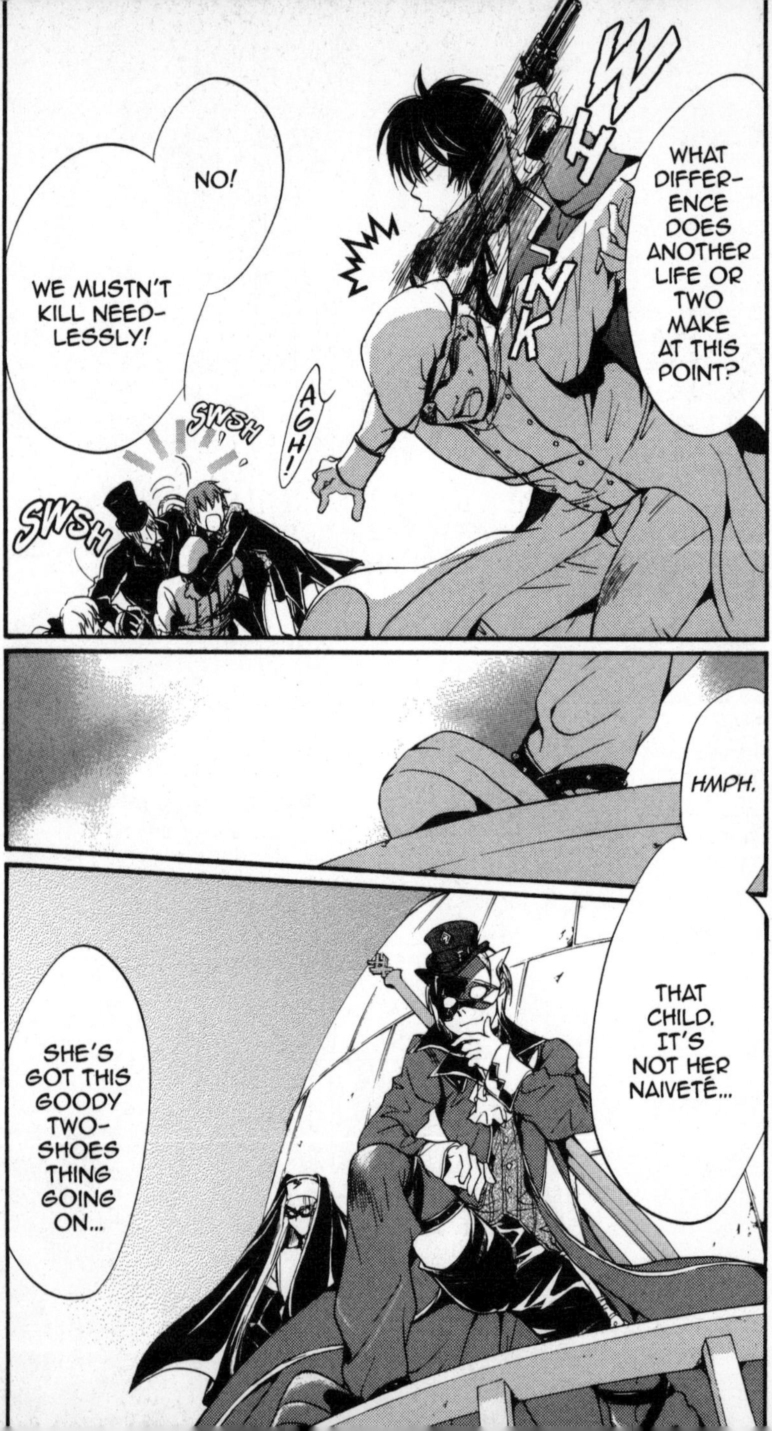
WHNK
WHAT DIFFERENCE DOES ANOTHER LIFE OR TWO MAKE AT THIS POINT?
NO!
WE MUSTN'T KILL NEEDLESSLY!
AGH!
SWSH
SWSH
HMPH.
THAT CHILD. IT'S NOT HER NAIVETÉ...
SHE'S GOT THIS GOODY TWO-SHOES THING GOING ON...

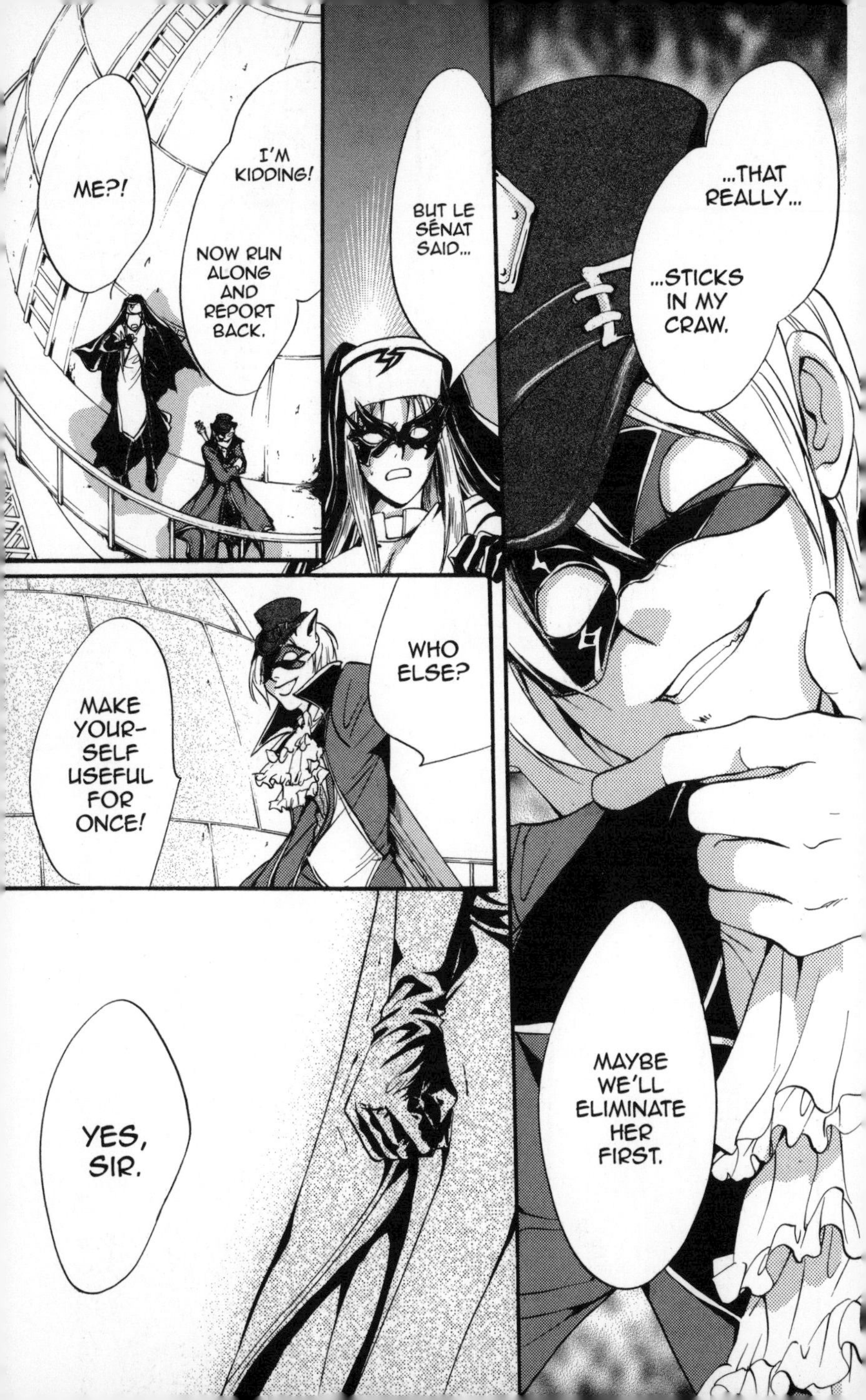
...THAT REALLY...
...STICKS IN MY CRAW.
MAYBE WE'LL ELIMINATE HER FIRST.
BUT LE SÉNAT SAID...
I'M KIDDING!
NOW RUN ALONG AND REPORT BACK.
ME?!
WHO ELSE?
MAKE YOURSELF USEFUL FOR ONCE!
YES, SIR.

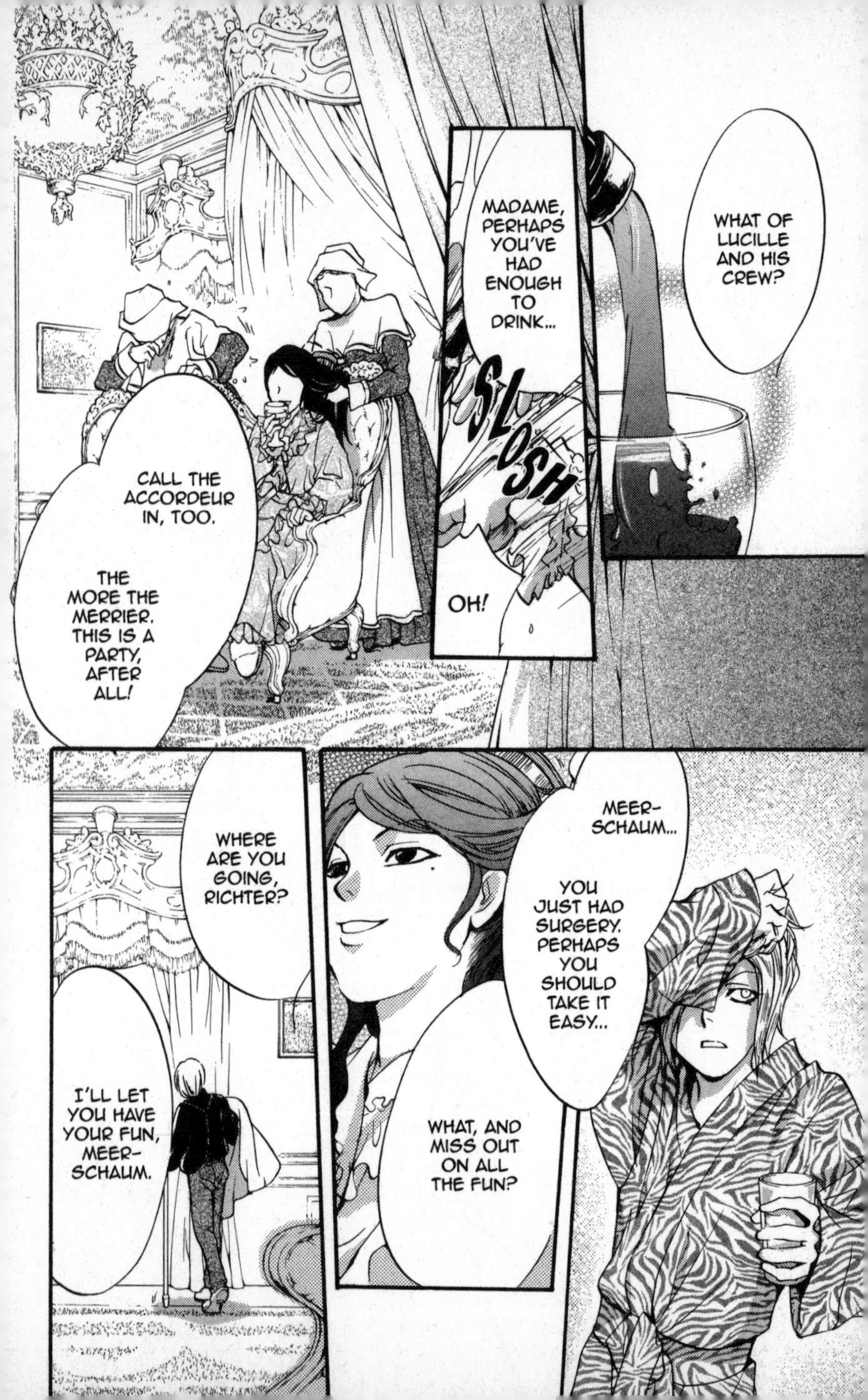
WHAT OF LUCILLE AND HIS CREW?
MADAME, PERHAPS YOU'VE HAD ENOUGH TO DRINK...
SLOSH
OH!
CALL THE ACCORDEUR IN, TOO.
THE MORE THE MERRIER. THIS IS A PARTY, AFTER ALL!
MEER-SCHAUM...
YOU JUST HAD SURGERY. PERHAPS YOU SHOULD TAKE IT EASY...
WHAT, AND MISS OUT ON ALL THE FUN?
WHERE ARE YOU GOING, RICHTER?
I'LL LET YOU HAVE YOUR FUN, MEER-SCHAUM.

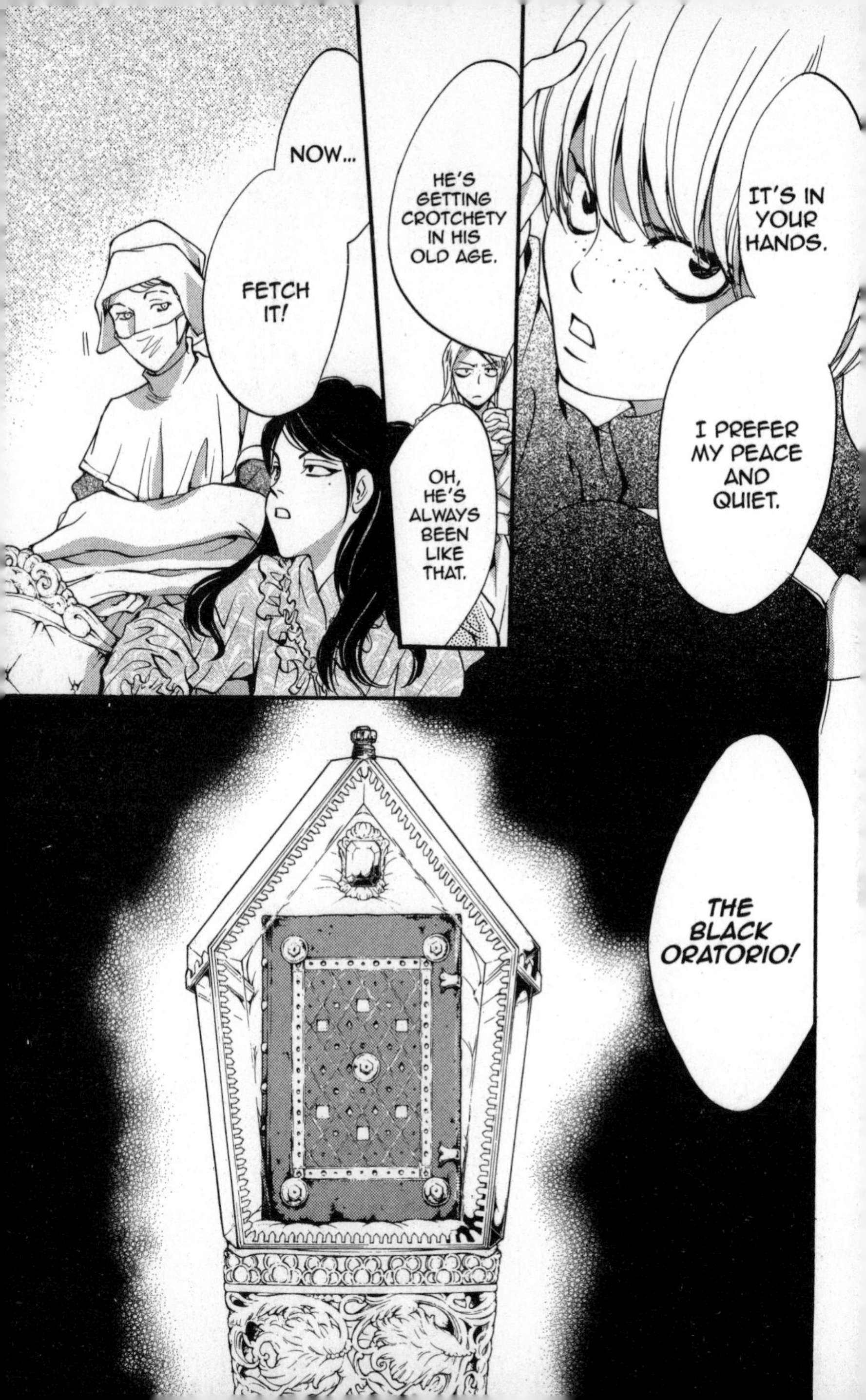
IT'S IN YOUR HANDS.
I PREFER MY PEACE AND QUIET.
HE'S GETTING CROTCHETY IN HIS OLD AGE.
OH, HE'S ALWAYS BEEN LIKE THAT.
NOW...
FETCH IT!
THE BLACK ORATORIO!

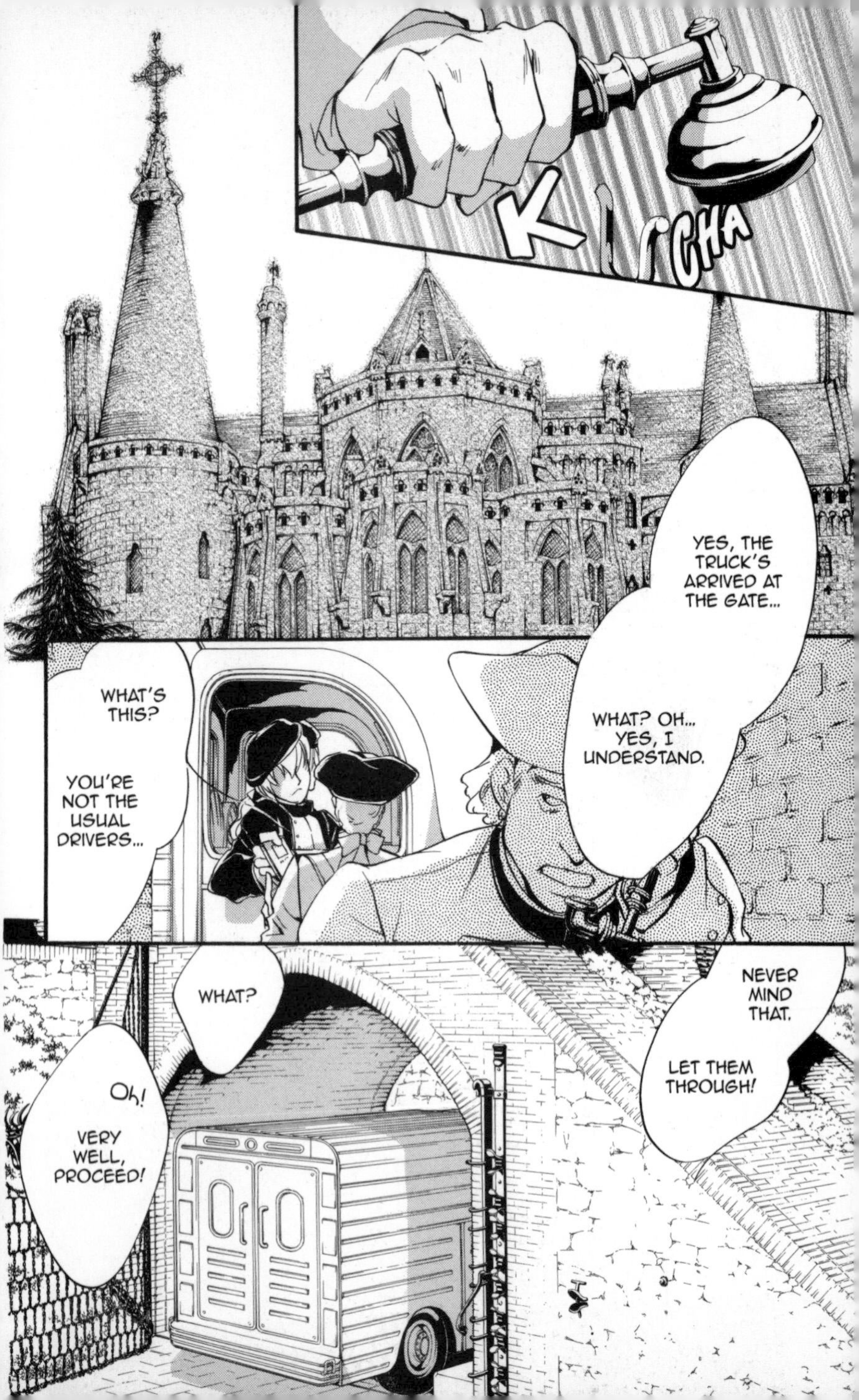
K CHA
YES, THE TRUCK'S ARRIVED AT THE GATE...
WHAT? OH... YES, I UNDERSTAND.
WHAT'S THIS?
YOU'RE NOT THE USUAL DRIVERS...
NEVER MIND THAT.
LET THEM THROUGH!
WHAT?
Oh!
VERY WELL, PROCEED!

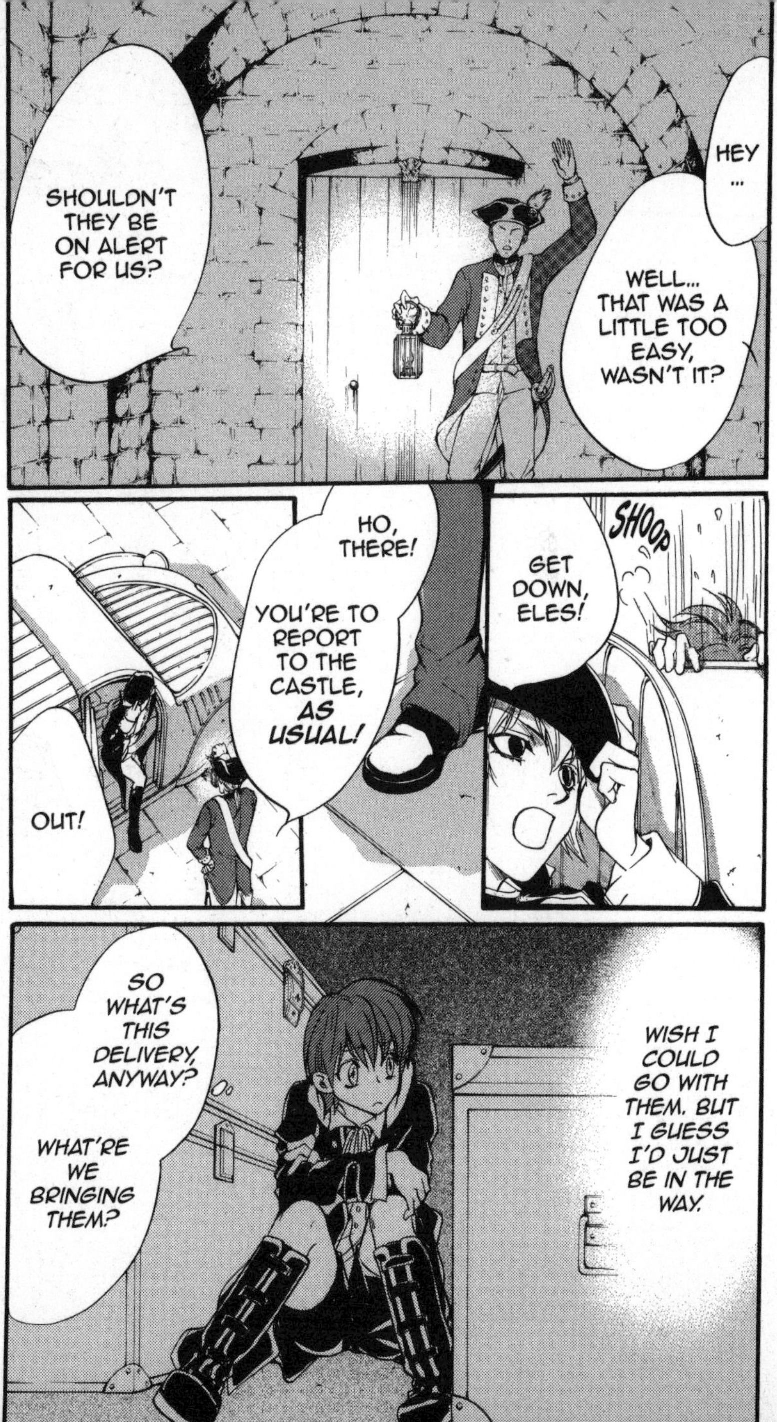
HEY ...
WELL... THAT WAS A LITTLE TOO EASY, WASN'T IT?
SHOULDN'T THEY BE ON ALERT FOR US?
SHOOP
GET DOWN, ELES!
HO, THERE!
YOU'RE TO REPORT TO THE CASTLE, AS USUAL!
OUT!
WISH I COULD GO WITH THEM. BUT I GUESS I'D JUST BE IN THE WAY.
SO WHAT'S THIS DELIVERY, ANYWAY?
WHAT'RE WE BRINGING THEM?

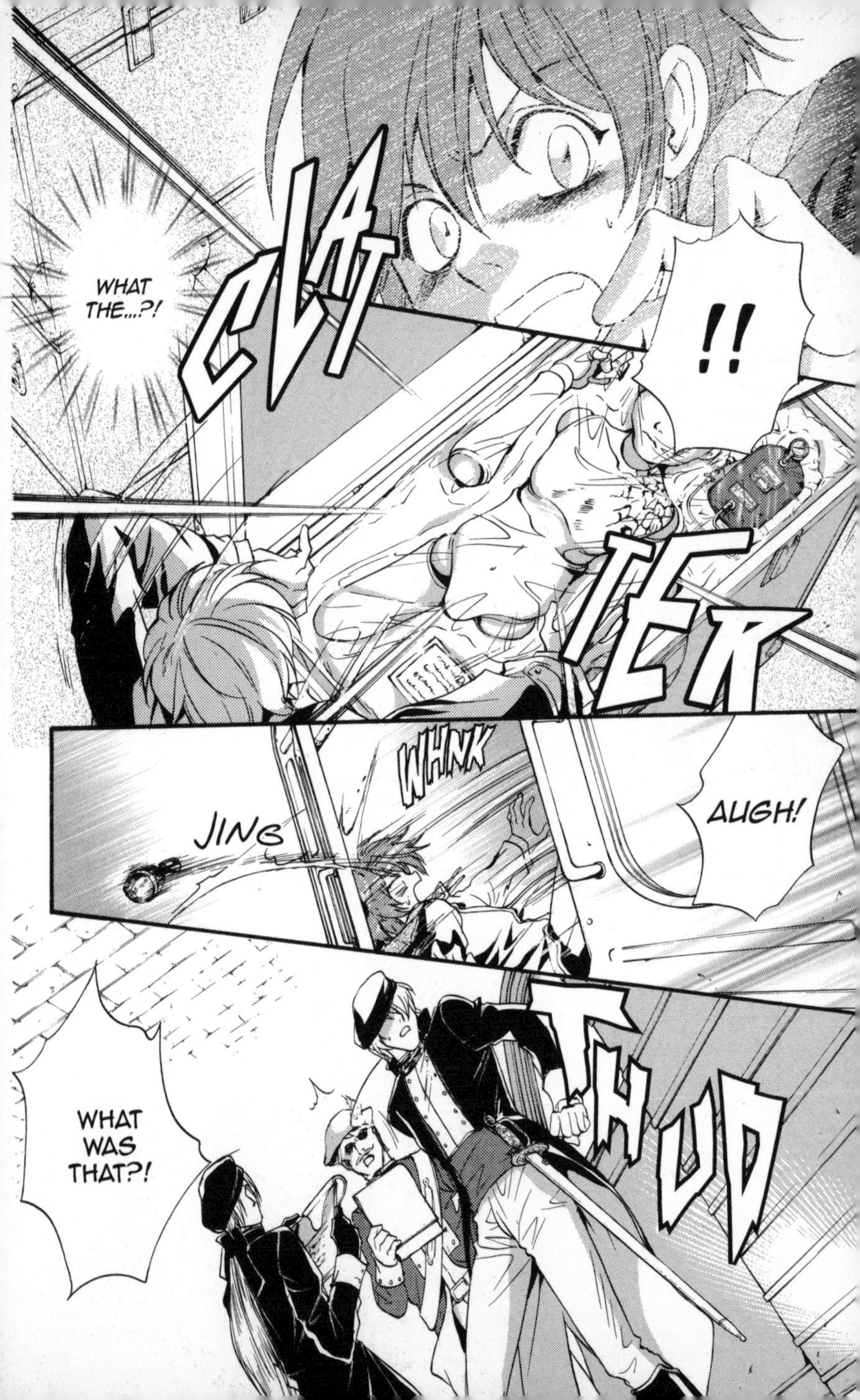

!!
CLATTER
WHAT THE...?!
AUGH!
WHNK
JING
THUD
WHAT WAS THAT?!

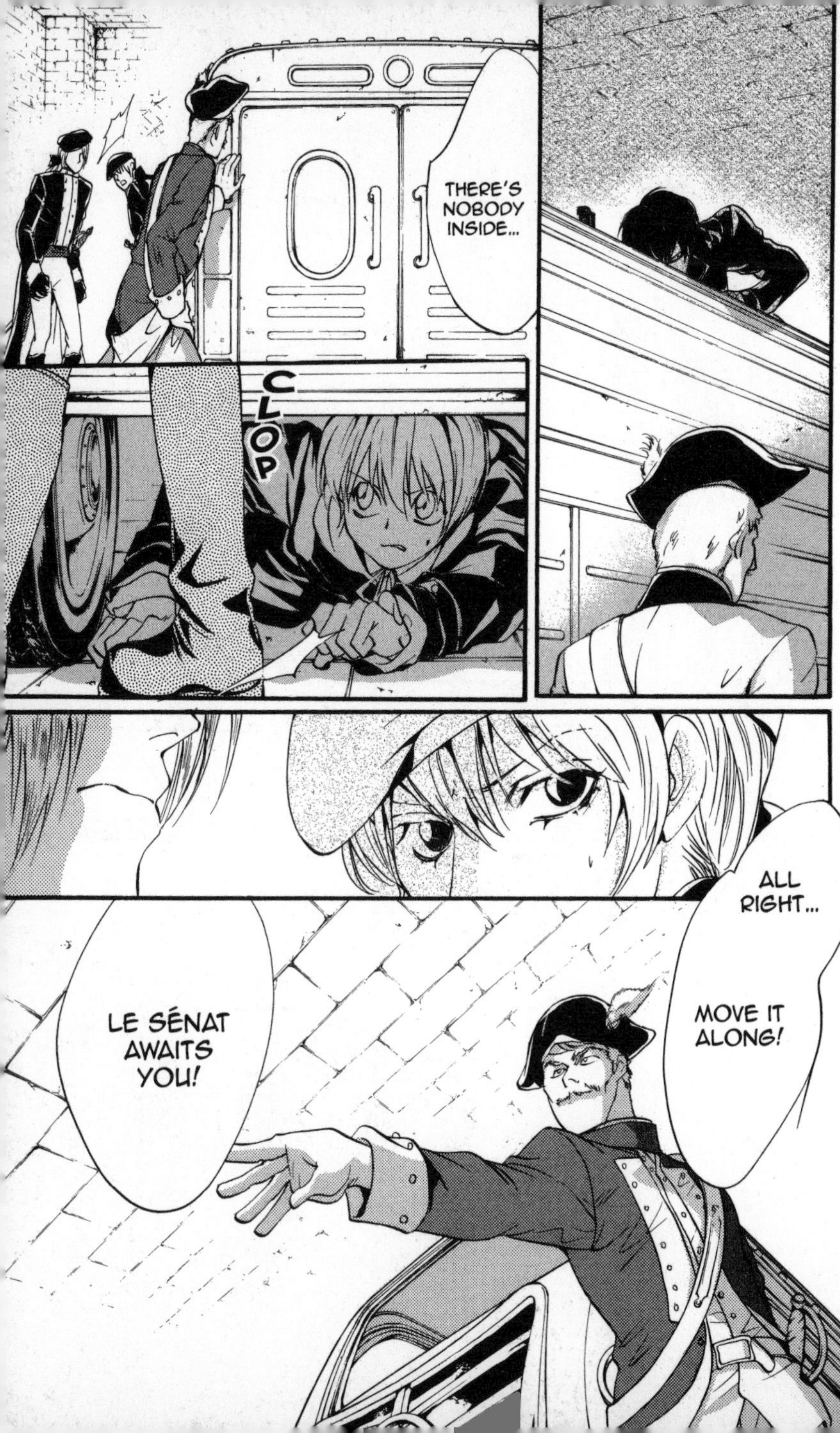
THERE'S NOBODY INSIDE...
CLOP
ALL RIGHT...
MOVE IT ALONG!
LE SÉNAT AWAITS YOU!

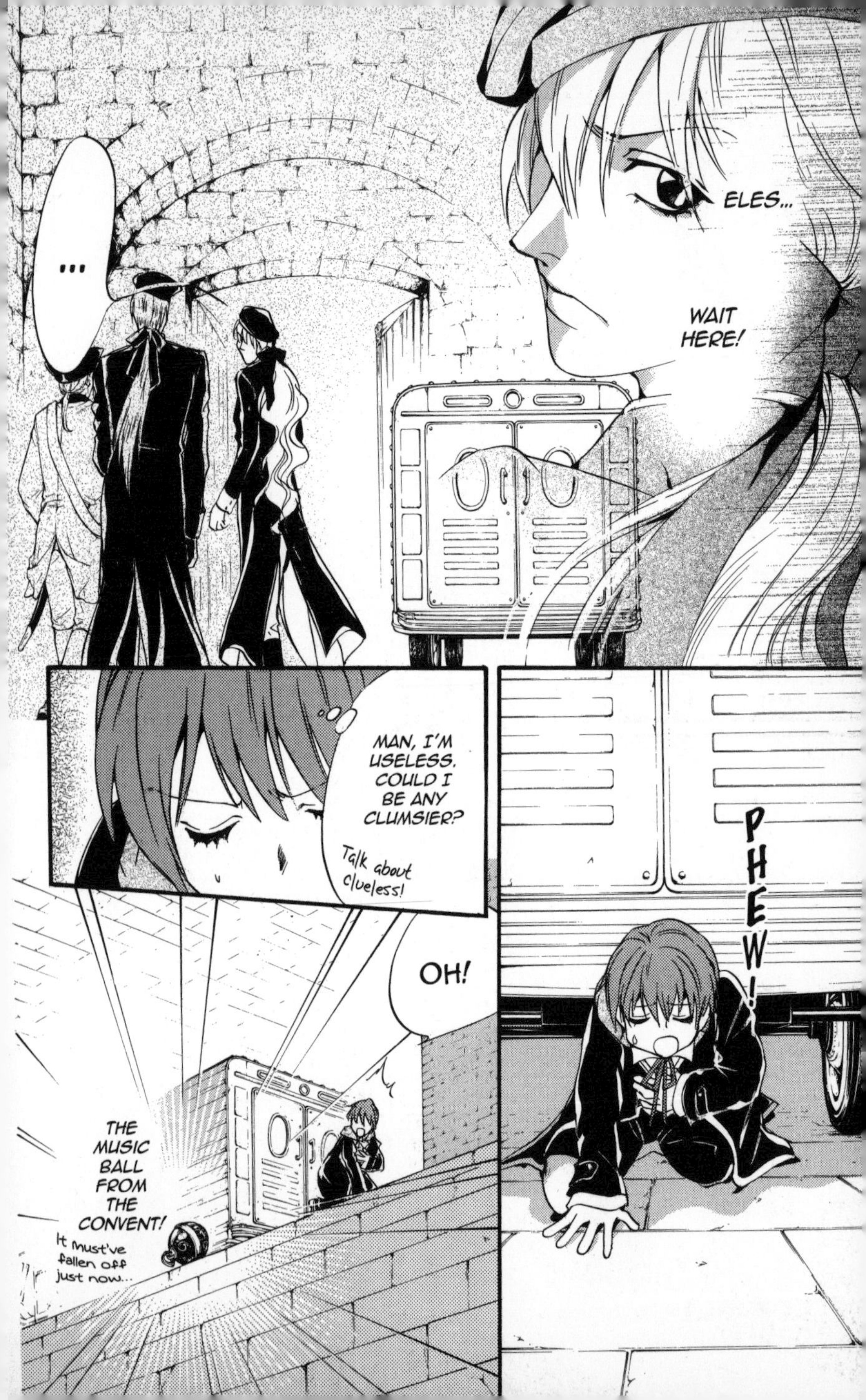

ELES...
WAIT HERE!
...
PHEW!
MAN, I'M USELESS. COULD I BE ANY CLUMSIER?
Talk about clueless!
OH!
THE MUSIC BALL FROM THE CONVENT!
It must've fallen off just now...

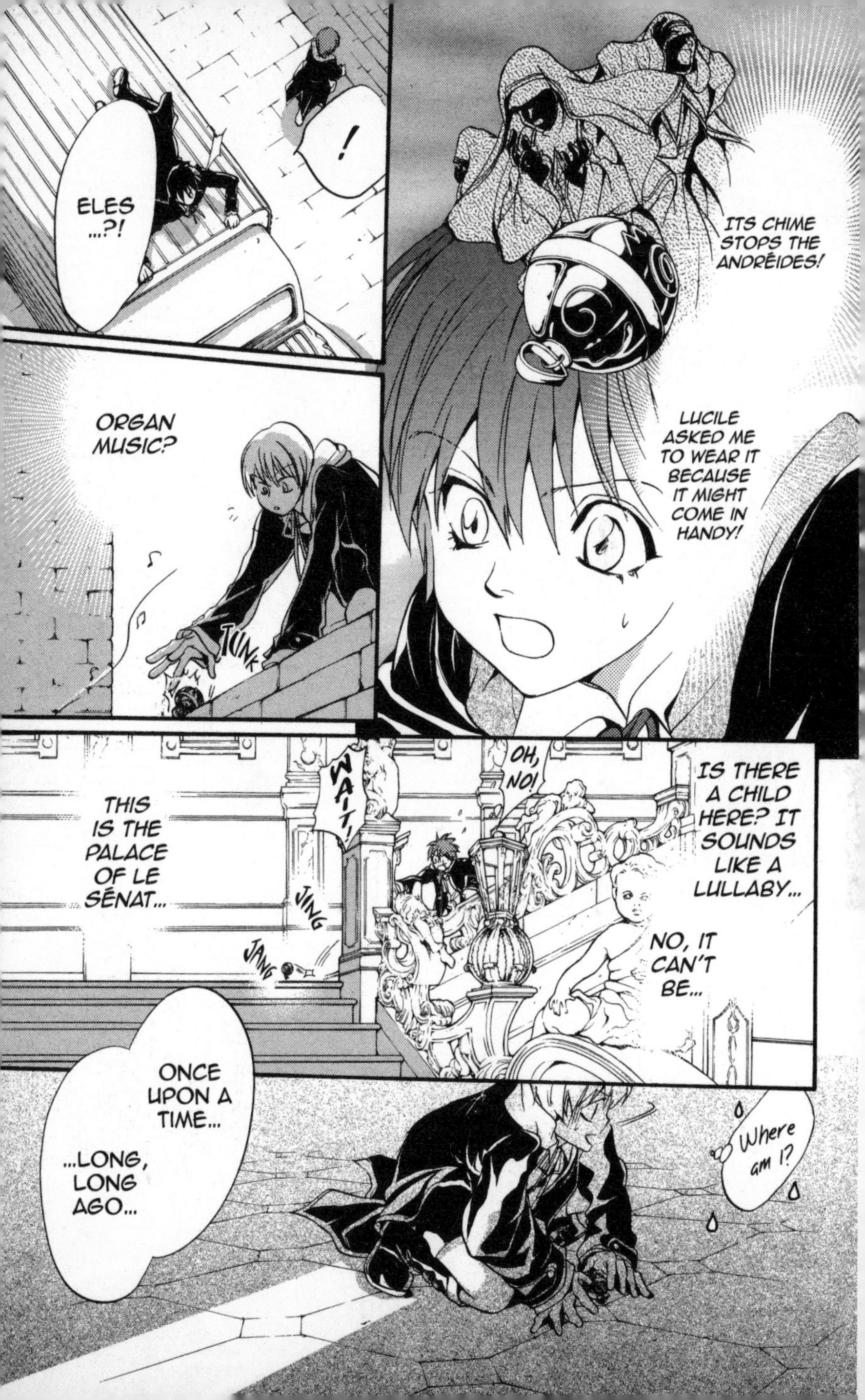
ITS CHIME STOPS THE ANDRÊIDES!
LUCILE ASKED ME TO WEAR IT BECAUSE IT MIGHT COME IN HANDY!
!
ELES ...?!
ORGAN MUSIC?
TUNK
IS THERE A CHILD HERE? IT SOUNDS LIKE A LULLABY...
NO, IT CAN'T BE...
OH, NO!
WAIT!
THIS IS THE PALACE OF LE SÉNAT...
JING
JANG
Where am I?
ONCE UPON A TIME...
...LONG, LONG AGO...

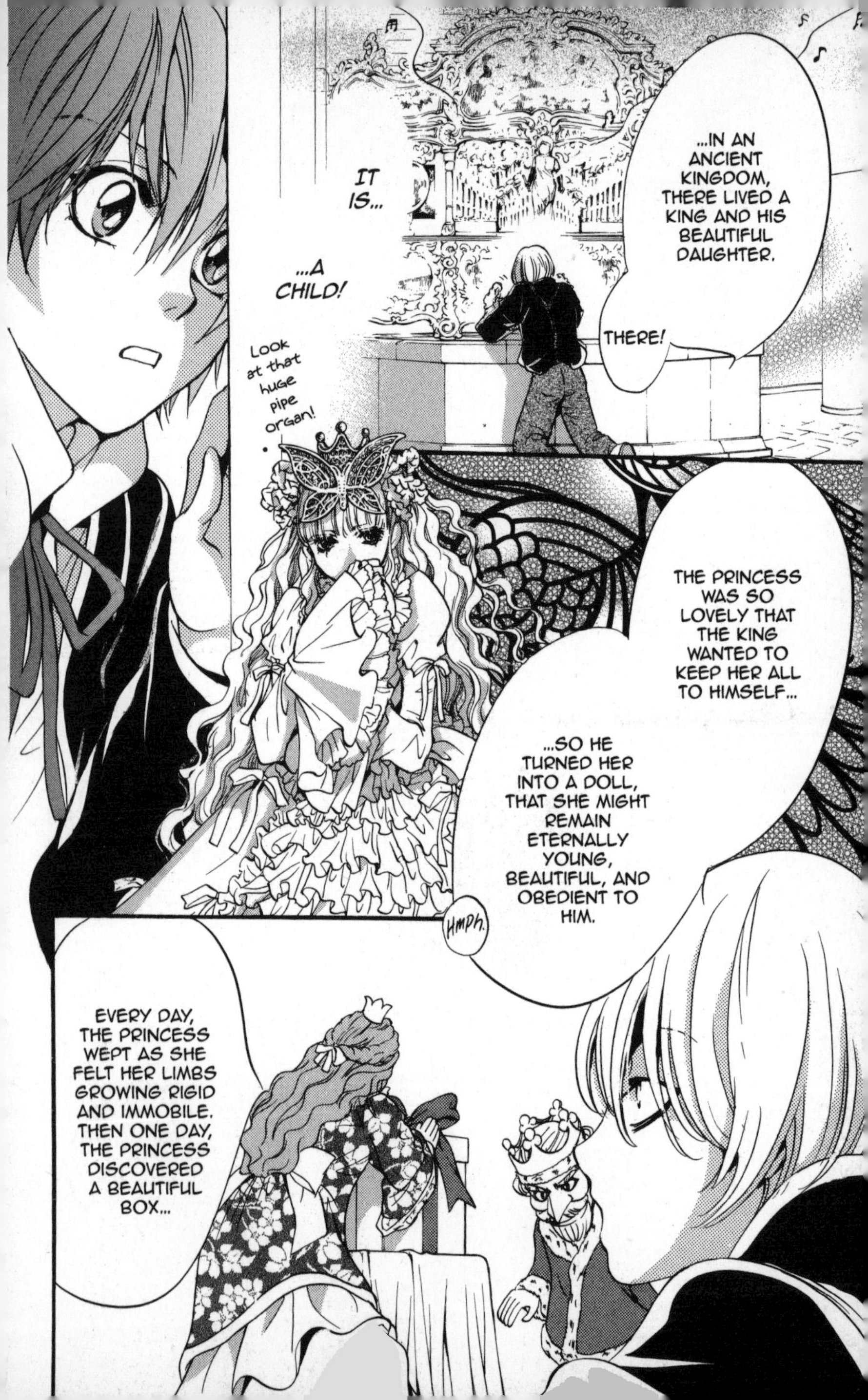
...IN AN ANCIENT KINGDOM, THERE LIVED A KING AND HIS BEAUTIFUL DAUGHTER.
THERE!
IT IS...
...A CHILD!
Look at that huge pipe organ!
THE PRINCESS WAS SO LOVELY THAT THE KING WANTED TO KEEP HER ALL TO HIMSELF...
...SO HE TURNED HER INTO A DOLL, THAT SHE MIGHT REMAIN ETERNALLY YOUNG, BEAUTIFUL, AND OBEDIENT TO HIM.
Hmph.
EVERY DAY, THE PRINCESS WEPT AS SHE FELT HER LIMBS GROWING RIGID AND IMMOBILE. THEN ONE DAY, THE PRINCESS DISCOVERED A BEAUTIFUL BOX...

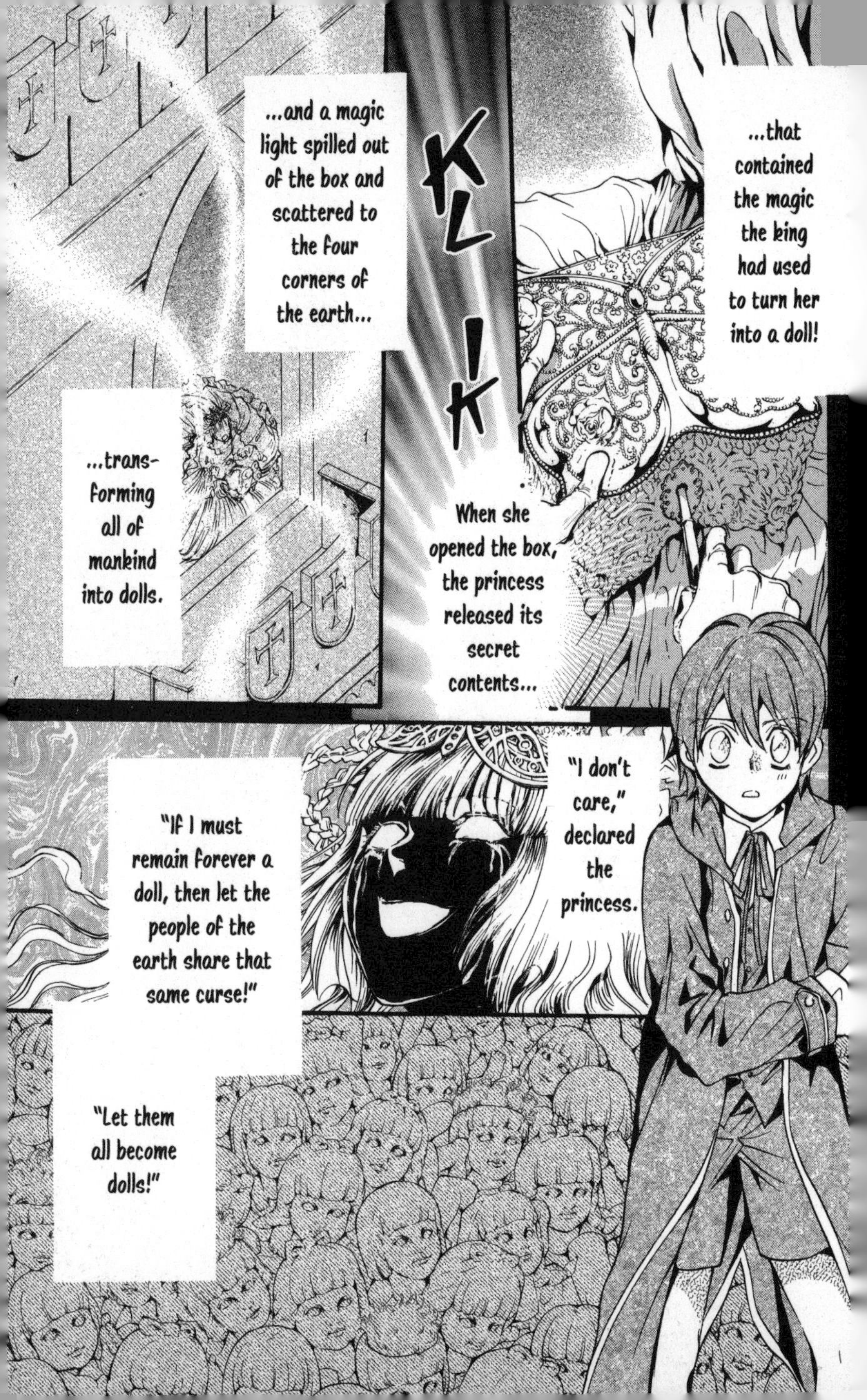
...that contained the magic the king had used to turn her into a doll!
KLIK
When she opened the box, the princess released its secret contents...
...and a magic light spilled out of the box and scattered to the four corners of the earth...
...trans-forming all of mankind into dolls.
"I don't care," declared the princess.
"If I must remain forever a doll, then let the people of the earth share that same curse!"
"Let them all become dolls!"

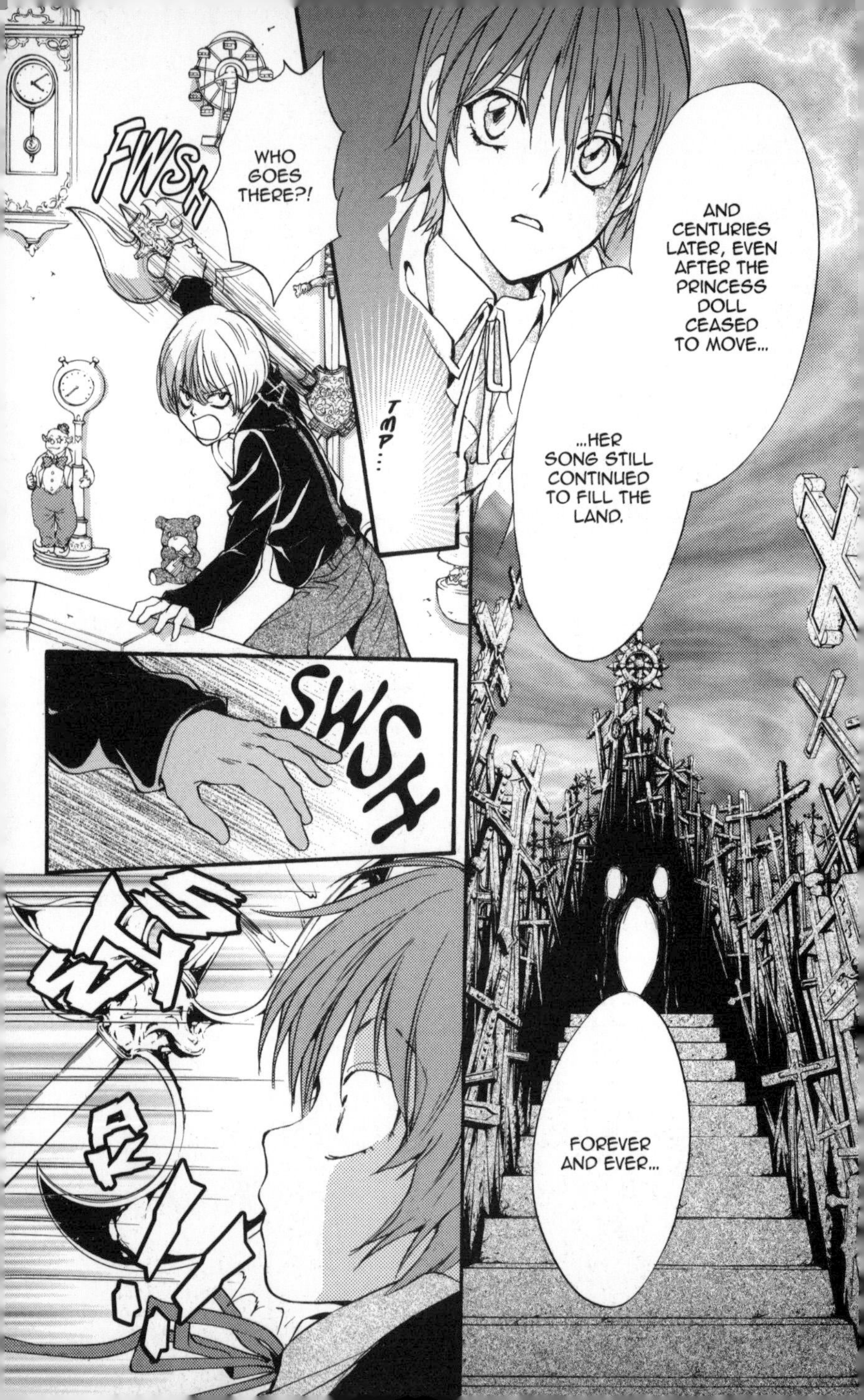
AND CENTURIES LATER, EVEN AFTER THE PRINCESS DOLL CEASED TO MOVE...
...HER SONG STILL CONTINUED TO FILL THE LAND.
FOREVER AND EVER...
TMP...
FWSH
WHO GOES THERE?!
SWSH

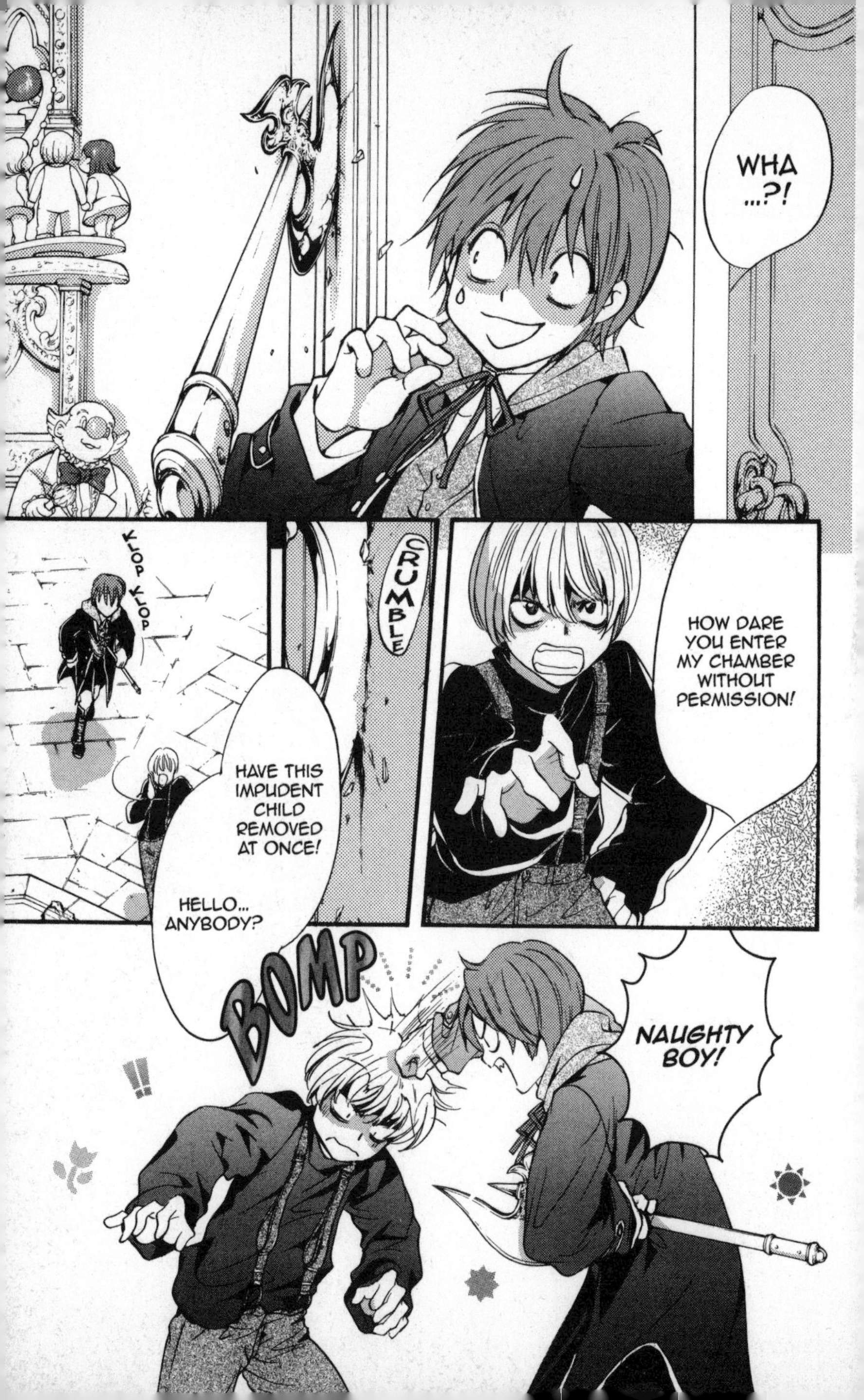
WHA ...?!
HOW DARE YOU ENTER MY CHAMBER WITHOUT PERMISSION!
CRUMBLE
HAVE THIS IMPUDENT CHILD REMOVED AT ONCE!
KLOP KLOP
HELLO... ANYBODY?
NAUGHTY BOY!
BOMP
!!

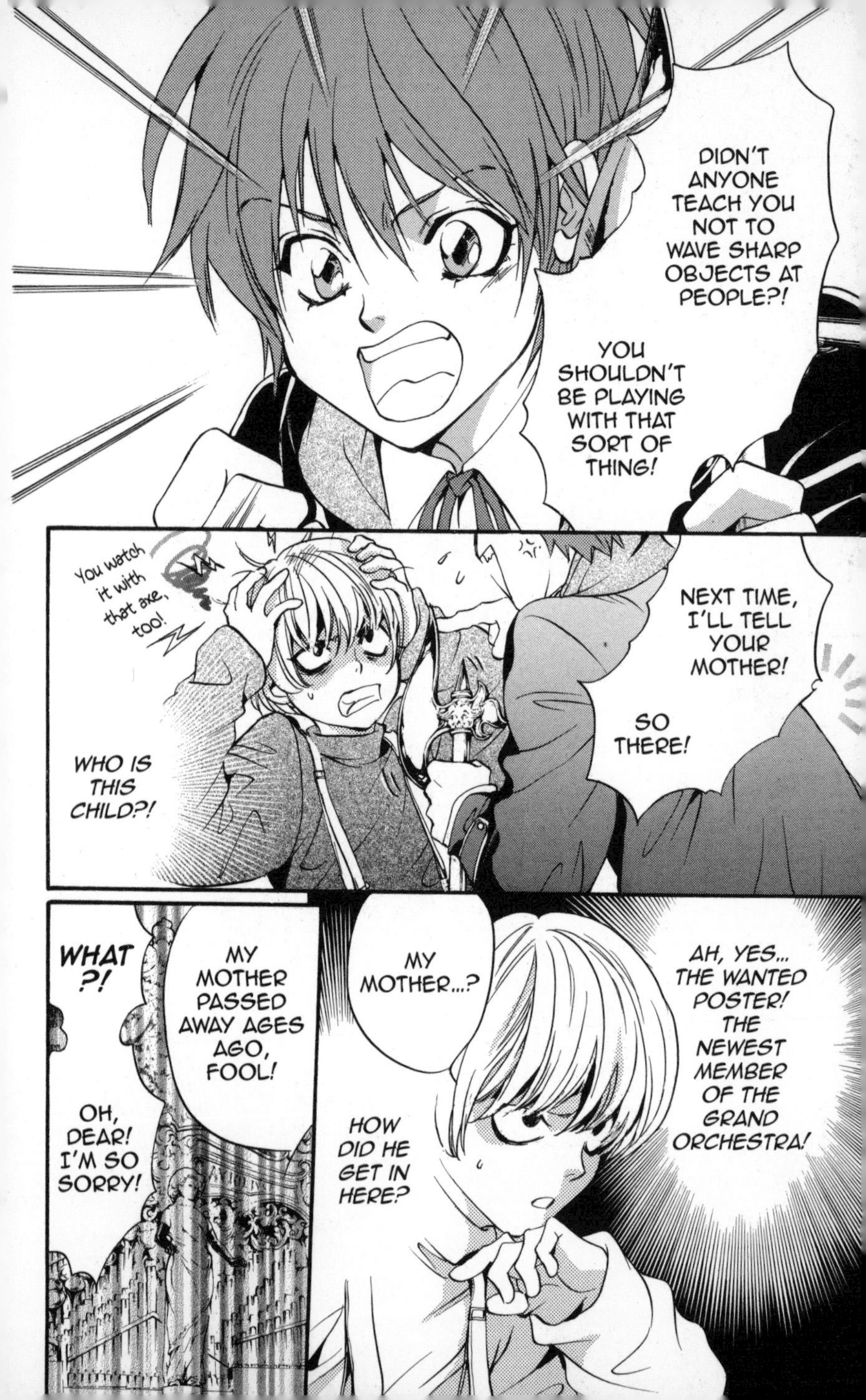
DIDN'T ANYONE TEACH YOU NOT TO WAVE SHARP OBJECTS AT PEOPLE?!
YOU SHOULDN'T BE PLAYING WITH THAT SORT OF THING!
NEXT TIME, I'LL TELL YOUR MOTHER!
SO THERE!
You watch it with that axe, too!
WHO IS THIS CHILD?!
AH, YES... THE WANTED POSTER! THE NEWEST MEMBER OF THE GRAND ORCHESTRA!
MY MOTHER...?
HOW DID HE GET IN HERE?
MY MOTHER PASSED AWAY AGES AGO, FOOL!
WHAT?!
OH, DEAR! I'M SO SORRY!

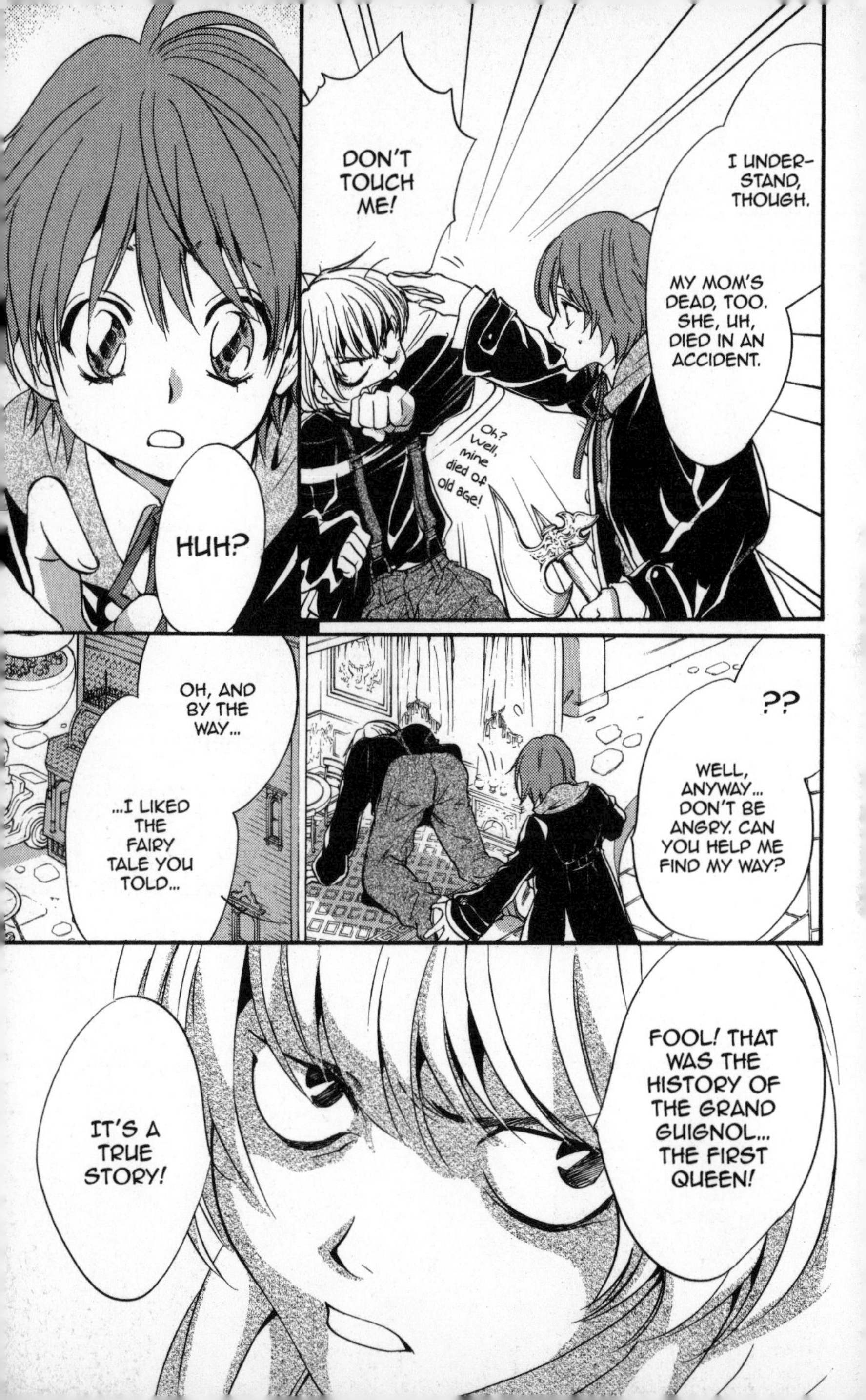
I UNDER-STAND, THOUGH.
MY MOM'S DEAD, TOO. SHE, UH, DIED IN AN ACCIDENT.
DON'T TOUCH ME!
Oh? Well, mine died of old age!
HUH?
??
WELL, ANYWAY... DON'T BE ANGRY. CAN YOU HELP ME FIND MY WAY?
OH, AND BY THE WAY...
...I LIKED THE FAIRY TALE YOU TOLD...
FOOL! THAT WAS THE HISTORY OF THE GRAND GUIGNOL... THE FIRST QUEEN!
IT'S A TRUE STORY!

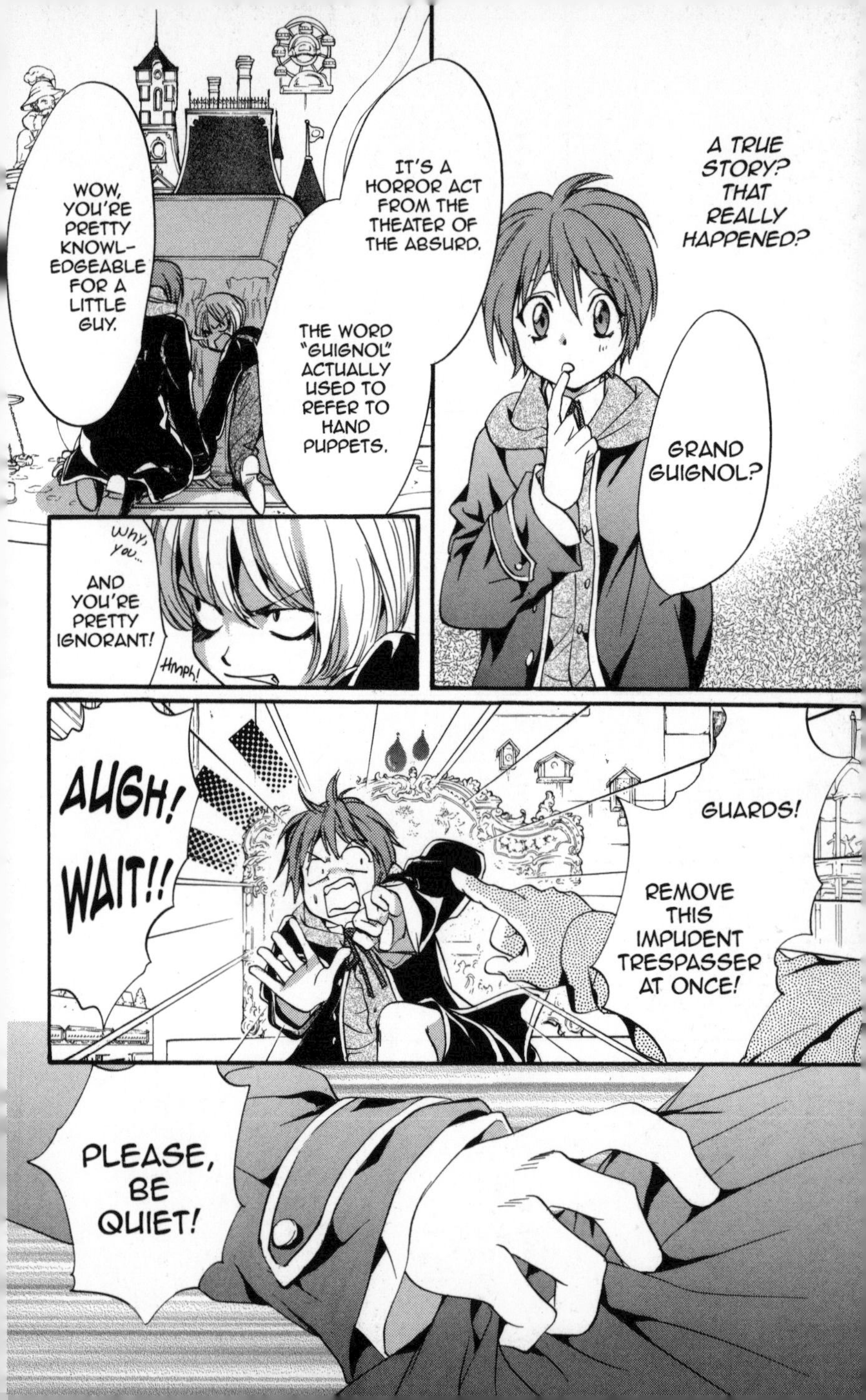
A TRUE STORY? THAT REALLY HAPPENED?
GRAND GUIGNOL?
IT'S A HORROR ACT FROM THE THEATER OF THE ABSURD.
THE WORD "GUIGNOL" ACTUALLY USED TO REFER TO HAND PUPPETS.
WOW, YOU'RE PRETTY KNOWL-EDGEABLE FOR A LITTLE GUY.
Why, you...
AND YOU'RE PRETTY IGNORANT!
Hmph!
GUARDS!
REMOVE THIS IMPUDENT TRESPASSER AT ONCE!
AUGH!
WAIT!!
PLEASE, BE QUIET!

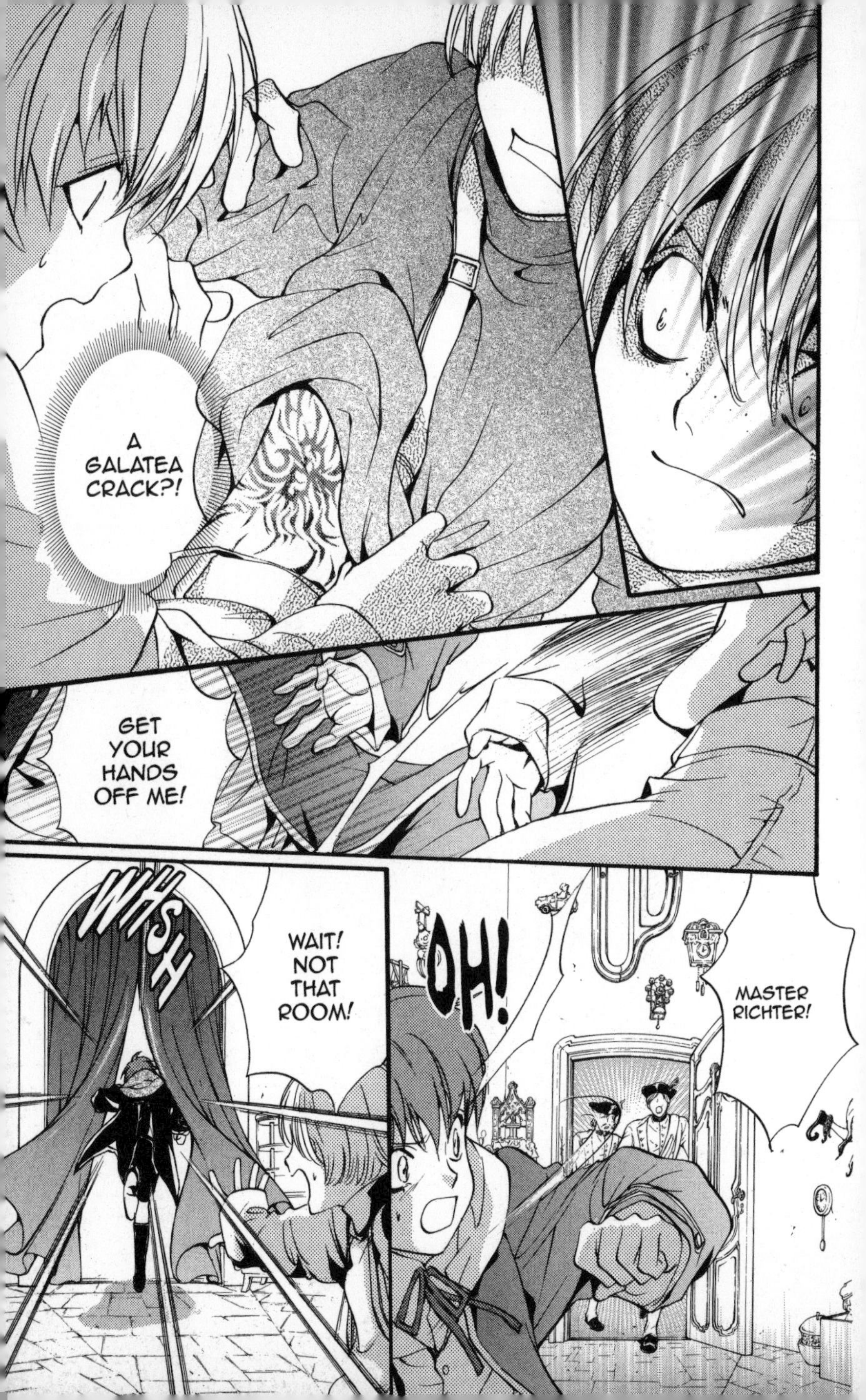
A GALATEA CRACK?!
GET YOUR HANDS OFF ME!
MASTER RICHTER!
OH!
WAIT! NOT THAT ROOM!
WHSH

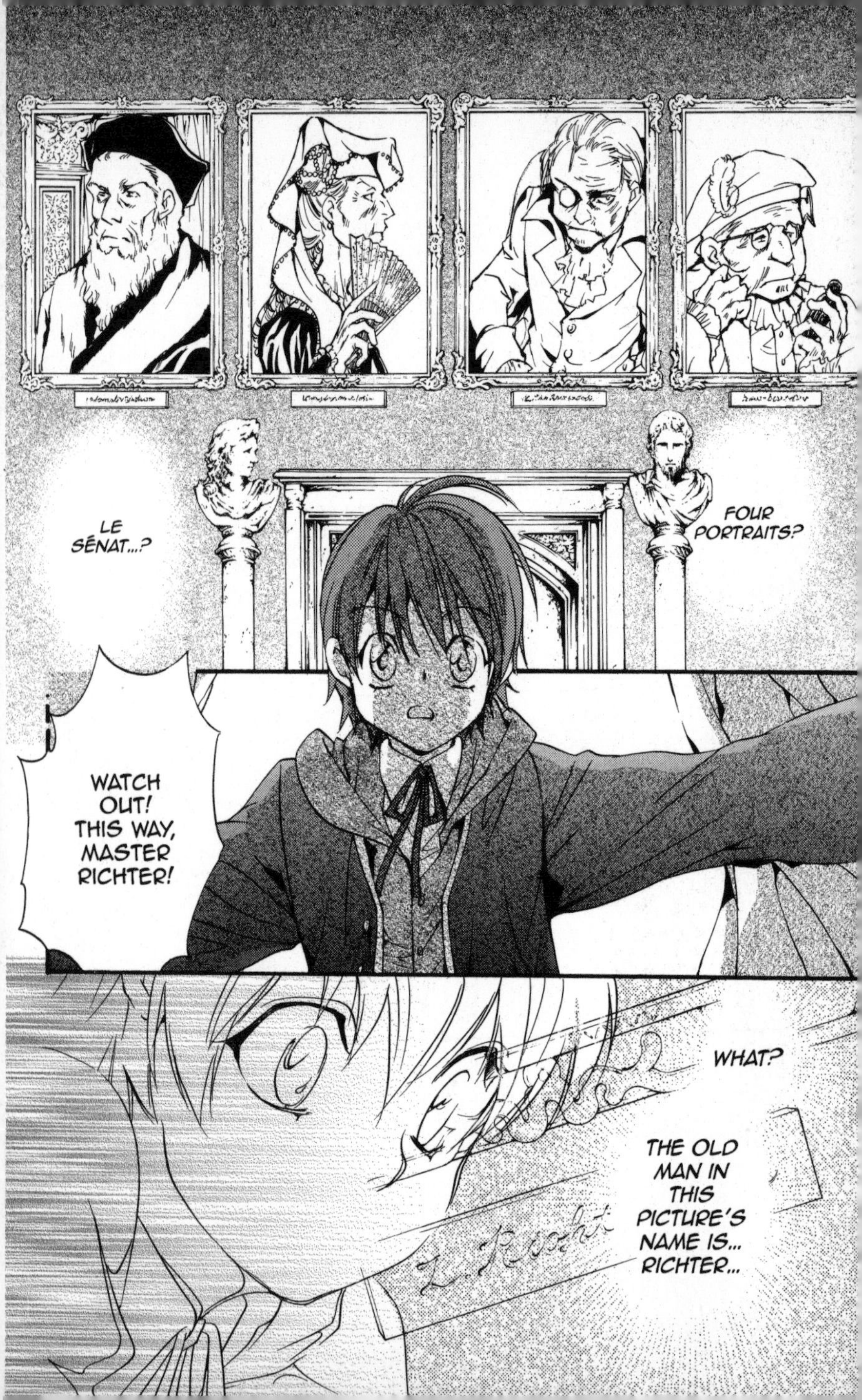
FOUR PORTRAITS?
LE SÉNAT...?
WATCH OUT! THIS WAY, MASTER RICHTER!
WHAT?
THE OLD MAN IN THIS PICTURE'S NAME IS... RICHTER...

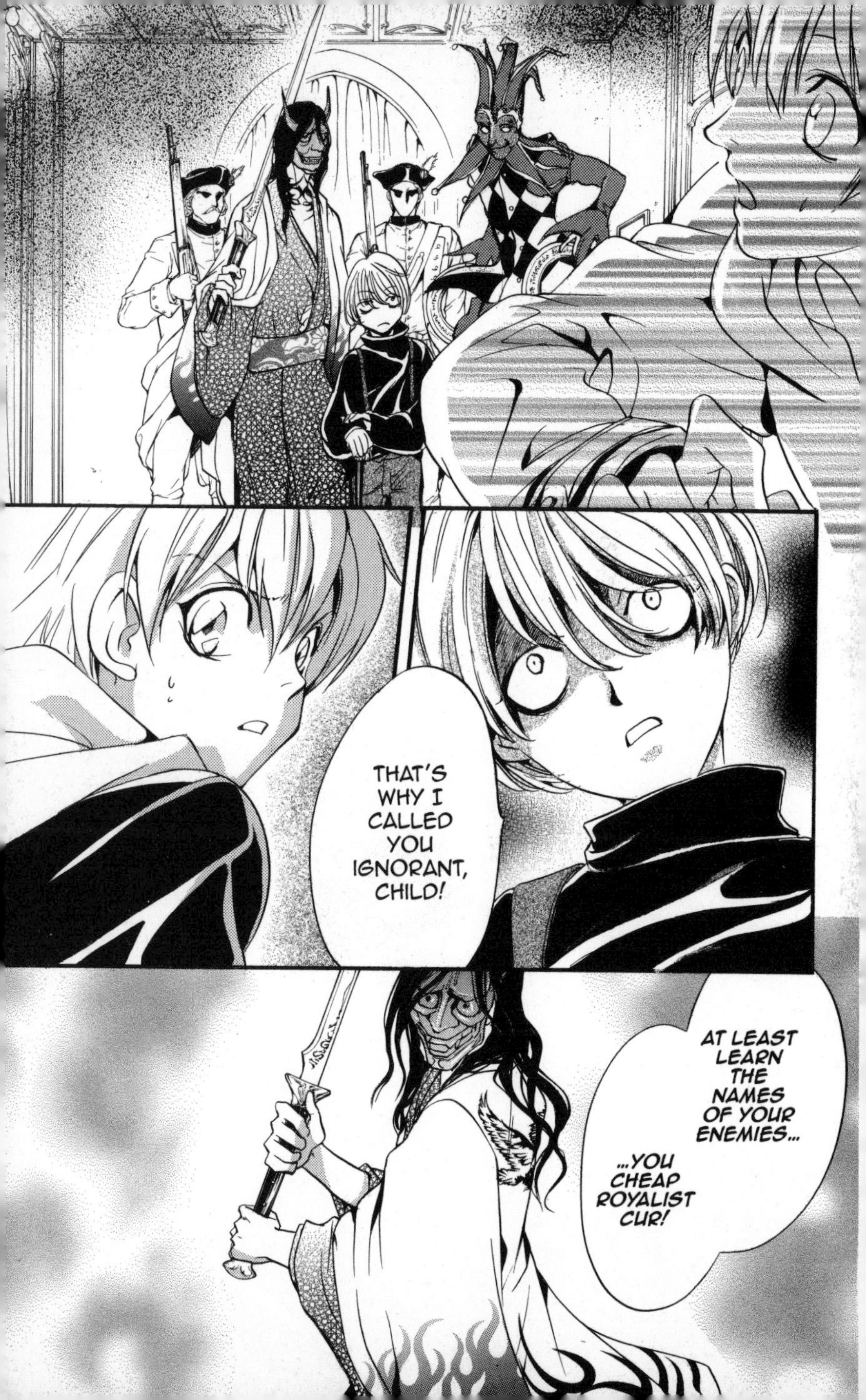
THAT'S WHY I CALLED YOU IGNORANT, CHILD!
AT LEAST LEARN THE NAMES OF YOUR ENEMIES...
...YOU CHEAP ROYALIST CUR!

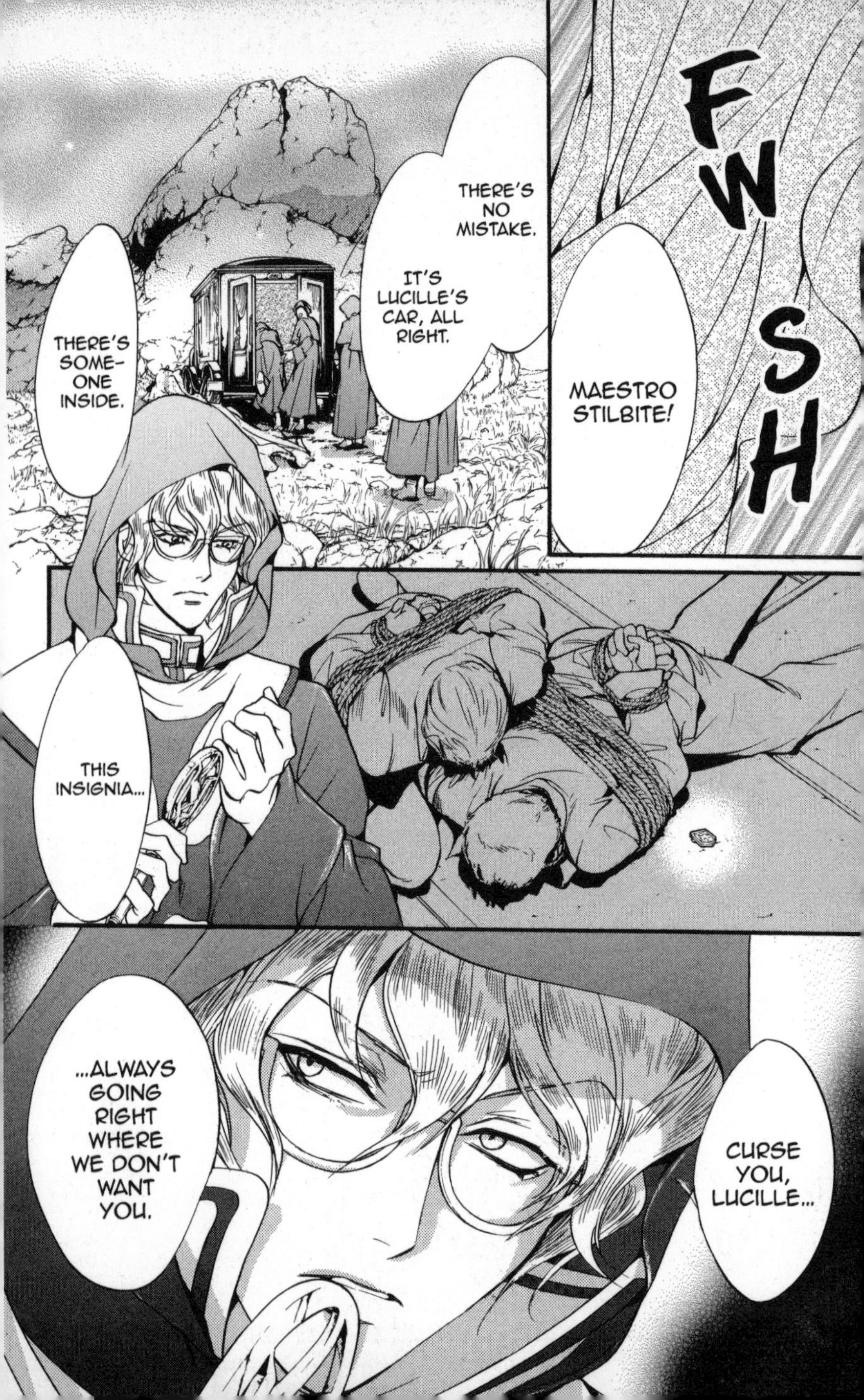
FWSH
MAESTRO STILBITE!
THERE'S NO MISTAKE.
IT'S LUCILLE'S CAR, ALL RIGHT.
THERE'S SOME-ONE INSIDE.
THIS INSIGNIA...
CURSE YOU, LUCILLE...
...ALWAYS GOING RIGHT WHERE WE DON'T WANT YOU.

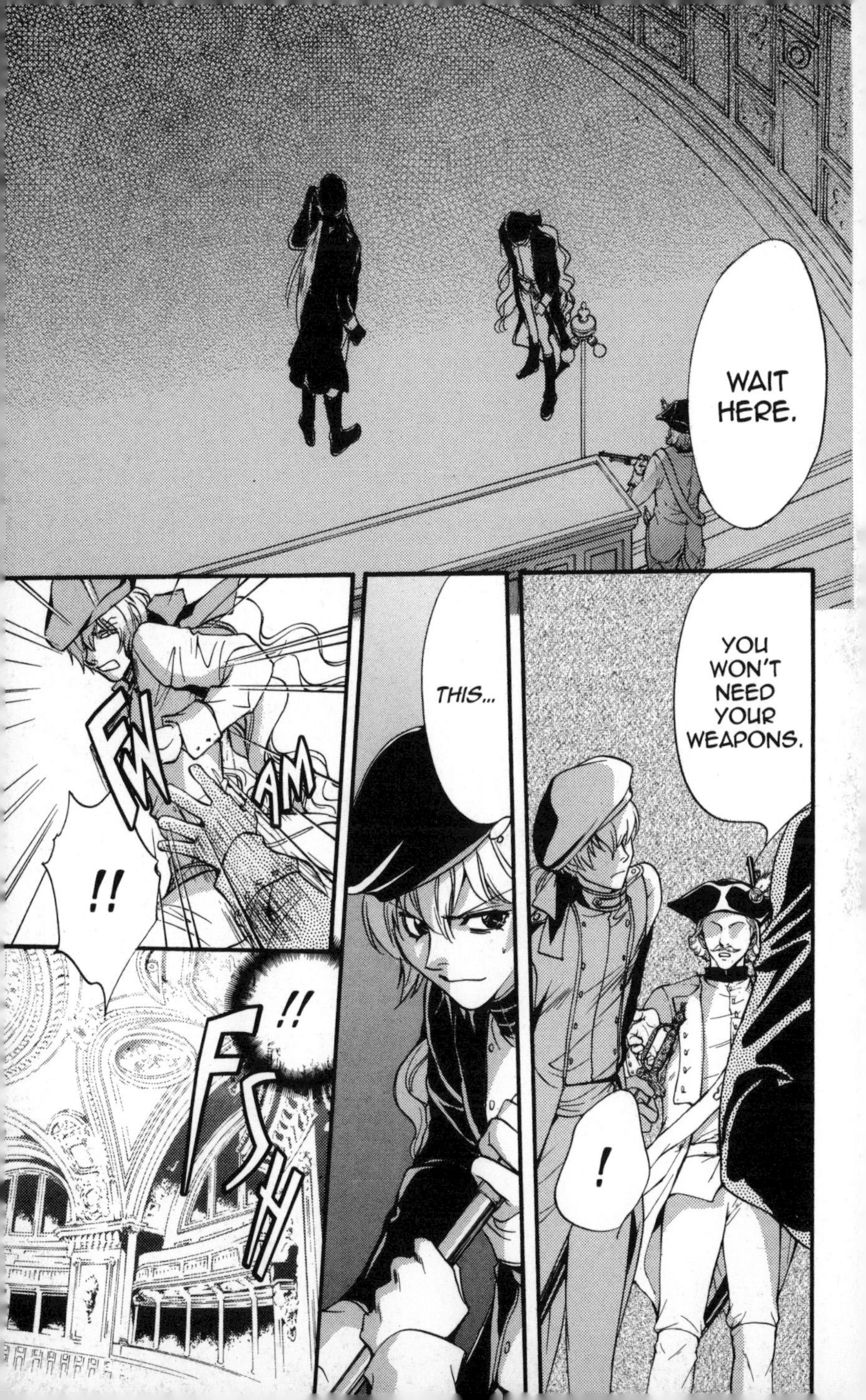
WAIT HERE.
YOU WON'T NEED YOUR WEAPONS.
!
THIS...
FWAM
!!
!!
FSHH

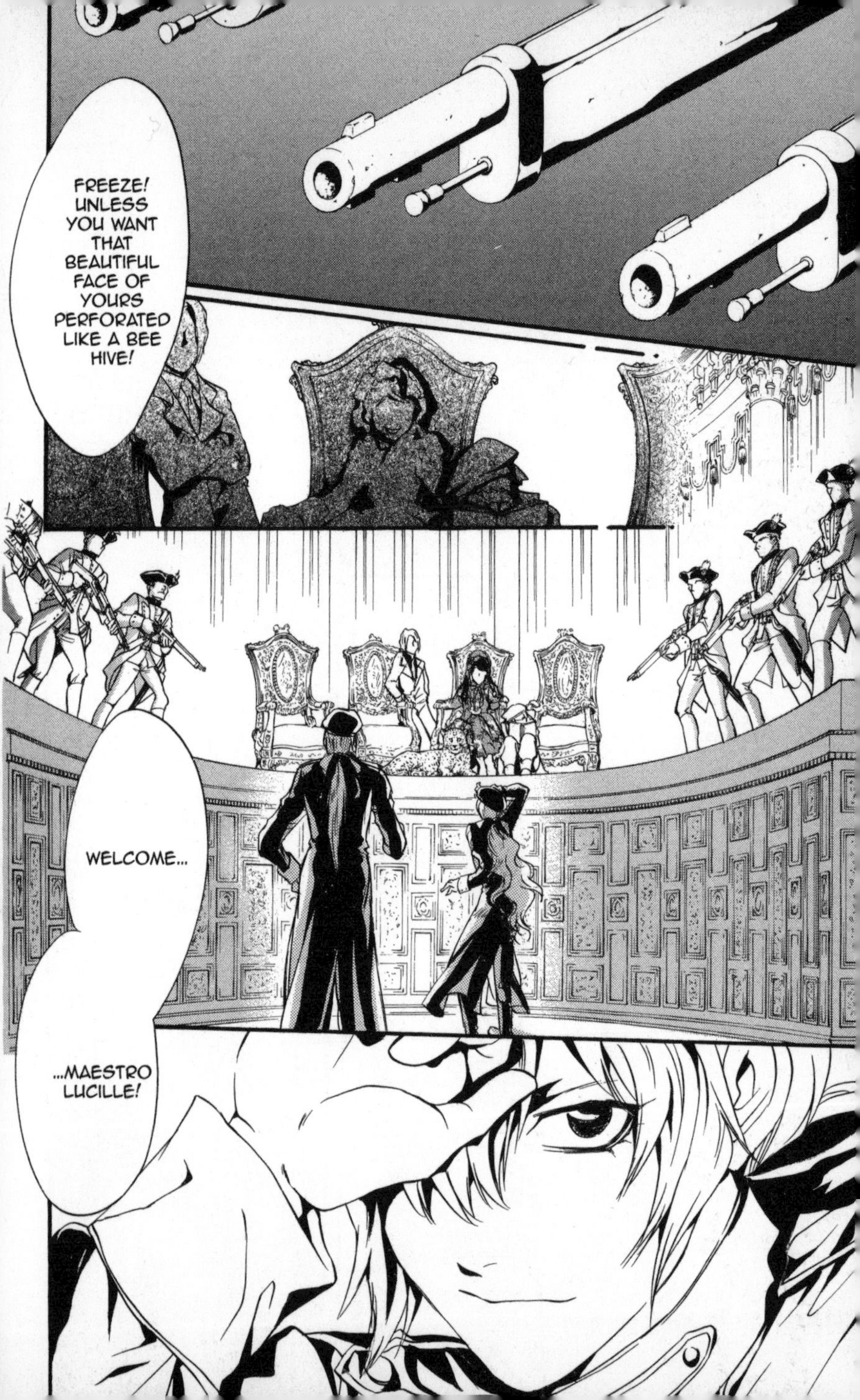
FREEZE! UNLESS YOU WANT THAT BEAUTIFUL FACE OF YOURS PERFORATED LIKE A BEE HIVE!
WELCOME...
...MAESTRO LUCILLE!

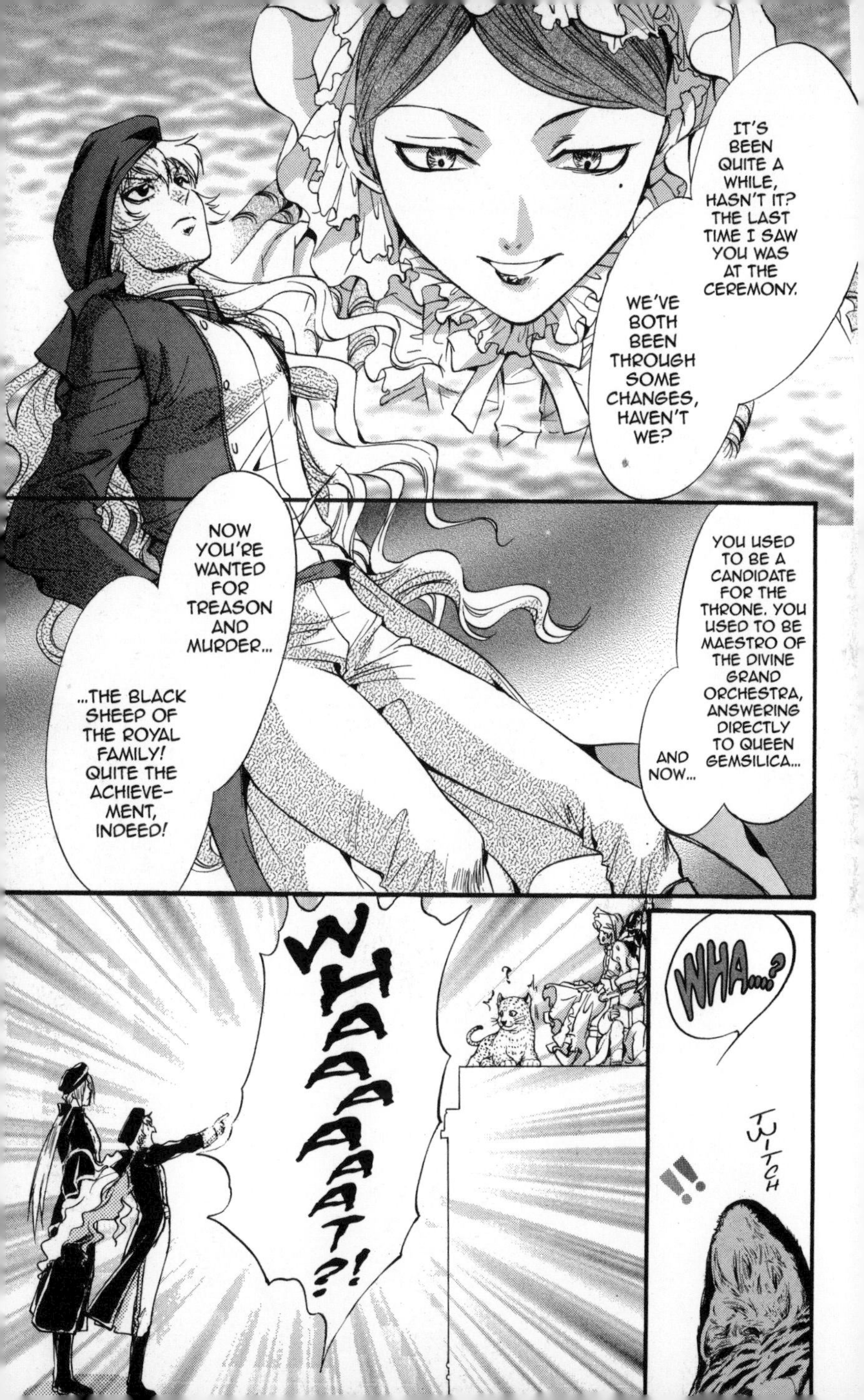
IT'S BEEN QUITE A WHILE, HASN'T IT? THE LAST TIME I SAW YOU WAS AT THE CEREMONY.
WE'VE BOTH BEEN THROUGH SOME CHANGES, HAVEN'T WE?
YOU USED TO BE A CANDIDATE FOR THE THRONE. YOU USED TO BE MAESTRO OF THE DIVINE GRAND ORCHESTRA, ANSWERING DIRECTLY TO QUEEN GEMSILICA...
AND NOW...
NOW YOU'RE WANTED FOR TREASON AND MURDER...
...THE BLACK SHEEP OF THE ROYAL FAMILY! QUITE THE ACHIEVEMENT, INDEED!
WHA...?
TWITCH
!!
WHAAAAAAAT?!

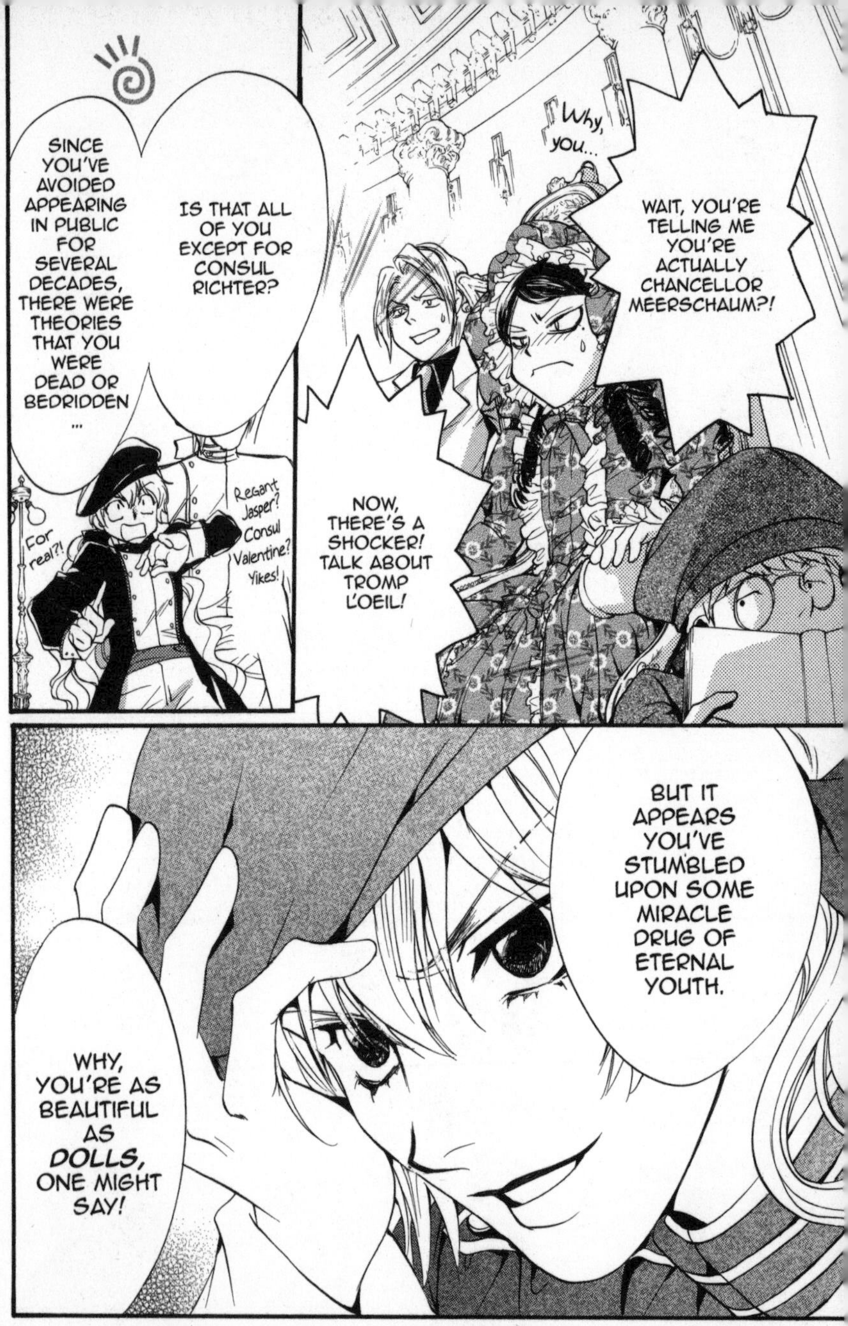
Why, you...
WAIT, YOU'RE TELLING ME YOU'RE ACTUALLY CHANCELLOR MEERSCHAUM?!
NOW, THERE'S A SHOCKER! TALK ABOUT TROMP L'OEIL!
IS THAT ALL OF YOU EXCEPT FOR CONSUL RICHTER?
SINCE YOU'VE AVOIDED APPEARING IN PUBLIC FOR SEVERAL DECADES, THERE WERE THEORIES THAT YOU WERE DEAD OR BEDRIDDEN ...
Regant Jasper? Consul Valentine? Yikes!
For real?!
BUT IT APPEARS YOU'VE STUMBLED UPON SOME MIRACLE DRUG OF ETERNAL YOUTH.
WHY, YOU'RE AS BEAUTIFUL AS *DOLLS*, ONE MIGHT SAY!

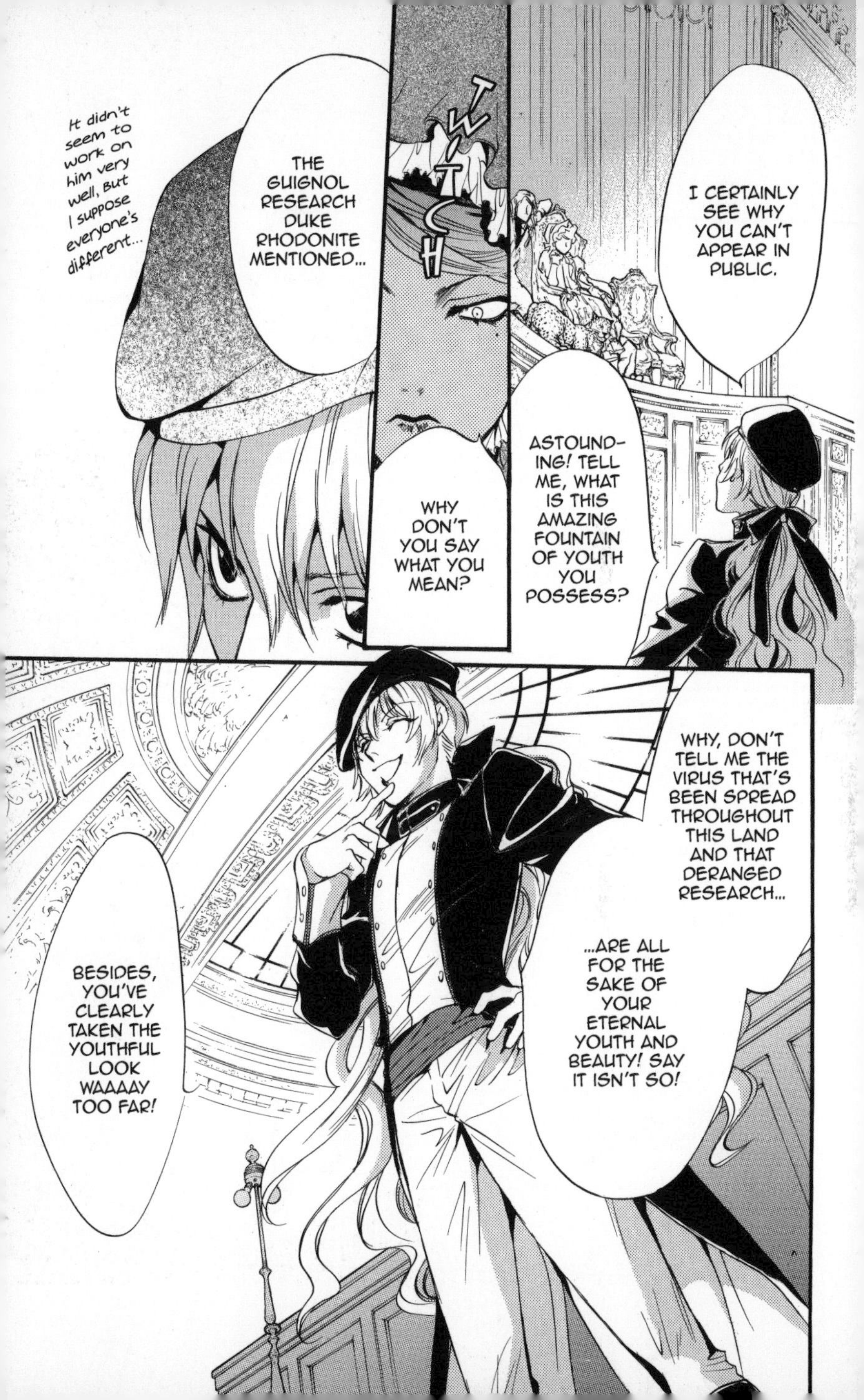
I CERTAINLY SEE WHY YOU CAN'T APPEAR IN PUBLIC.
ASTOUNDING! TELL ME, WHAT IS THIS AMAZING FOUNTAIN OF YOUTH YOU POSSESS?
TWITCH
WHY DON'T YOU SAY WHAT YOU MEAN?
THE GUIGNOL RESEARCH DUKE RHODONITE MENTIONED...
It didn't seem to work on him very well, but I suppose everyone's different...
WHY, DON'T TELL ME THE VIRUS THAT'S BEEN SPREAD THROUGHOUT THIS LAND AND THAT DERANGED RESEARCH...
...ARE ALL FOR THE SAKE OF YOUR ETERNAL YOUTH AND BEAUTY! SAY IT ISN'T SO!
BESIDES, YOU'VE CLEARLY TAKEN THE YOUTHFUL LOOK WAAAAY TOO FAR!

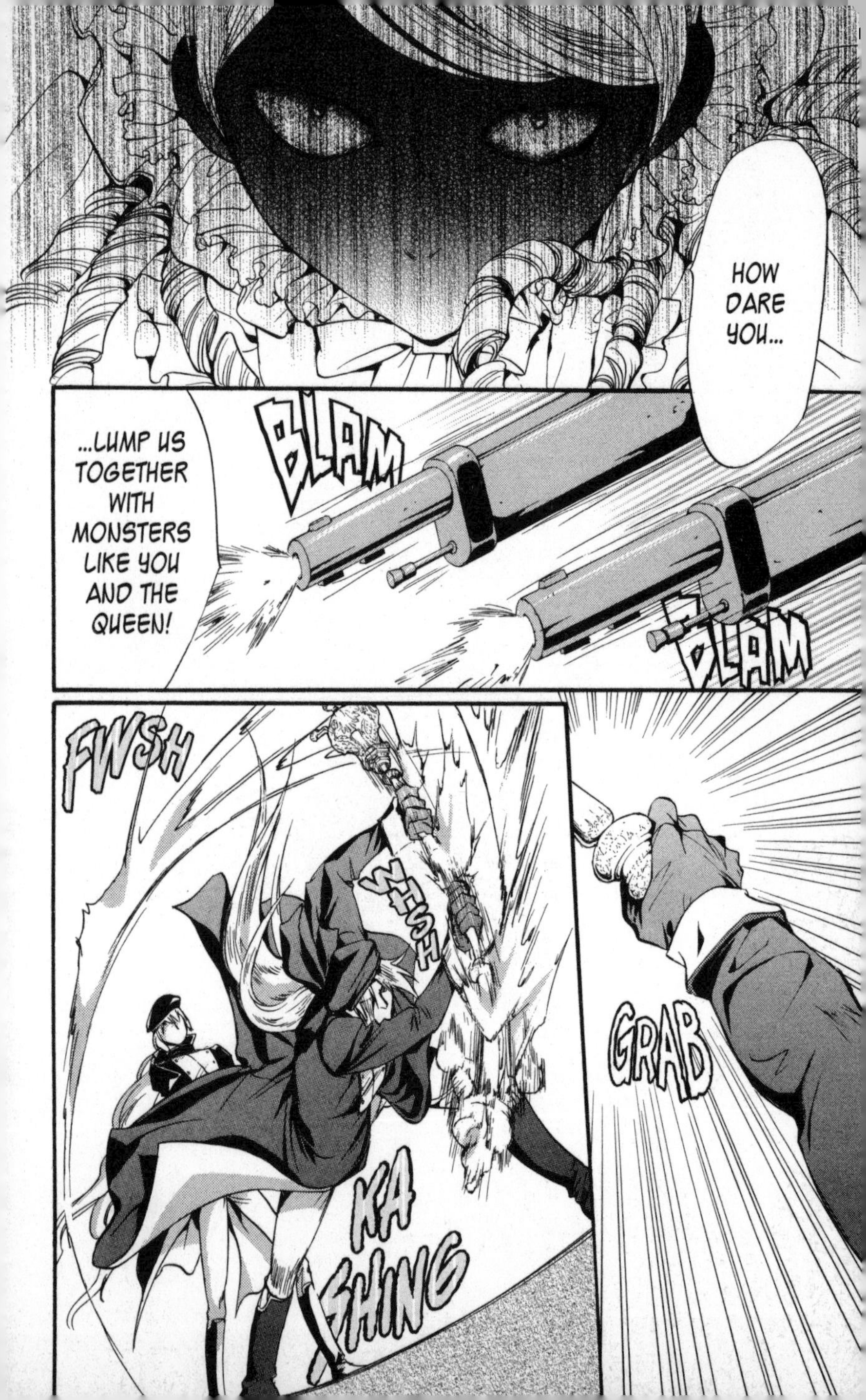
HOW DARE YOU...
BLAM
BLAM
...LUMP US TOGETHER WITH MONSTERS LIKE YOU AND THE QUEEN!
GRAB
FWSH
WHSH
KA SHING

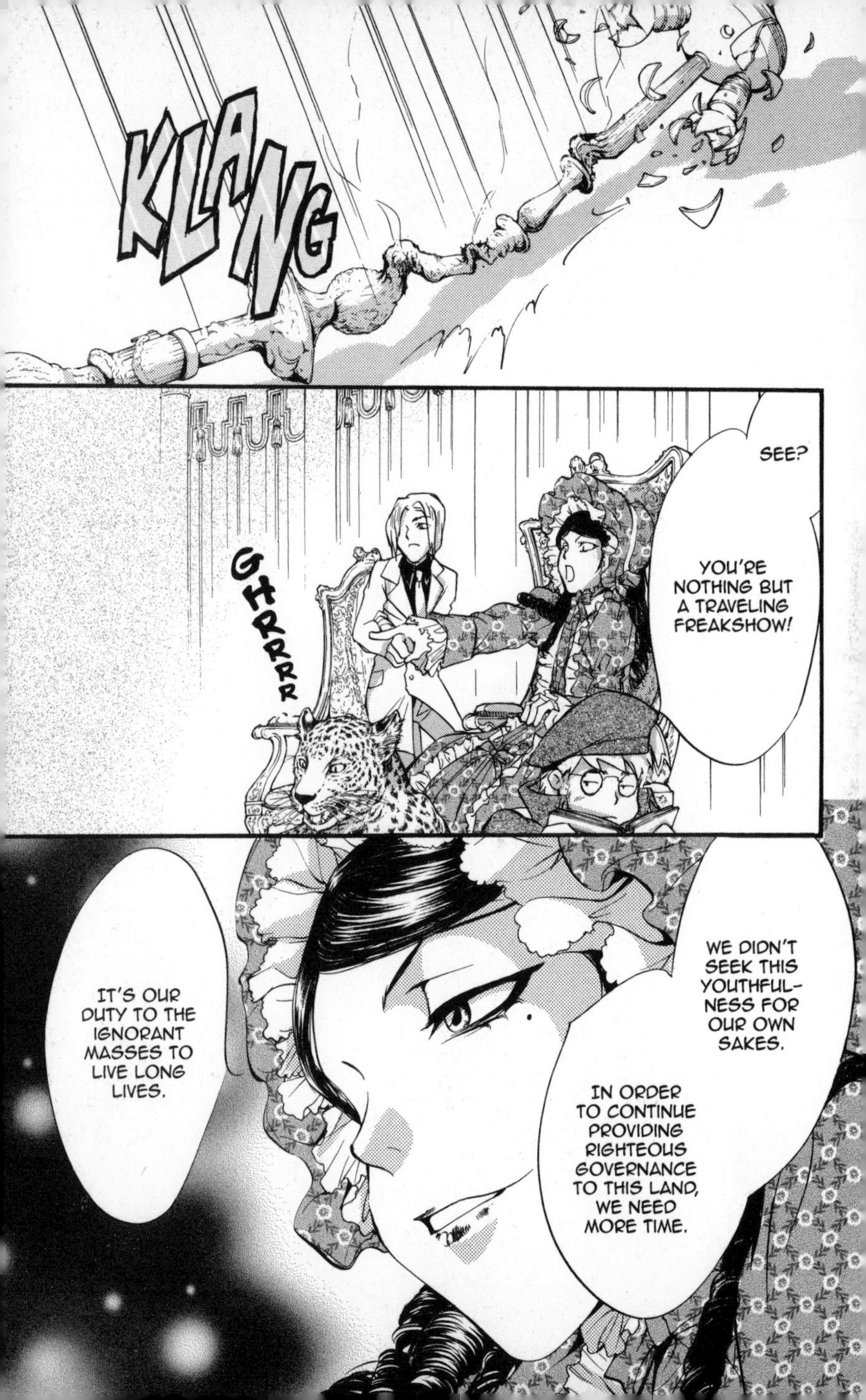
KLANG
SEE?
YOU'RE NOTHING BUT A TRAVELING FREAKSHOW!
GHRRRR
WE DIDN'T SEEK THIS YOUTHFUL-NESS FOR OUR OWN SAKES.
IN ORDER TO CONTINUE PROVIDING RIGHTEOUS GOVERNANCE TO THIS LAND, WE NEED MORE TIME.
IT'S OUR DUTY TO THE IGNORANT MASSES TO LIVE LONG LIVES.

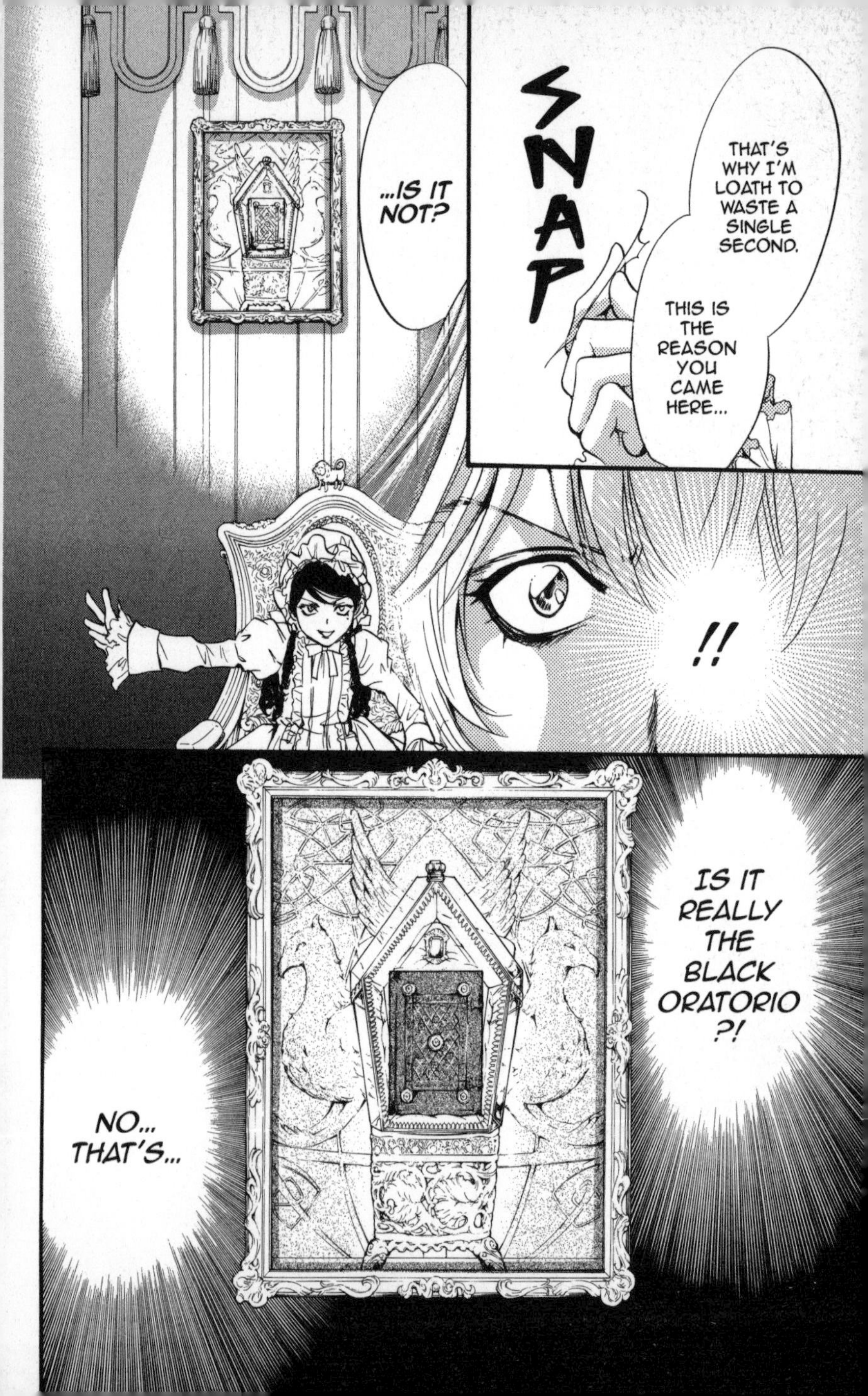
SNAP
THAT'S WHY I'M LOATH TO WASTE A SINGLE SECOND.
THIS IS THE REASON YOU CAME HERE...
...IS IT NOT?
!!
IS IT REALLY THE BLACK ORATORIO?!
NO... THAT'S...

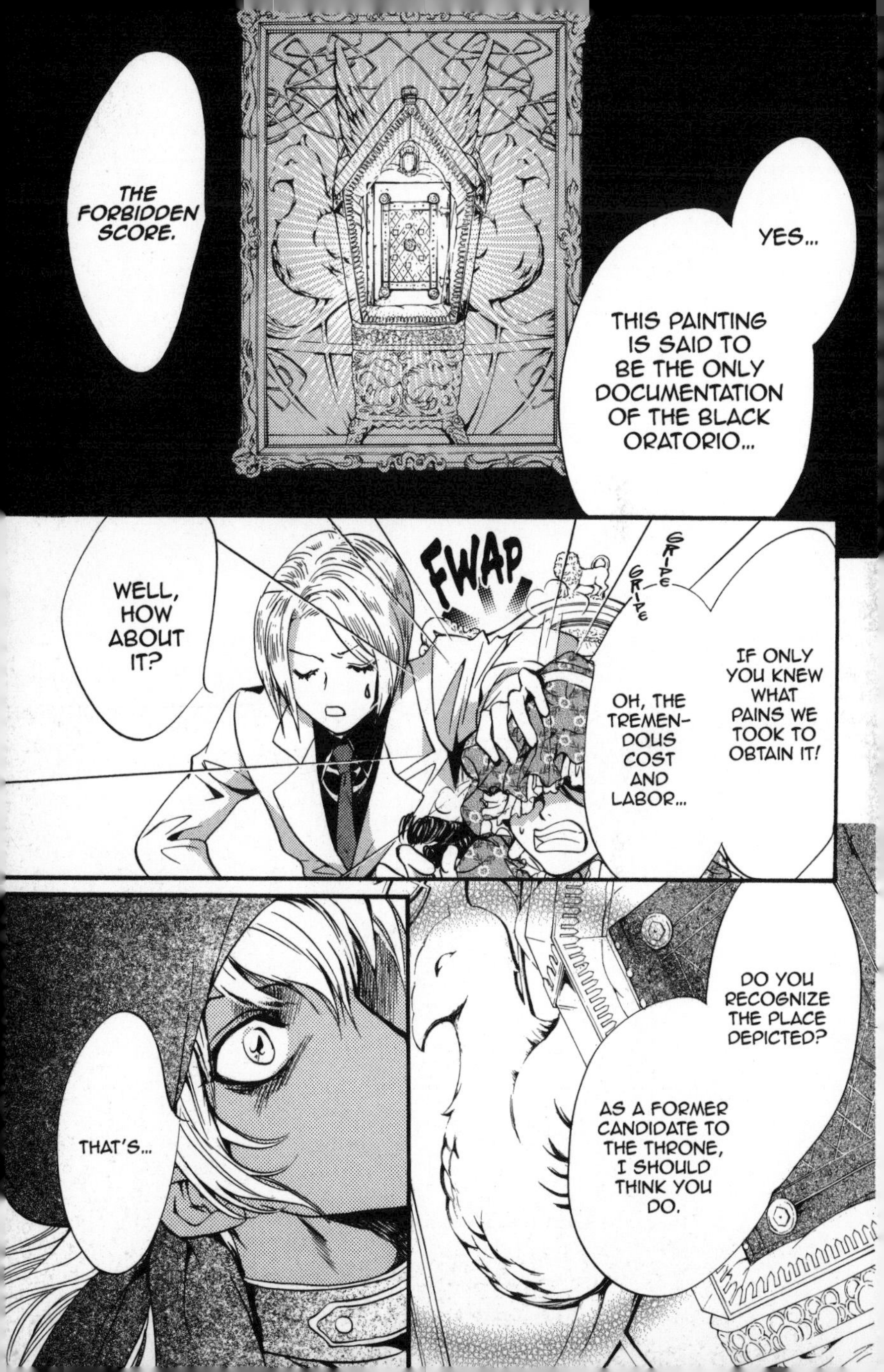
YES...
THIS PAINTING IS SAID TO BE THE ONLY DOCUMENTATION OF THE BLACK ORATORIO...
THE FORBIDDEN SCORE.
IF ONLY YOU KNEW WHAT PAINS WE TOOK TO OBTAIN IT!
OH, THE TREMEN-DOUS COST AND LABOR...
GRIPE GRIPE
FWAP
WELL, HOW ABOUT IT?
DO YOU RECOGNIZE THE PLACE DEPICTED?
AS A FORMER CANDIDATE TO THE THRONE, I SHOULD THINK YOU DO.
THAT'S...

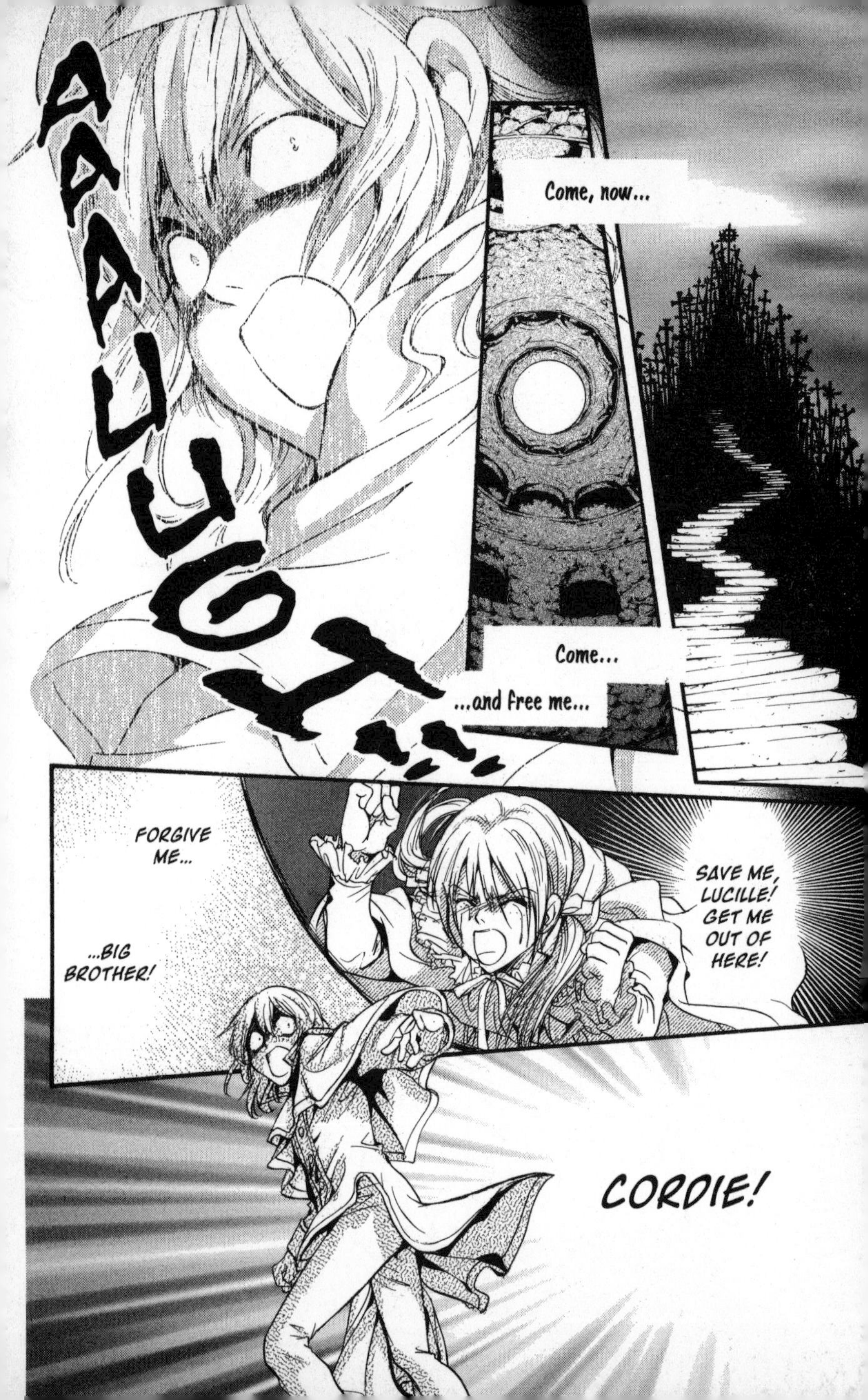
Come, now...
Come...
...and free me...
AAAUUGH!!!
SAVE ME, LUCILLE! GET ME OUT OF HERE!
FORGIVE ME...
...BIG BROTHER!
CORDIE!

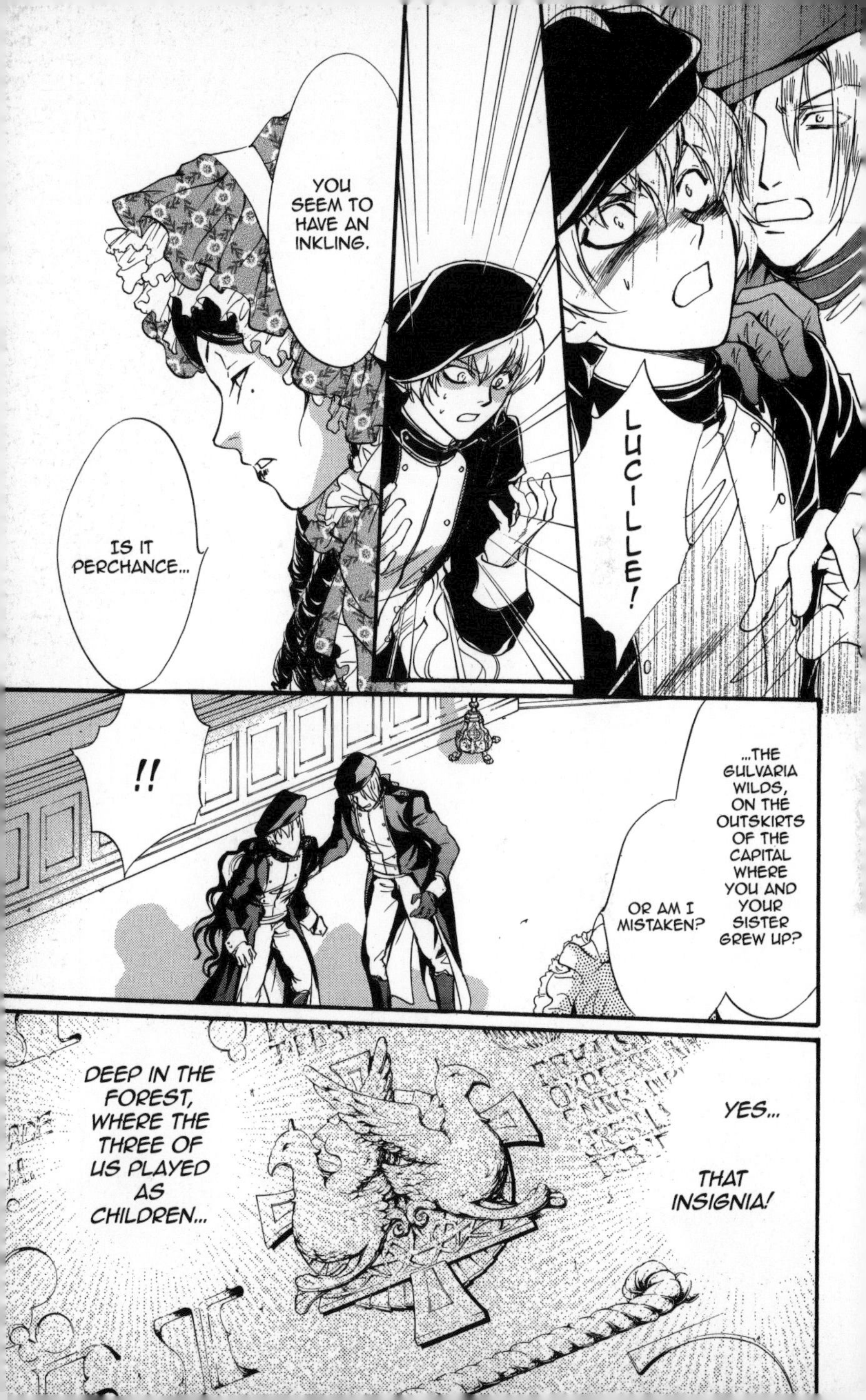
LUCILLE!
YOU SEEM TO HAVE AN INKLING.
IS IT PERCHANCE...
...THE GULVARIA WILDS, ON THE OUTSKIRTS OF THE CAPITAL WHERE YOU AND YOUR SISTER GREW UP?
OR AM I MISTAKEN?
!!
YES...
THAT INSIGNIA!
DEEP IN THE FOREST, WHERE THE THREE OF US PLAYED AS CHILDREN...

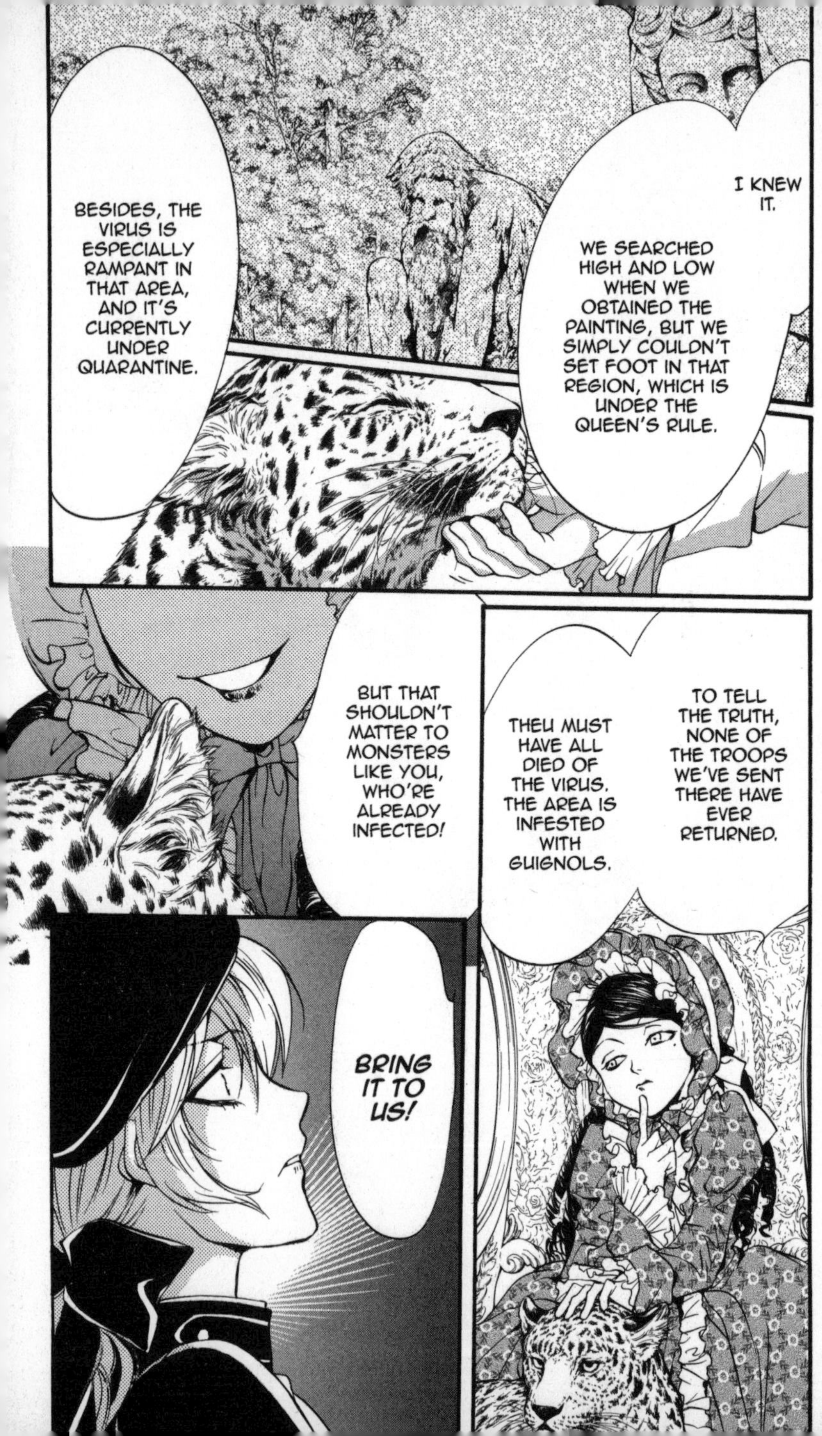
I KNEW IT.
WE SEARCHED HIGH AND LOW WHEN WE OBTAINED THE PAINTING, BUT WE SIMPLY COULDN'T SET FOOT IN THAT REGION, WHICH IS UNDER THE QUEEN'S RULE.
BESIDES, THE VIRUS IS ESPECIALLY RAMPANT IN THAT AREA, AND IT'S CURRENTLY UNDER QUARANTINE.
TO TELL THE TRUTH, NONE OF THE TROOPS WE'VE SENT THERE HAVE EVER RETURNED.
THEY MUST HAVE ALL DIED OF THE VIRUS. THE AREA IS INFESTED WITH GUIGNOLS.
BUT THAT SHOULDN'T MATTER TO MONSTERS LIKE YOU, WHO'RE ALREADY INFECTED!
BRING IT TO US!

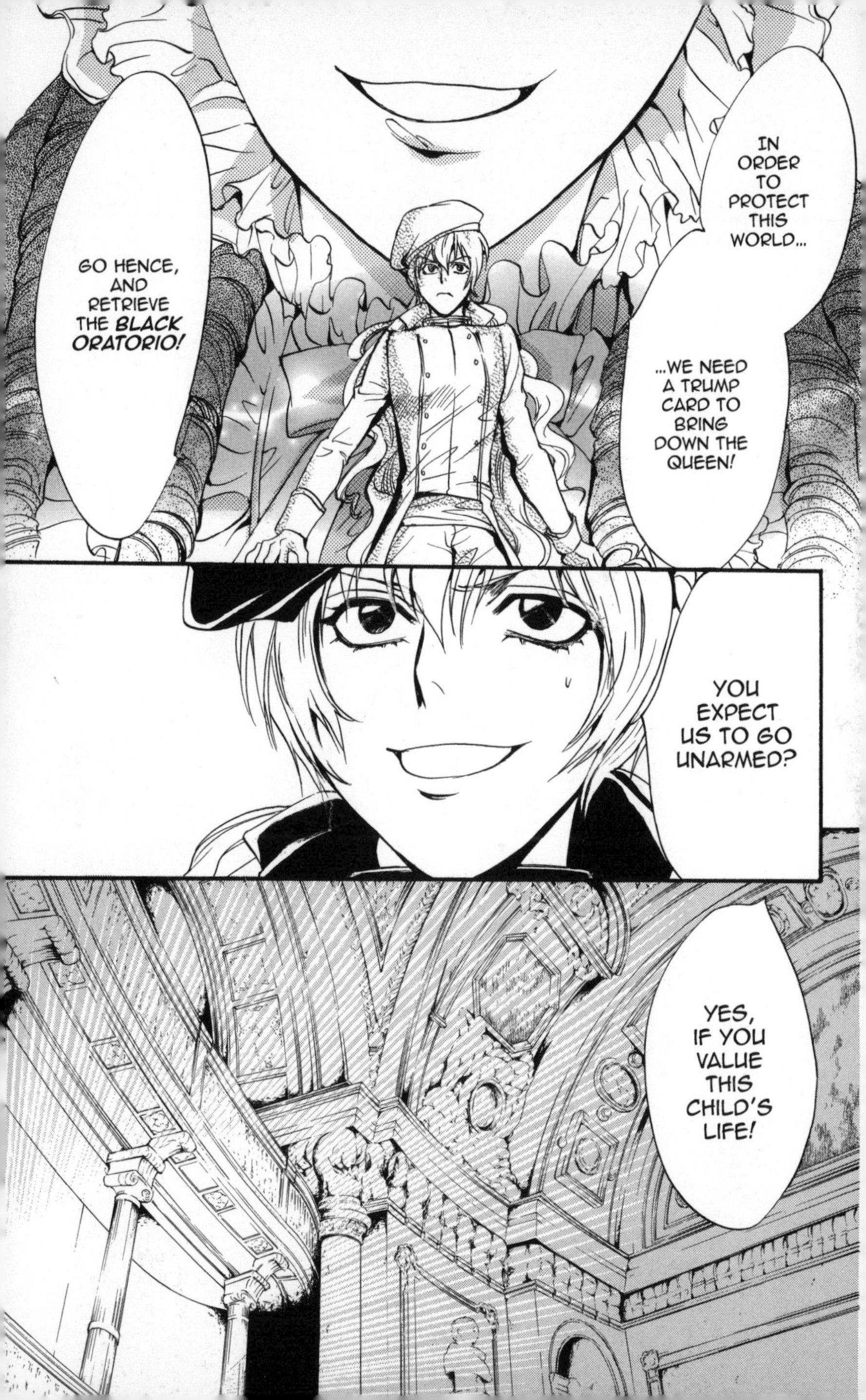
IN ORDER TO PROTECT THIS WORLD...
...WE NEED A TRUMP CARD TO BRING DOWN THE QUEEN!
GO HENCE, AND RETRIEVE THE *BLACK ORATORIO!*
YOU EXPECT US TO GO UNARMED?
YES, IF YOU VALUE THIS CHILD'S LIFE!

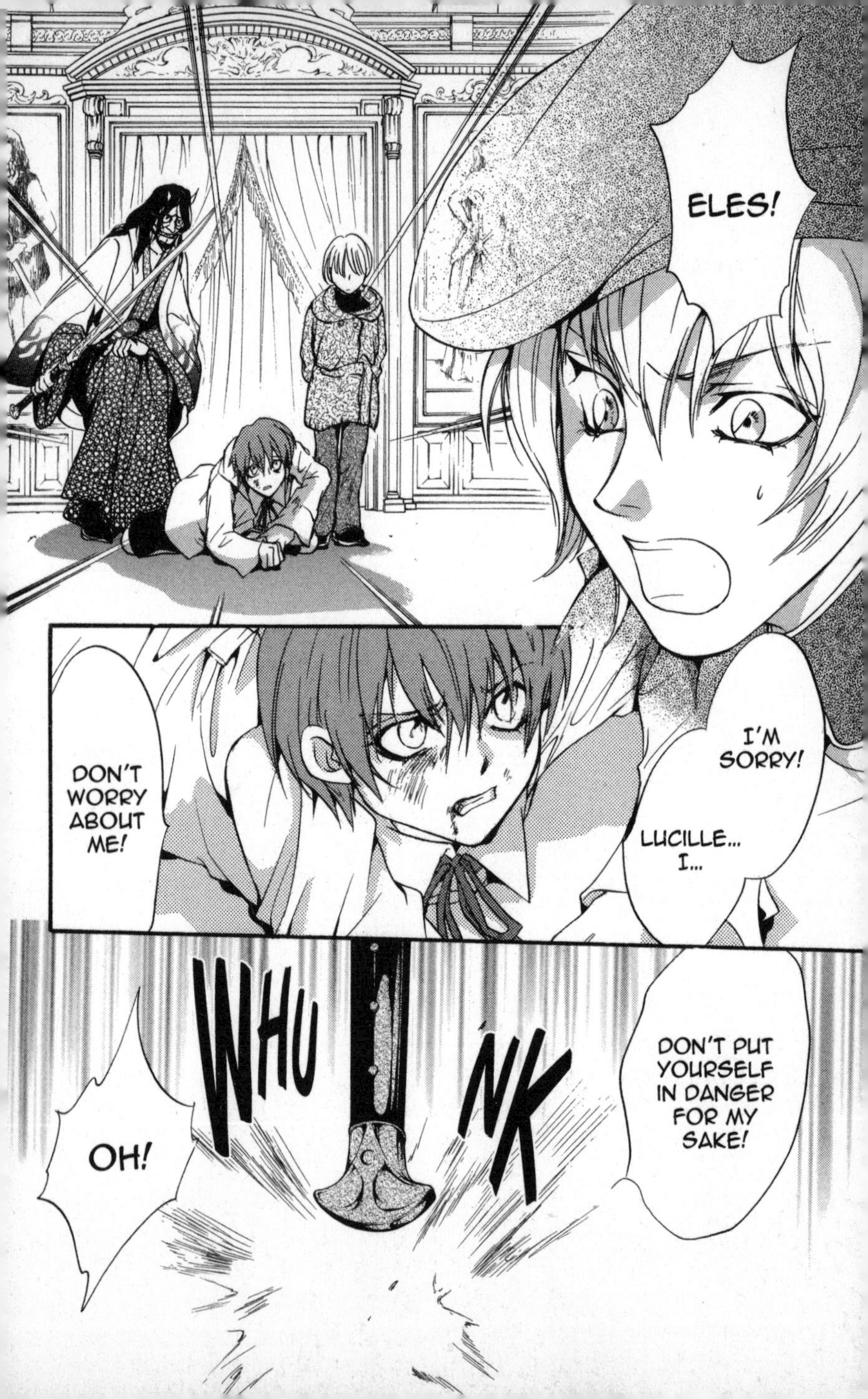
ELES!
I'M SORRY!
LUCILLE... I...
DON'T WORRY ABOUT ME!
DON'T PUT YOURSELF IN DANGER FOR MY SAKE!
WHUNK
OH!

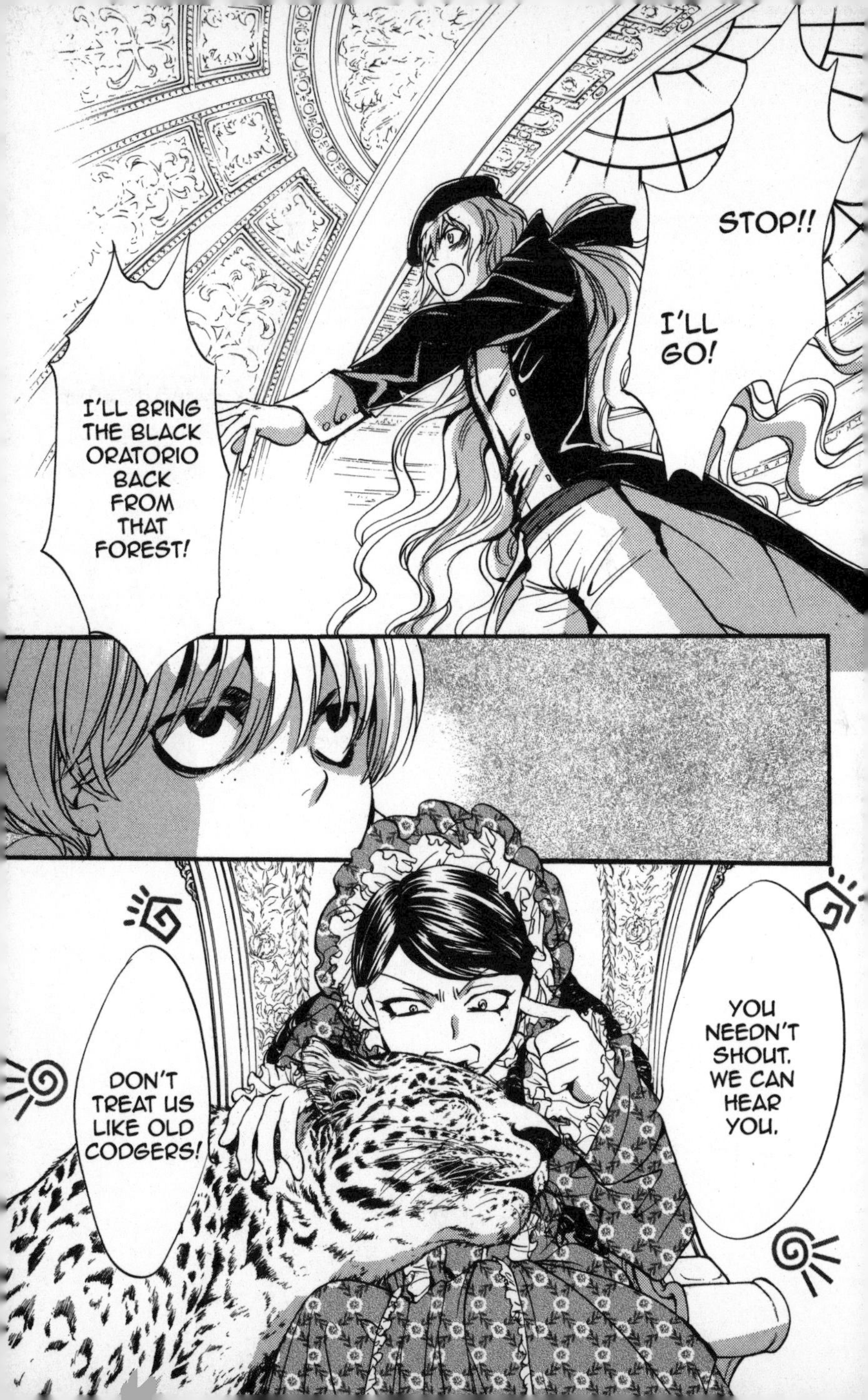
STOP!!
I'LL GO!
I'LL BRING THE BLACK ORATORIO BACK FROM THAT FOREST!
YOU NEEDN'T SHOUT. WE CAN HEAR YOU.
DON'T TREAT US LIKE OLD CODGERS!

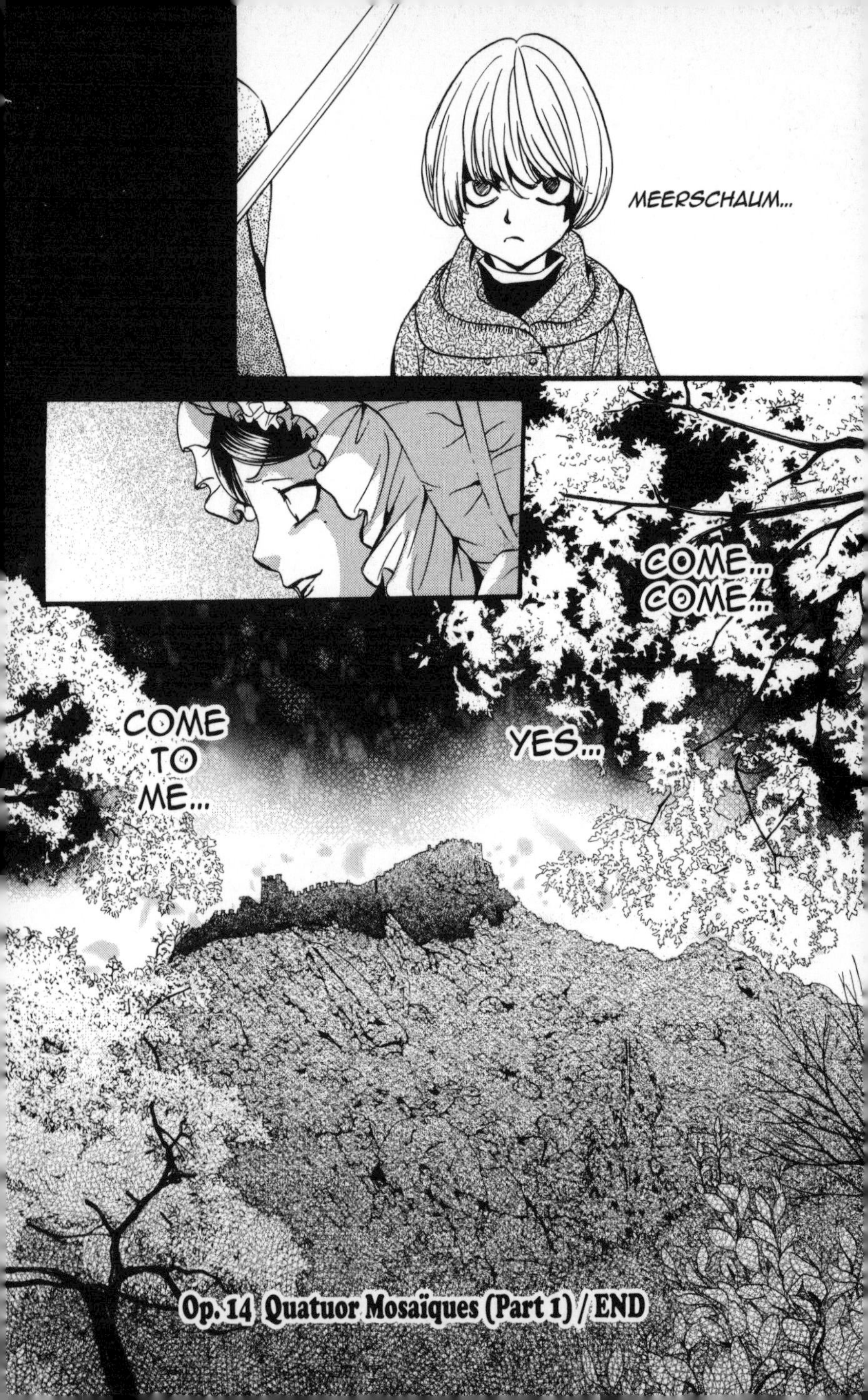
MEERSCHAUM...
COME... COME...
YES...
COME TO ME...
Op. 14 Quatuor Mosaïques (Part 1) / END

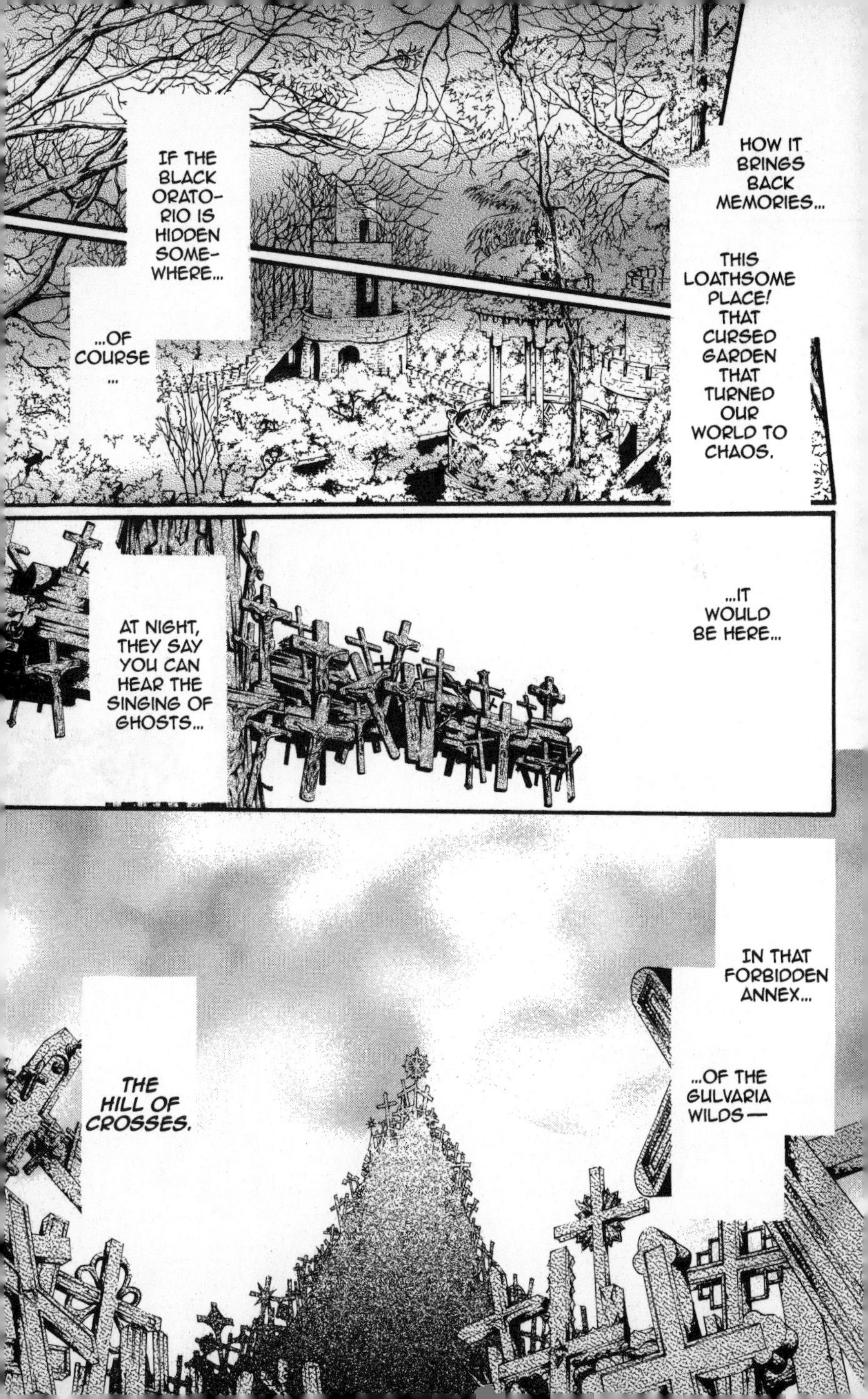
HOW IT BRINGS BACK MEMORIES...
THIS LOATHSOME PLACE! THAT CURSED GARDEN THAT TURNED OUR WORLD TO CHAOS.
IF THE BLACK ORATO-RIO IS HIDDEN SOME-WHERE...
...OF COURSE...
...IT WOULD BE HERE...
AT NIGHT, THEY SAY YOU CAN HEAR THE SINGING OF GHOSTS...
IN THAT FORBIDDEN ANNEX...
...OF THE GULVARIA WILDS—
THE HILL OF CROSSES.

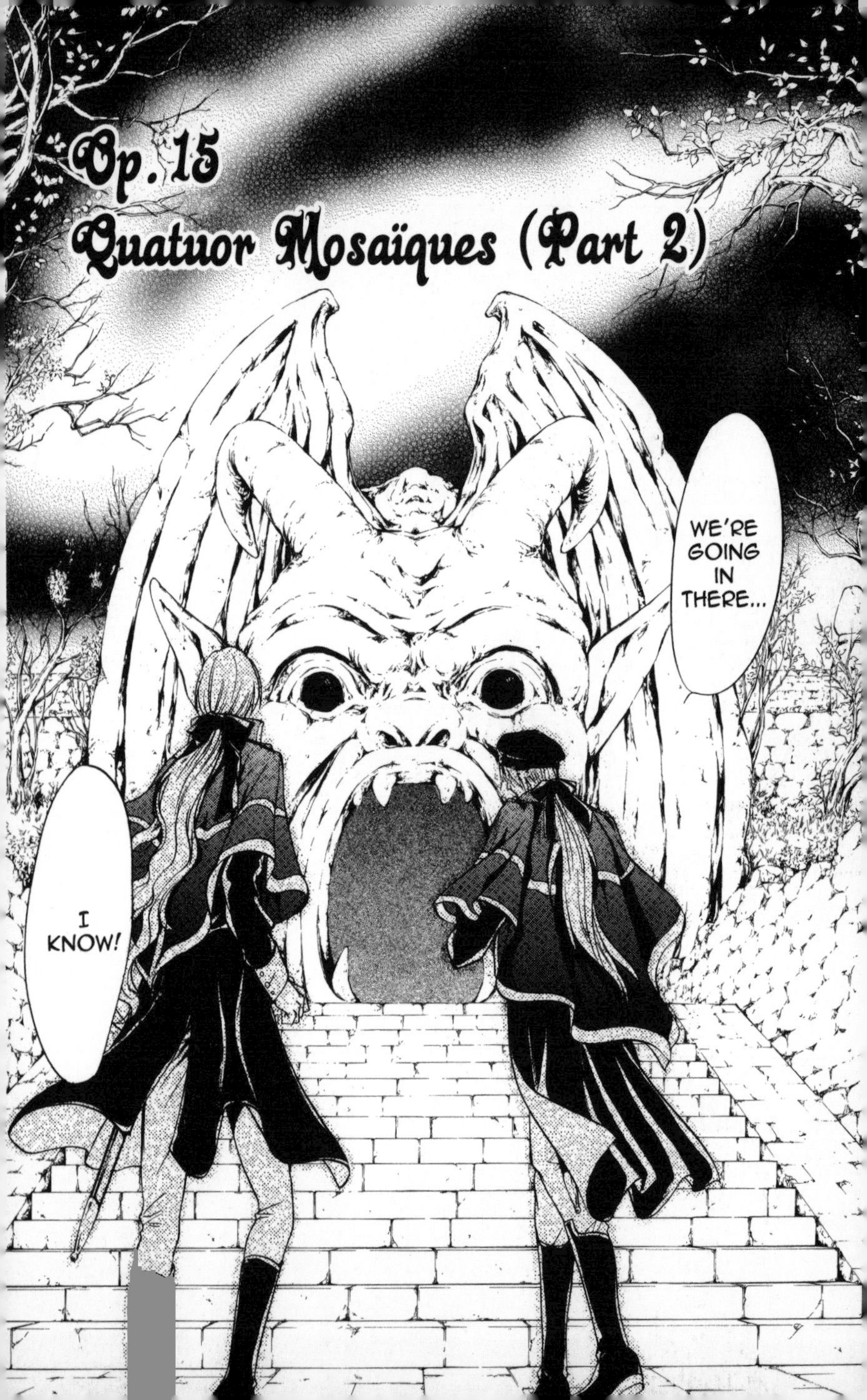
Op. 15
Quatuor Mosaïques (Part 2)
WE'RE GOING IN THERE...
I KNOW!

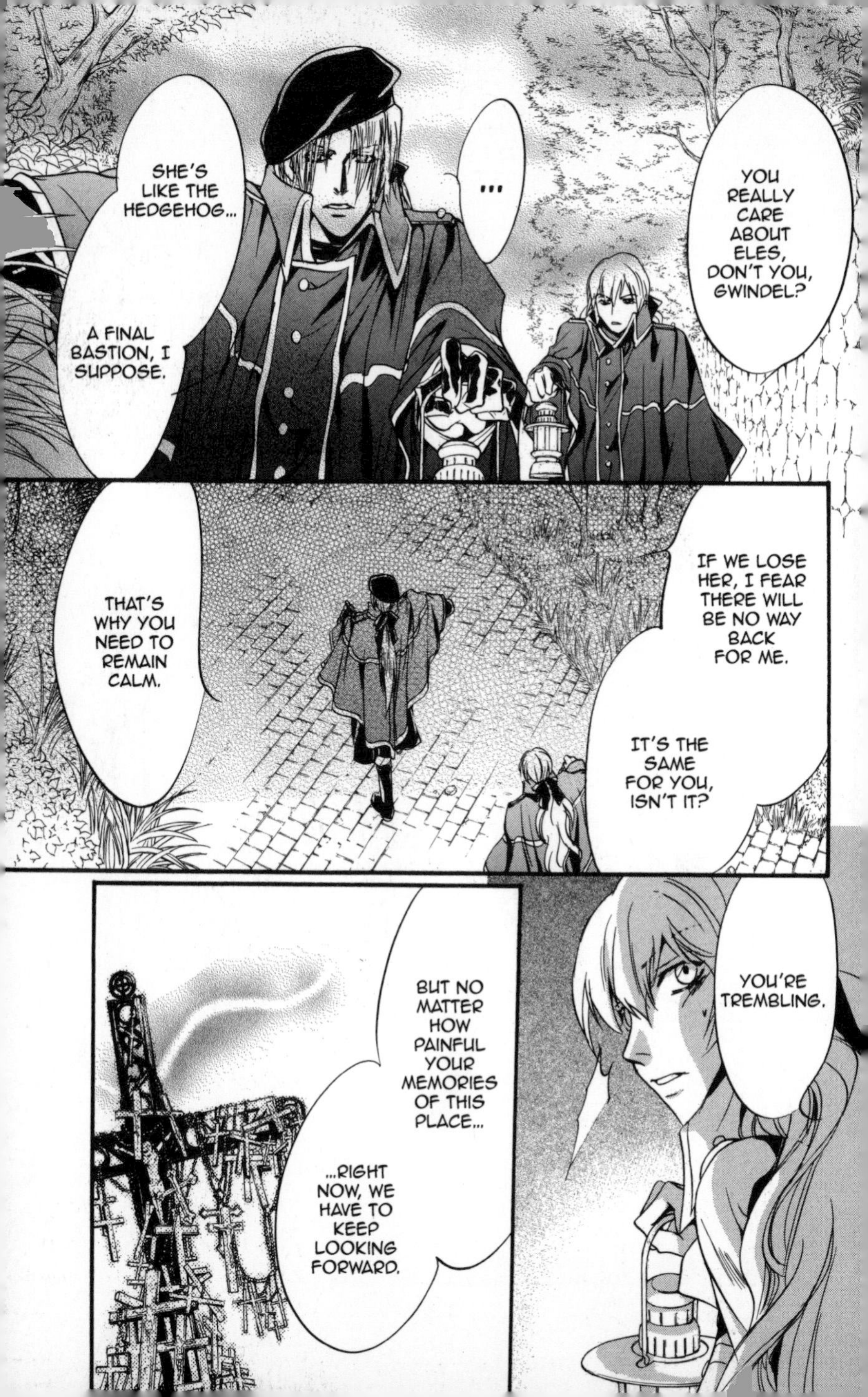
YOU REALLY CARE ABOUT ELES, DON'T YOU, GWINDEL?
...
SHE'S LIKE THE HEDGEHOG...
A FINAL BASTION, I SUPPOSE.
IF WE LOSE HER, I FEAR THERE WILL BE NO WAY BACK FOR ME.
IT'S THE SAME FOR YOU, ISN'T IT?
THAT'S WHY YOU NEED TO REMAIN CALM.
YOU'RE TREMBLING.
BUT NO MATTER HOW PAINFUL YOUR MEMORIES OF THIS PLACE...
...RIGHT NOW, WE HAVE TO KEEP LOOKING FORWARD.

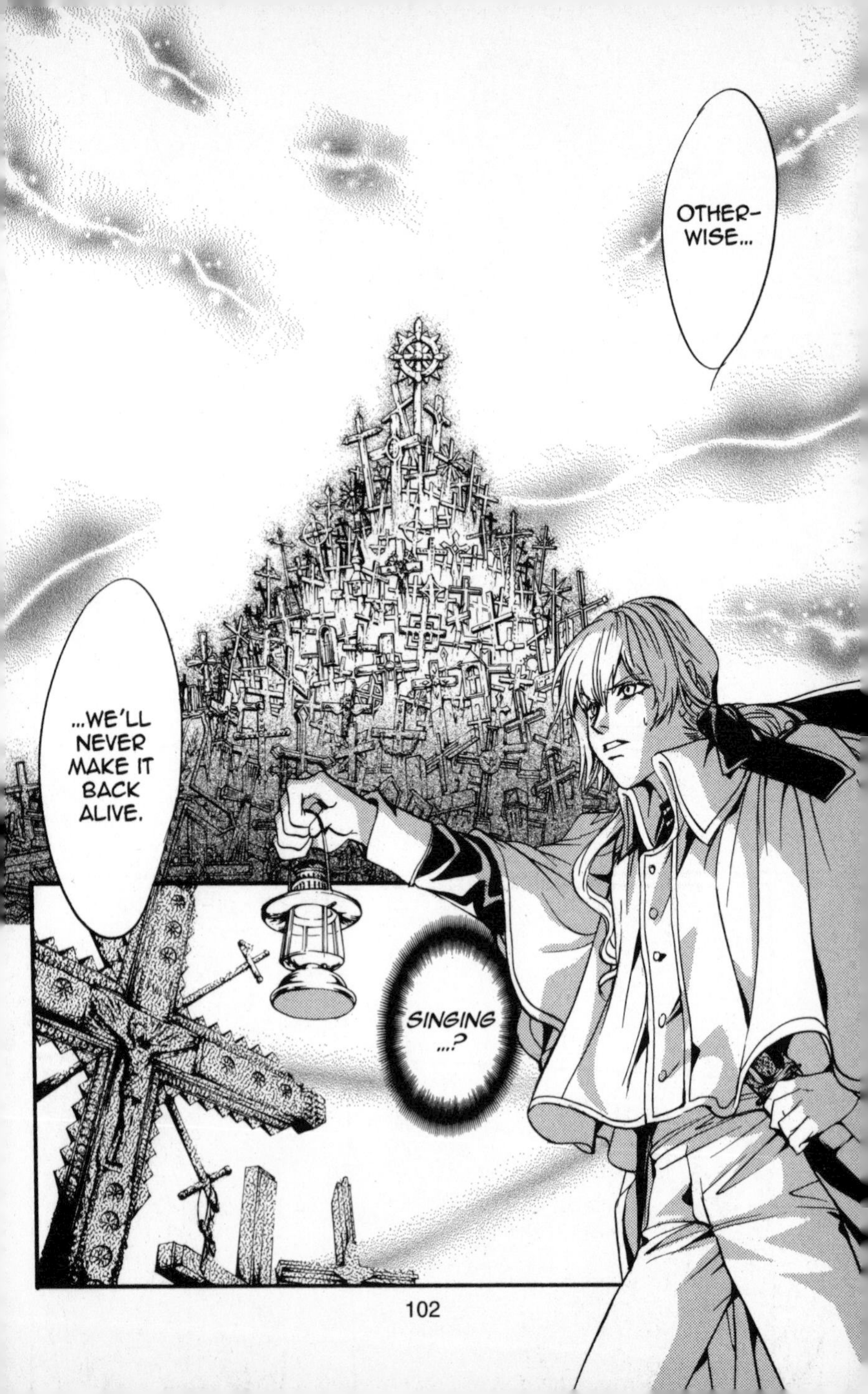
OTHER-WISE...
...WE'LL NEVER MAKE IT BACK ALIVE.
SINGING ...?

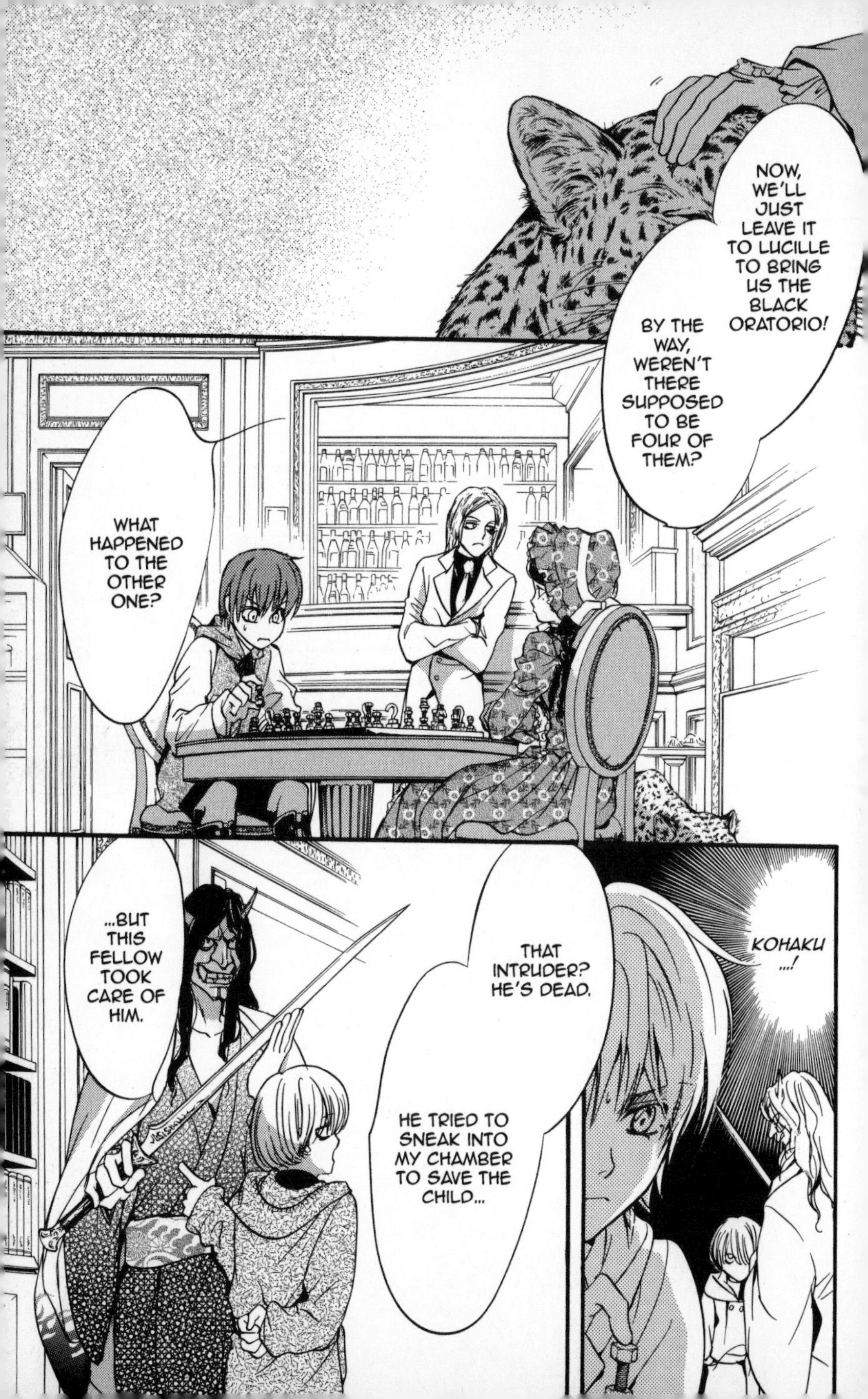
NOW, WE'LL JUST LEAVE IT TO LUCILLE TO BRING US THE BLACK ORATORIO!
BY THE WAY, WEREN'T THERE SUPPOSED TO BE FOUR OF THEM?
WHAT HAPPENED TO THE OTHER ONE?
KOHAKU ...!
THAT INTRUDER? HE'S DEAD.
HE TRIED TO SNEAK INTO MY CHAMBER TO SAVE THE CHILD...
...BUT THIS FELLOW TOOK CARE OF HIM.

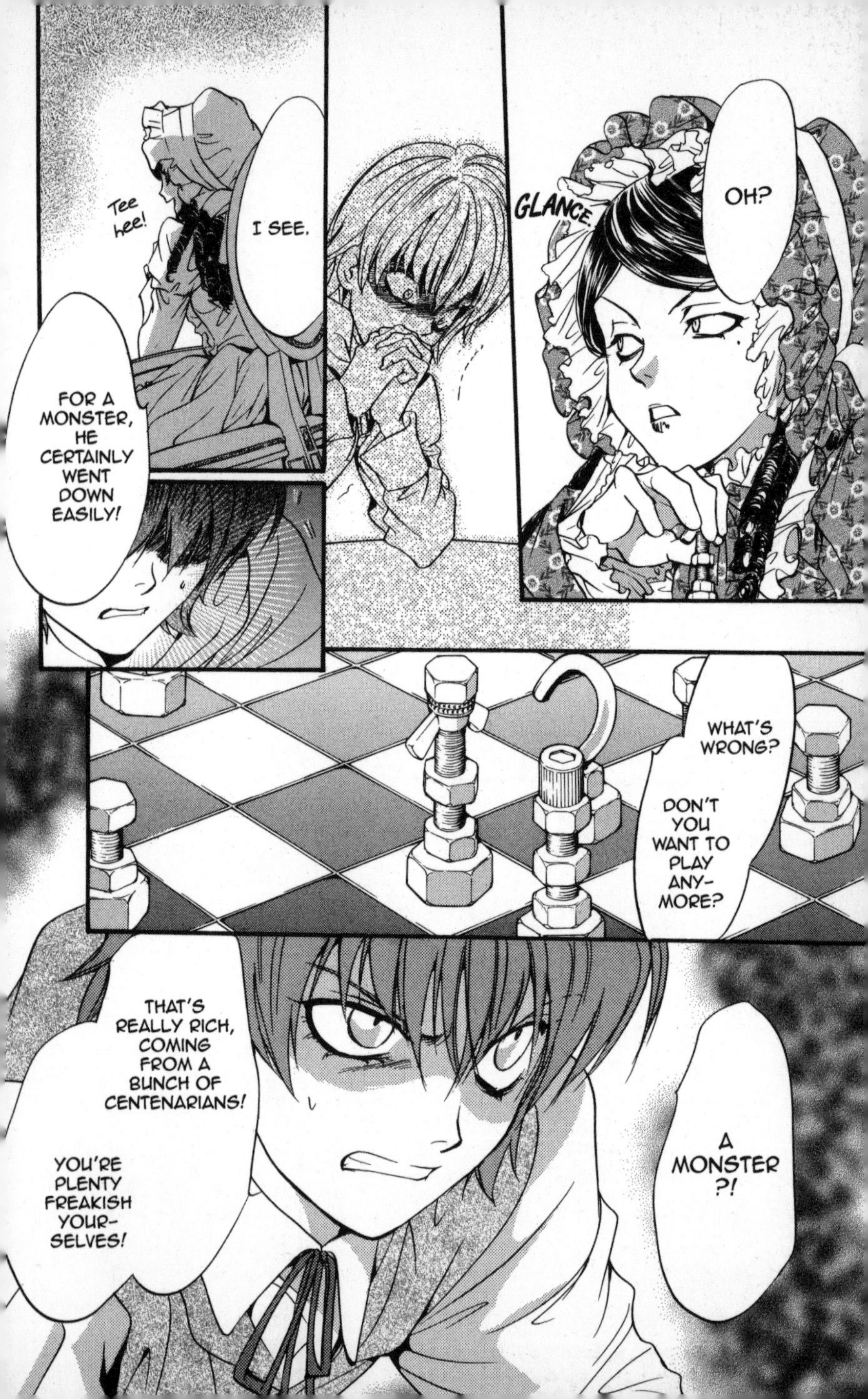
OH?
GLANCE.
I SEE.
Tee hee!
FOR A MONSTER, HE CERTAINLY WENT DOWN EASILY!
WHAT'S WRONG?
DON'T YOU WANT TO PLAY ANY-MORE?
A MONSTER ?!
THAT'S REALLY RICH, COMING FROM A BUNCH OF CENTENARIANS!
YOU'RE PLENTY FREAKISH YOUR-SELVES!

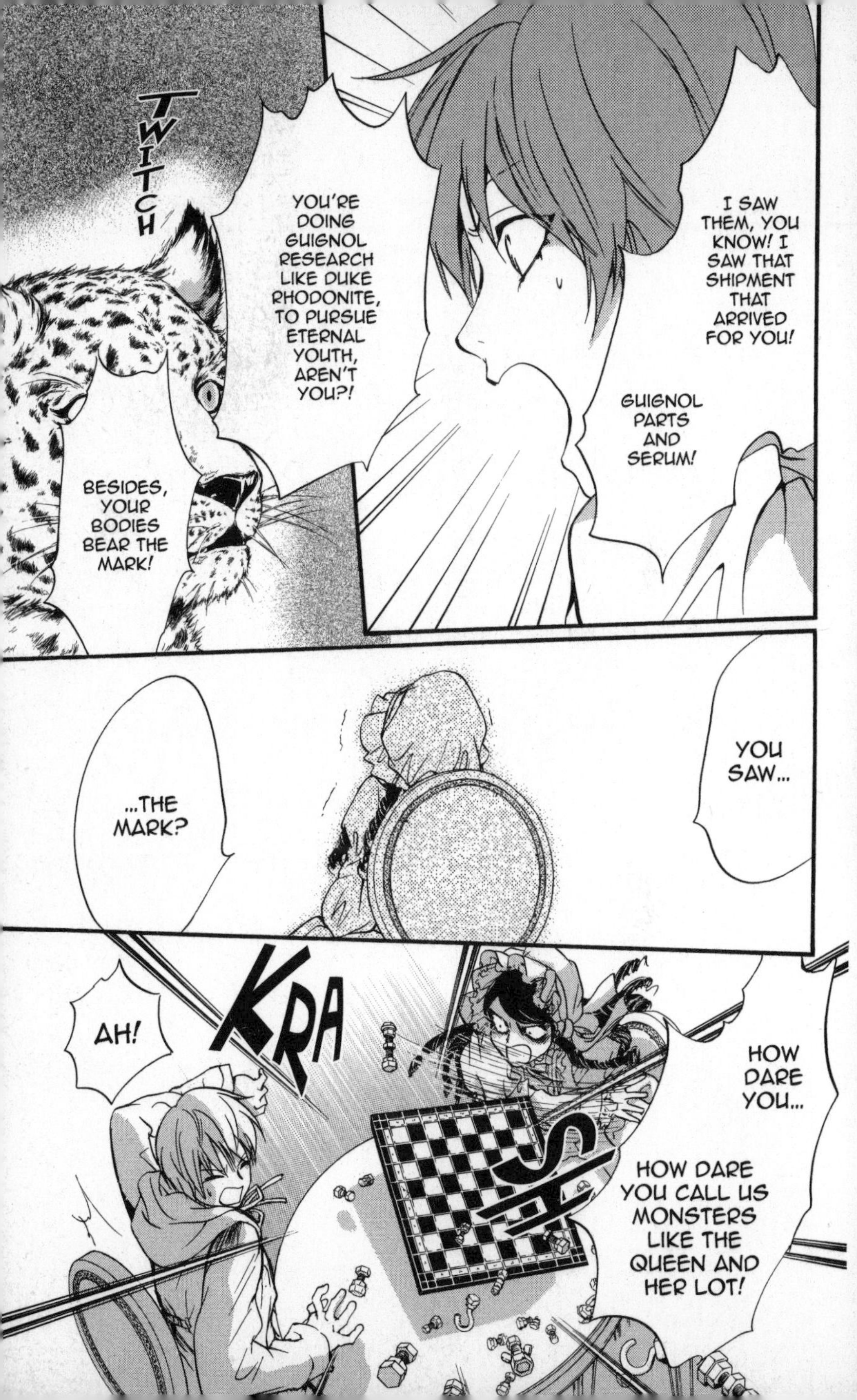
I SAW THEM, YOU KNOW! I SAW THAT SHIPMENT THAT ARRIVED FOR YOU!
GUIGNOL PARTS AND SERUM!
YOU'RE DOING GUIGNOL RESEARCH LIKE DUKE RHODONITE, TO PURSUE ETERNAL YOUTH, AREN'T YOU?!
BESIDES, YOUR BODIES BEAR THE MARK!
TWITCH
YOU SAW...
...THE MARK?
HOW DARE YOU...
HOW DARE YOU CALL US MONSTERS LIKE THE QUEEN AND HER LOT!
SH
KRA
AH!

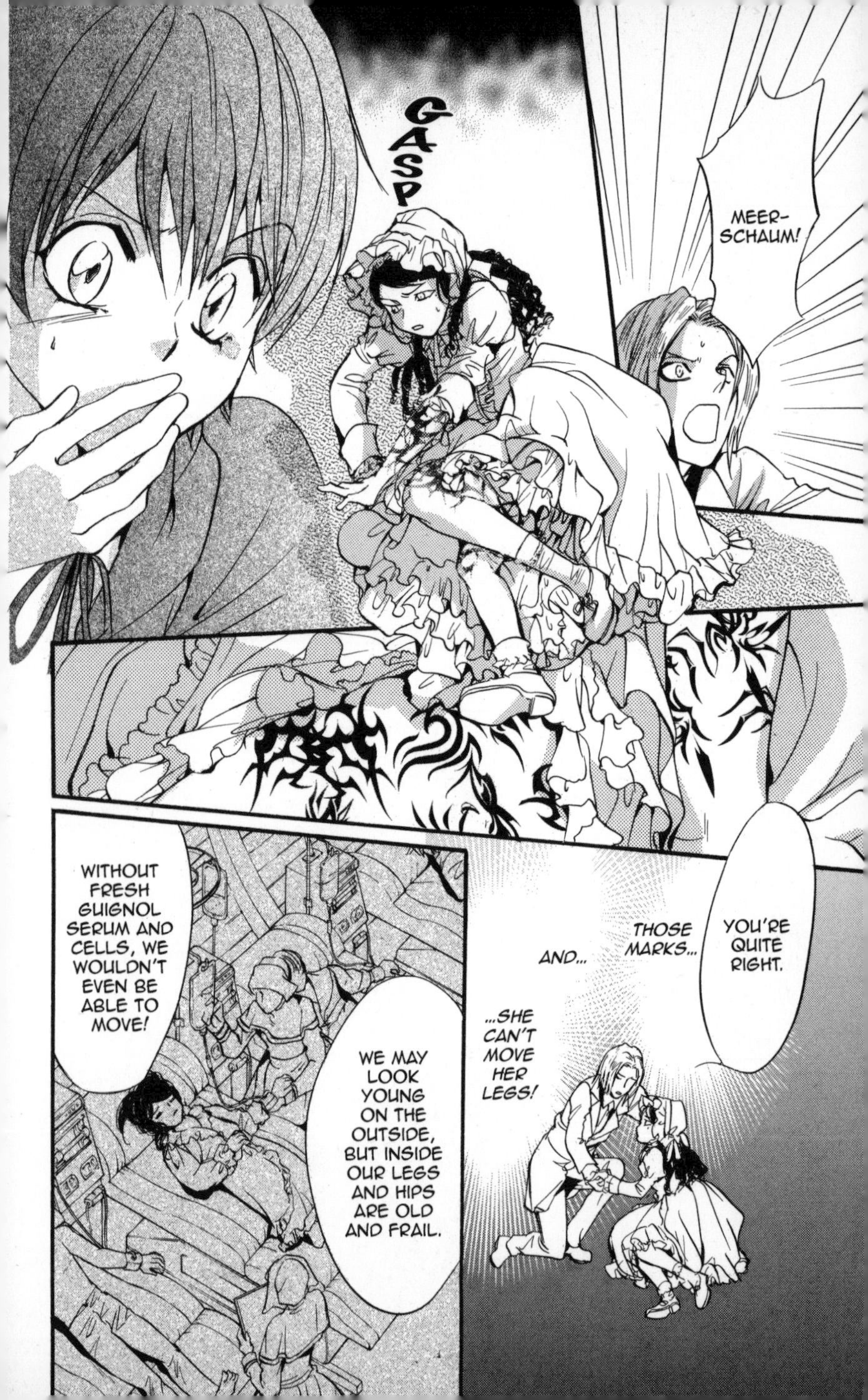
MEER-SCHAUM!
GASP
YOU'RE QUITE RIGHT.
THOSE MARKS...
AND...
...SHE CAN'T MOVE HER LEGS!
WE MAY LOOK YOUNG ON THE OUTSIDE, BUT INSIDE OUR LEGS AND HIPS ARE OLD AND FRAIL.
WITHOUT FRESH GUIGNOL SERUM AND CELLS, WE WOULDN'T EVEN BE ABLE TO MOVE!

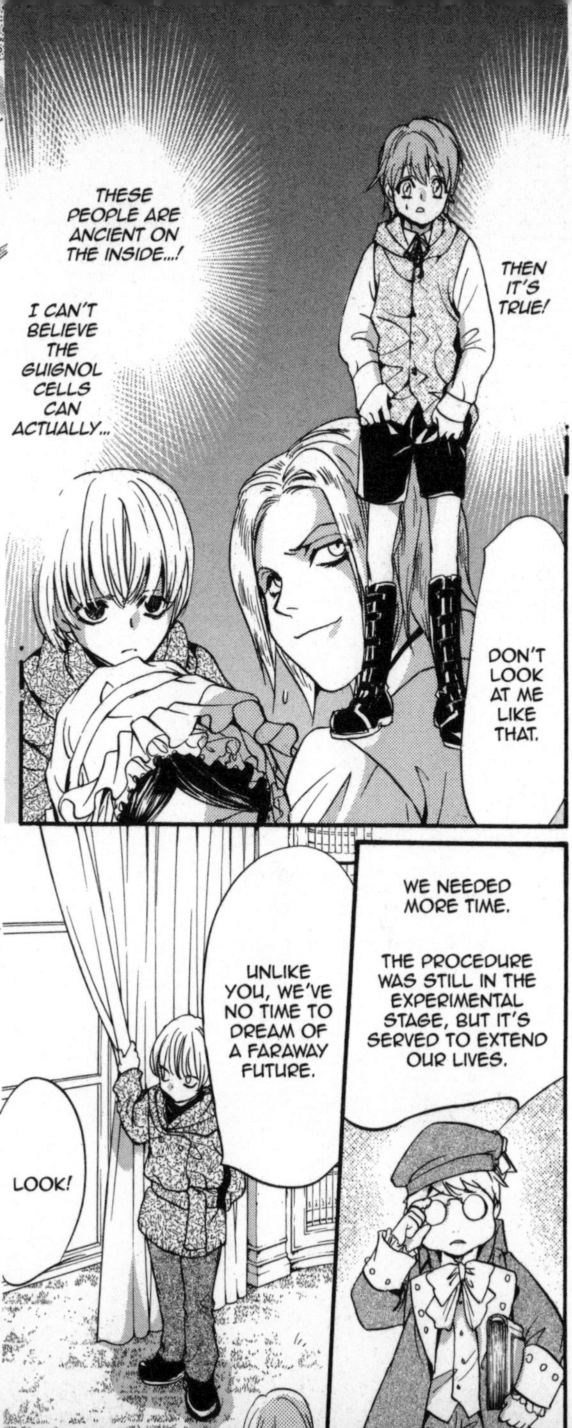
THEN IT'S TRUE!
THESE PEOPLE ARE ANCIENT ON THE INSIDE...!
I CAN'T BELIEVE THE GUIGNOL CELLS CAN ACTUALLY...
DON'T LOOK AT ME LIKE THAT.
WE NEEDED MORE TIME.
THE PROCEDURE WAS STILL IN THE EXPERIMENTAL STAGE, BUT IT'S SERVED TO EXTEND OUR LIVES.
UNLIKE YOU, WE'VE NO TIME TO DREAM OF A FARAWAY FUTURE.
LOOK!

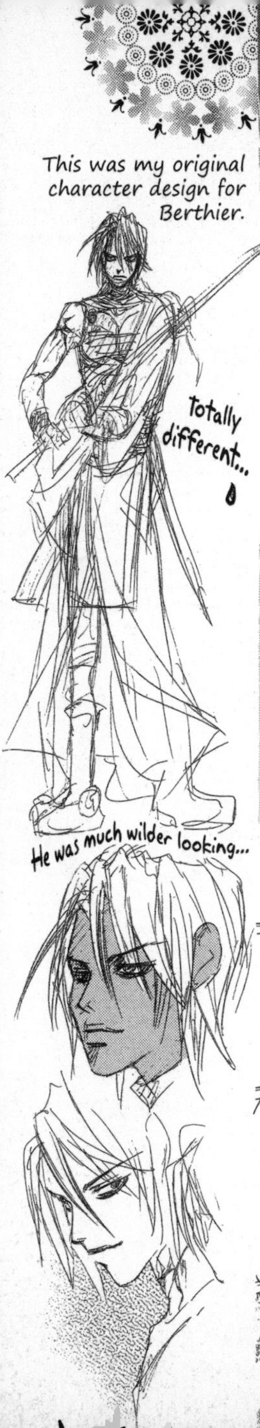
This was my original character design for Berthier.
totally different...
He was much wilder looking...

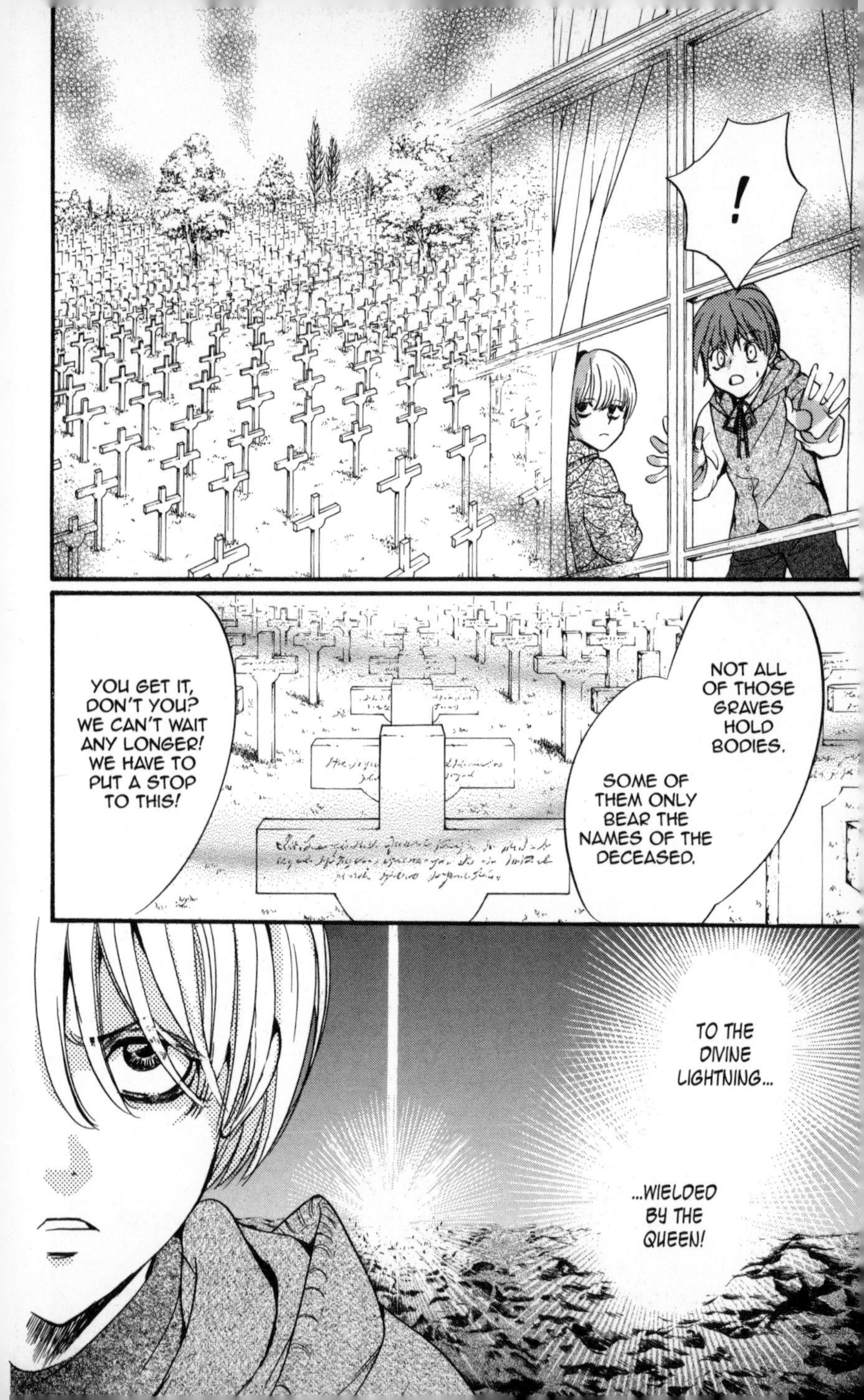
!
NOT ALL OF THOSE GRAVES HOLD BODIES.
SOME OF THEM ONLY BEAR THE NAMES OF THE DECEASED.
YOU GET IT, DON'T YOU? WE CAN'T WAIT ANY LONGER! WE HAVE TO PUT A STOP TO THIS!
TO THE DIVINE LIGHTNING...
...WIELDED BY THE QUEEN!

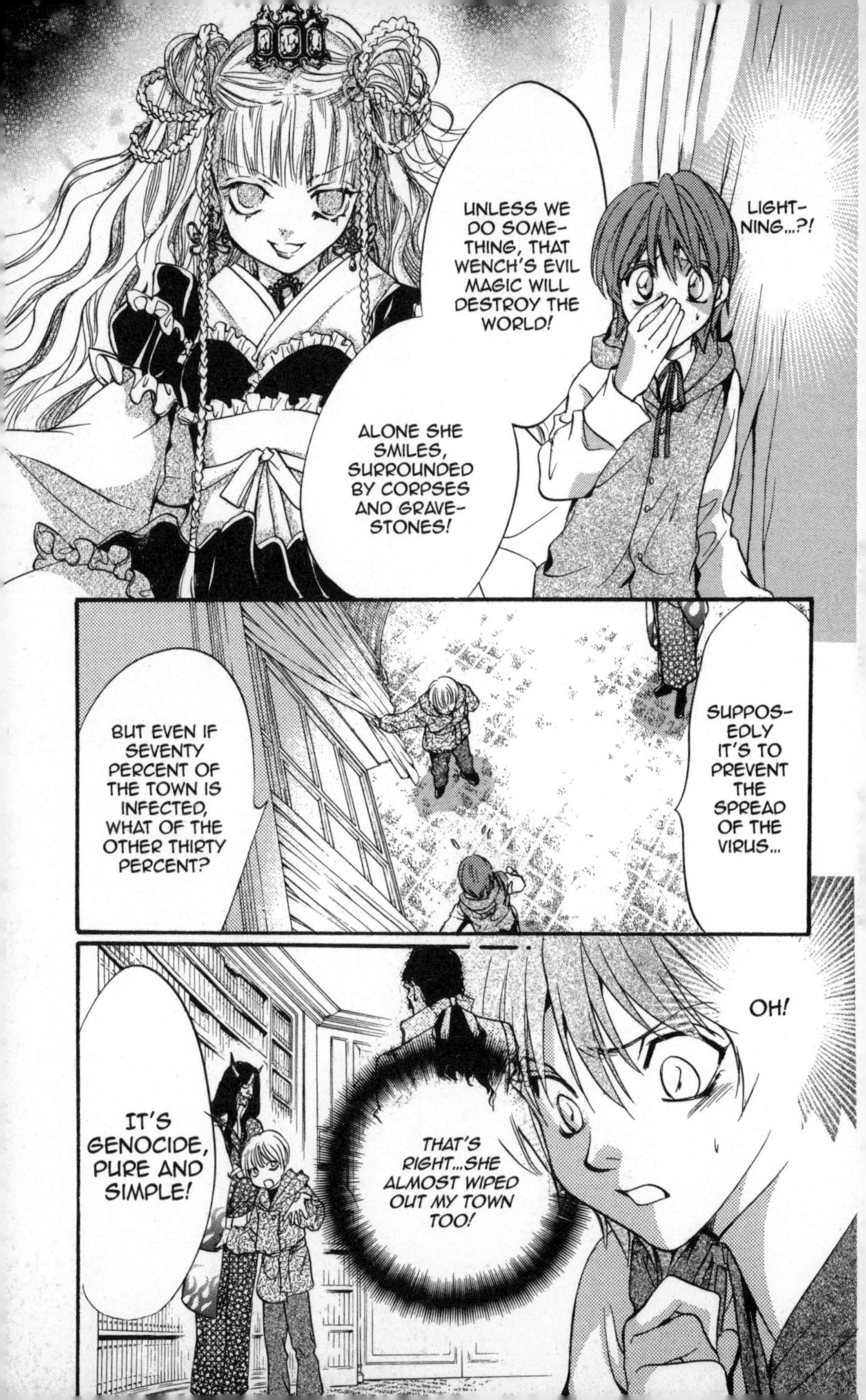
LIGHTNING...?!
UNLESS WE DO SOMETHING, THAT WENCH'S EVIL MAGIC WILL DESTROY THE WORLD!
ALONE SHE SMILES, SURROUNDED BY CORPSES AND GRAVESTONES!
SUPPOSEDLY IT'S TO PREVENT THE SPREAD OF THE VIRUS...
BUT EVEN IF SEVENTY PERCENT OF THE TOWN IS INFECTED, WHAT OF THE OTHER THIRTY PERCENT?
OH!
THAT'S RIGHT...SHE ALMOST WIPED OUT MY TOWN TOO!
IT'S GENOCIDE, PURE AND SIMPLE!

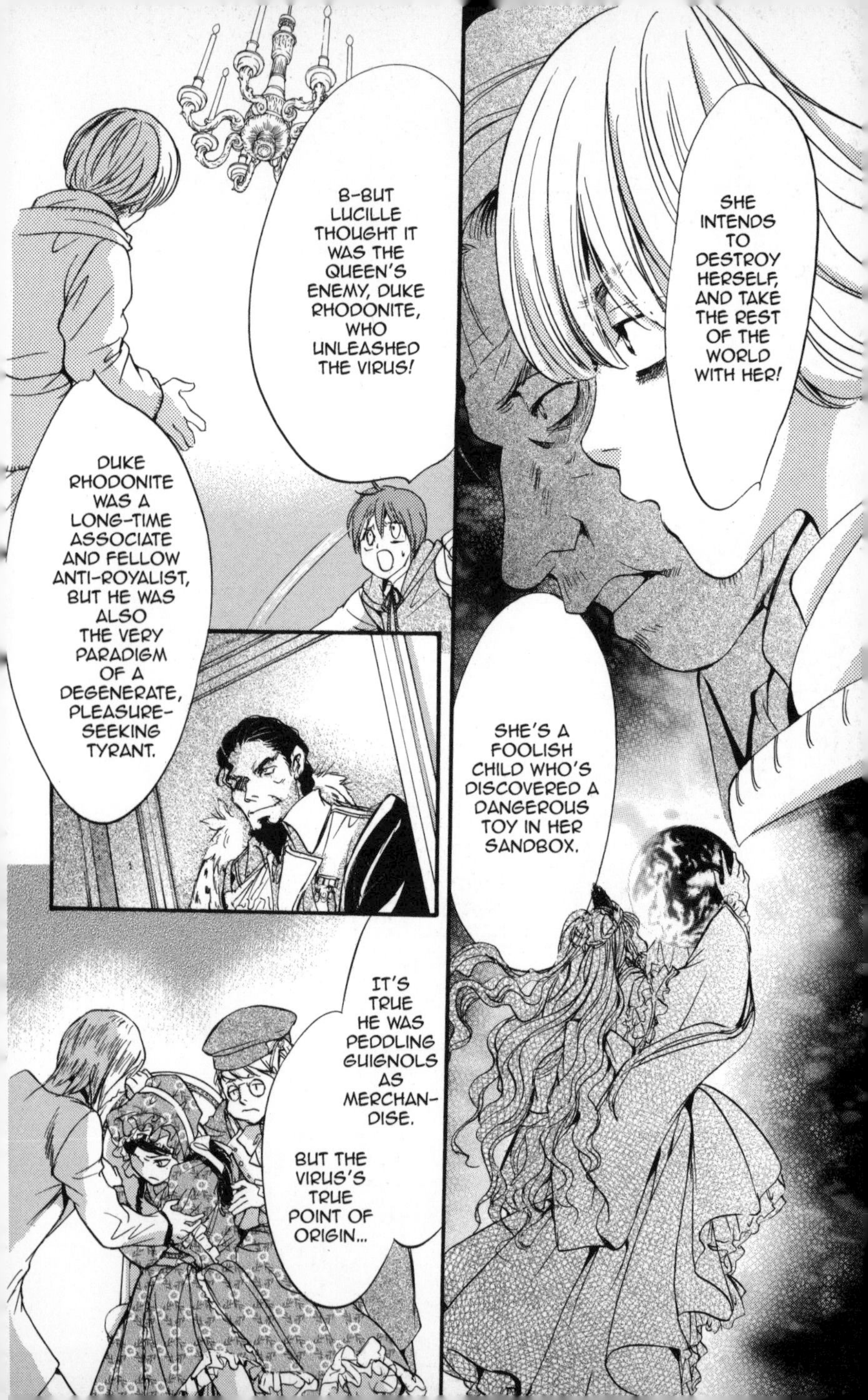
SHE INTENDS TO DESTROY HERSELF, AND TAKE THE REST OF THE WORLD WITH HER!
SHE'S A FOOLISH CHILD WHO'S DISCOVERED A DANGEROUS TOY IN HER SANDBOX.
B-BUT LUCILLE THOUGHT IT WAS THE QUEEN'S ENEMY, DUKE RHODONITE, WHO UNLEASHED THE VIRUS!
DUKE RHODONITE WAS A LONG-TIME ASSOCIATE AND FELLOW ANTI-ROYALIST, BUT HE WAS ALSO THE VERY PARADIGM OF A DEGENERATE, PLEASURE-SEEKING TYRANT.
IT'S TRUE HE WAS PEDDLING GUIGNOLS AS MERCHAN-DISE.
BUT THE VIRUS'S TRUE POINT OF ORIGIN...

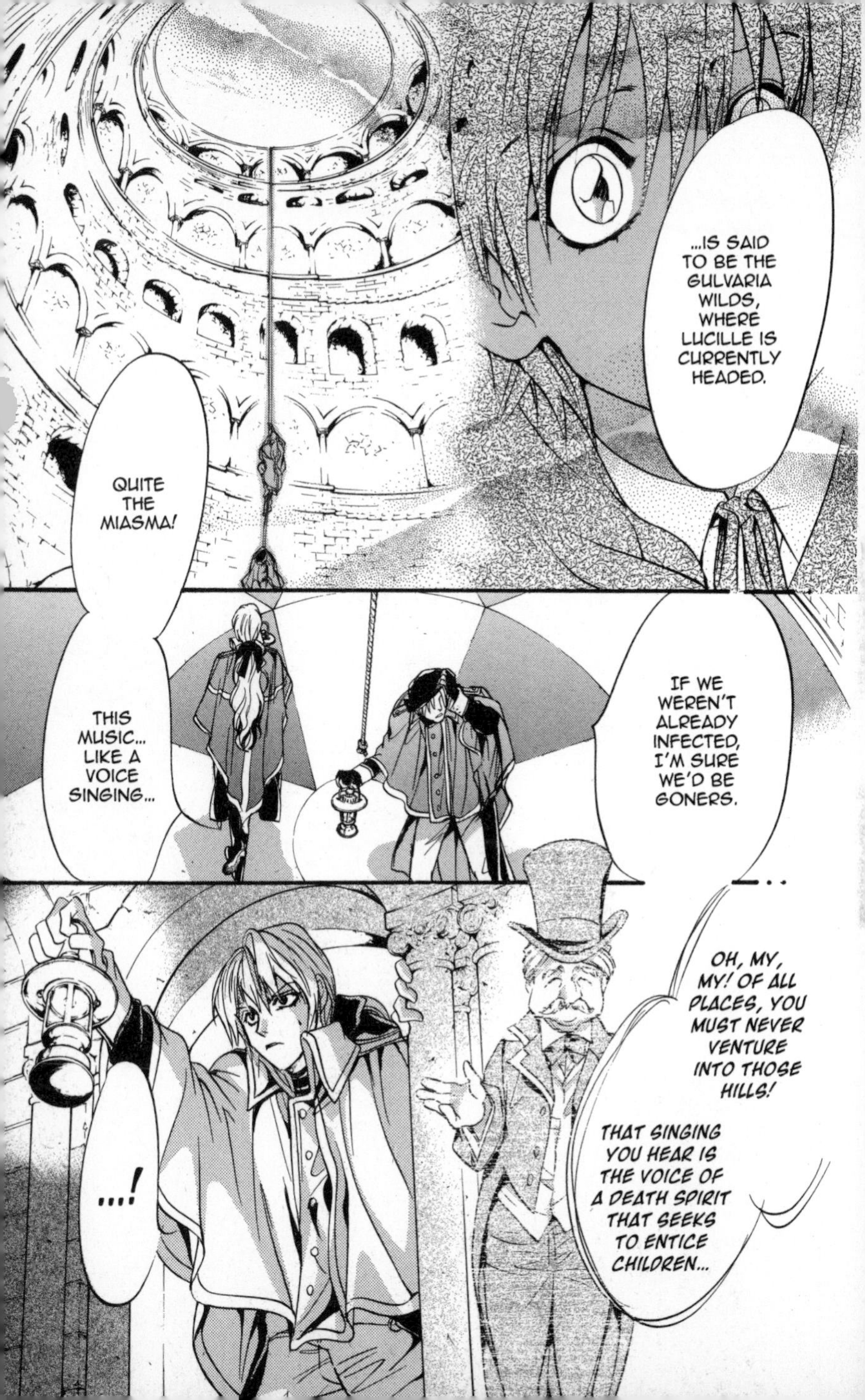
...IS SAID TO BE THE GULVARIA WILDS, WHERE LUCILLE IS CURRENTLY HEADED.
QUITE THE MIASMA!
IF WE WEREN'T ALREADY INFECTED, I'M SURE WE'D BE GONERS.
THIS MUSIC... LIKE A VOICE SINGING...
OH, MY, MY! OF ALL PLACES, YOU MUST NEVER VENTURE INTO THOSE HILLS!
THAT SINGING YOU HEAR IS THE VOICE OF A DEATH SPIRIT THAT SEEKS TO ENTICE CHILDREN...
...!

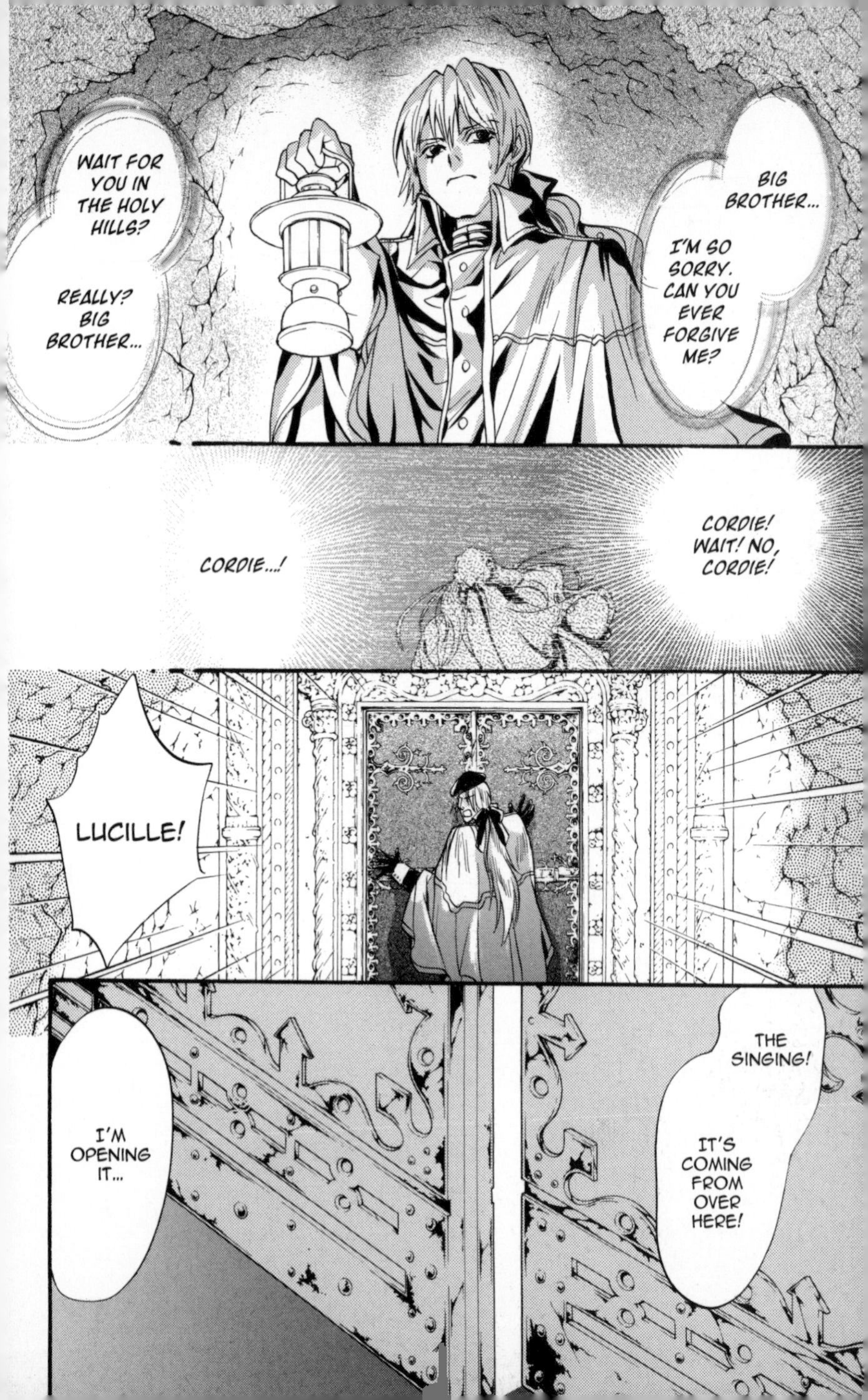
BIG BROTHER...
I'M SO SORRY. CAN YOU EVER FORGIVE ME?
WAIT FOR YOU IN THE HOLY HILLS?
REALLY? BIG BROTHER...
CORDIE! WAIT! NO, CORDIE!
CORDIE...!
LUCILLE!
THE SINGING!
IT'S COMING FROM OVER HERE!
I'M OPENING IT...

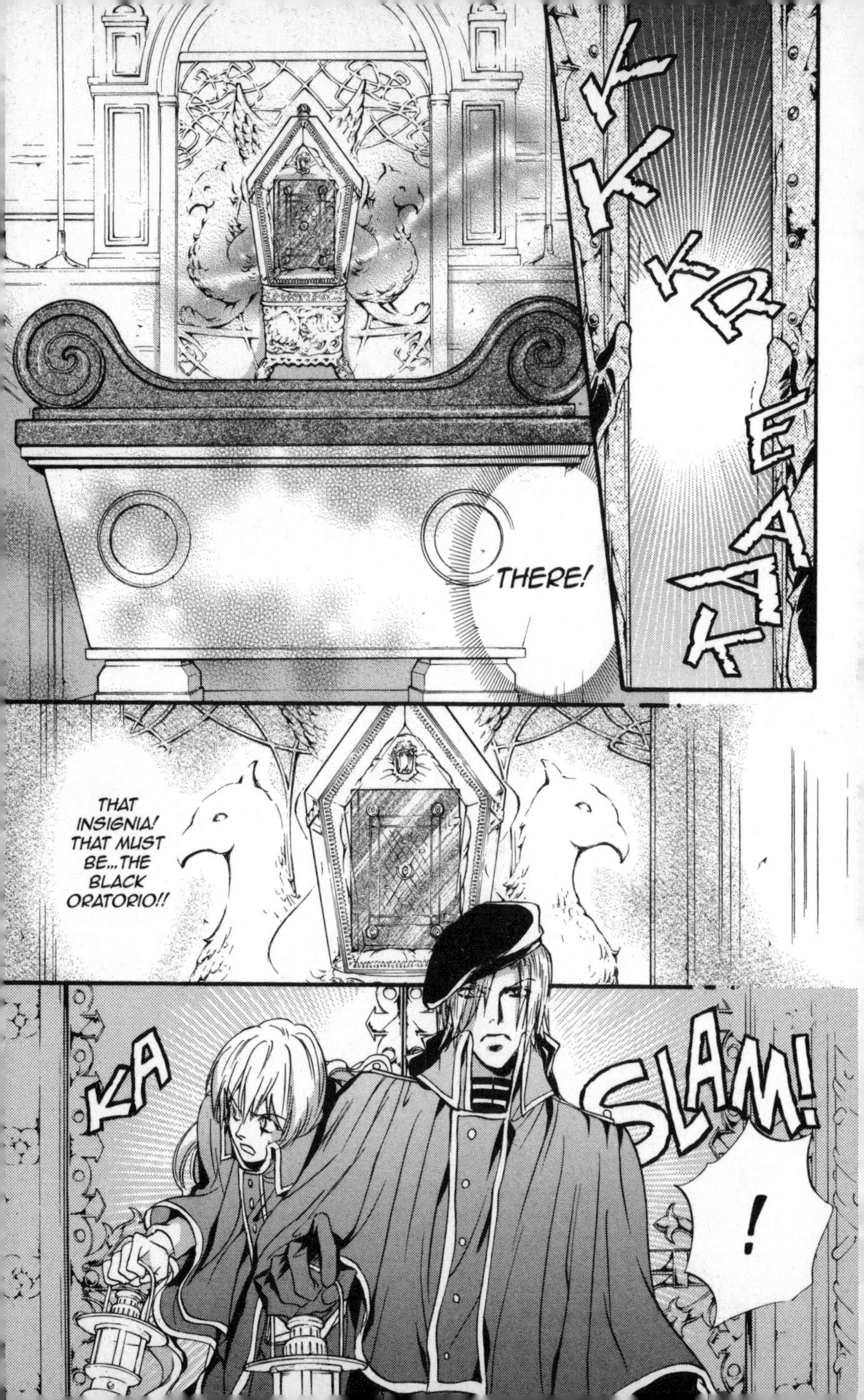
KKKREAAK
THERE!
THAT INSIGNIA! THAT MUST BE...THE BLACK ORATORIO!!
KA SLAM!
!

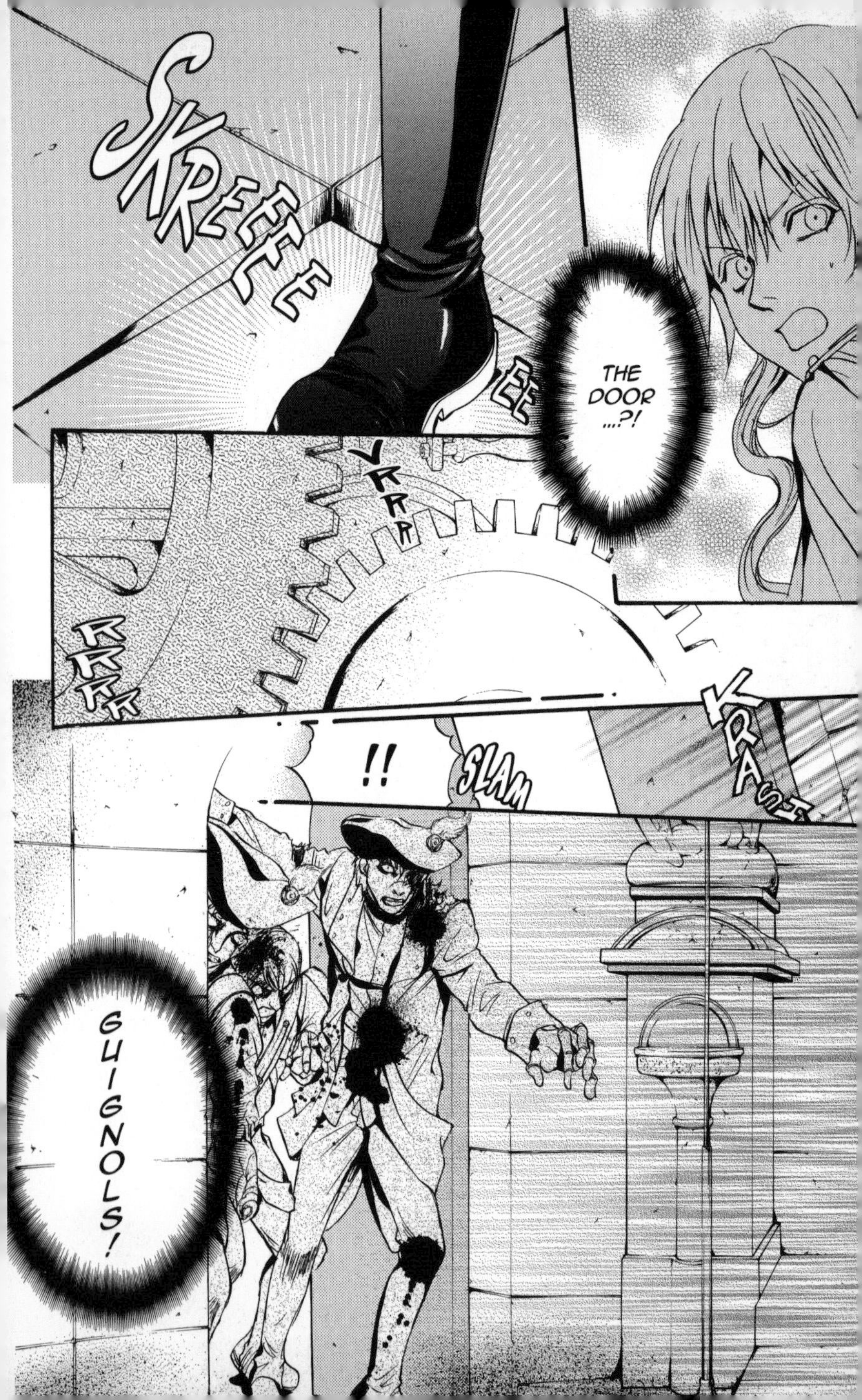
THE DOOR ...?!
SKREEEE
EE
VRRR
RRRR
KRASH
SLAM
!!
GUIGNOLS!

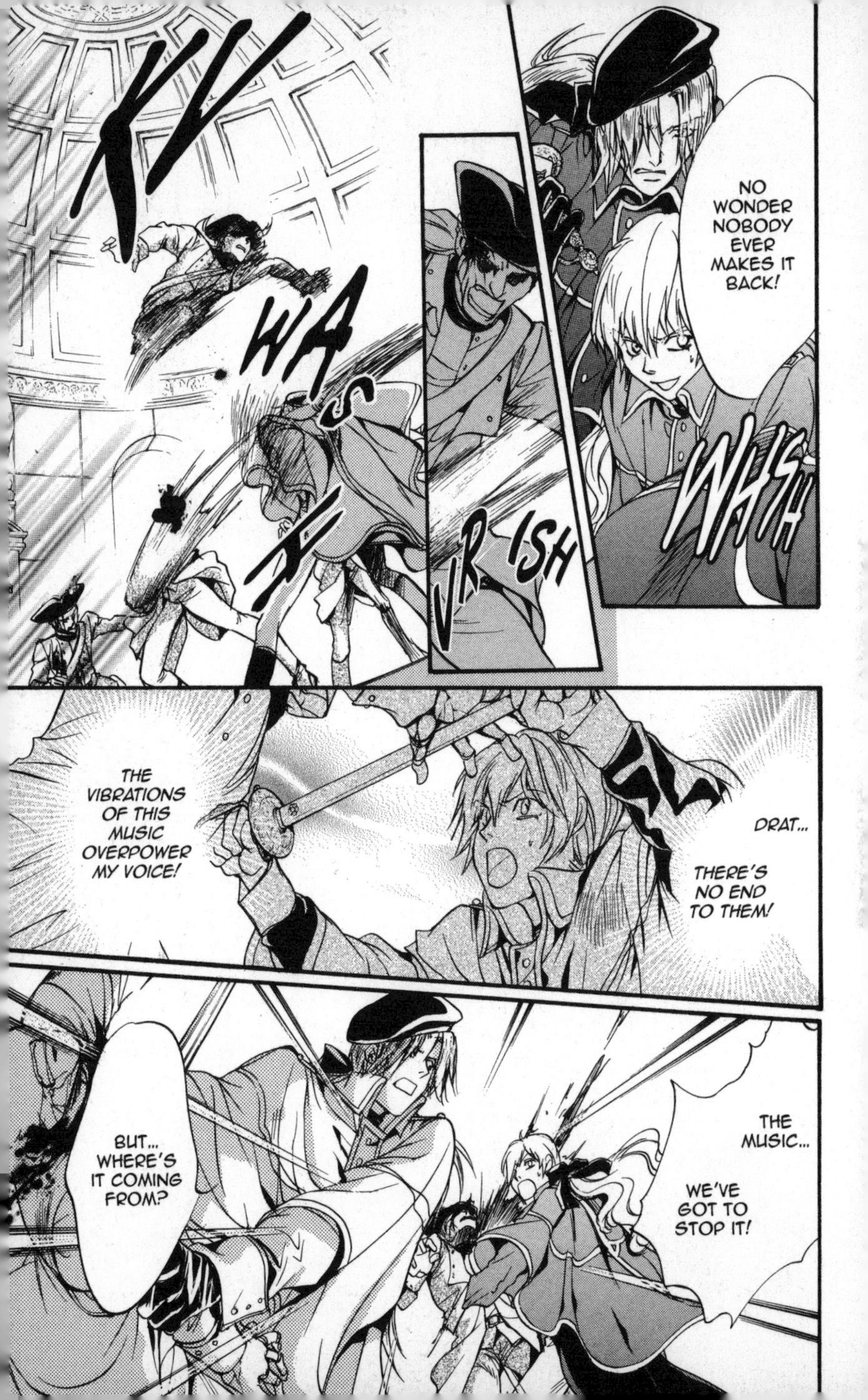
NO WONDER NOBODY EVER MAKES IT BACK!
WHISH
VRISH
DRAT...
THERE'S NO END TO THEM!
THE VIBRATIONS OF THIS MUSIC OVERPOWER MY VOICE!
THE MUSIC...
WE'VE GOT TO STOP IT!
BUT... WHERE'S IT COMING FROM?

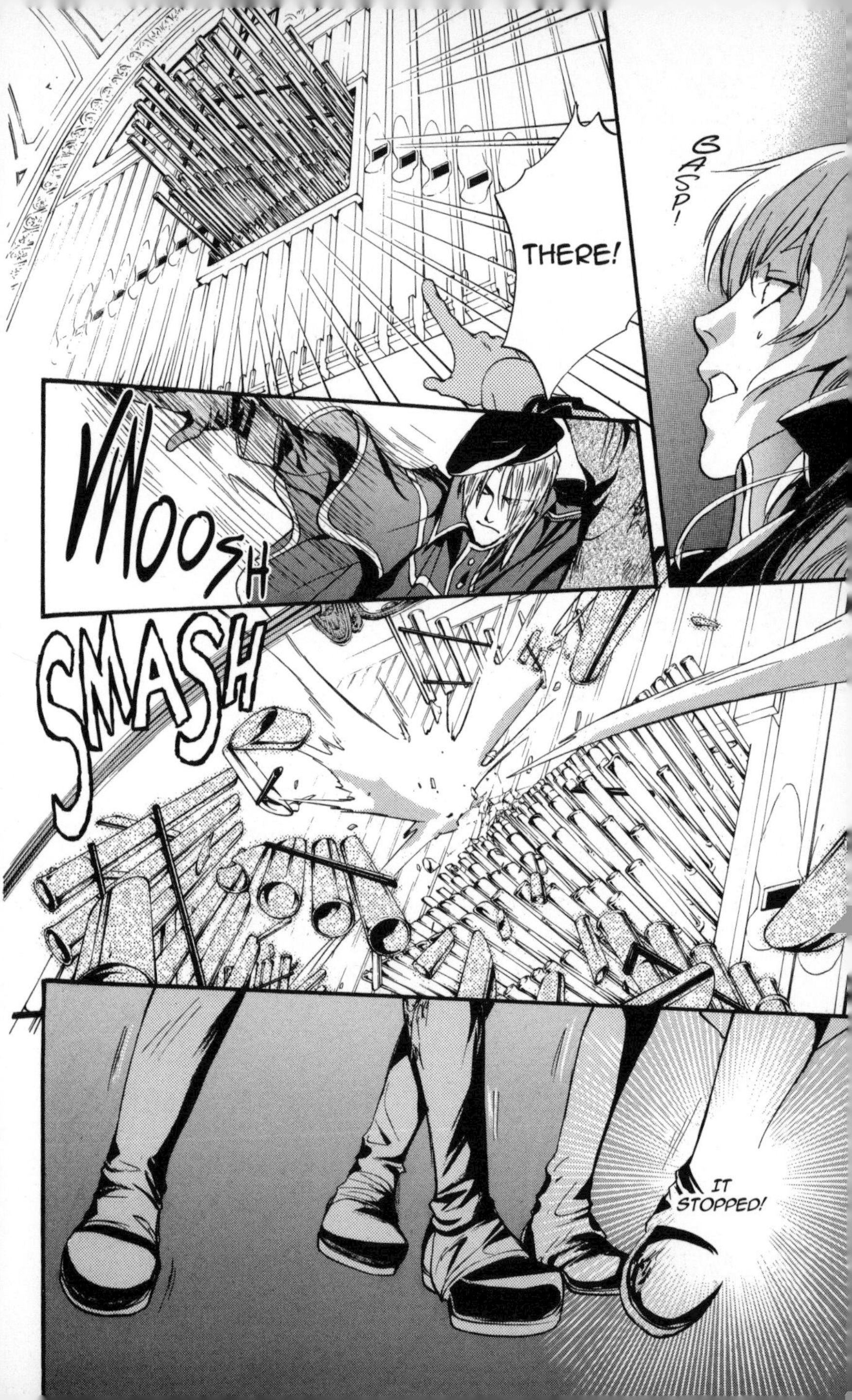
GASP!
THERE!
WHOOSH
SMASH
IT STOPPED!

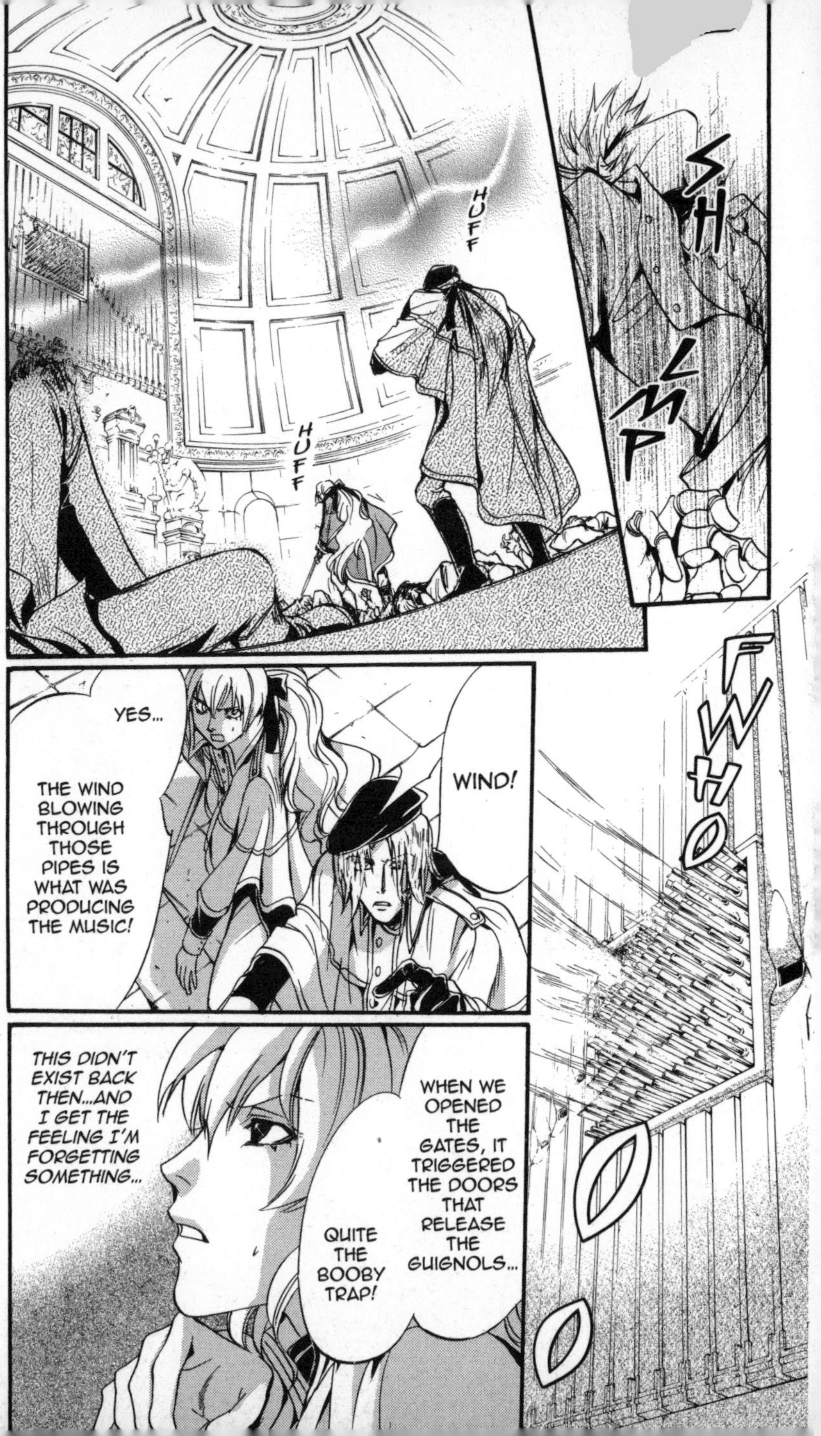
SHLMP
HUFF
HUFF
FWHOOO
WIND!
YES...
THE WIND BLOWING THROUGH THOSE PIPES IS WHAT WAS PRODUCING THE MUSIC!
WHEN WE OPENED THE GATES, IT TRIGGERED THE DOORS THAT RELEASE THE GUIGNOLS...
QUITE THE BOOBY TRAP!
THIS DIDN'T EXIST BACK THEN...AND I GET THE FEELING I'M FORGETTING SOMETHING...

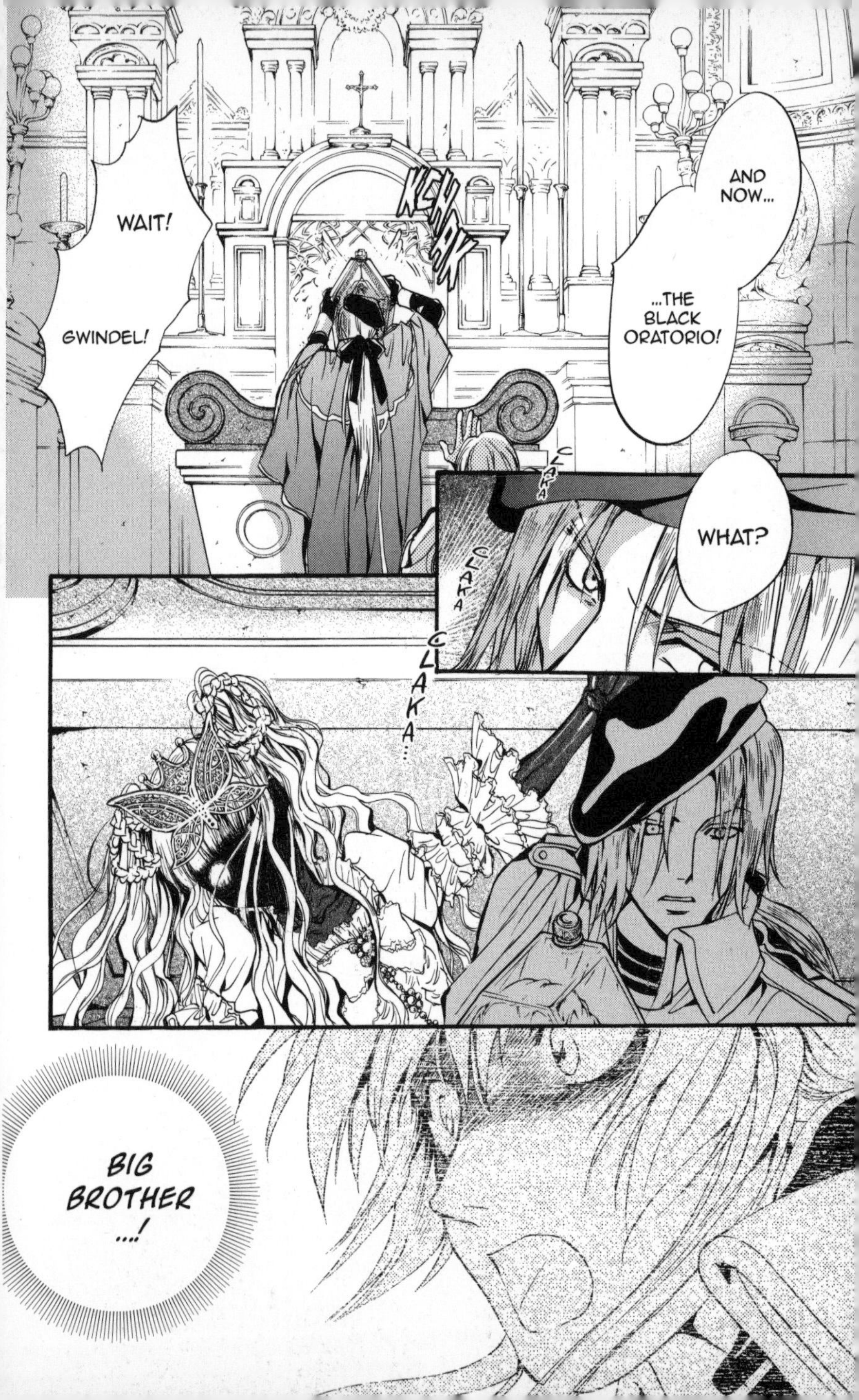
AND NOW...
...THE BLACK ORATORIO!
KCHAK
WAIT!
GWINDEL!
WHAT?
CLAKA
CLAKA
CLAKA...
BIG BROTHER ...!

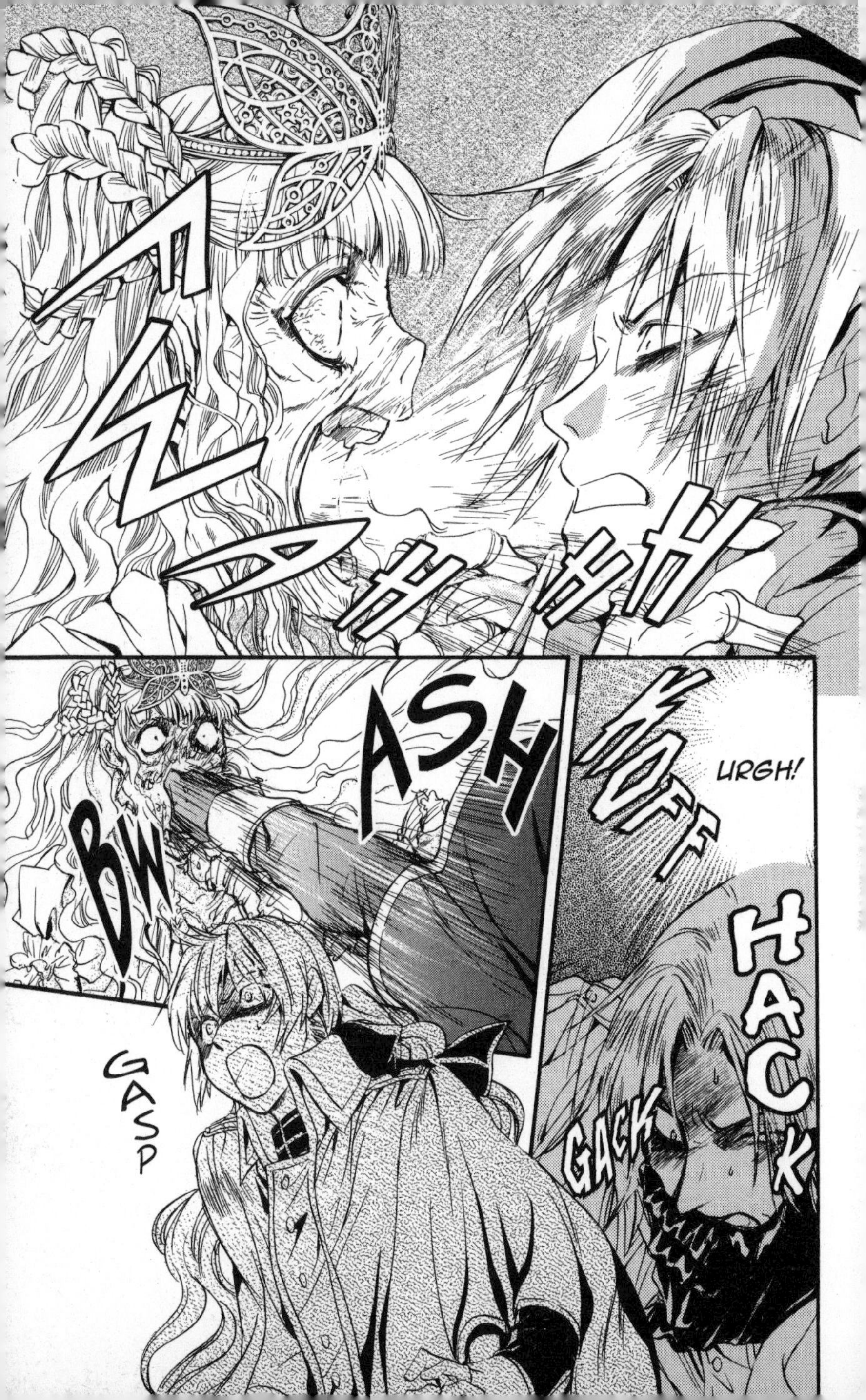
URGH!
HACK
GACK
BWASH
GASP

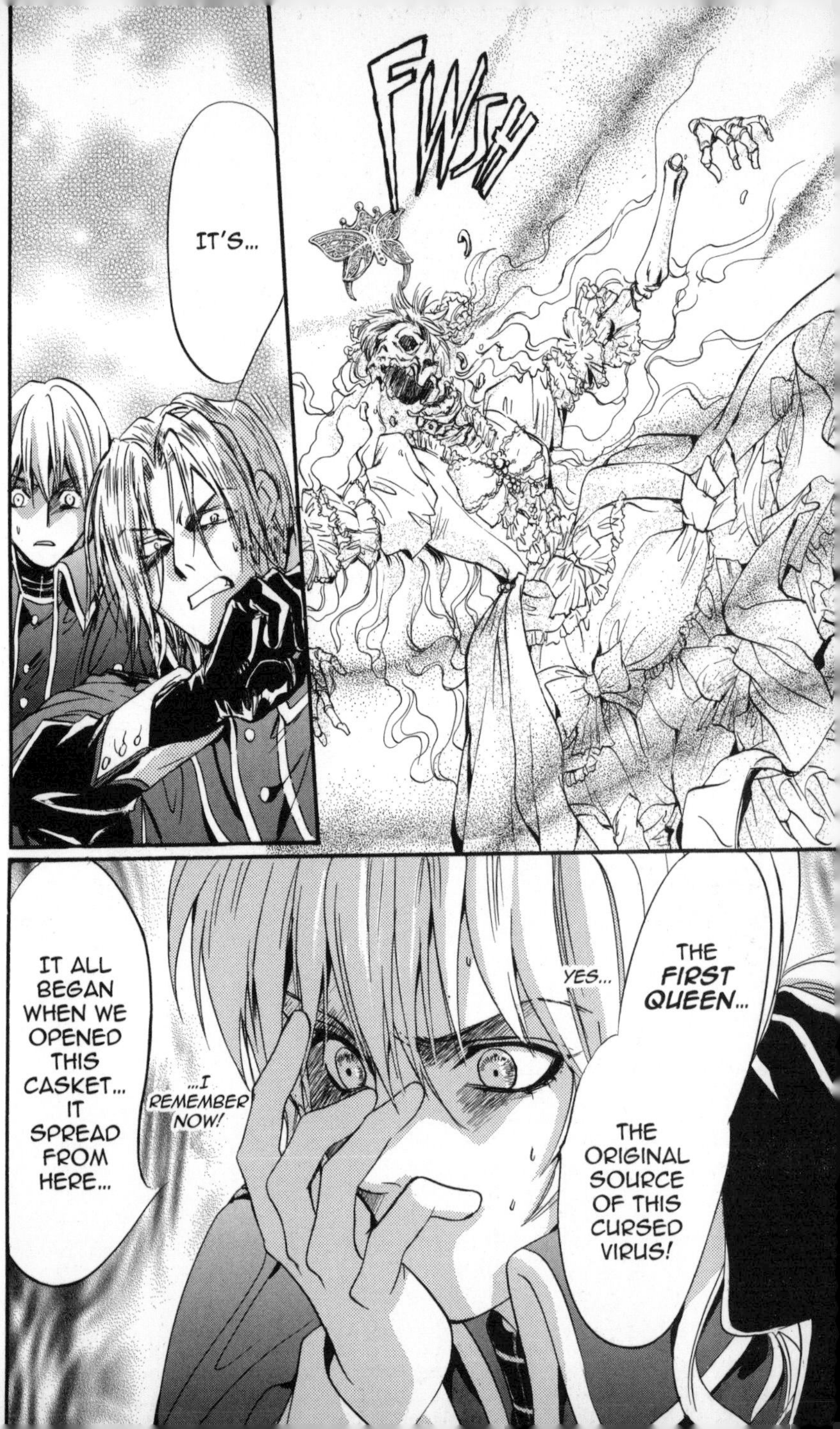
FWSH
IT'S...
THE FIRST QUEEN...
THE ORIGINAL SOURCE OF THIS CURSED VIRUS!
YES...
...I REMEMBER NOW!
IT ALL BEGAN WHEN WE OPENED THIS CASKET... IT SPREAD FROM HERE...

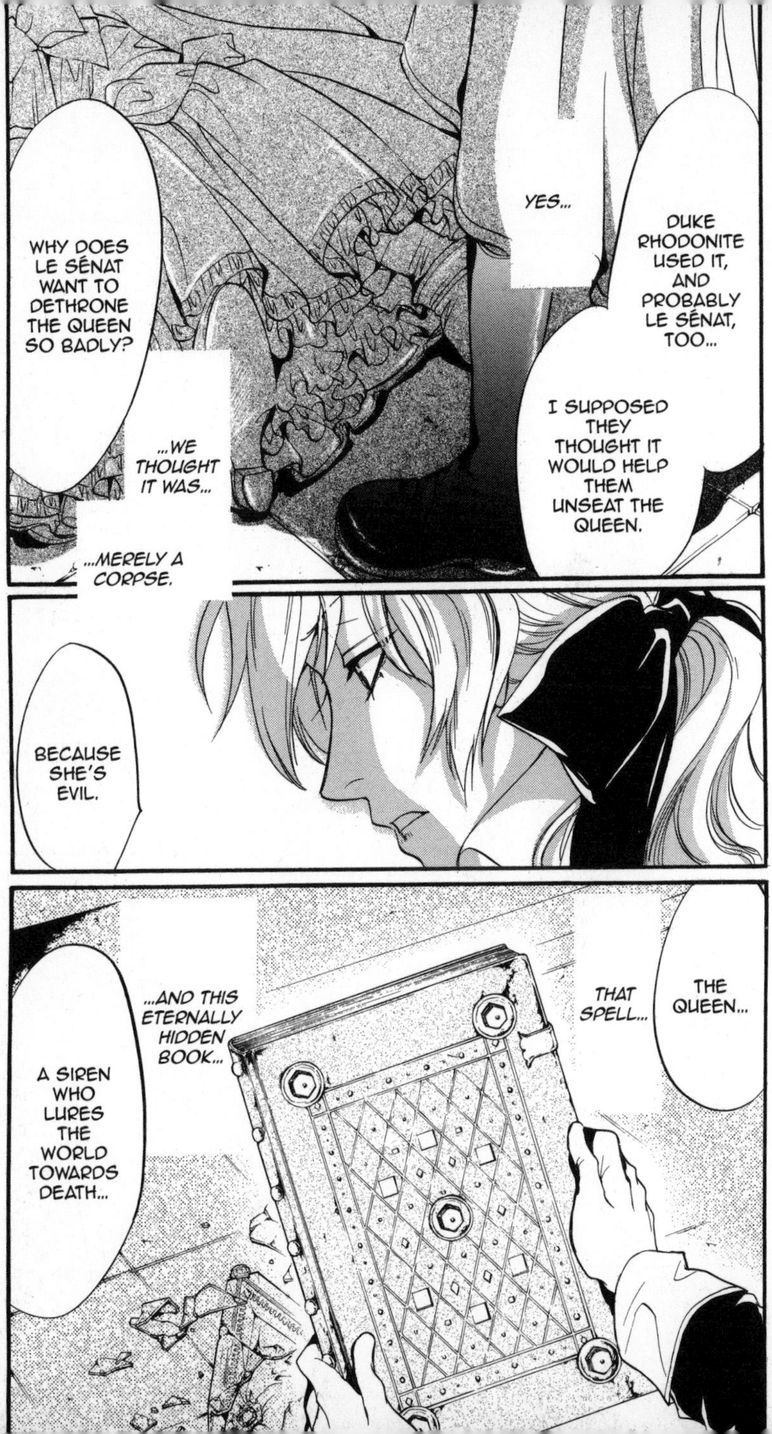

DUKE RHODONITE USED IT, AND PROBABLY LE SÉNAT, TOO...
YES...
I SUPPOSED THEY THOUGHT IT WOULD HELP THEM UNSEAT THE QUEEN.
WHY DOES LE SÉNAT WANT TO DETHRONE THE QUEEN SO BADLY?
...WE THOUGHT IT WAS...
...MERELY A CORPSE.
BECAUSE SHE'S EVIL.
THE QUEEN...
THAT SPELL...
...AND THIS ETERNALLY HIDDEN BOOK...
A SIREN WHO LURES THE WORLD TOWARDS DEATH...

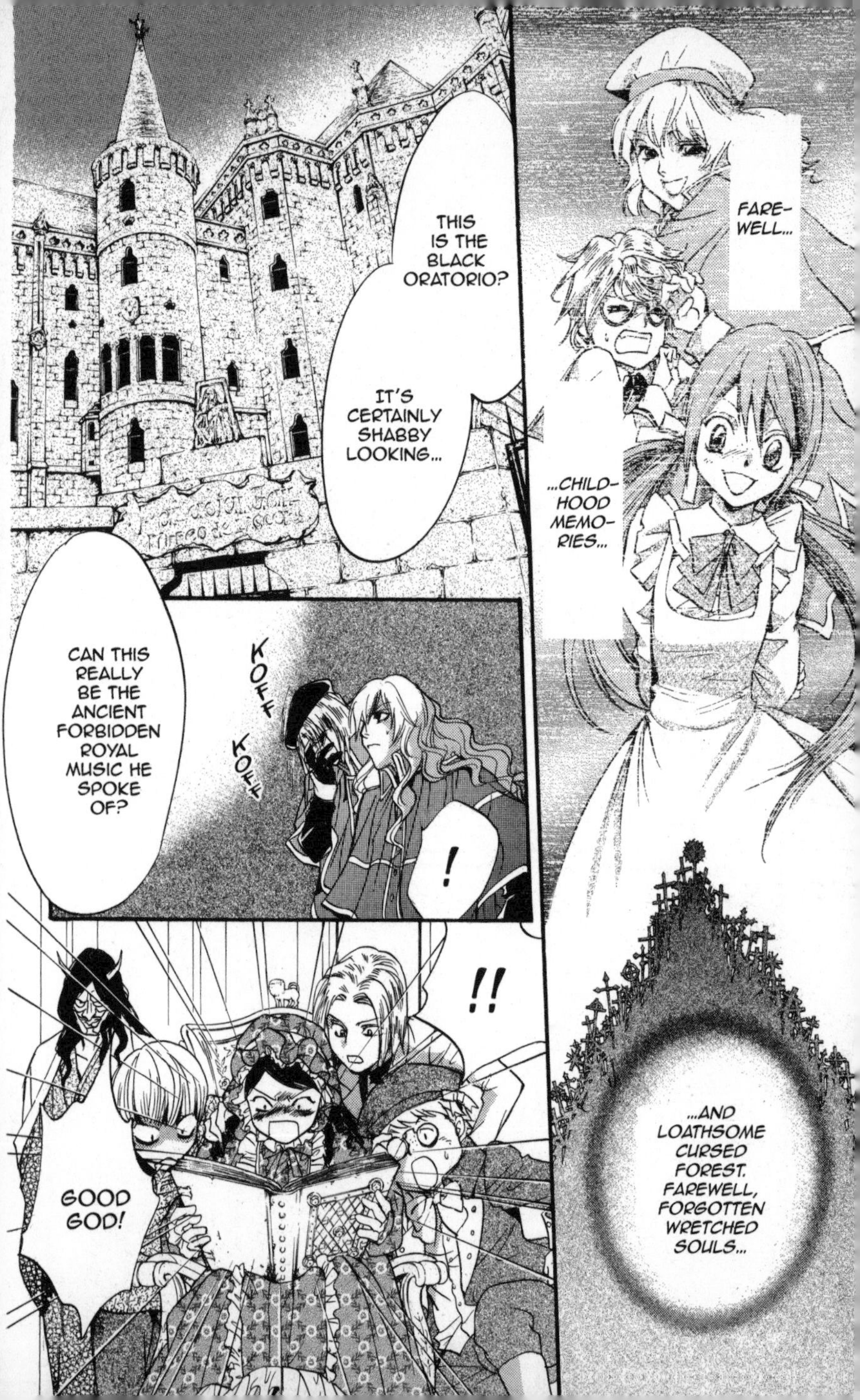
FARE-WELL...
...CHILD-HOOD MEMO-RIES...
...AND LOATHSOME CURSED FOREST. FAREWELL, FORGOTTEN WRETCHED SOULS...
THIS IS THE BLACK ORATORIO?
IT'S CERTAINLY SHABBY LOOKING...
CAN THIS REALLY BE THE ANCIENT FORBIDDEN ROYAL MUSIC HE SPOKE OF?
KOFF
KOFF
!
!!
GOOD GOD!

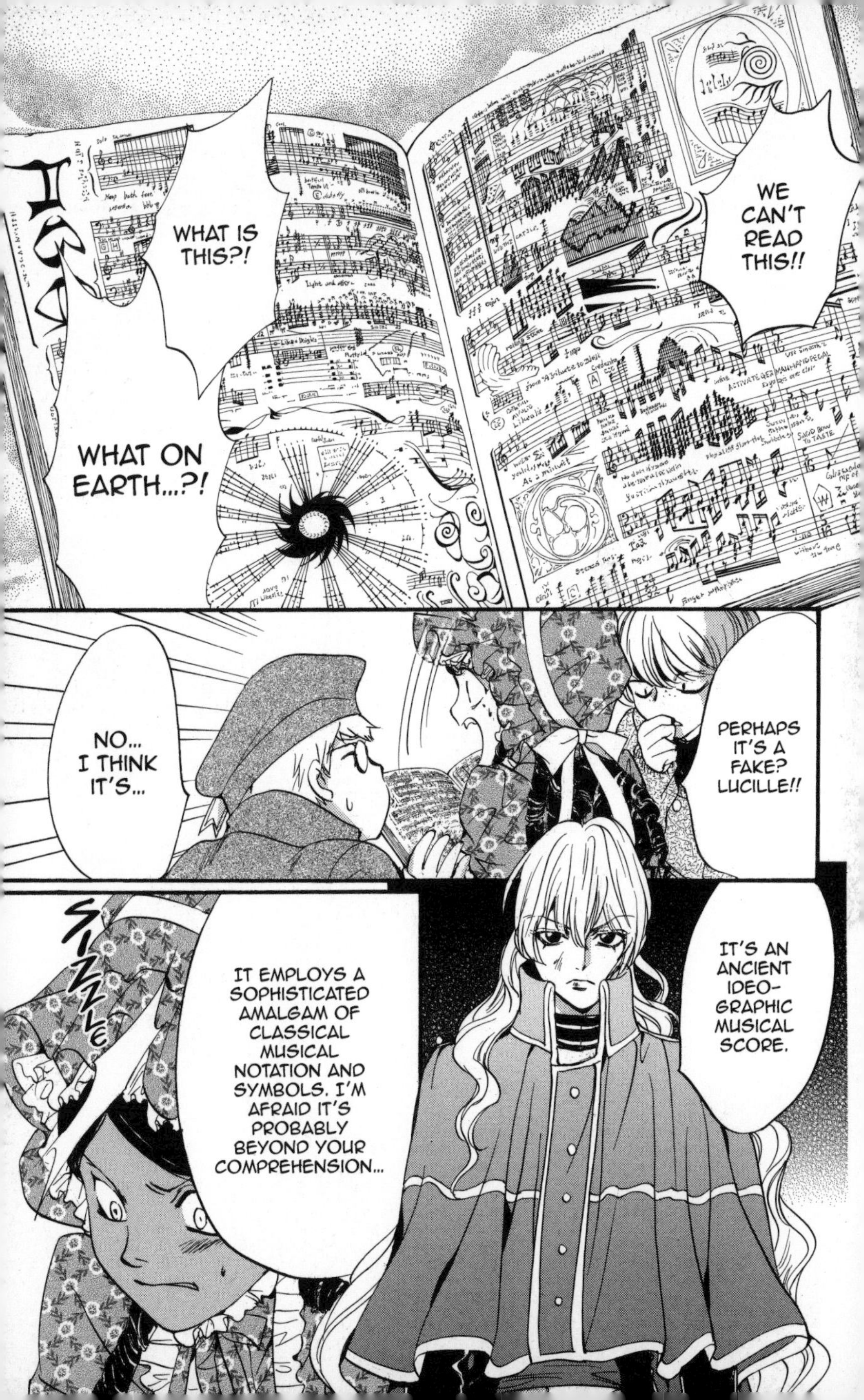
WE CAN'T READ THIS!!
WHAT IS THIS?!
WHAT ON EARTH...?!
PERHAPS IT'S A FAKE? LUCILLE!!
NO... I THINK IT'S...
IT'S AN ANCIENT IDEO-GRAPHIC MUSICAL SCORE.
IT EMPLOYS A SOPHISTICATED AMALGAM OF CLASSICAL MUSICAL NOTATION AND SYMBOLS. I'M AFRAID IT'S PROBABLY BEYOND YOUR COMPREHENSION...
SIZZLE

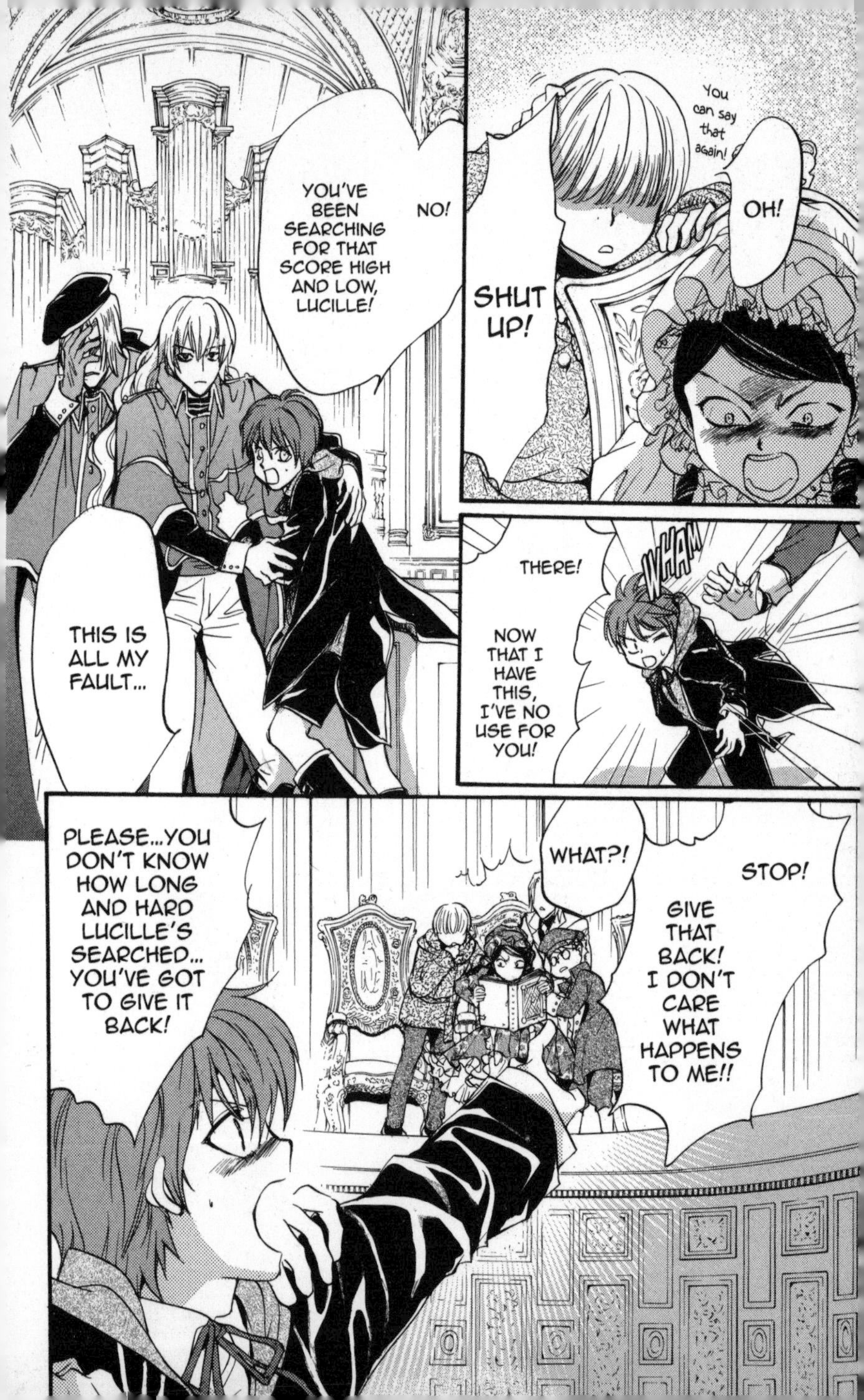
You can say that again!
OH!
SHUT UP!
WHAM
THERE!
NOW THAT I HAVE THIS, I'VE NO USE FOR YOU!
NO!
YOU'VE BEEN SEARCHING FOR THAT SCORE HIGH AND LOW, LUCILLE!
THIS IS ALL MY FAULT...
STOP!
GIVE THAT BACK! I DON'T CARE WHAT HAPPENS TO ME!!
WHAT?!
PLEASE...YOU DON'T KNOW HOW LONG AND HARD LUCILLE'S SEARCHED... YOU'VE GOT TO GIVE IT BACK!

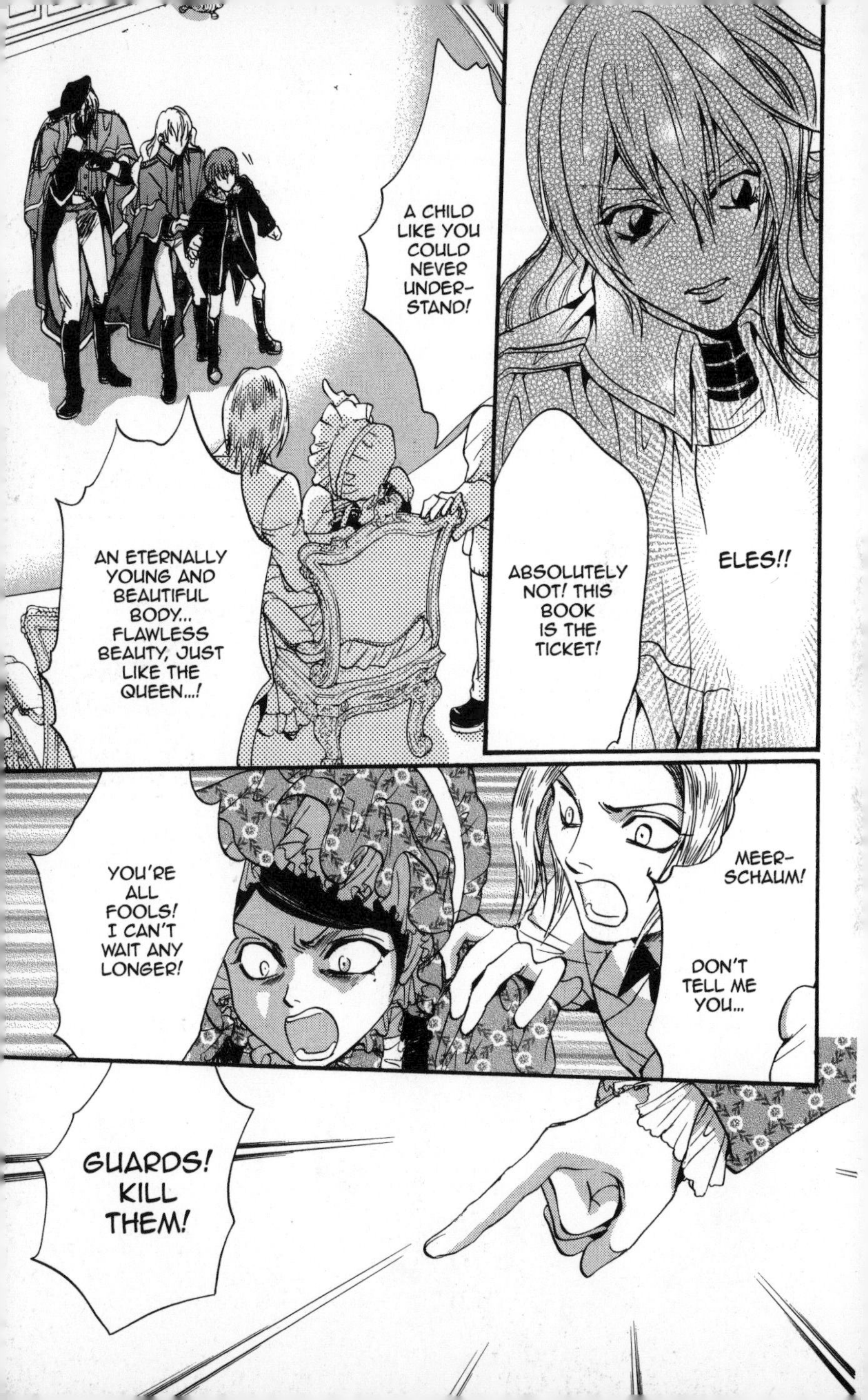
ELES!!
ABSOLUTELY NOT! THIS BOOK IS THE TICKET!
A CHILD LIKE YOU COULD NEVER UNDER-STAND!
AN ETERNALLY YOUNG AND BEAUTIFUL BODY... FLAWLESS BEAUTY, JUST LIKE THE QUEEN...!
MEER-SCHAUM!
DON'T TELL ME YOU...
YOU'RE ALL FOOLS! I CAN'T WAIT ANY LONGER!
GUARDS! KILL THEM!

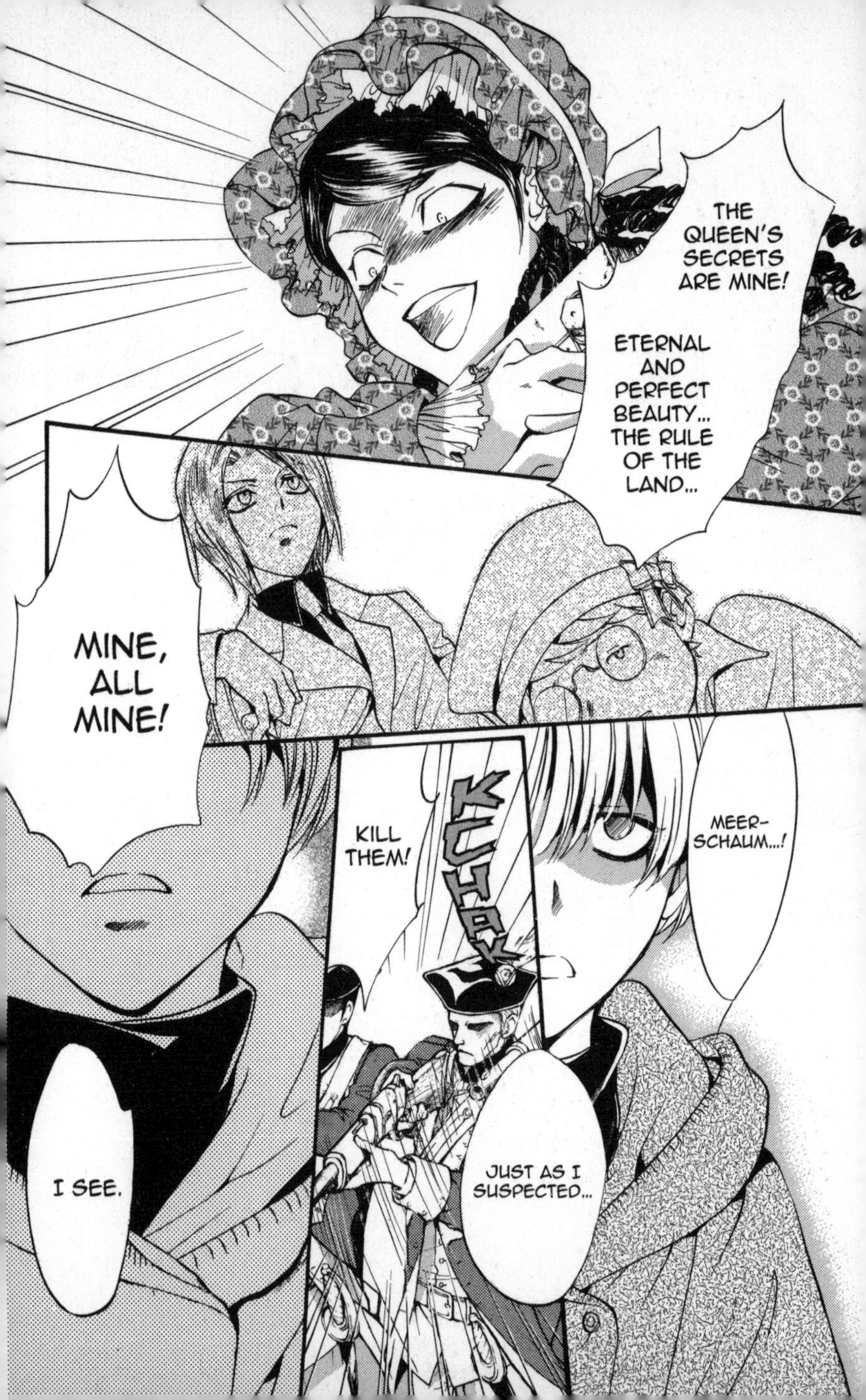
THE QUEEN'S SECRETS ARE MINE!
ETERNAL AND PERFECT BEAUTY... THE RULE OF THE LAND...
MINE, ALL MINE!
MEER-SCHAUM...!
KILL THEM!
KCHAK
JUST AS I SUSPECTED...
I SEE.

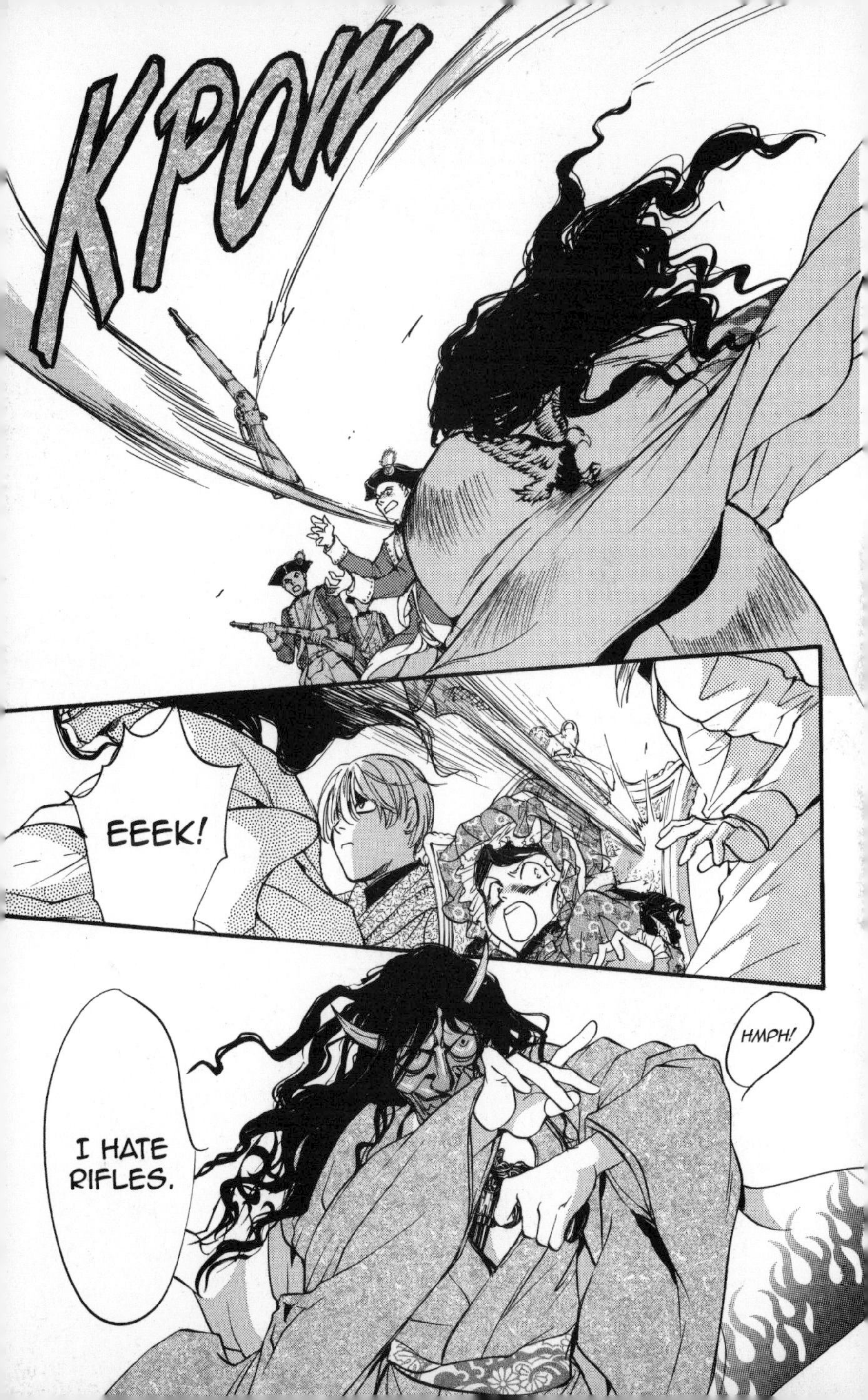
KPOW
EEEK!
HMPH!
I HATE RIFLES.

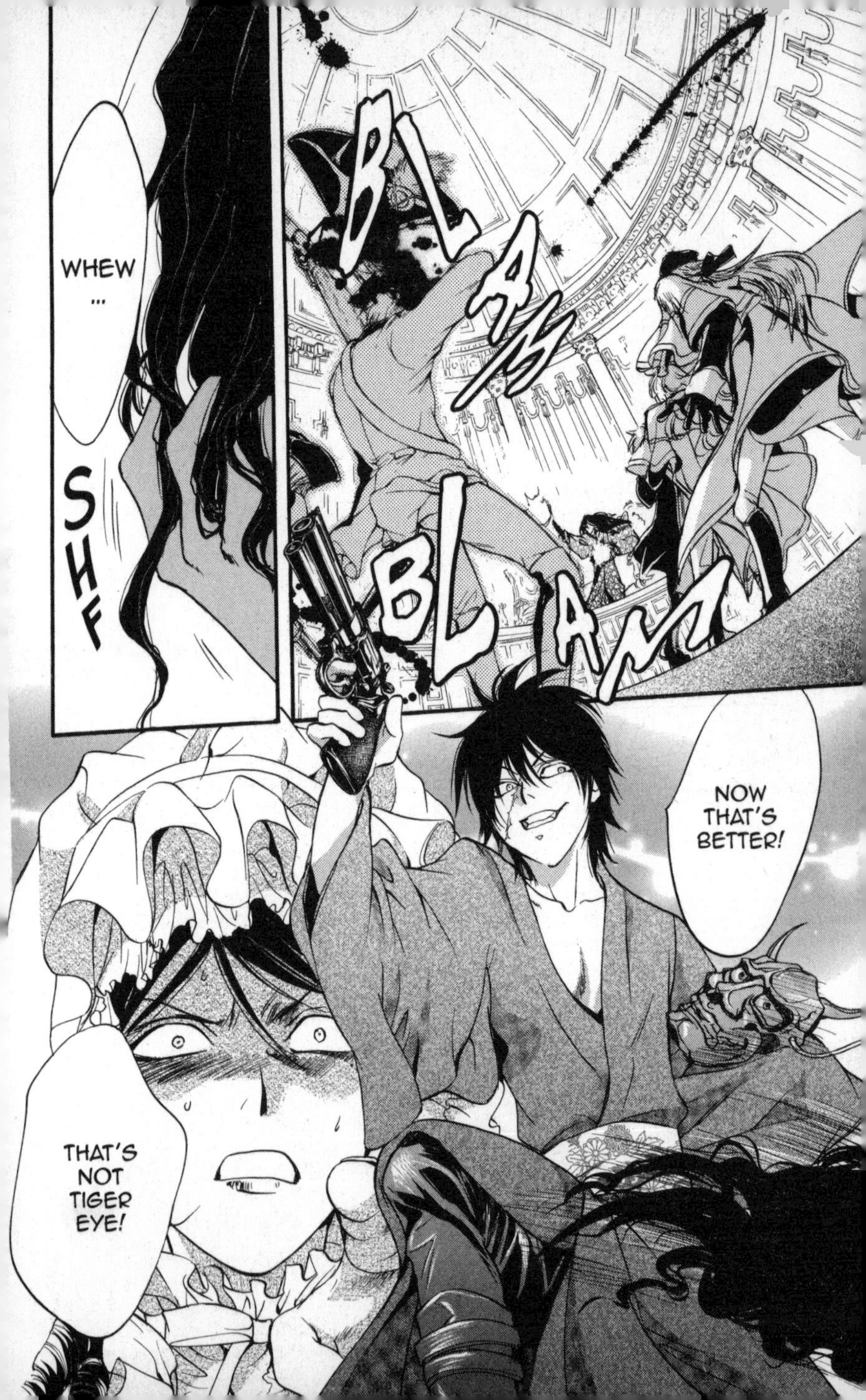
BLAM
BLAM
WHEW...
SHF
NOW THAT'S BETTER!
THAT'S NOT TIGER EYE!

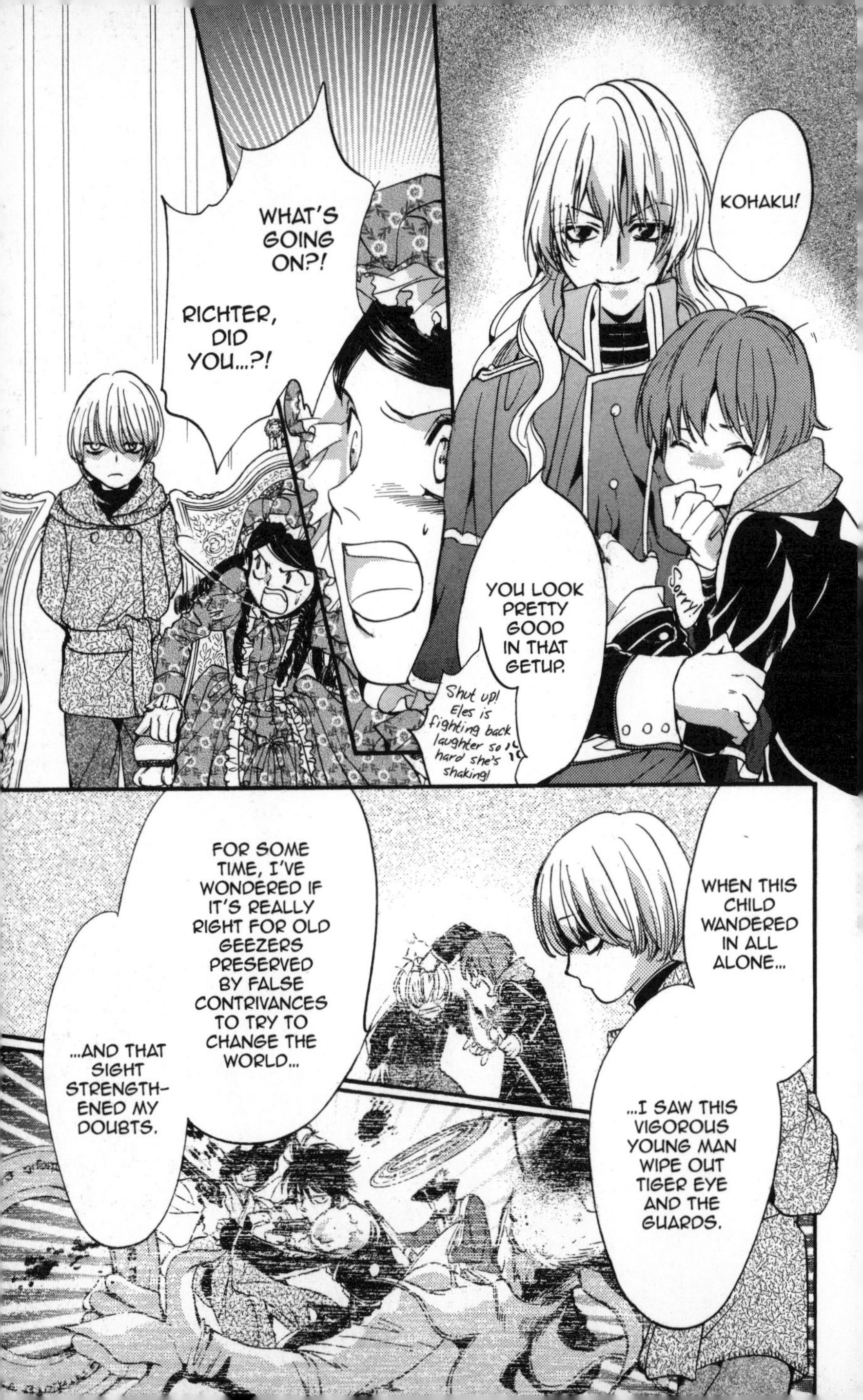
KOHAKU!
Sorry!
YOU LOOK PRETTY GOOD IN THAT GETUP.
Shut up! Eles is fighting back laughter so hard she's shaking!
WHAT'S GOING ON?!
RICHTER, DID YOU...?!
WHEN THIS CHILD WANDERED IN ALL ALONE...
...I SAW THIS VIGOROUS YOUNG MAN WIPE OUT TIGER EYE AND THE GUARDS.
FOR SOME TIME, I'VE WONDERED IF IT'S REALLY RIGHT FOR OLD GEEZERS PRESERVED BY FALSE CONTRIVANCES TO TRY TO CHANGE THE WORLD...
...AND THAT SIGHT STRENGTHENED MY DOUBTS.

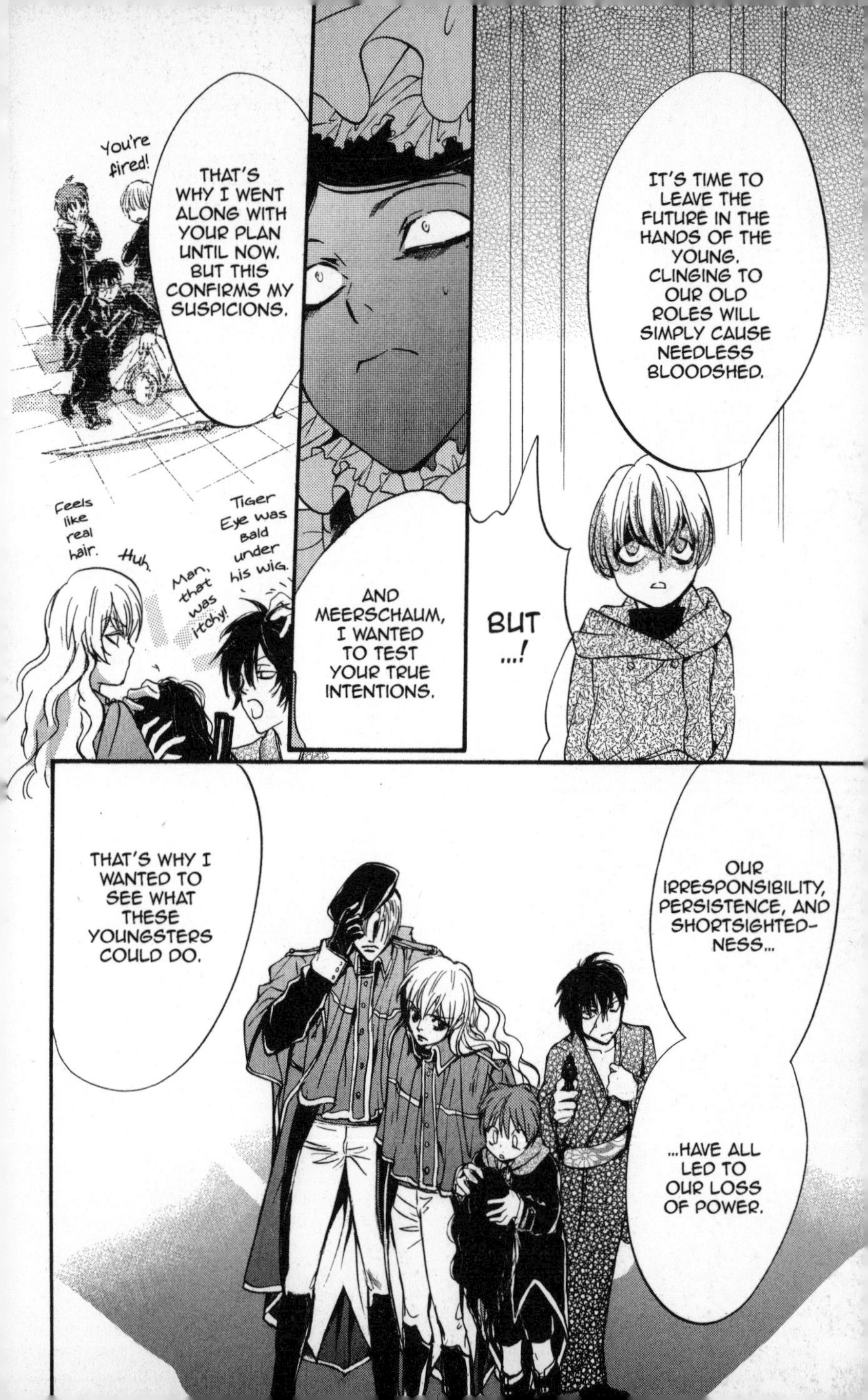
IT'S TIME TO LEAVE THE FUTURE IN THE HANDS OF THE YOUNG. CLINGING TO OUR OLD ROLES WILL SIMPLY CAUSE NEEDLESS BLOODSHED.
BUT ...!
THAT'S WHY I WENT ALONG WITH YOUR PLAN UNTIL NOW. BUT THIS CONFIRMS MY SUSPICIONS.
AND MEERSCHAUM, I WANTED TO TEST YOUR TRUE INTENTIONS.
You're fired!
Tiger Eye was bald under his wig.
Man, that was itchy!
Huh.
Feels like real hair.
OUR IRRESPONSIBILITY, PERSISTENCE, AND SHORTSIGHTED-NESS...
...HAVE ALL LED TO OUR LOSS OF POWER.
THAT'S WHY I WANTED TO SEE WHAT THESE YOUNGSTERS COULD DO.

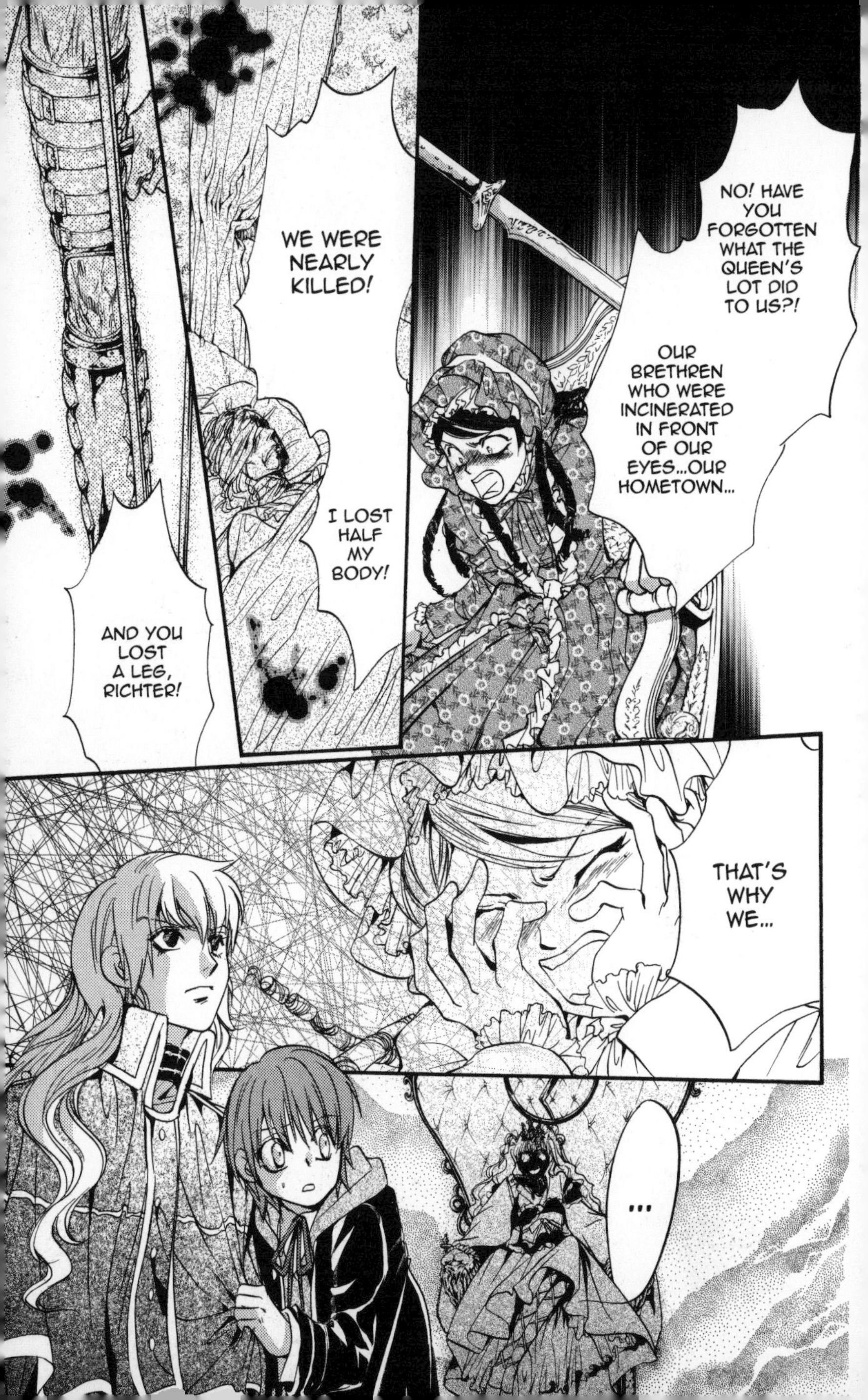
NO! HAVE YOU FORGOTTEN WHAT THE QUEEN'S LOT DID TO US?!
OUR BRETHREN WHO WERE INCINERATED IN FRONT OF OUR EYES...OUR HOMETOWN...
WE WERE NEARLY KILLED!
I LOST HALF MY BODY!
AND YOU LOST A LEG, RICHTER!
THAT'S WHY WE...
...

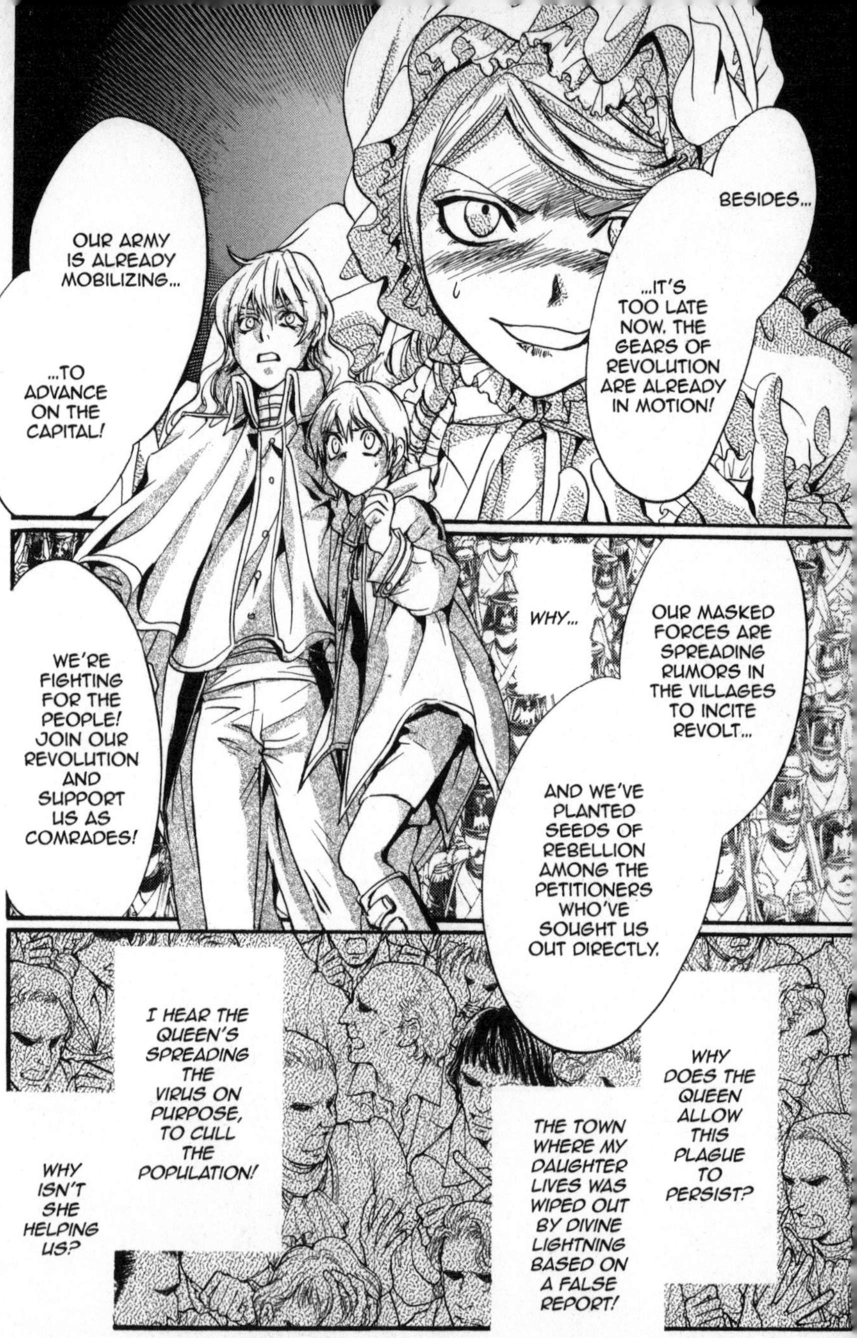
BESIDES...
...IT'S TOO LATE NOW. THE GEARS OF REVOLUTION ARE ALREADY IN MOTION!
OUR ARMY IS ALREADY MOBILIZING...
...TO ADVANCE ON THE CAPITAL!
OUR MASKED FORCES ARE SPREADING RUMORS IN THE VILLAGES TO INCITE REVOLT...
AND WE'VE PLANTED SEEDS OF REBELLION AMONG THE PETITIONERS WHO'VE SOUGHT US OUT DIRECTLY.
WHY...
WE'RE FIGHTING FOR THE PEOPLE! JOIN OUR REVOLUTION AND SUPPORT US AS COMRADES!
WHY DOES THE QUEEN ALLOW THIS PLAGUE TO PERSIST?
THE TOWN WHERE MY DAUGHTER LIVES WAS WIPED OUT BY DIVINE LIGHTNING BASED ON A FALSE REPORT!
I HEAR THE QUEEN'S SPREADING THE VIRUS ON PURPOSE, TO CULL THE POPULATION!
WHY ISN'T SHE HELPING US?

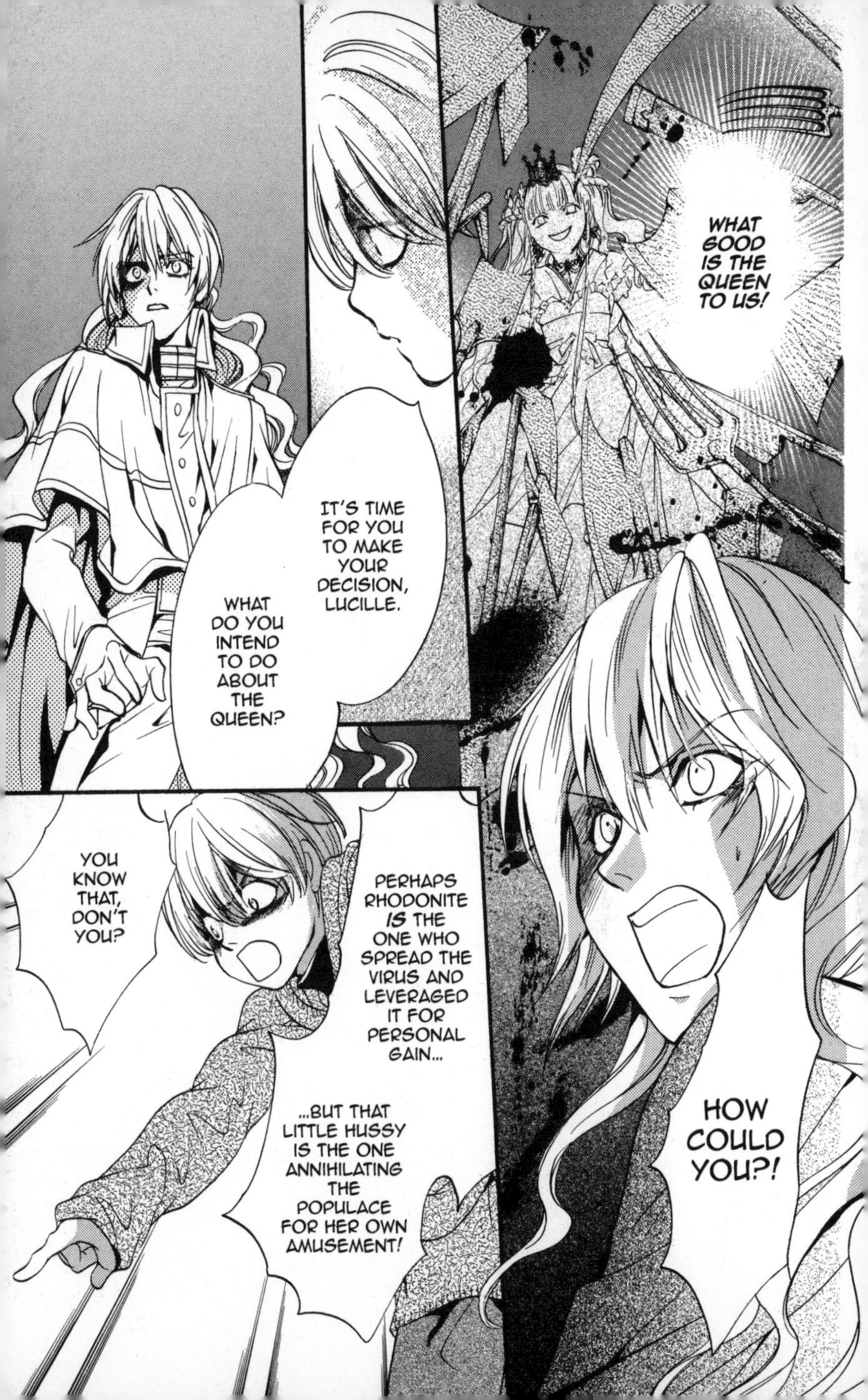
WHAT GOOD IS THE QUEEN TO US!
IT'S TIME FOR YOU TO MAKE YOUR DECISION, LUCILLE.
WHAT DO YOU INTEND TO DO ABOUT THE QUEEN?
HOW COULD YOU?!
PERHAPS RHODONITE *IS* THE ONE WHO SPREAD THE VIRUS AND LEVERAGED IT FOR PERSONAL GAIN...
...BUT THAT LITTLE HUSSY IS THE ONE ANNIHILATING THE POPULACE FOR HER OWN AMUSEMENT!
YOU KNOW THAT, DON'T YOU?

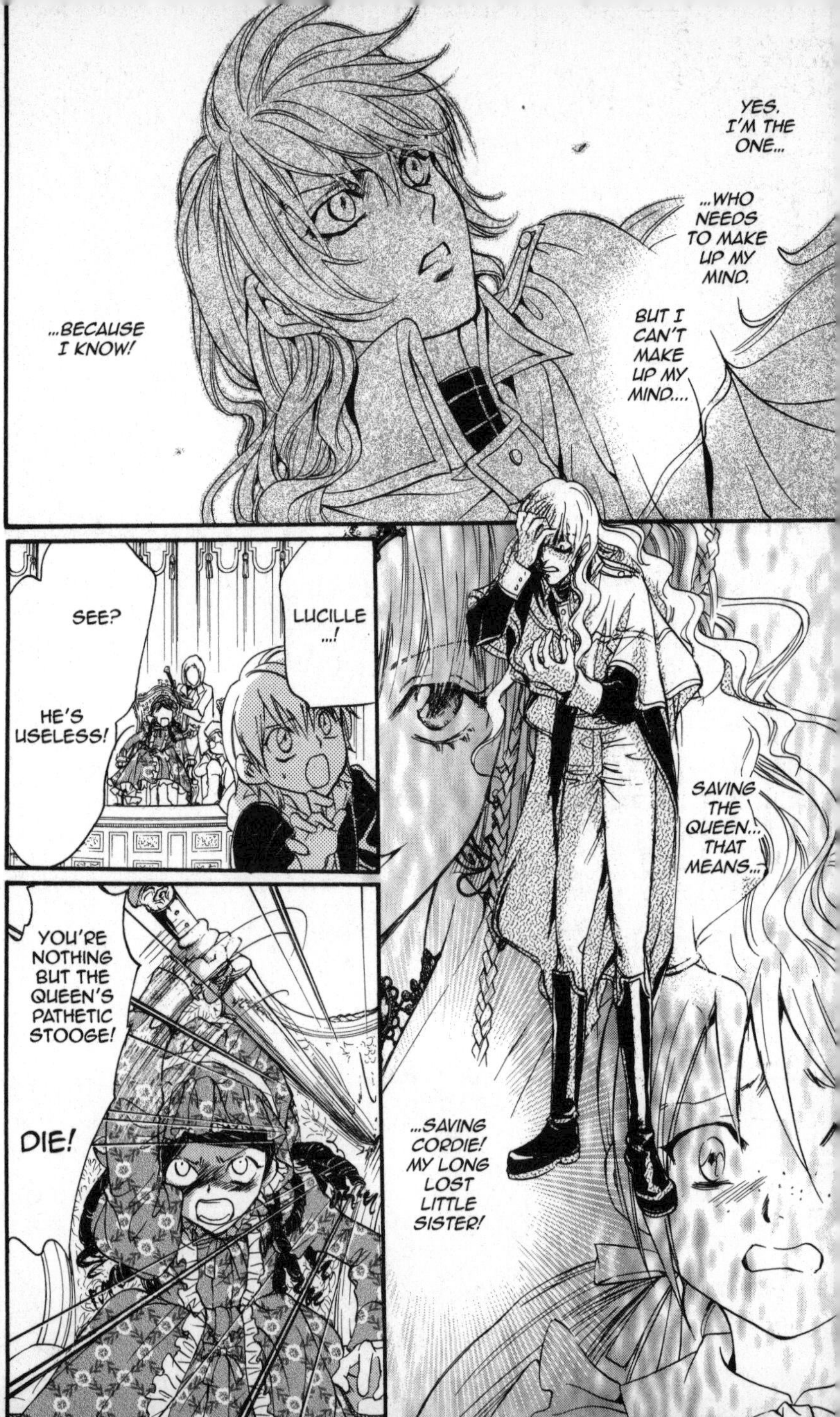
YES. I'M THE ONE...
...WHO NEEDS TO MAKE UP MY MIND.
BUT I CAN'T MAKE UP MY MIND....
...BECAUSE I KNOW!
SAVING THE QUEEN... THAT MEANS...
...SAVING CORDIE! MY LONG LOST LITTLE SISTER!
LUCILLE ...!
SEE?
HE'S USELESS!
YOU'RE NOTHING BUT THE QUEEN'S PATHETIC STOOGE!
DIE!

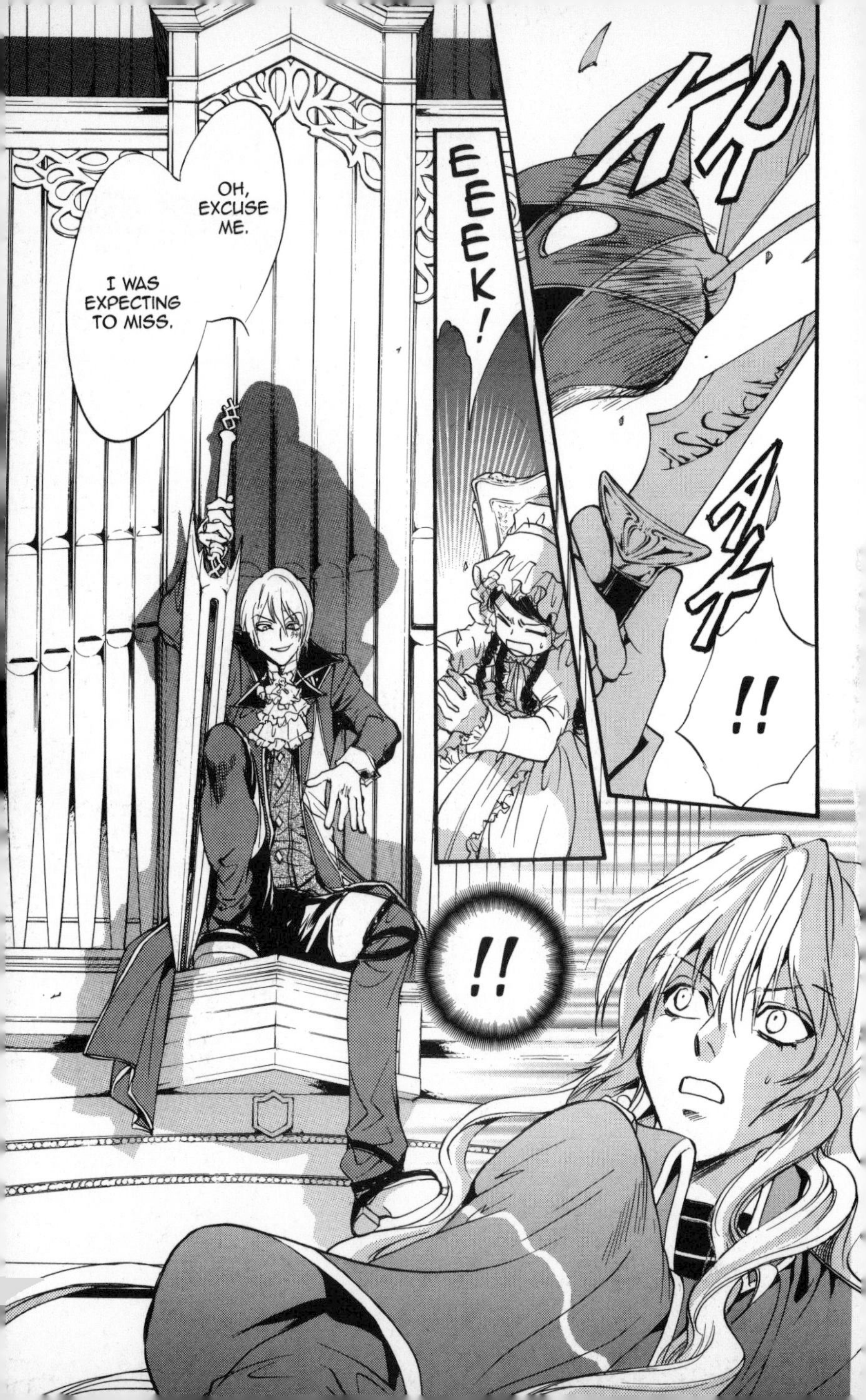
KR
AAK
!!
EEEK!
OH, EXCUSE ME. I WAS EXPECTING TO MISS.
!!

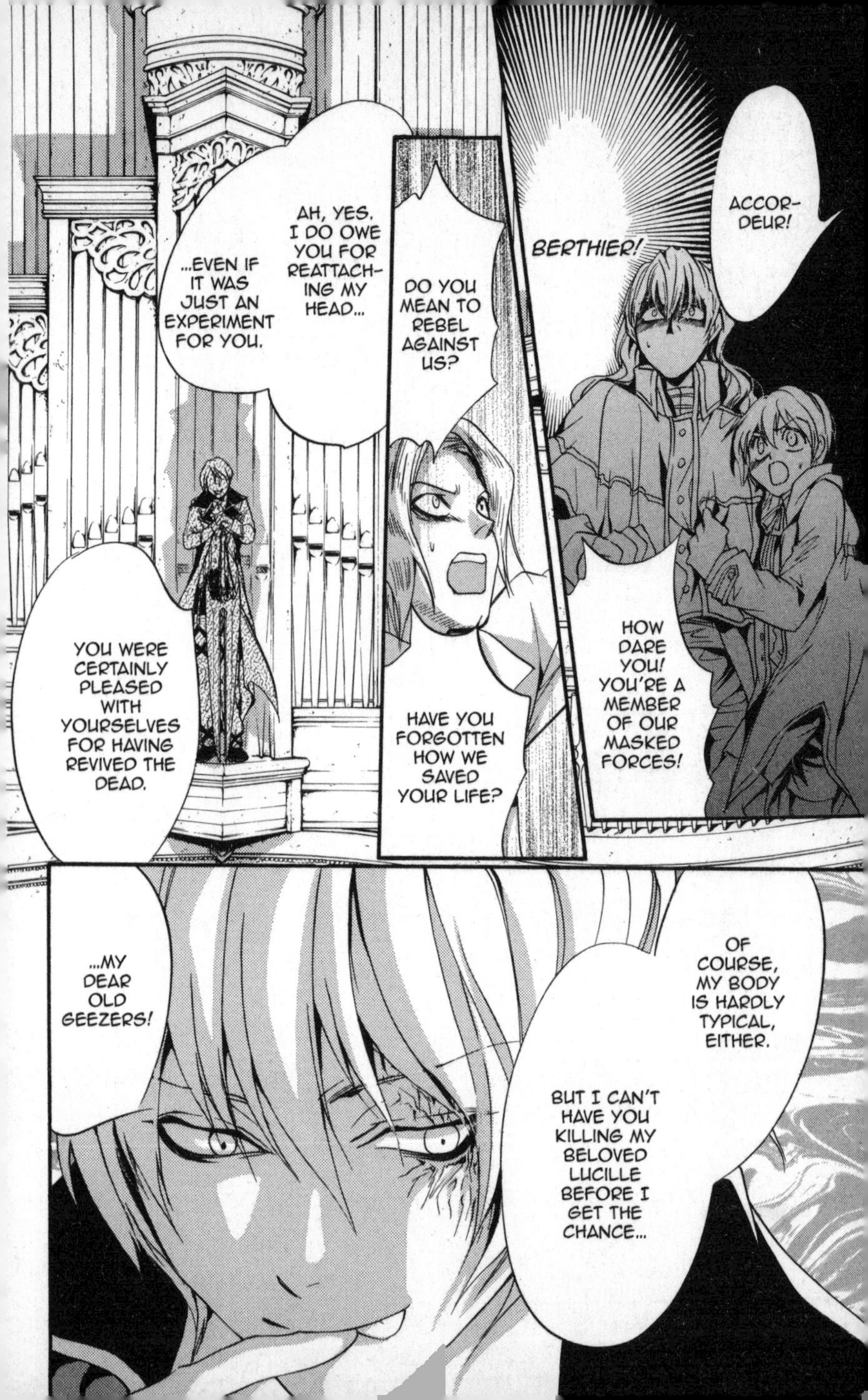
ACCOR-DEUR!
BERTHIER!
HOW DARE YOU! YOU'RE A MEMBER OF OUR MASKED FORCES!
DO YOU MEAN TO REBEL AGAINST US?
HAVE YOU FORGOTTEN HOW WE SAVED YOUR LIFE?
AH, YES. I DO OWE YOU FOR REATTACHING MY HEAD...
...EVEN IF IT WAS JUST AN EXPERIMENT FOR YOU.
YOU WERE CERTAINLY PLEASED WITH YOURSELVES FOR HAVING REVIVED THE DEAD.
OF COURSE, MY BODY IS HARDLY TYPICAL, EITHER.
BUT I CAN'T HAVE YOU KILLING MY BELOVED LUCILLE BEFORE I GET THE CHANCE...
...MY DEAR OLD GEEZERS!

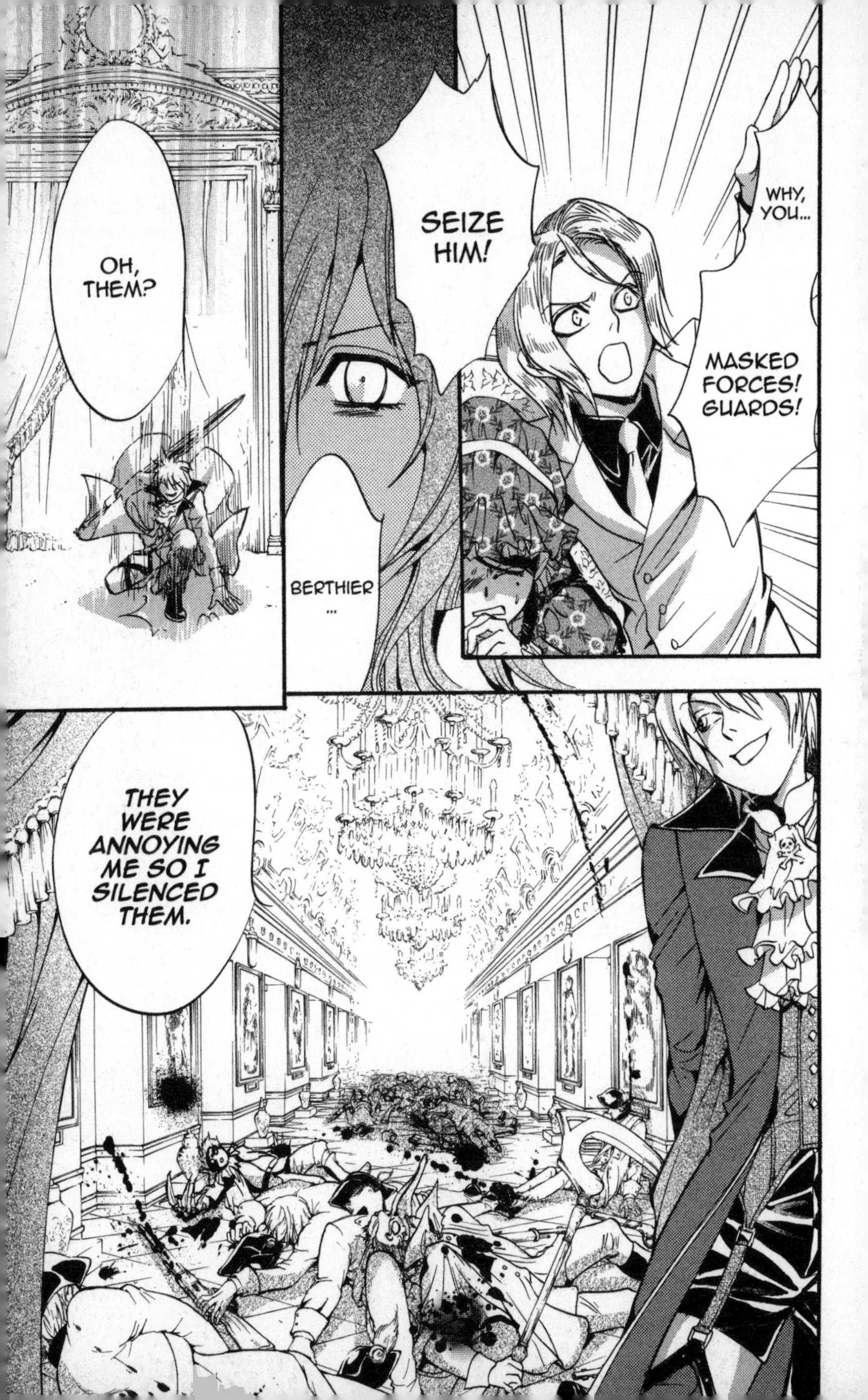
WHY, YOU...
MASKED FORCES! GUARDS!
SEIZE HIM!
BERTHIER...
OH, THEM?
THEY WERE ANNOYING ME SO I SILENCED THEM.

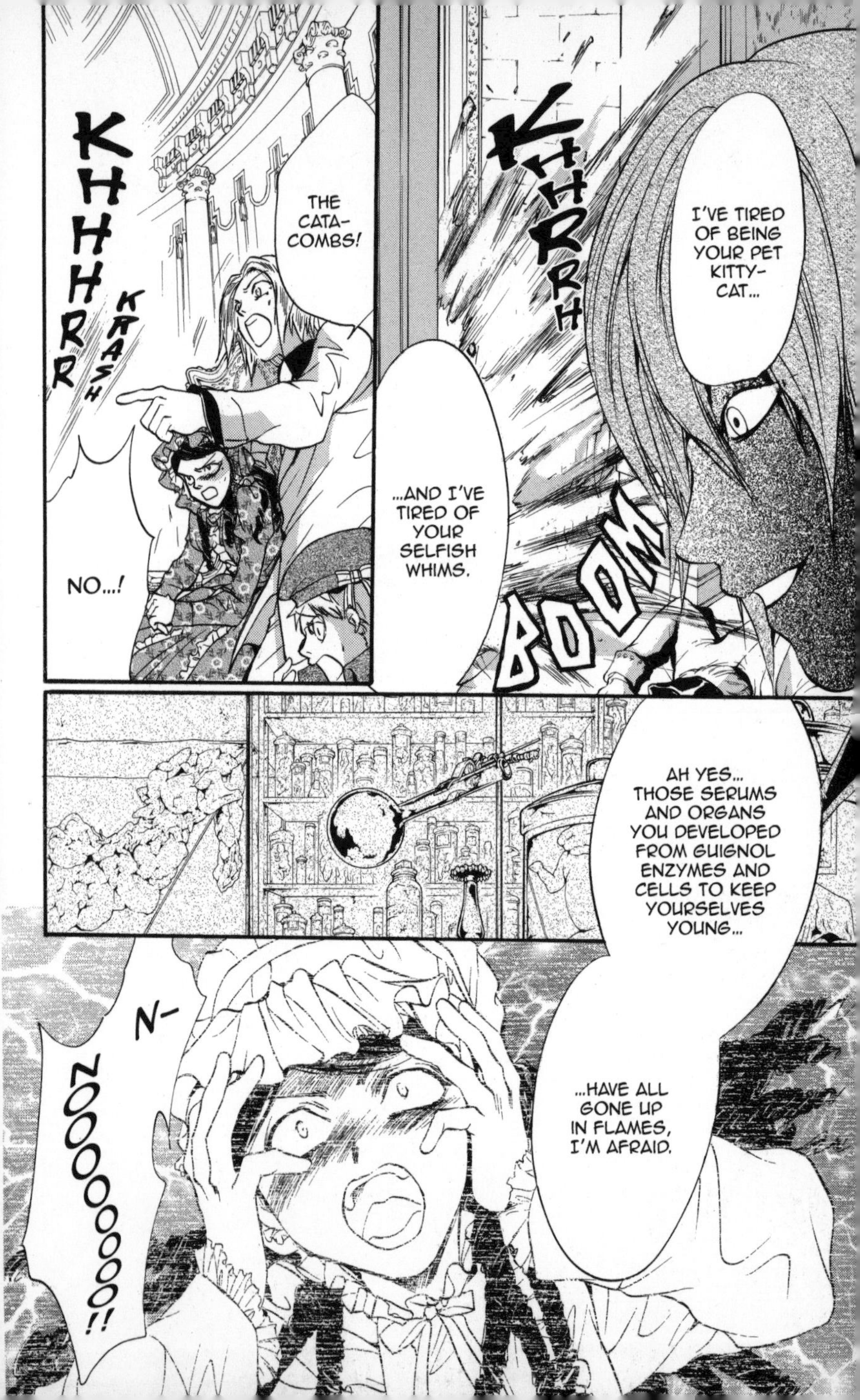
KHHRRH
I'VE TIRED OF BEING YOUR PET KITTY-CAT...
...AND I'VE TIRED OF YOUR SELFISH WHIMS.
BOOM
KHHHHRR
KRASH
THE CATA-COMBS!
NO...!
AH YES... THOSE SERUMS AND ORGANS YOU DEVELOPED FROM GUIGNOL ENZYMES AND CELLS TO KEEP YOURSELVES YOUNG...
...HAVE ALL GONE UP IN FLAMES, I'M AFRAID.
N-
NOOOOOOOO!!

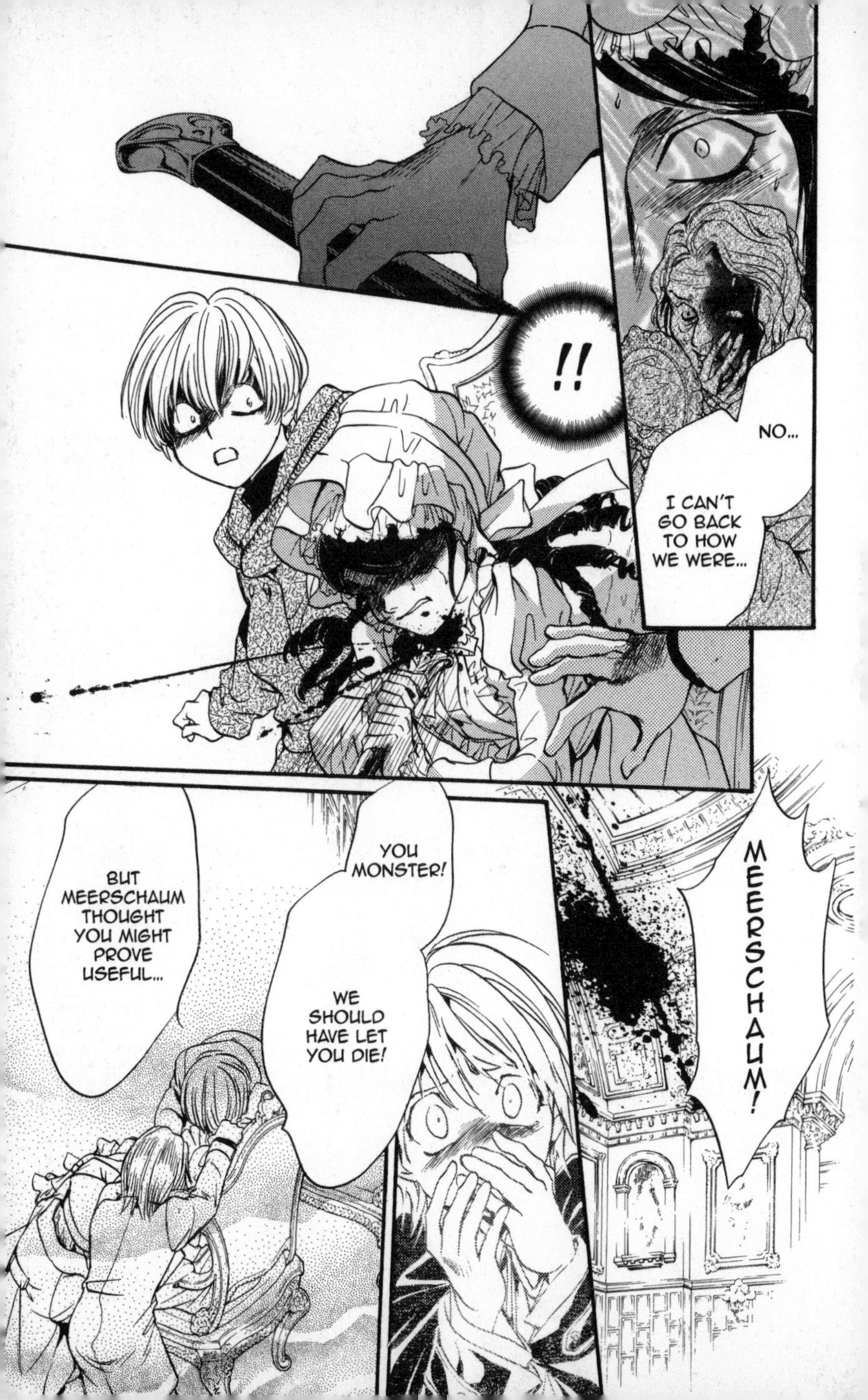
NO...
I CAN'T GO BACK TO HOW WE WERE...
!!
MEERSCHAUM!
YOU MONSTER!
WE SHOULD HAVE LET YOU DIE!
BUT MEERSCHAUM THOUGHT YOU MIGHT PROVE USEFUL...

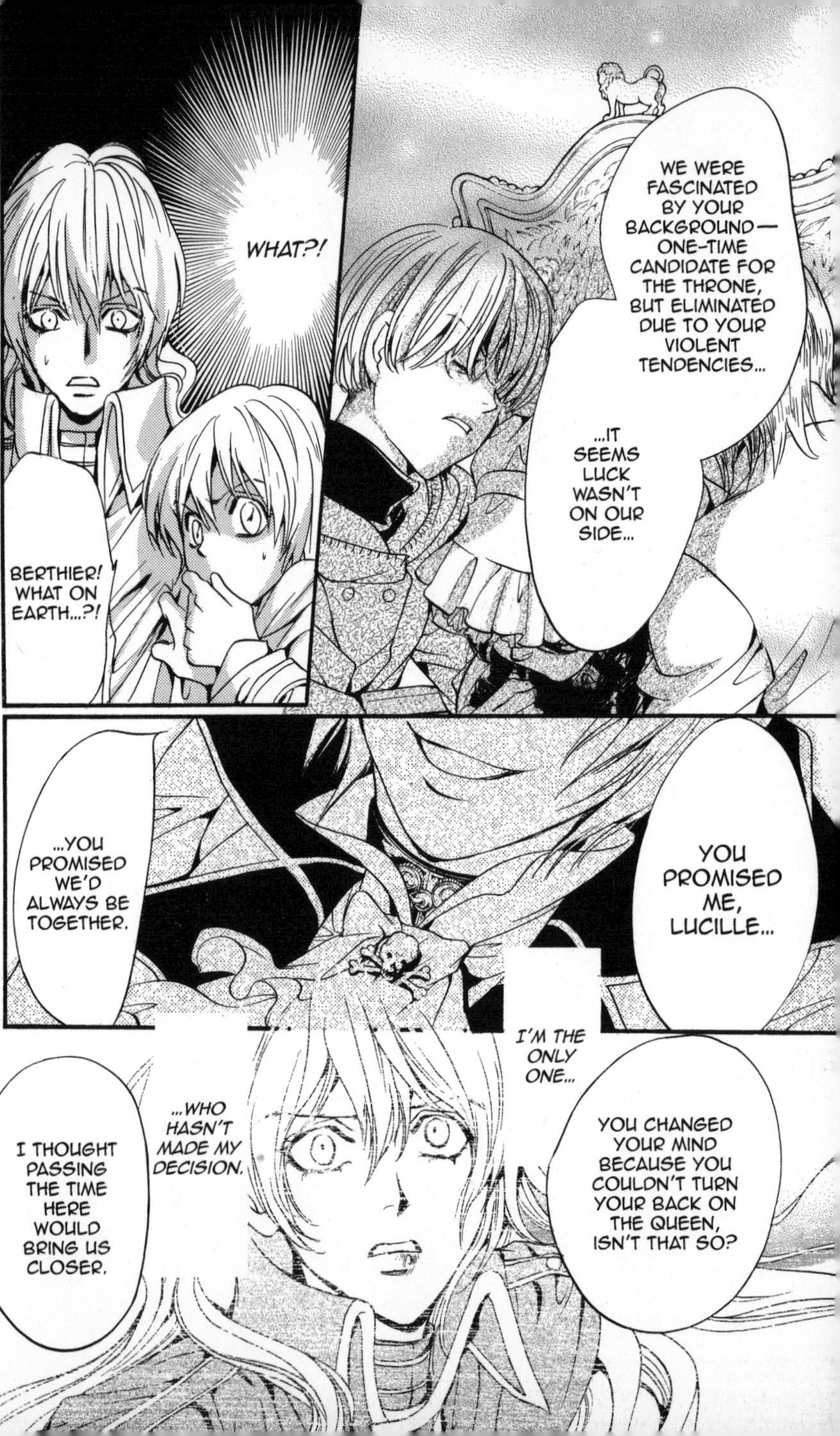
WE WERE FASCINATED BY YOUR BACKGROUND—ONE-TIME CANDIDATE FOR THE THRONE, BUT ELIMINATED DUE TO YOUR VIOLENT TENDENCIES...
...IT SEEMS LUCK WASN'T ON OUR SIDE...
WHAT?!
BERTHIER! WHAT ON EARTH...?!
YOU PROMISED ME, LUCILLE...
...YOU PROMISED WE'D ALWAYS BE TOGETHER.
I'M THE ONLY ONE...
YOU CHANGED YOUR MIND BECAUSE YOU COULDN'T TURN YOUR BACK ON THE QUEEN, ISN'T THAT SO?
...WHO HASN'T MADE MY DECISION.
I THOUGHT PASSING THE TIME HERE WOULD BRING US CLOSER.

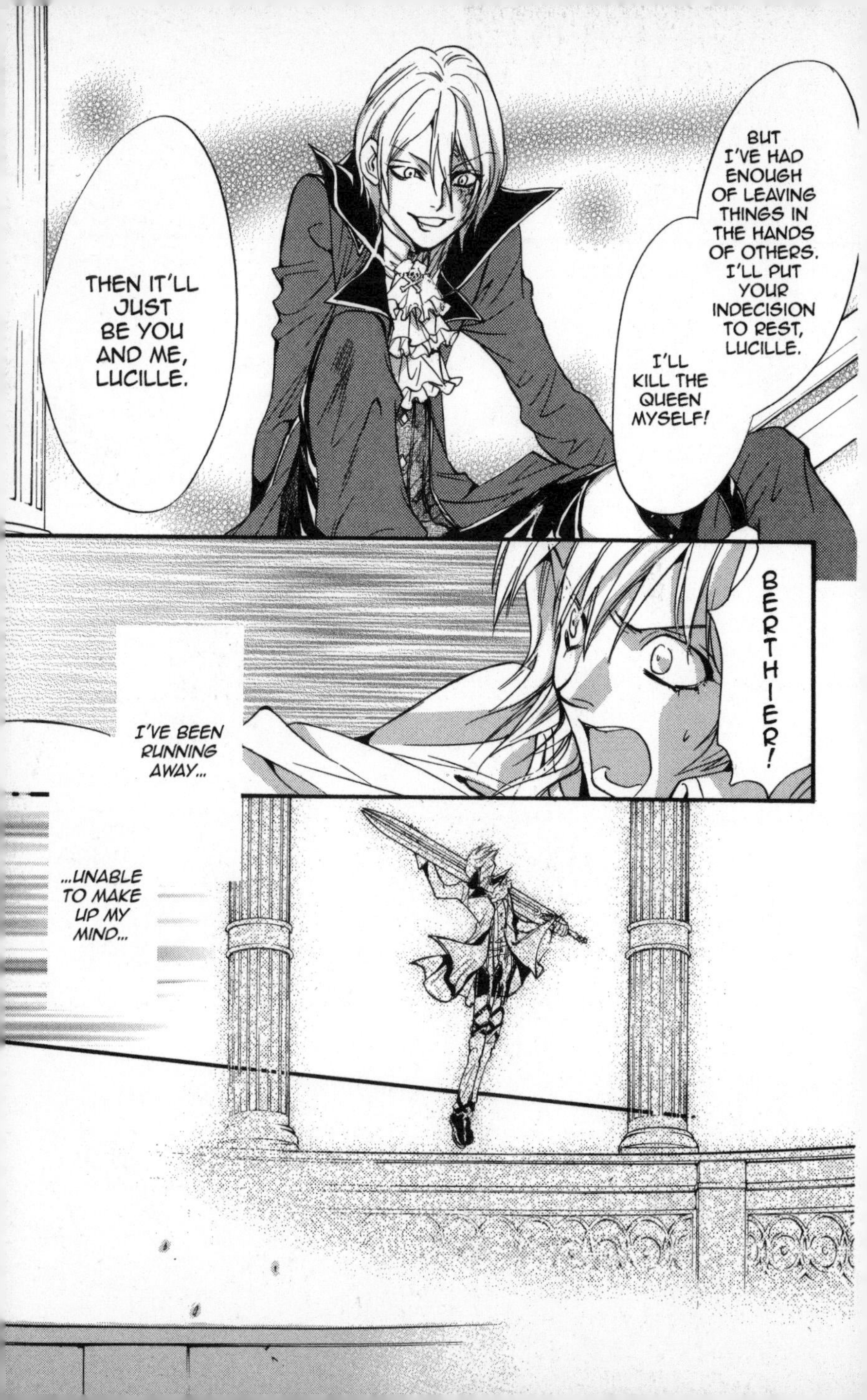
BUT I'VE HAD ENOUGH OF LEAVING THINGS IN THE HANDS OF OTHERS. I'LL PUT YOUR INDECISION TO REST, LUCILLE.
I'LL KILL THE QUEEN MYSELF!
THEN IT'LL JUST BE YOU AND ME, LUCILLE.
BERTHIER!
I'VE BEEN RUNNING AWAY...
...UNABLE TO MAKE UP MY MIND...

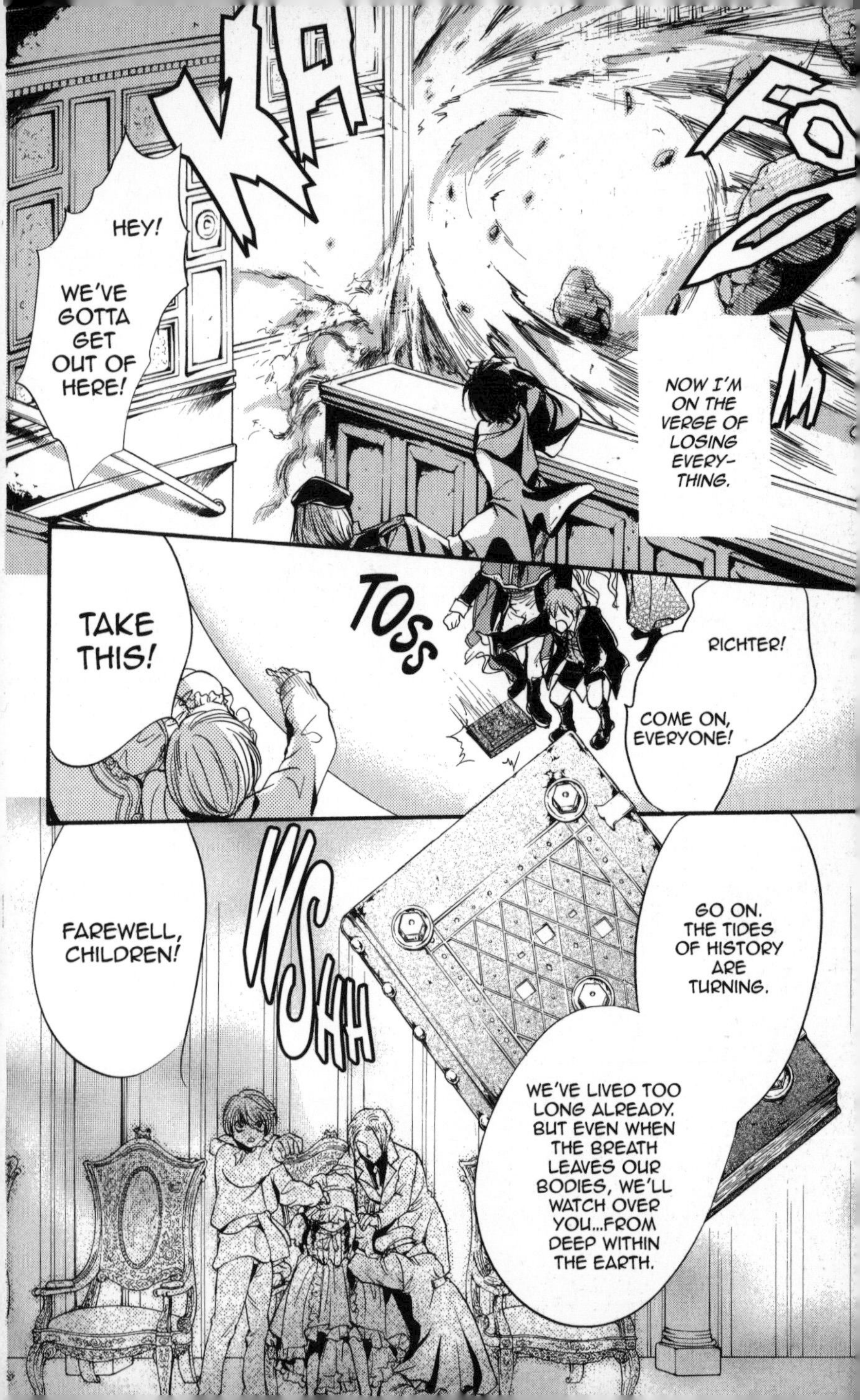
FOOM
NOW I'M ON THE VERGE OF LOSING EVERY-THING.
KA
HEY!
WE'VE GOTTA GET OUT OF HERE!
RICHTER!
COME ON, EVERYONE!
TOSS
TAKE THIS!
GO ON. THE TIDES OF HISTORY ARE TURNING.
WE'VE LIVED TOO LONG ALREADY. BUT EVEN WHEN THE BREATH LEAVES OUR BODIES, WE'LL WATCH OVER YOU...FROM DEEP WITHIN THE EARTH.
WSHH
FAREWELL, CHILDREN!

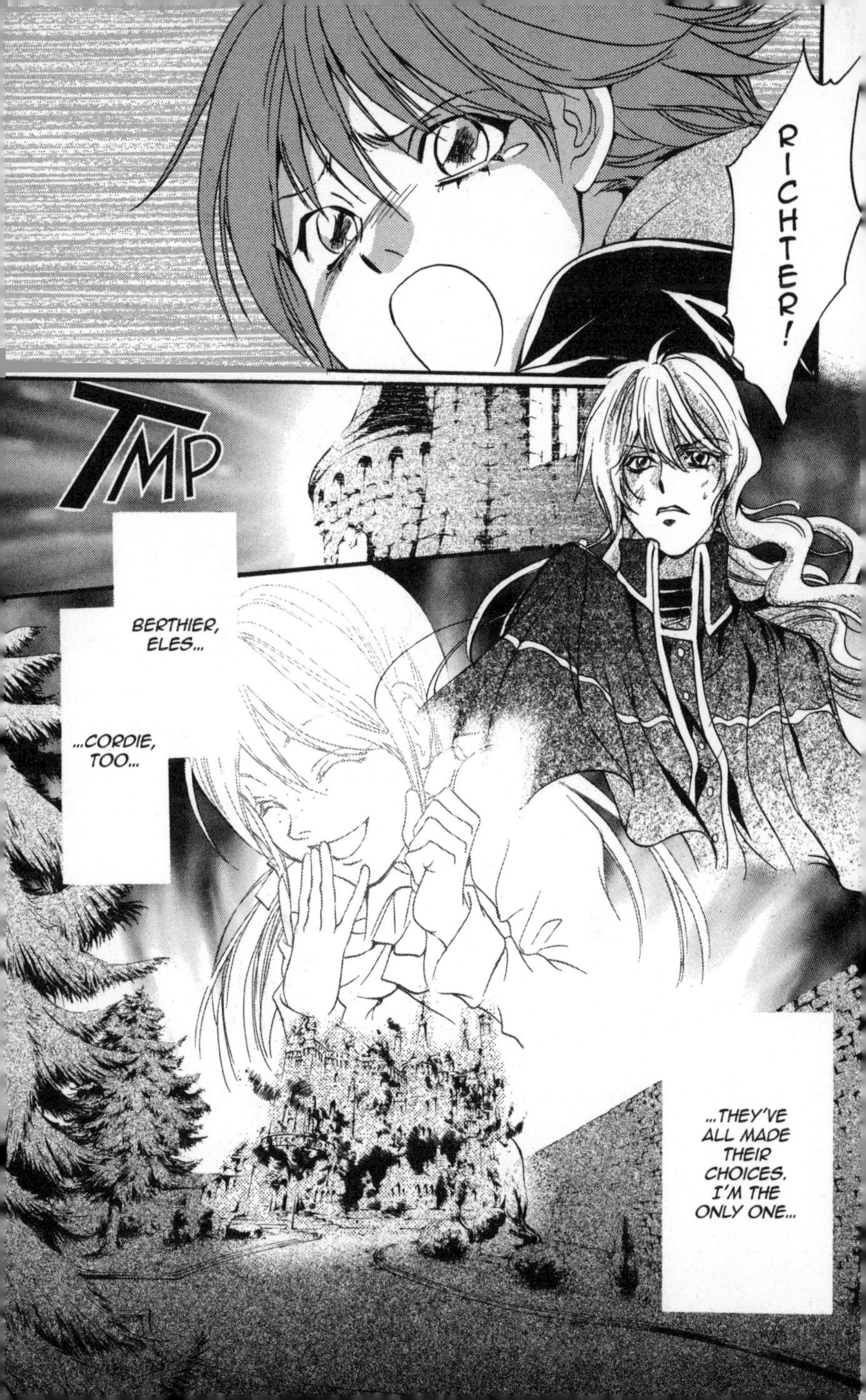
RICHTER!
TMP
BERTHIER, ELES...
...CORDIE, TOO...
...THEY'VE ALL MADE THEIR CHOICES. I'M THE ONLY ONE...

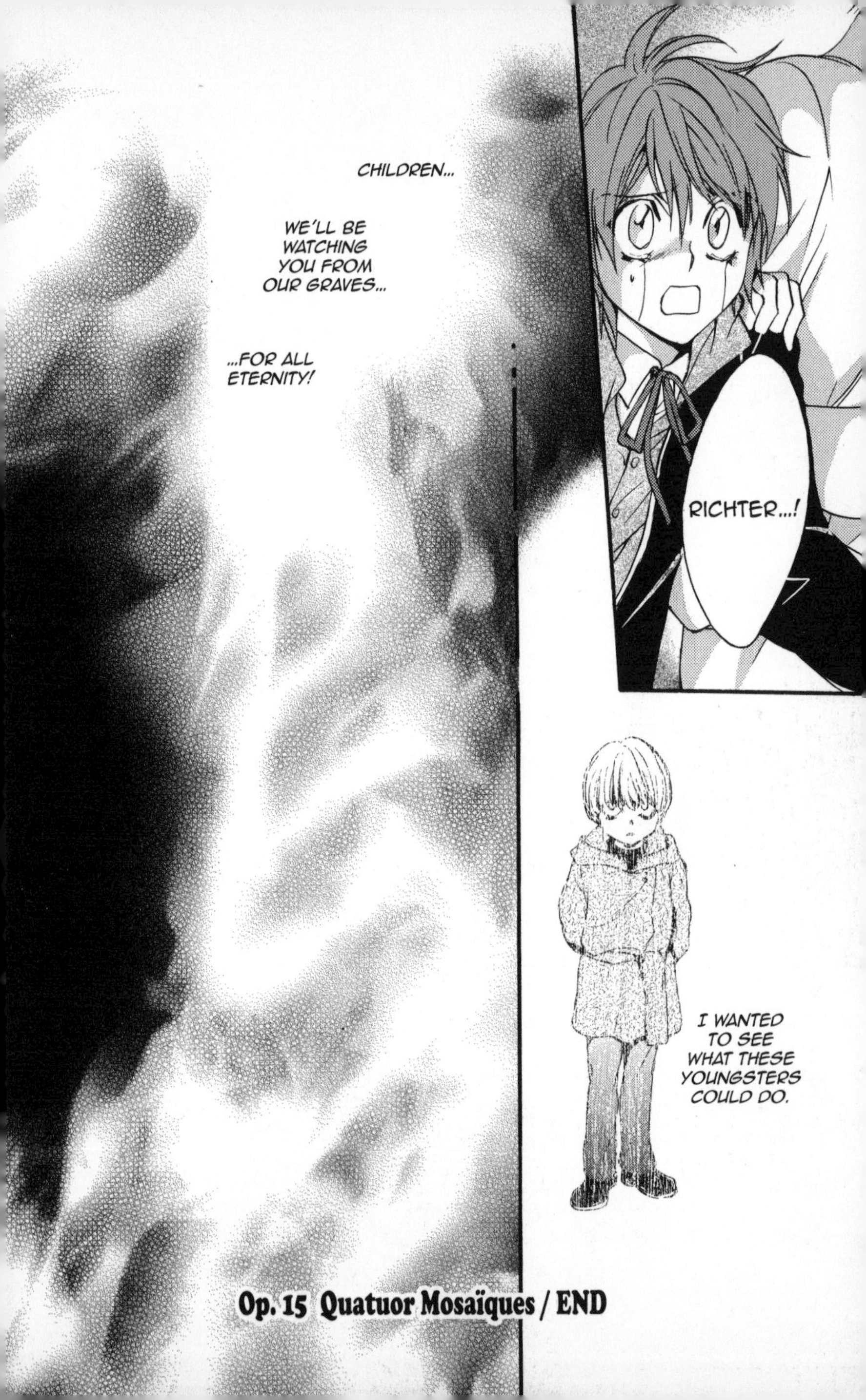
RICHTER...!
I WANTED TO SEE WHAT THESE YOUNGSTERS COULD DO.
CHILDREN...
WE'LL BE WATCHING YOU FROM OUR GRAVES...
...FOR ALL ETERNITY!

Op. 15 Quatuor Mosaïques / END

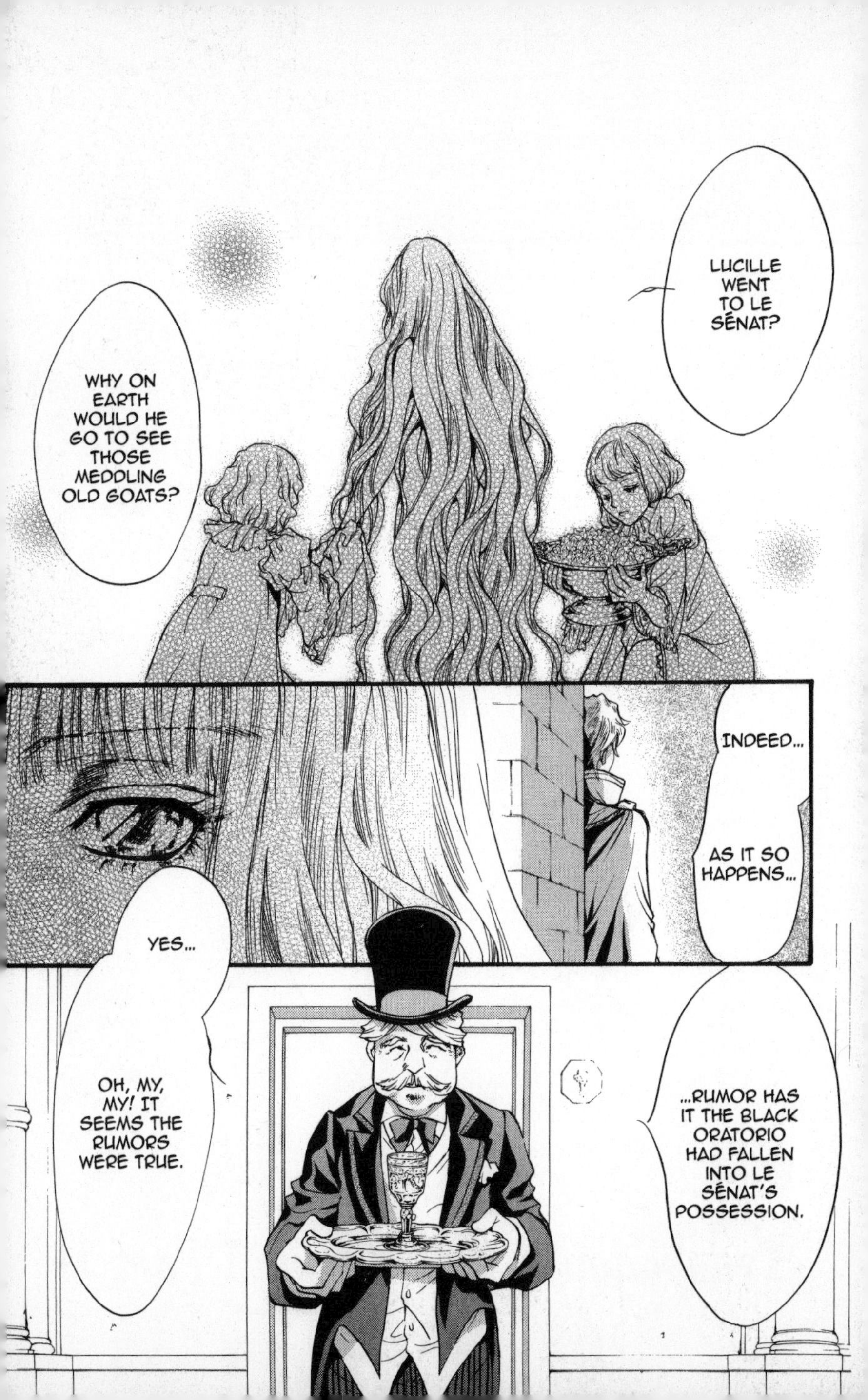

LUCILLE WENT TO LE SÉNAT?
WHY ON EARTH WOULD HE GO TO SEE THOSE MEDDLING OLD GOATS?
INDEED...
AS IT SO HAPPENS...
...RUMOR HAS IT THE BLACK ORATORIO HAD FALLEN INTO LE SÉNAT'S POSSESSION.
YES...
OH, MY, MY! IT SEEMS THE RUMORS WERE TRUE.

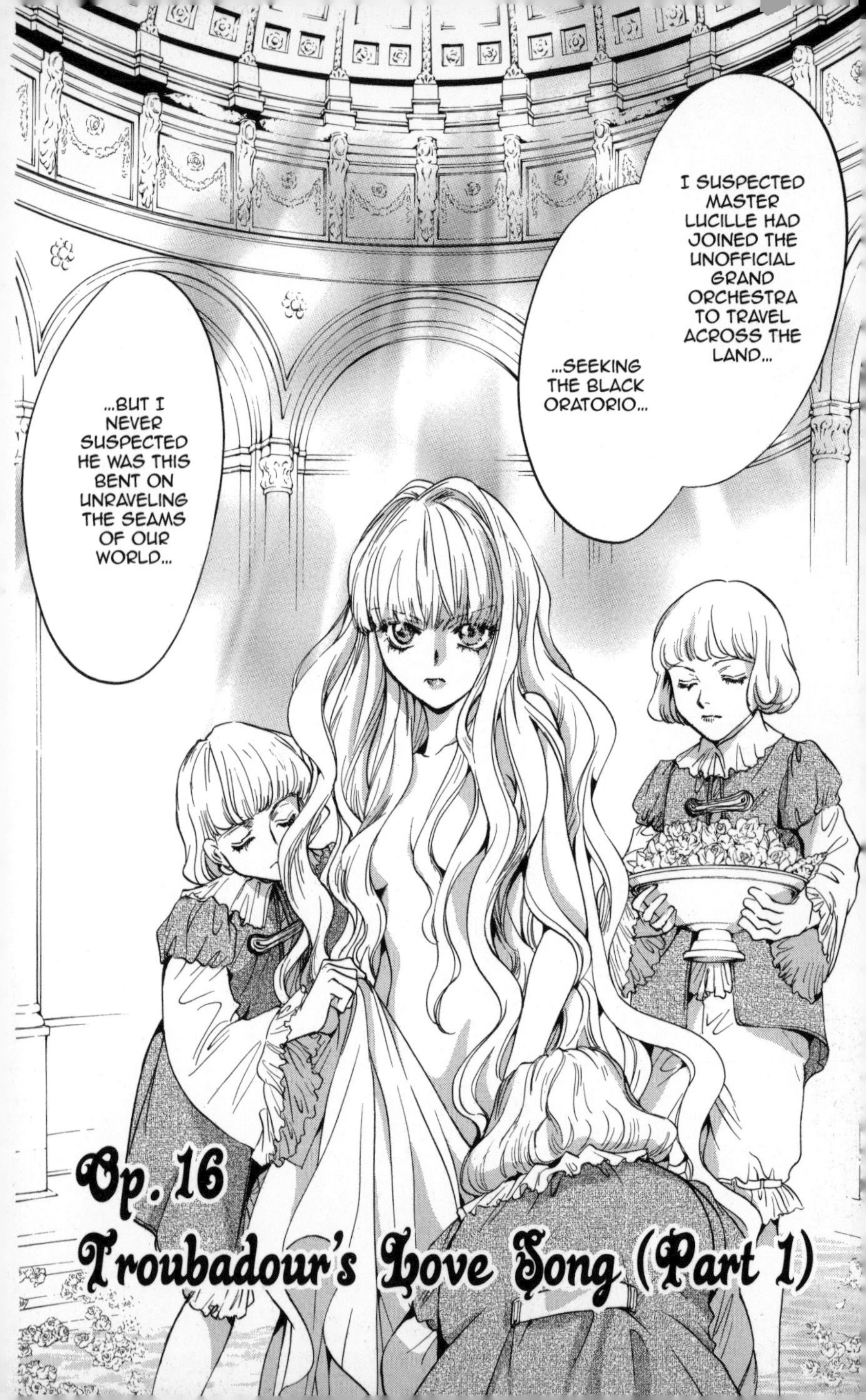
I SUSPECTED MASTER LUCILLE HAD JOINED THE UNOFFICIAL GRAND ORCHESTRA TO TRAVEL ACROSS THE LAND...
...SEEKING THE BLACK ORATORIO...
...BUT I NEVER SUSPECTED HE WAS THIS BENT ON UNRAVELING THE SEAMS OF OUR WORLD...

Op. 16 Troubadour's Love Song (Part 1)

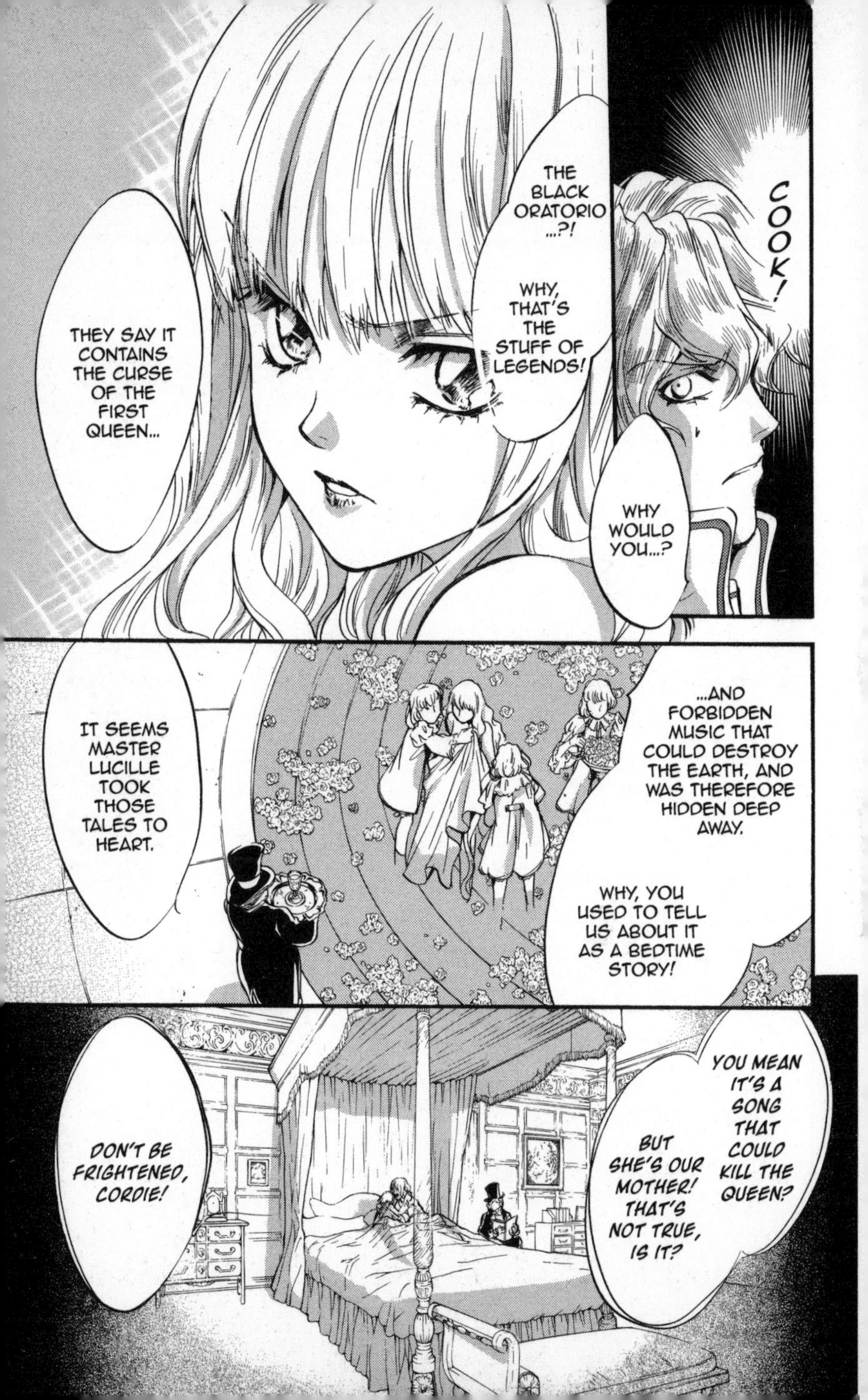
COOK!
THE BLACK ORATORIO ...?!
WHY, THAT'S THE STUFF OF LEGENDS!
WHY WOULD YOU...?
THEY SAY IT CONTAINS THE CURSE OF THE FIRST QUEEN...
...AND FORBIDDEN MUSIC THAT COULD DESTROY THE EARTH, AND WAS THEREFORE HIDDEN DEEP AWAY.
WHY, YOU USED TO TELL US ABOUT IT AS A BEDTIME STORY!
IT SEEMS MASTER LUCILLE TOOK THOSE TALES TO HEART.
YOU MEAN IT'S A SONG THAT COULD KILL THE QUEEN?
BUT SHE'S OUR MOTHER! THAT'S NOT TRUE, IS IT?
DON'T BE FRIGHTENED, CORDIE!

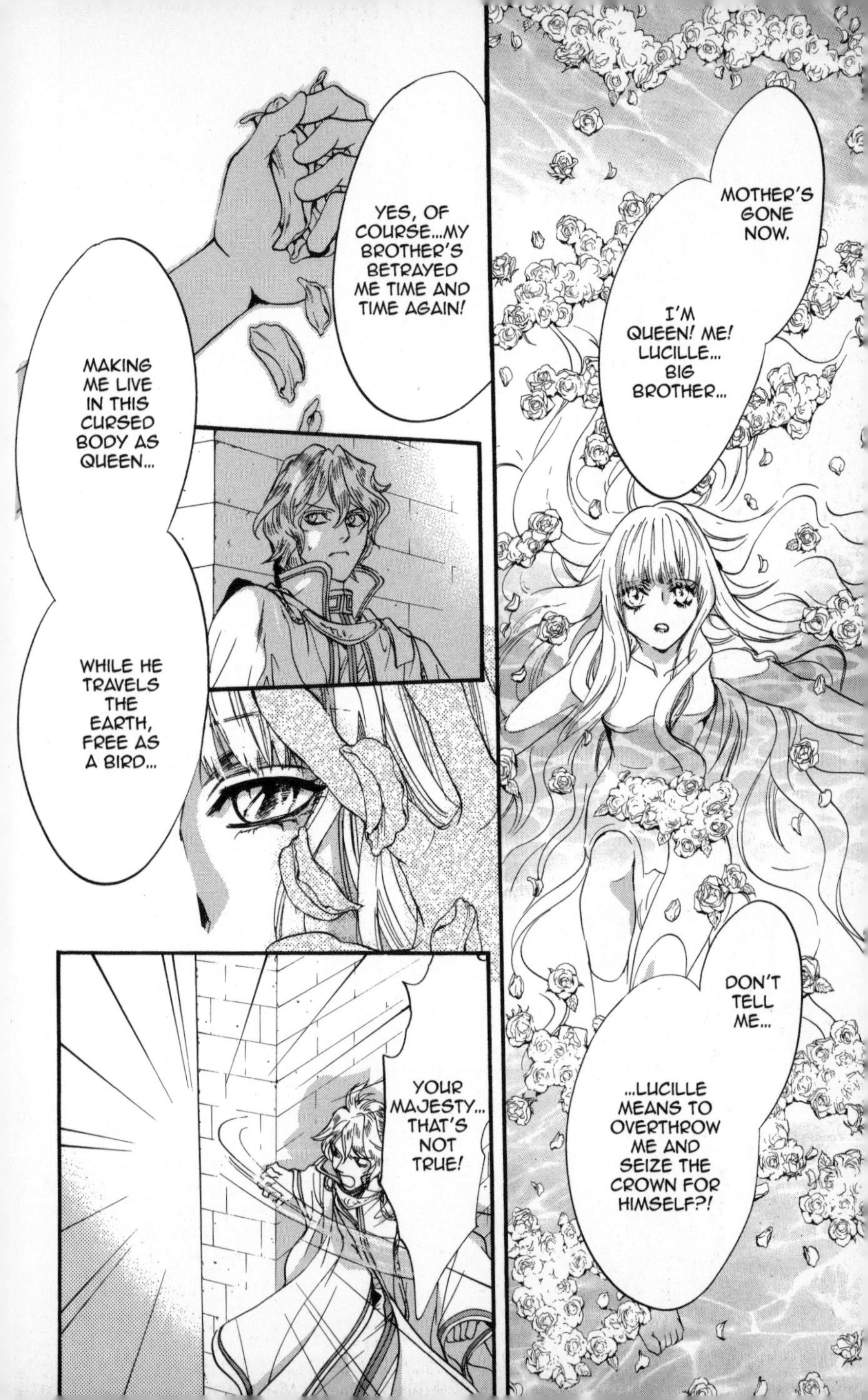
MOTHER'S GONE NOW.
I'M QUEEN! ME! LUCILLE... BIG BROTHER...
DON'T TELL ME...
...LUCILLE MEANS TO OVERTHROW ME AND SEIZE THE CROWN FOR HIMSELF?!
YES, OF COURSE...MY BROTHER'S BETRAYED ME TIME AND TIME AGAIN!
MAKING ME LIVE IN THIS CURSED BODY AS QUEEN...
WHILE HE TRAVELS THE EARTH, FREE AS A BIRD...
YOUR MAJESTY... THAT'S NOT TRUE!

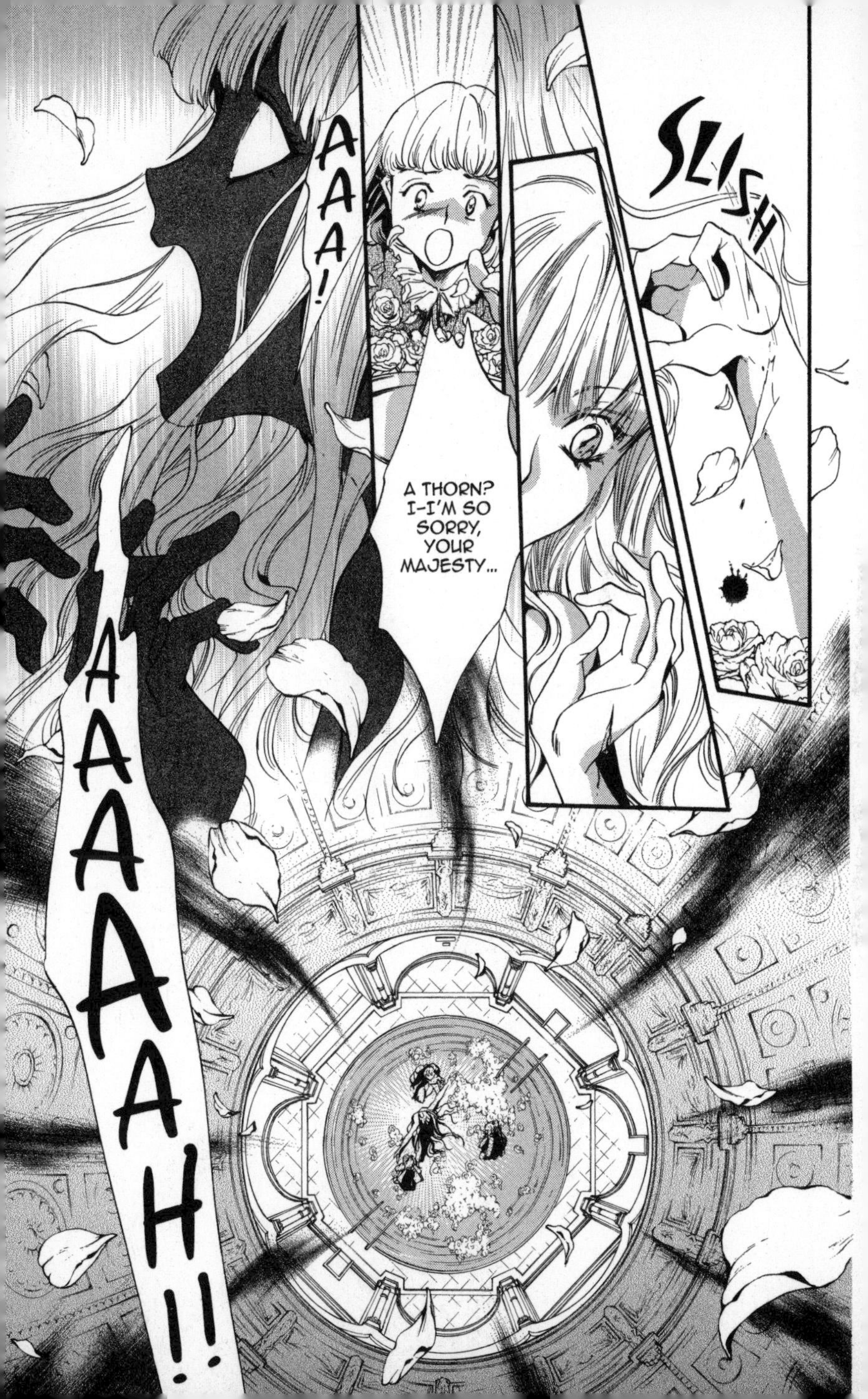
SLISH
A THORN? I-I'M SO SORRY, YOUR MAJESTY...
AAAA!
AAAAAAAH!!

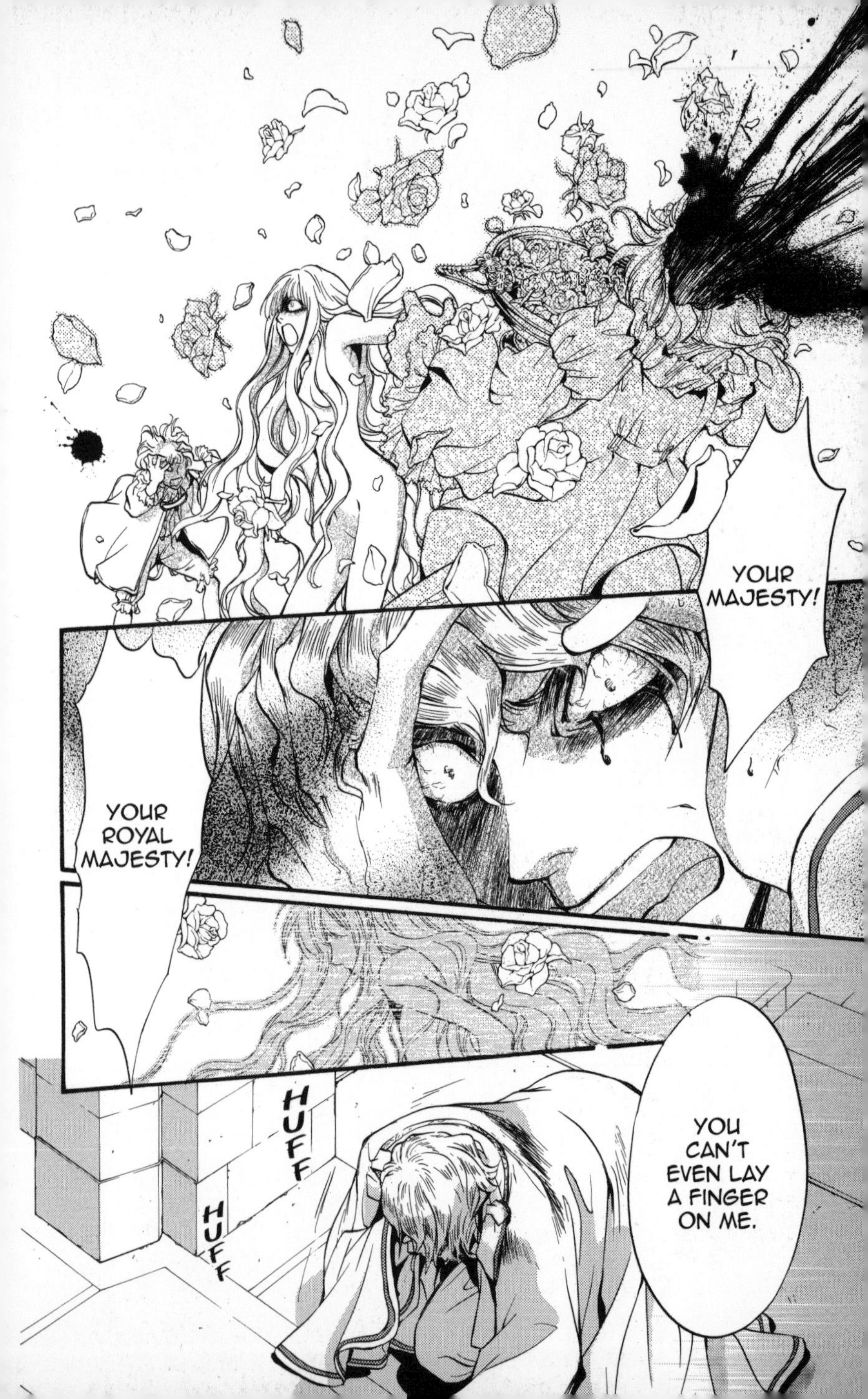
YOUR MAJESTY!
YOUR ROYAL MAJESTY!
YOU CAN'T EVEN LAY A FINGER ON ME.
HUFF
HUFF

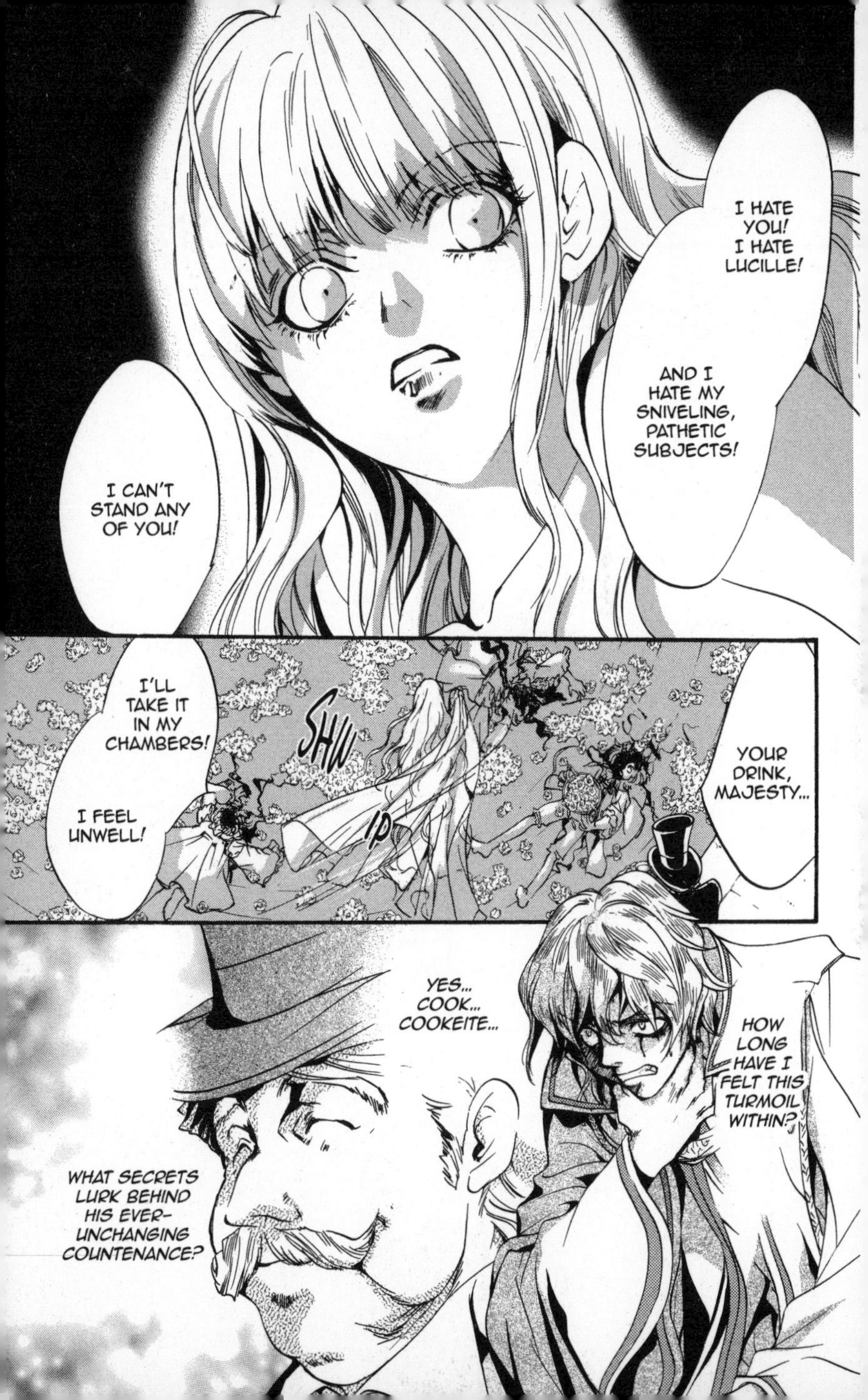
I HATE YOU! I HATE LUCILLE!
AND I HATE MY SNIVELING, PATHETIC SUBJECTS!
I CAN'T STAND ANY OF YOU!
YOUR DRINK, MAJESTY...
I'LL TAKE IT IN MY CHAMBERS!
I FEEL UNWELL!
SHW IP
HOW LONG HAVE I FELT THIS TURMOIL WITHIN?
YES... COOK... COOKEITE...
WHAT SECRETS LURK BEHIND HIS EVER-UNCHANGING COUNTENANCE?

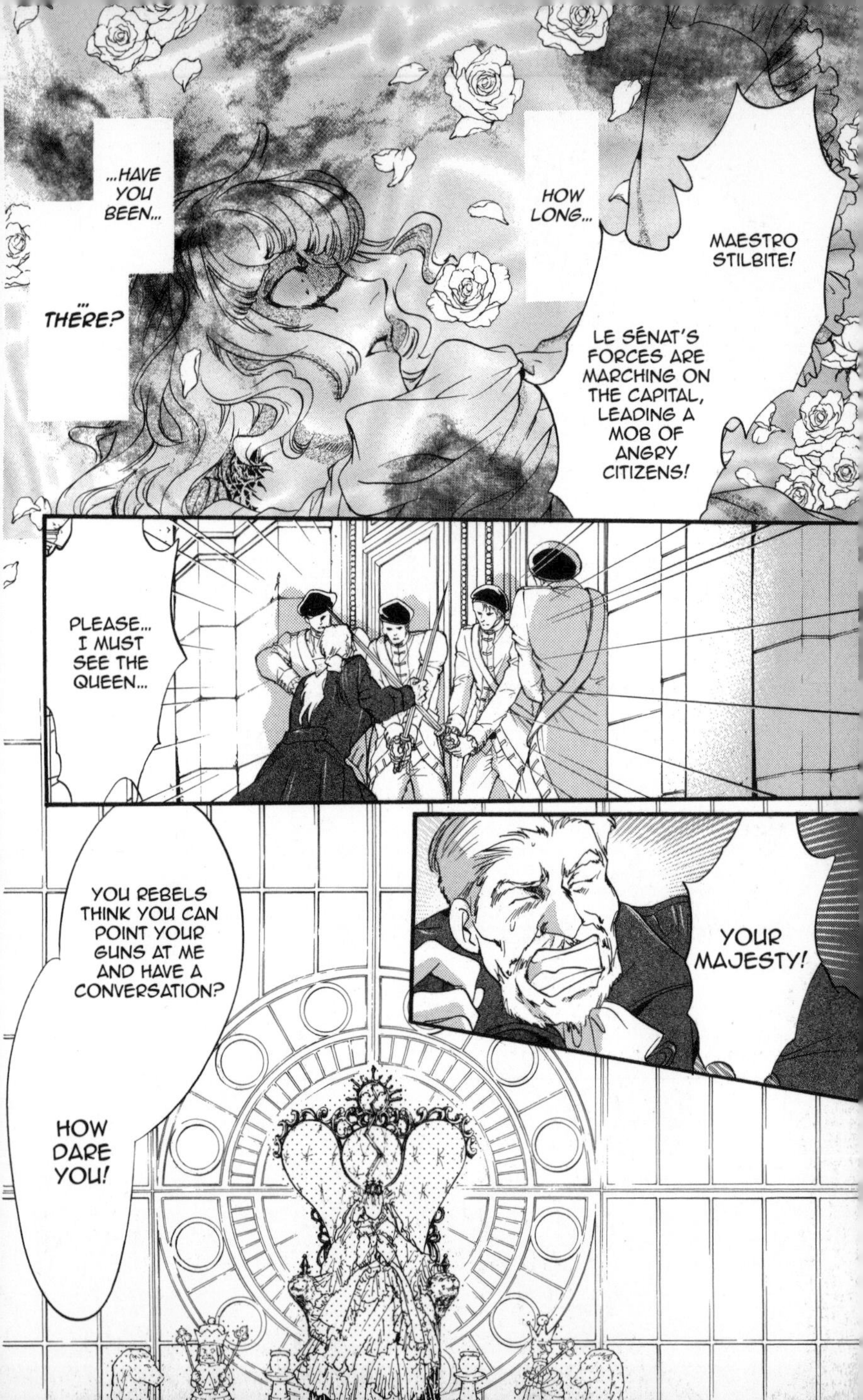
MAESTRO STILBITE!
LE SÉNAT'S FORCES ARE MARCHING ON THE CAPITAL, LEADING A MOB OF ANGRY CITIZENS!
HOW LONG...
...HAVE YOU BEEN...
...THERE?
PLEASE... I MUST SEE THE QUEEN...
YOUR MAJESTY!
YOU REBELS THINK YOU CAN POINT YOUR GUNS AT ME AND HAVE A CONVERSATION?
HOW DARE YOU!

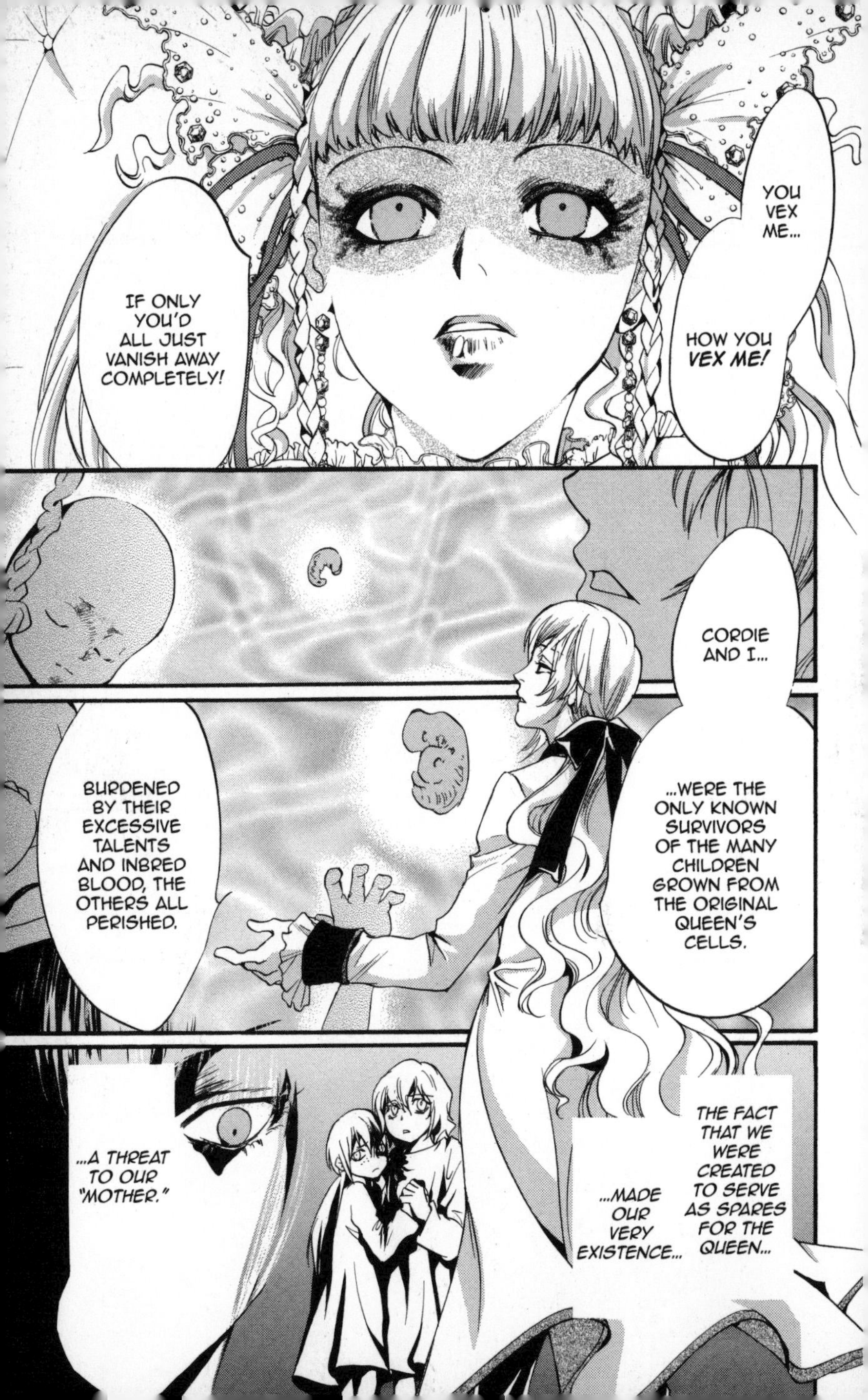
YOU VEX ME...
HOW YOU *VEX ME!*
IF ONLY YOU'D ALL JUST VANISH AWAY COMPLETELY!
CORDIE AND I...
...WERE THE ONLY KNOWN SURVIVORS OF THE MANY CHILDREN GROWN FROM THE ORIGINAL QUEEN'S CELLS.
BURDENED BY THEIR EXCESSIVE TALENTS AND INBRED BLOOD, THE OTHERS ALL PERISHED.
THE FACT THAT WE WERE CREATED TO SERVE AS SPARES FOR THE QUEEN...
...MADE OUR VERY EXISTENCE...
...A THREAT TO OUR "MOTHER."

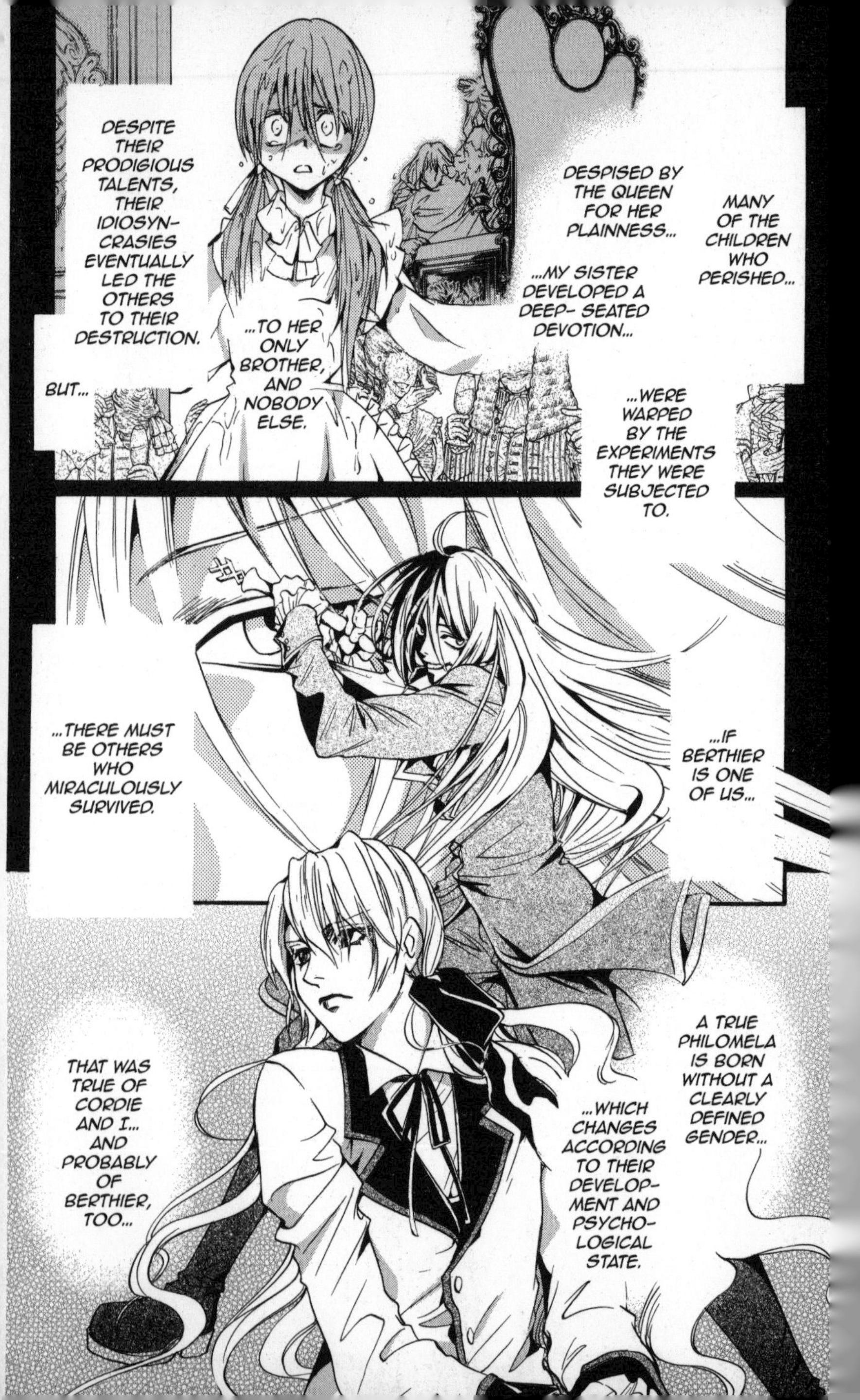
MANY OF THE CHILDREN WHO PERISHED...
...WERE WARPED BY THE EXPERIMENTS THEY WERE SUBJECTED TO.
DESPISED BY THE QUEEN FOR HER PLAINNESS...
...MY SISTER DEVELOPED A DEEP- SEATED DEVOTION...
...TO HER ONLY BROTHER, AND NOBODY ELSE.
DESPITE THEIR PRODIGIOUS TALENTS, THEIR IDIOSYN-CRASIES EVENTUALLY LED THE OTHERS TO THEIR DESTRUCTION.
BUT...
...IF BERTHIER IS ONE OF US...
...THERE MUST BE OTHERS WHO MIRACULOUSLY SURVIVED.
A TRUE PHILOMELA IS BORN WITHOUT A CLEARLY DEFINED GENDER...
...WHICH CHANGES ACCORDING TO THEIR DEVELOP-MENT AND PSYCHO-LOGICAL STATE.
THAT WAS TRUE OF CORDIE AND I... AND PROBABLY OF BERTHIER, TOO...

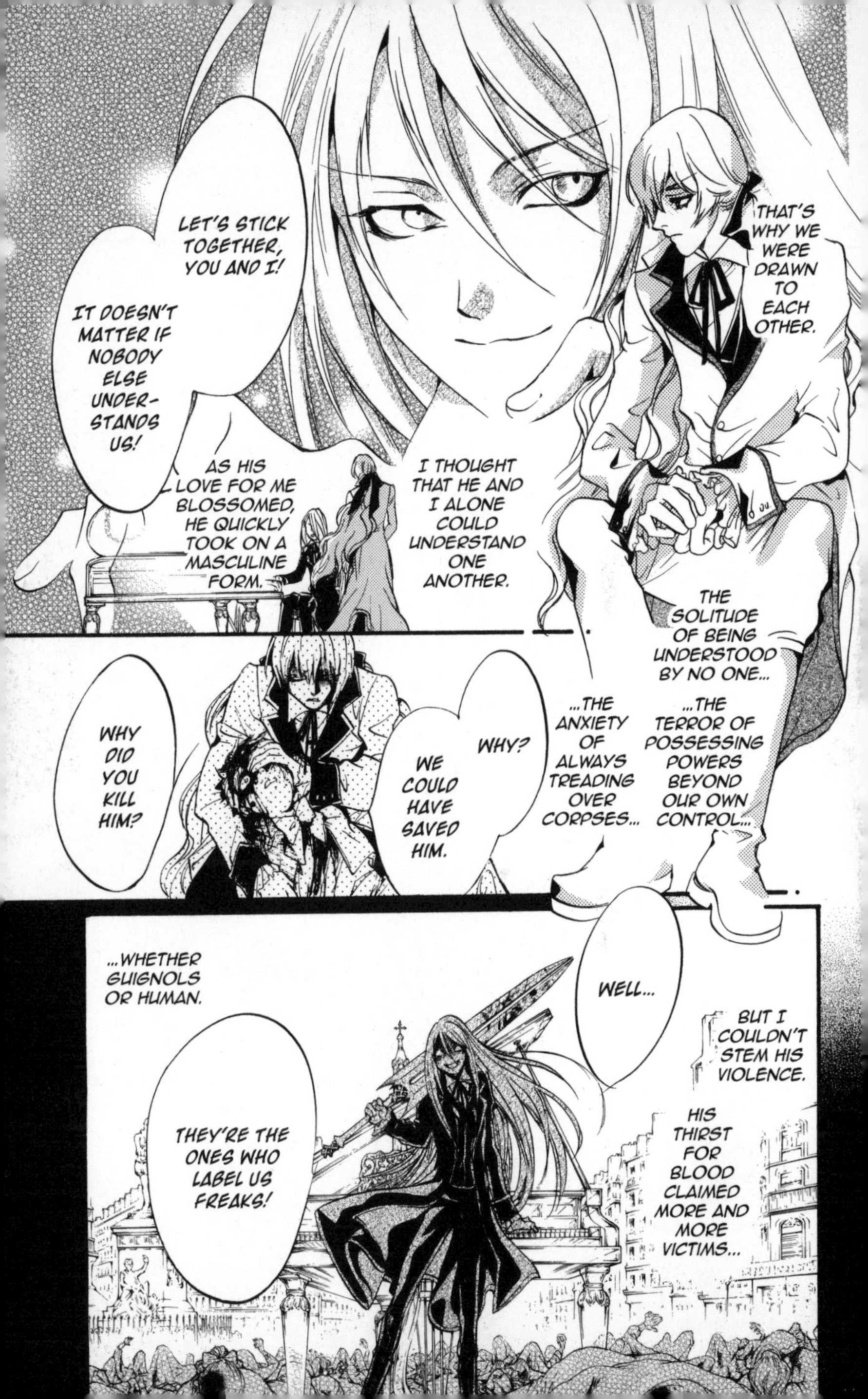
THAT'S WHY WE WERE DRAWN TO EACH OTHER.
I THOUGHT THAT HE AND I ALONE COULD UNDERSTAND ONE ANOTHER.
AS HIS LOVE FOR ME BLOSSOMED, HE QUICKLY TOOK ON A MASCULINE FORM.
LET'S STICK TOGETHER, YOU AND I!
IT DOESN'T MATTER IF NOBODY ELSE UNDER-STANDS US!
THE SOLITUDE OF BEING UNDERSTOOD BY NO ONE...
...THE TERROR OF POSSESSING POWERS BEYOND OUR OWN CONTROL...
...THE ANXIETY OF ALWAYS TREADING OVER CORPSES...
WHY?
WE COULD HAVE SAVED HIM.
WHY DID YOU KILL HIM?
BUT I COULDN'T STEM HIS VIOLENCE.
HIS THIRST FOR BLOOD CLAIMED MORE AND MORE VICTIMS...
WELL...
THEY'RE THE ONES WHO LABEL US FREAKS!
...WHETHER GUIGNOLS OR HUMAN.

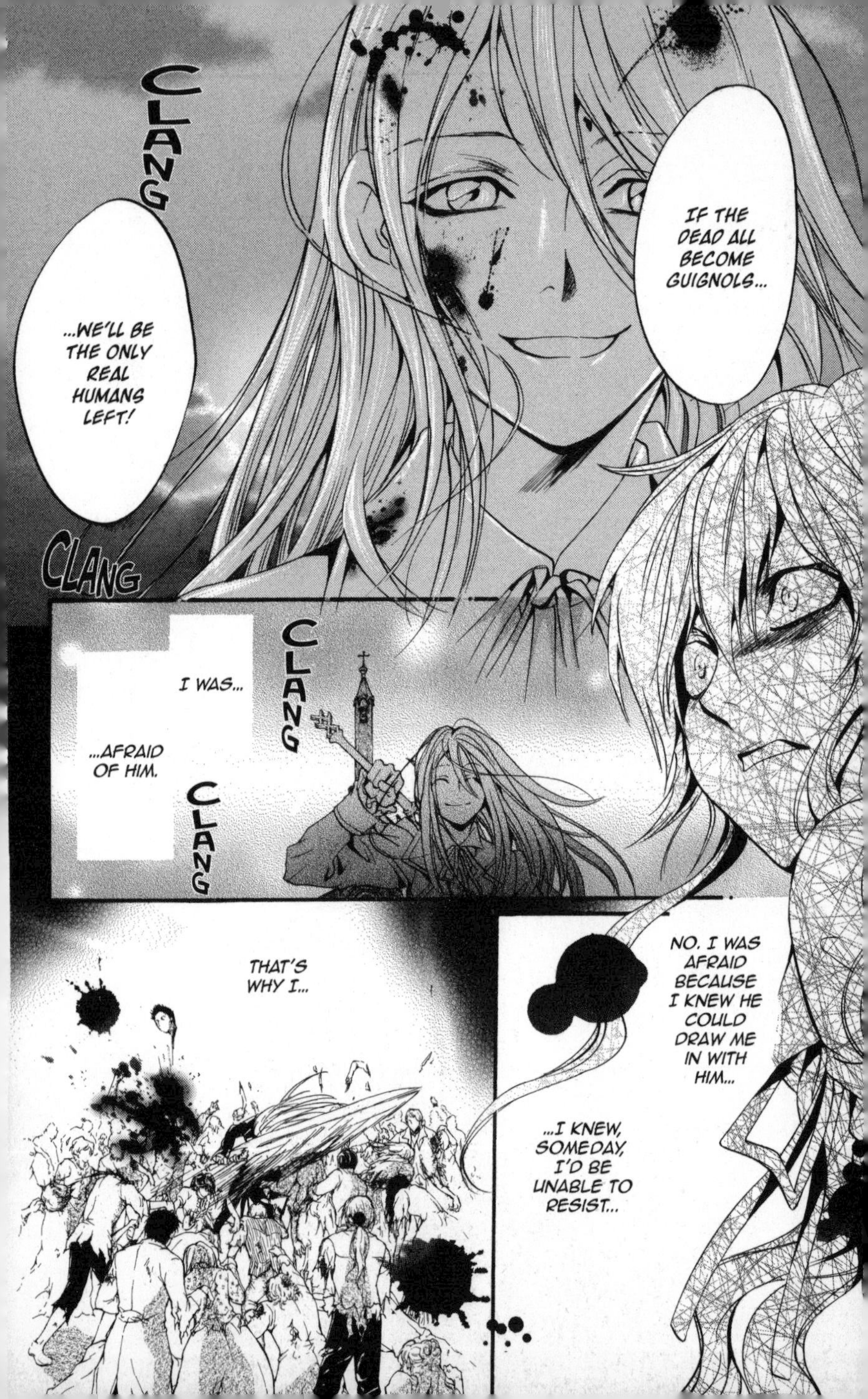
IF THE DEAD ALL BECOME GUIGNOLS...
CLANG
...WE'LL BE THE ONLY REAL HUMANS LEFT!
CLANG
CLANG
I WAS...
...AFRAID OF HIM.
CLANG
NO. I WAS AFRAID BECAUSE I KNEW HE COULD DRAW ME IN WITH HIM...
...I KNEW, SOMEDAY, I'D BE UNABLE TO RESIST...
THAT'S WHY I...

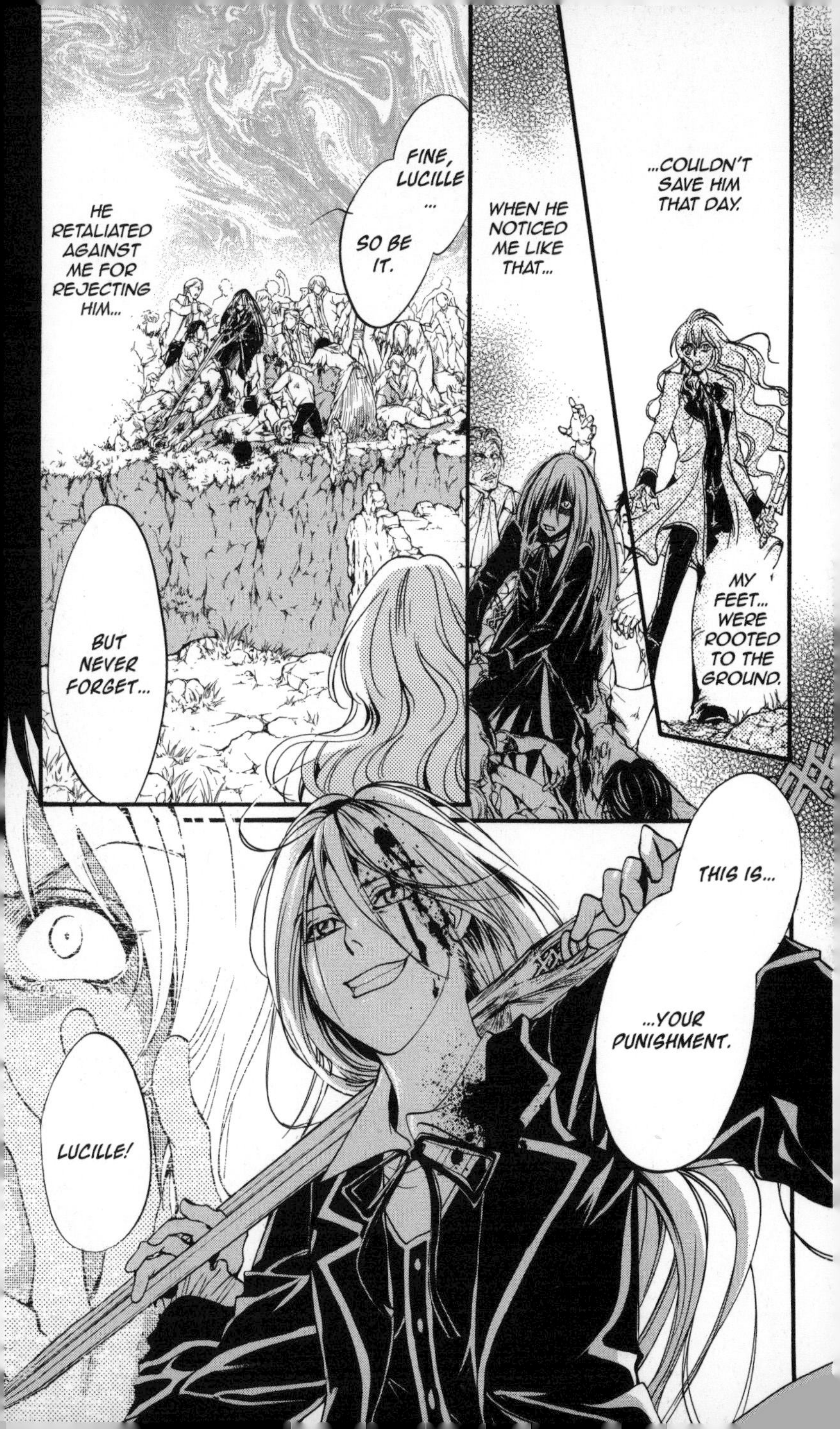
...COULDN'T SAVE HIM THAT DAY.
MY FEET... WERE ROOTED TO THE GROUND.
WHEN HE NOTICED ME LIKE THAT...
FINE, LUCILLE ... SO BE IT.
HE RETALIATED AGAINST ME FOR REJECTING HIM...
BUT NEVER FORGET...
THIS IS...
...YOUR PUNISHMENT.
LUCILLE!

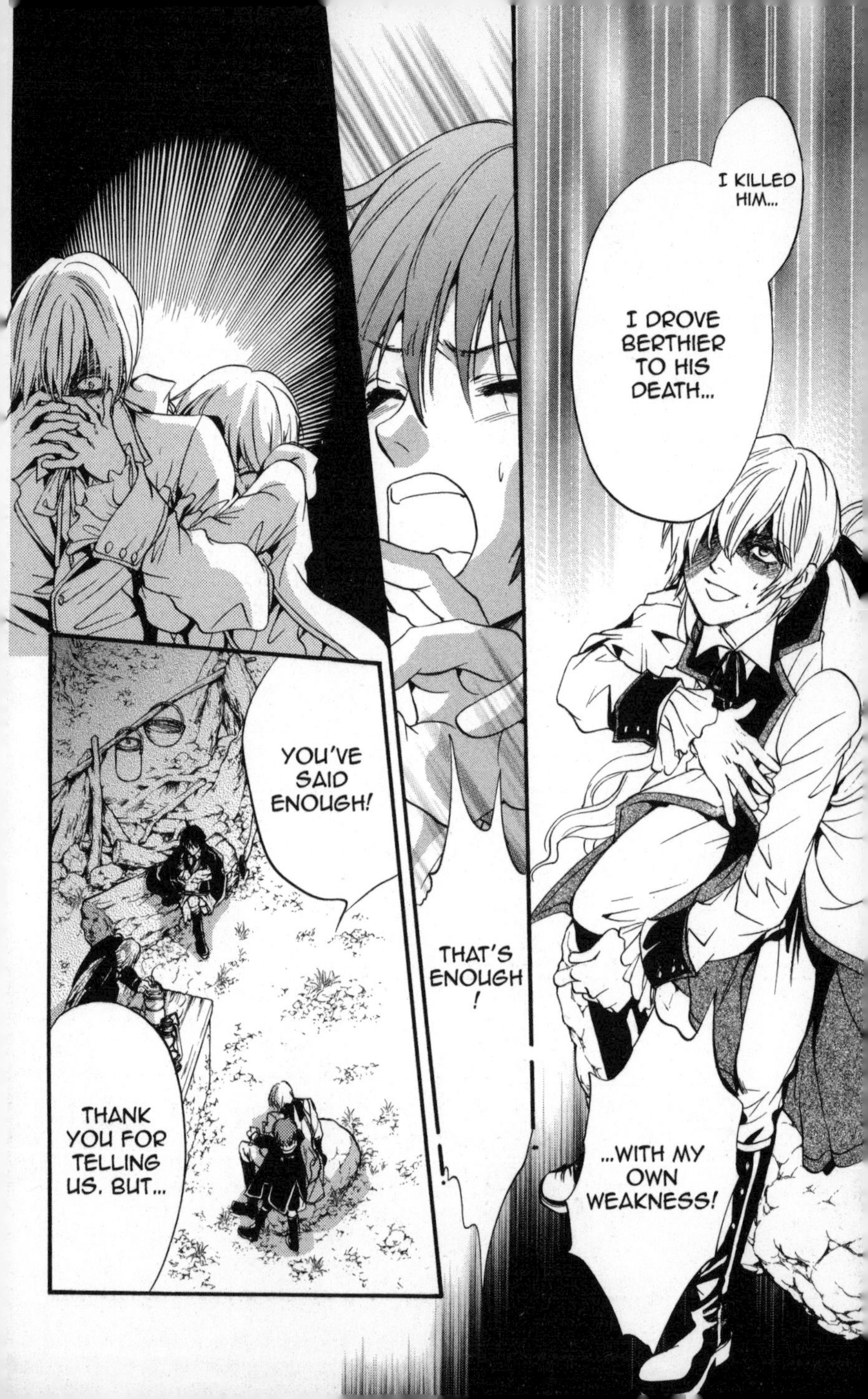
I KILLED HIM...
I DROVE BERTHIER TO HIS DEATH...
...WITH MY OWN WEAKNESS!
THAT'S ENOUGH!
YOU'VE SAID ENOUGH!
THANK YOU FOR TELLING US. BUT...

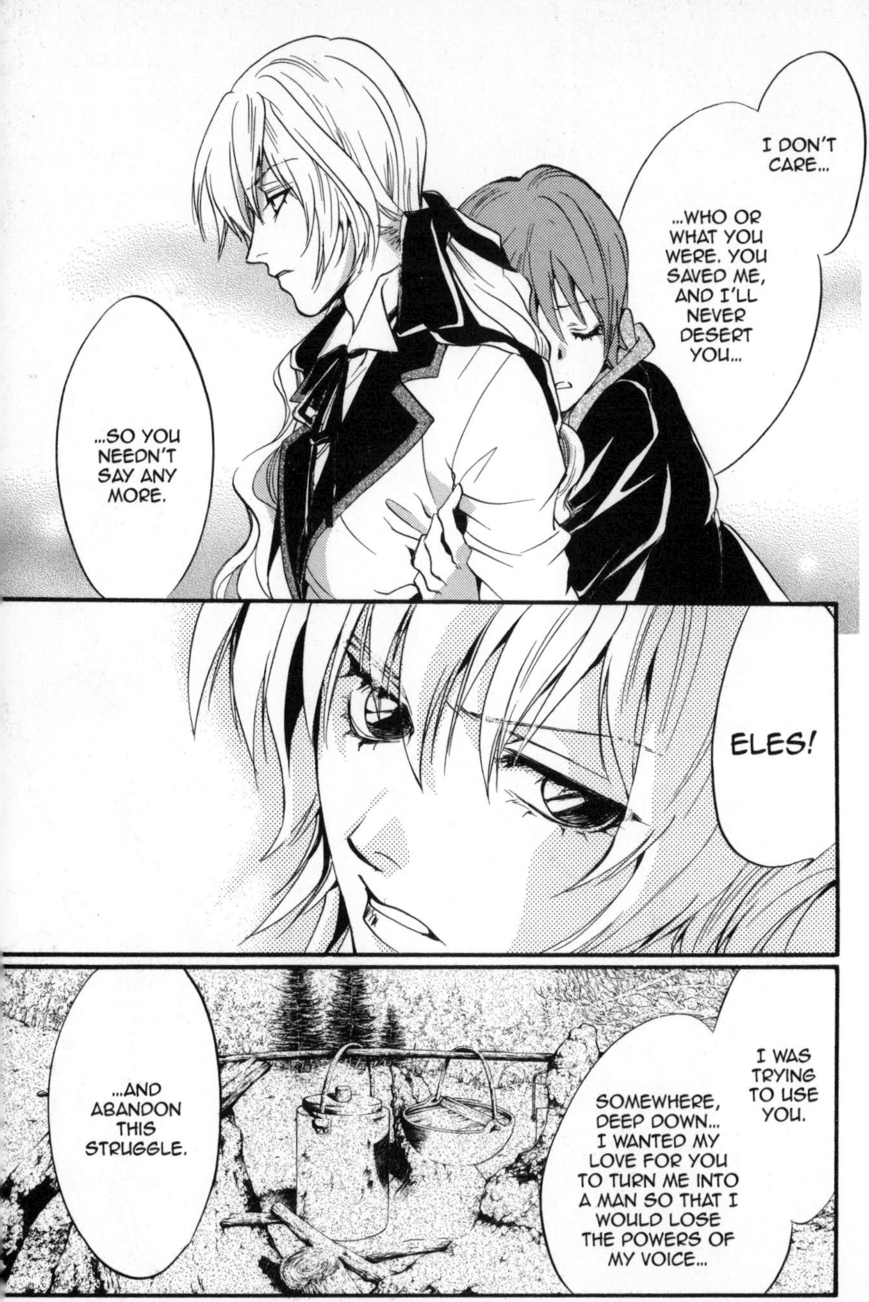
I DON'T CARE...
...WHO OR WHAT YOU WERE. YOU SAVED ME, AND I'LL NEVER DESERT YOU...
...SO YOU NEEDN'T SAY ANY MORE.
ELES!
I WAS TRYING TO USE YOU.
SOMEWHERE, DEEP DOWN... I WANTED MY LOVE FOR YOU TO TURN ME INTO A MAN SO THAT I WOULD LOSE THE POWERS OF MY VOICE...
...AND ABANDON THIS STRUGGLE.

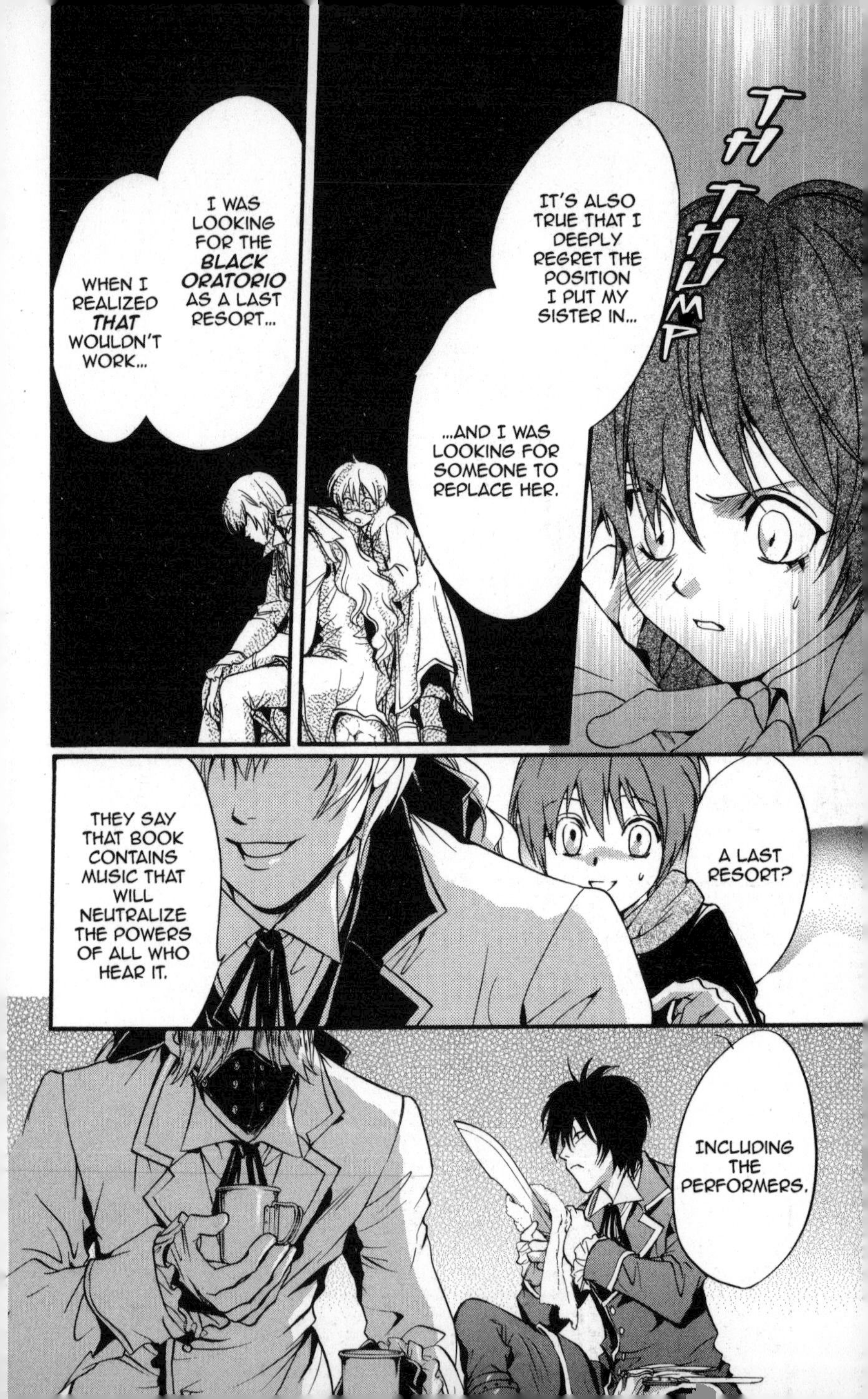
TH TH THUMP
IT'S ALSO TRUE THAT I DEEPLY REGRET THE POSITION I PUT MY SISTER IN...
...AND I WAS LOOKING FOR SOMEONE TO REPLACE HER.
I WAS LOOKING FOR THE *BLACK ORATORIO* AS A LAST RESORT...
WHEN I REALIZED *THAT* WOULDN'T WORK...
A LAST RESORT?
THEY SAY THAT BOOK CONTAINS MUSIC THAT WILL NEUTRALIZE THE POWERS OF ALL WHO HEAR IT.
INCLUDING THE PERFORMERS.

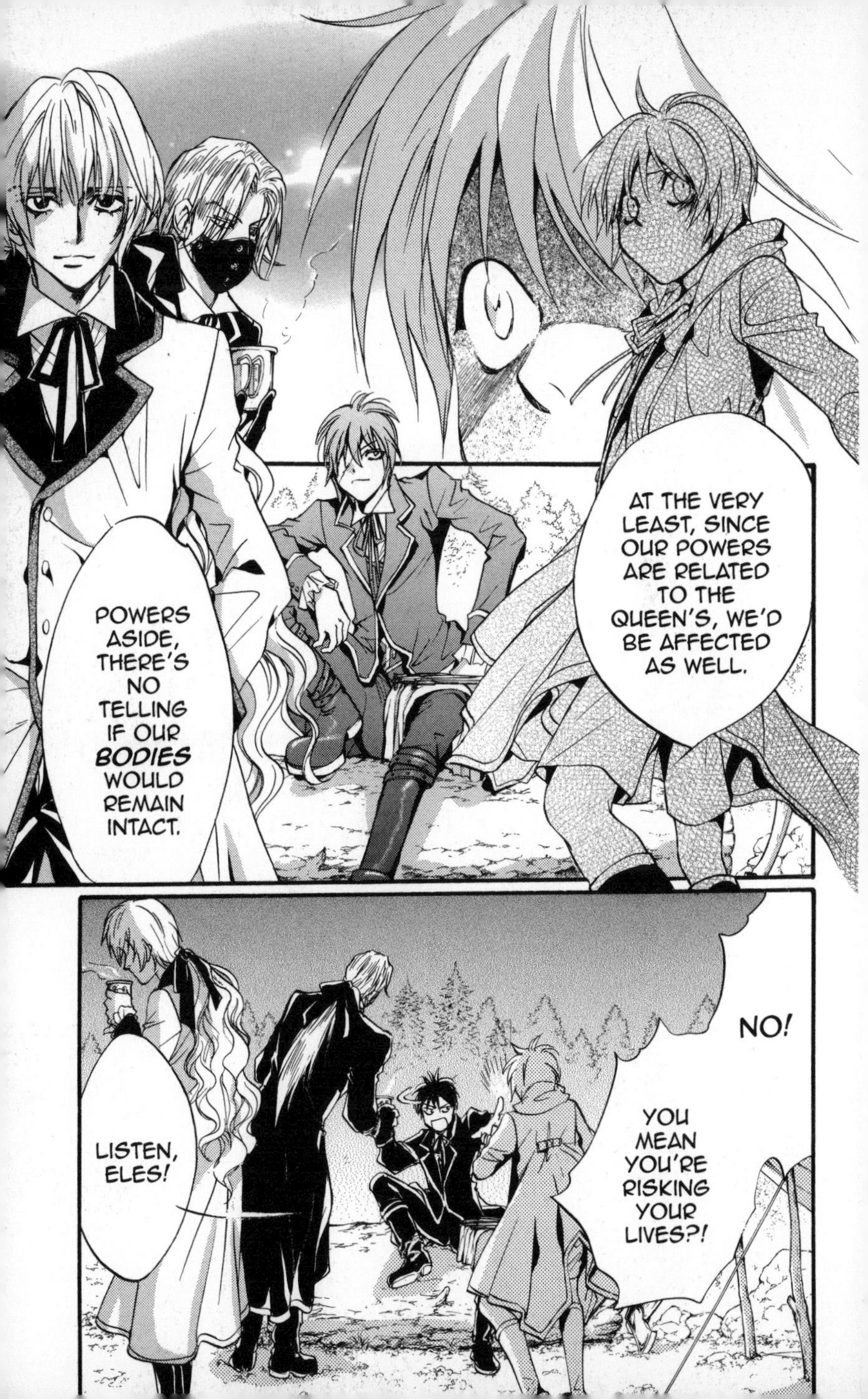
AT THE VERY LEAST, SINCE OUR POWERS ARE RELATED TO THE QUEEN'S, WE'D BE AFFECTED AS WELL.
POWERS ASIDE, THERE'S NO TELLING IF OUR *BODIES* WOULD REMAIN INTACT.
NO!
YOU MEAN YOU'RE RISKING YOUR LIVES?!
LISTEN, ELES!

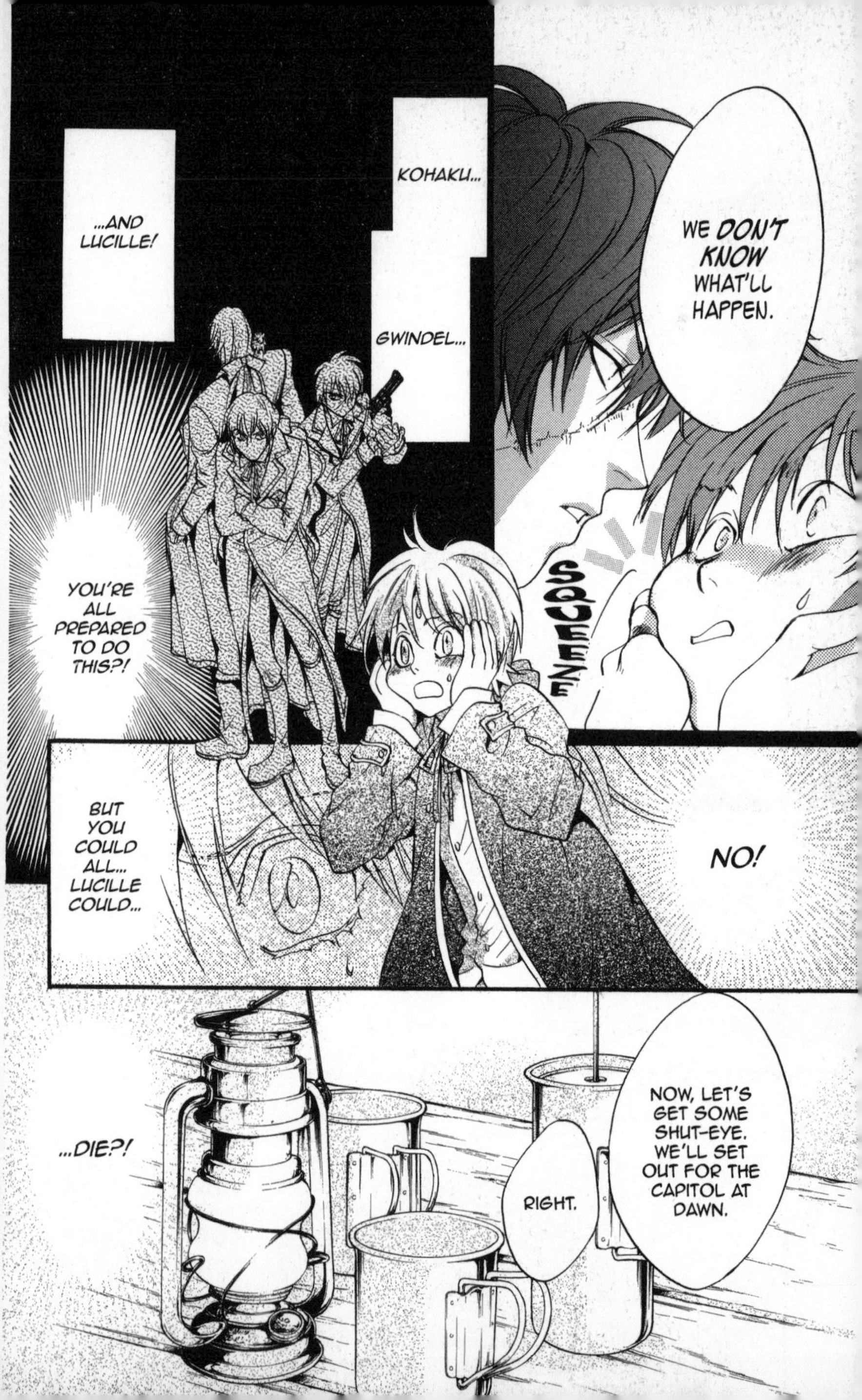
WE DON'T KNOW WHAT'LL HAPPEN.
SQUEEENE
KOHAKU...
GWINDEL...
...AND LUCILLE!
YOU'RE ALL PREPARED TO DO THIS?!
NO!
BUT YOU COULD ALL... LUCILLE COULD...
...DIE?!
NOW, LET'S GET SOME SHUT-EYE. WE'LL SET OUT FOR THE CAPITOL AT DAWN.
RIGHT.

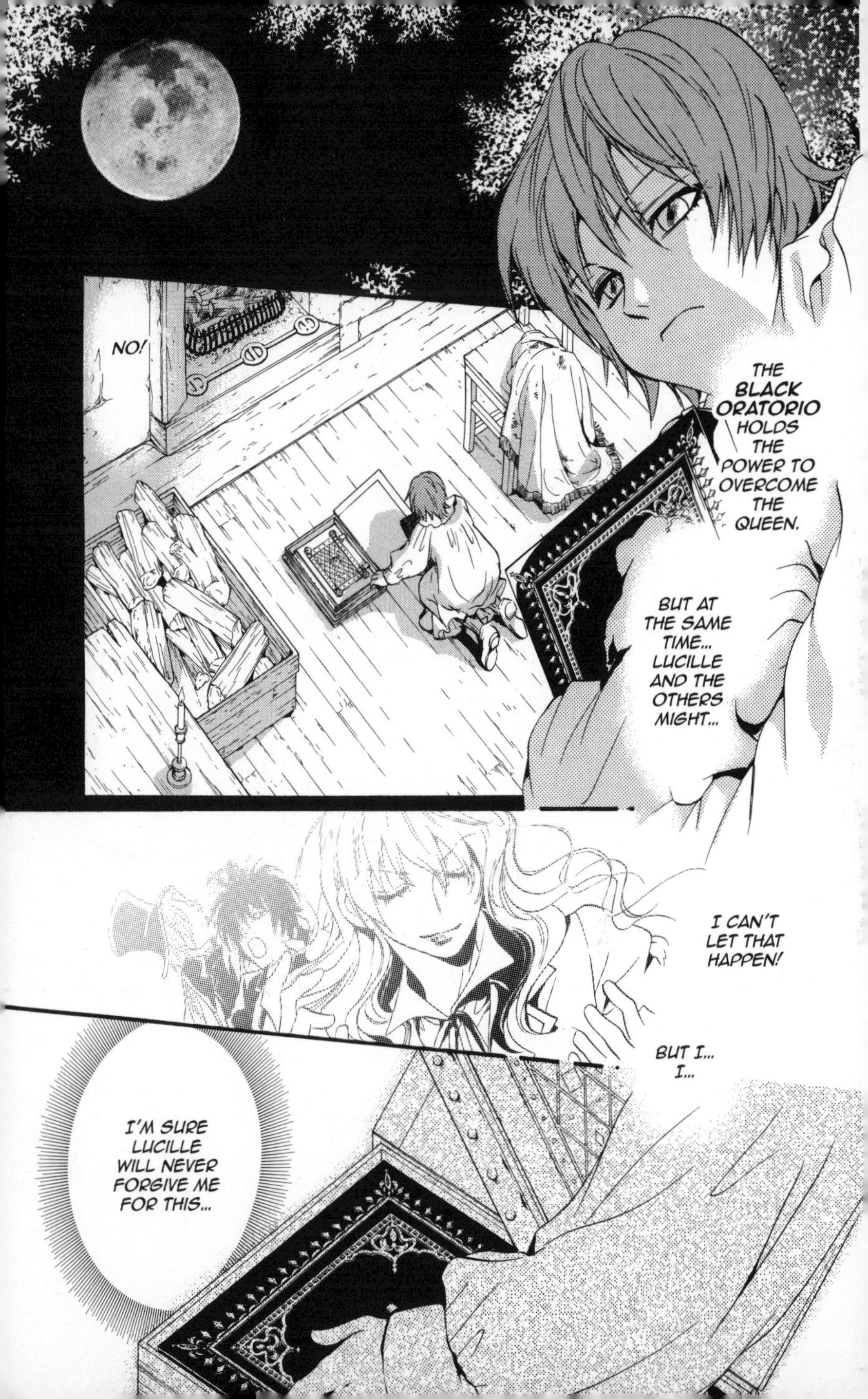
THE BLACK ORATORIO HOLDS THE POWER TO OVERCOME THE QUEEN.
BUT AT THE SAME TIME... LUCILLE AND THE OTHERS MIGHT...
NO!
I CAN'T LET THAT HAPPEN!
BUT I... I...
I'M SURE LUCILLE WILL NEVER FORGIVE ME FOR THIS...

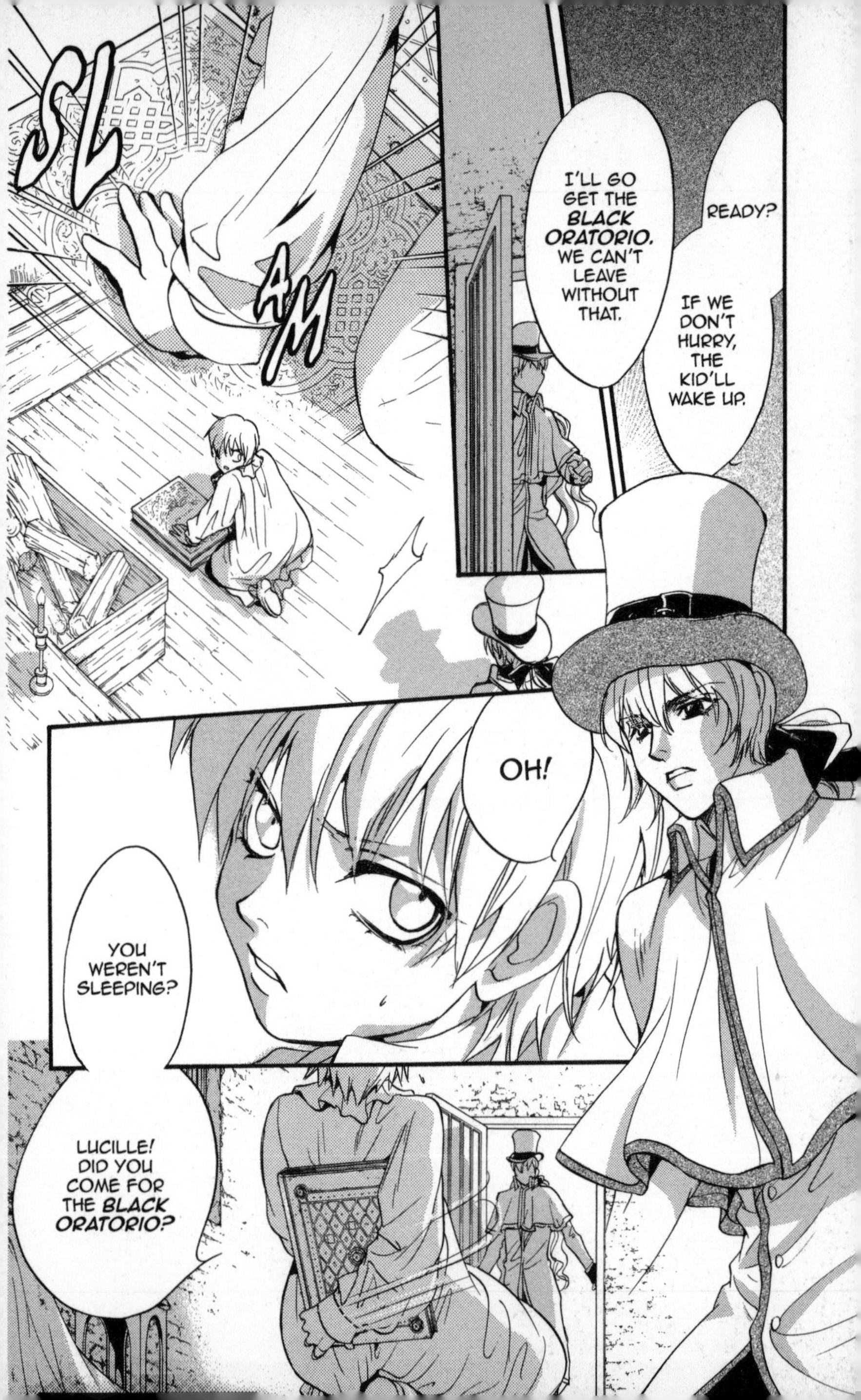
READY?
I'LL GO GET THE BLACK ORATORIO. WE CAN'T LEAVE WITHOUT THAT.
IF WE DON'T HURRY, THE KID'LL WAKE UP.
SLAM
OH!
YOU WEREN'T SLEEPING?
LUCILLE! DID YOU COME FOR THE BLACK ORATORIO?

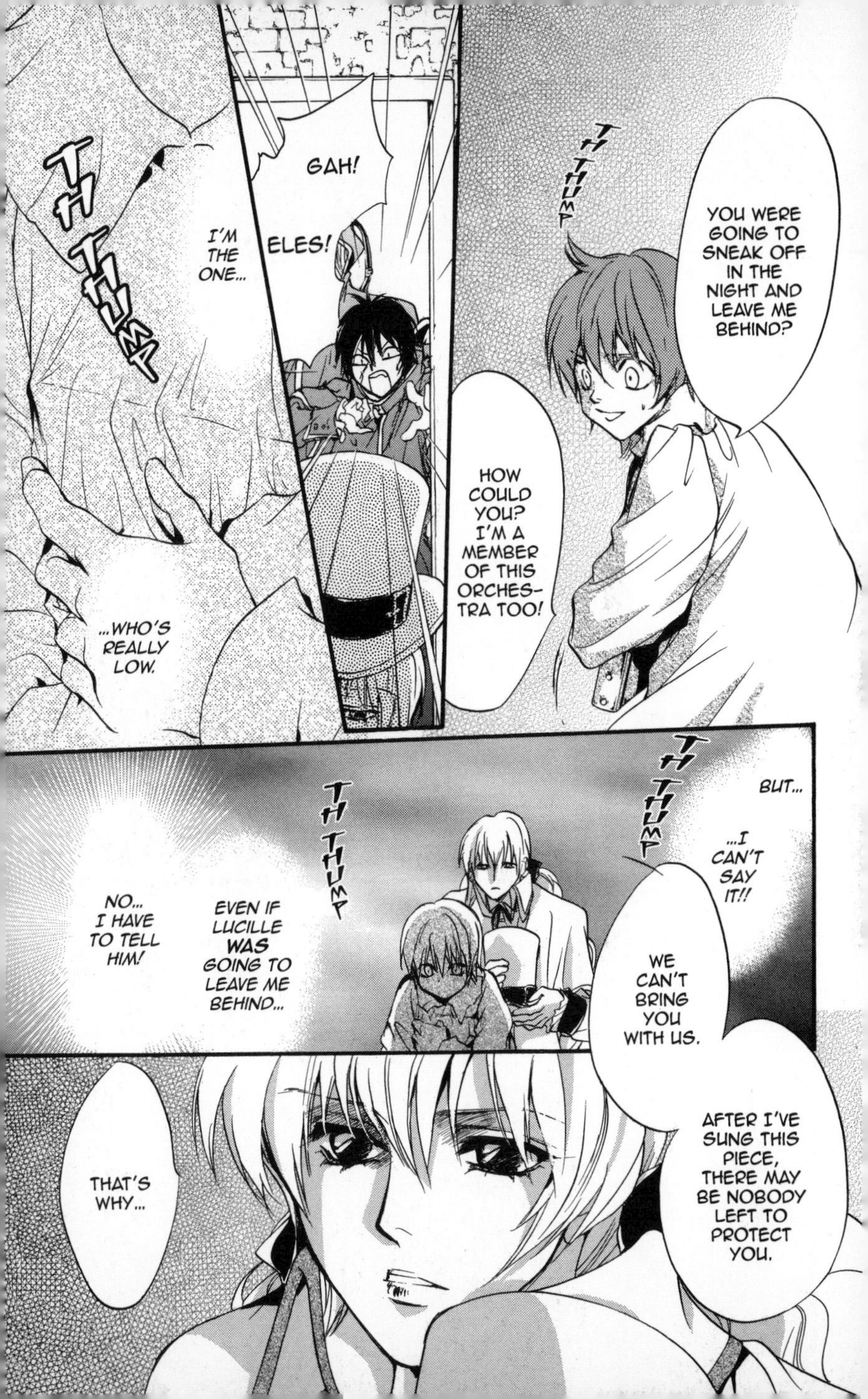
TH THUMP
YOU WERE GOING TO SNEAK OFF IN THE NIGHT AND LEAVE ME BEHIND?
HOW COULD YOU? I'M A MEMBER OF THIS ORCHESTRA TOO!
GAH!
ELES!
I'M THE ONE...
TH THUMP
...WHO'S REALLY LOW.
BUT...
TH THUMP
...I CAN'T SAY IT!!
WE CAN'T BRING YOU WITH US.
TH THUMP
EVEN IF LUCILLE **WAS** GOING TO LEAVE ME BEHIND...
NO... I HAVE TO TELL HIM!
AFTER I'VE SUNG THIS PIECE, THERE MAY BE NOBODY LEFT TO PROTECT YOU.
THAT'S WHY...

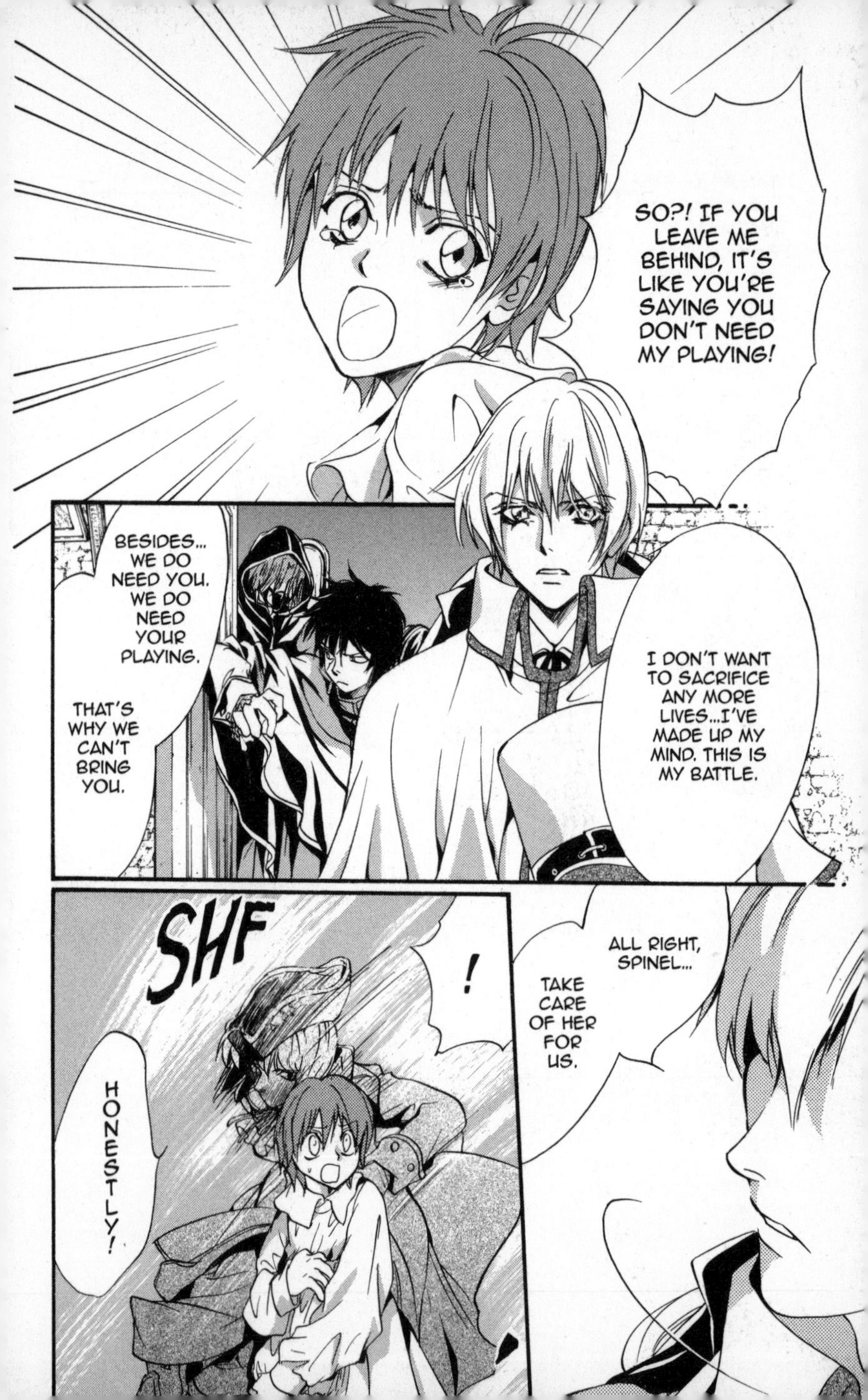
SO?! IF YOU LEAVE ME BEHIND, IT'S LIKE YOU'RE SAYING YOU DON'T NEED MY PLAYING!
I DON'T WANT TO SACRIFICE ANY MORE LIVES...I'VE MADE UP MY MIND. THIS IS MY BATTLE.
BESIDES... WE DO NEED YOU. WE DO NEED YOUR PLAYING.
THAT'S WHY WE CAN'T BRING YOU.
ALL RIGHT, SPINEL...
TAKE CARE OF HER FOR US.
!
SHF
HONESTLY!

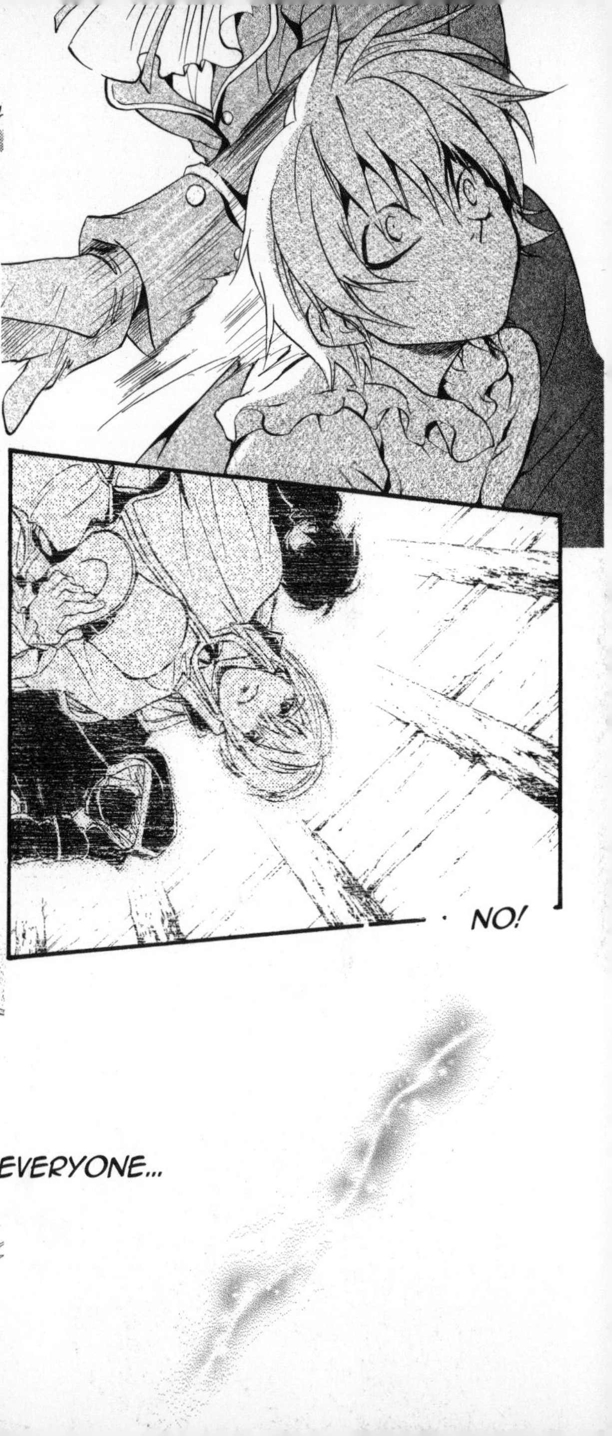
NO!
EVERYONE...

The sketch below is another early version of Berthier. I'd forgotten how much I agonized over his design.

This one got reused as one of the masked forces. Recycling!

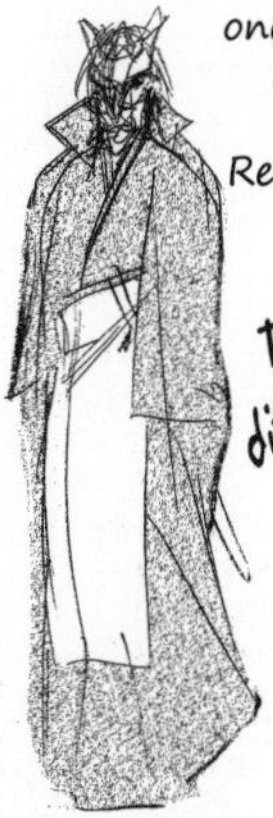
totally different!

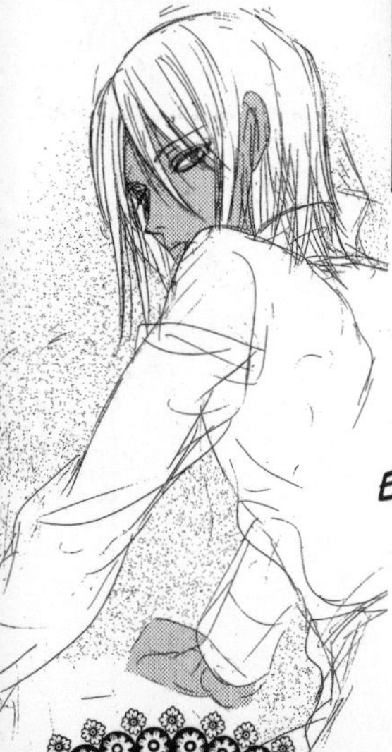

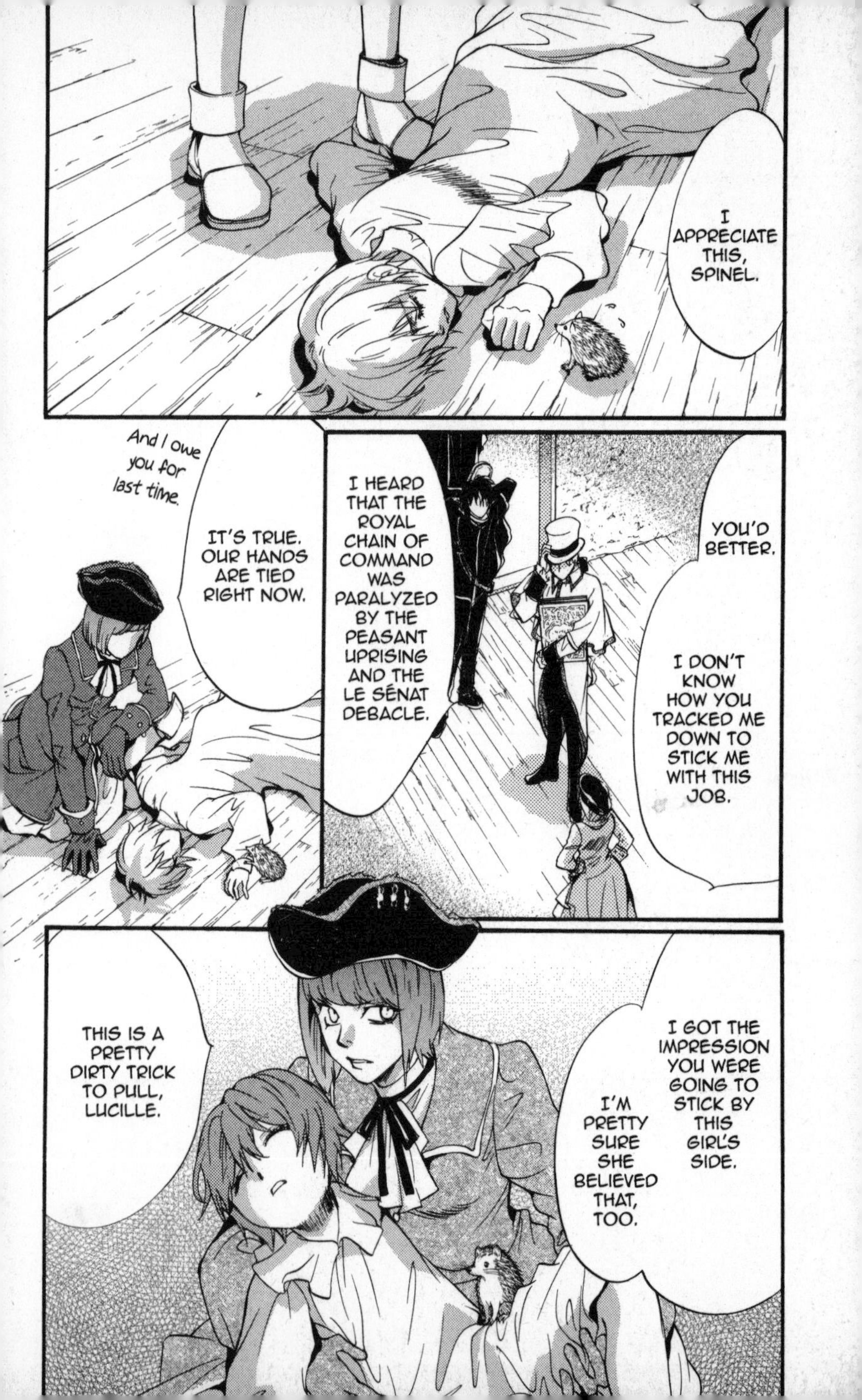
I APPRECIATE THIS, SPINEL.
YOU'D BETTER.
I DON'T KNOW HOW YOU TRACKED ME DOWN TO STICK ME WITH THIS JOB.
I HEARD THAT THE ROYAL CHAIN OF COMMAND WAS PARALYZED BY THE PEASANT UPRISING AND THE LE SÉNAT DEBACLE.
IT'S TRUE. OUR HANDS ARE TIED RIGHT NOW.
And I owe you for last time.
I GOT THE IMPRESSION YOU WERE GOING TO STICK BY THIS GIRL'S SIDE.
I'M PRETTY SURE SHE BELIEVED THAT, TOO.
THIS IS A PRETTY DIRTY TRICK TO PULL, LUCILLE.

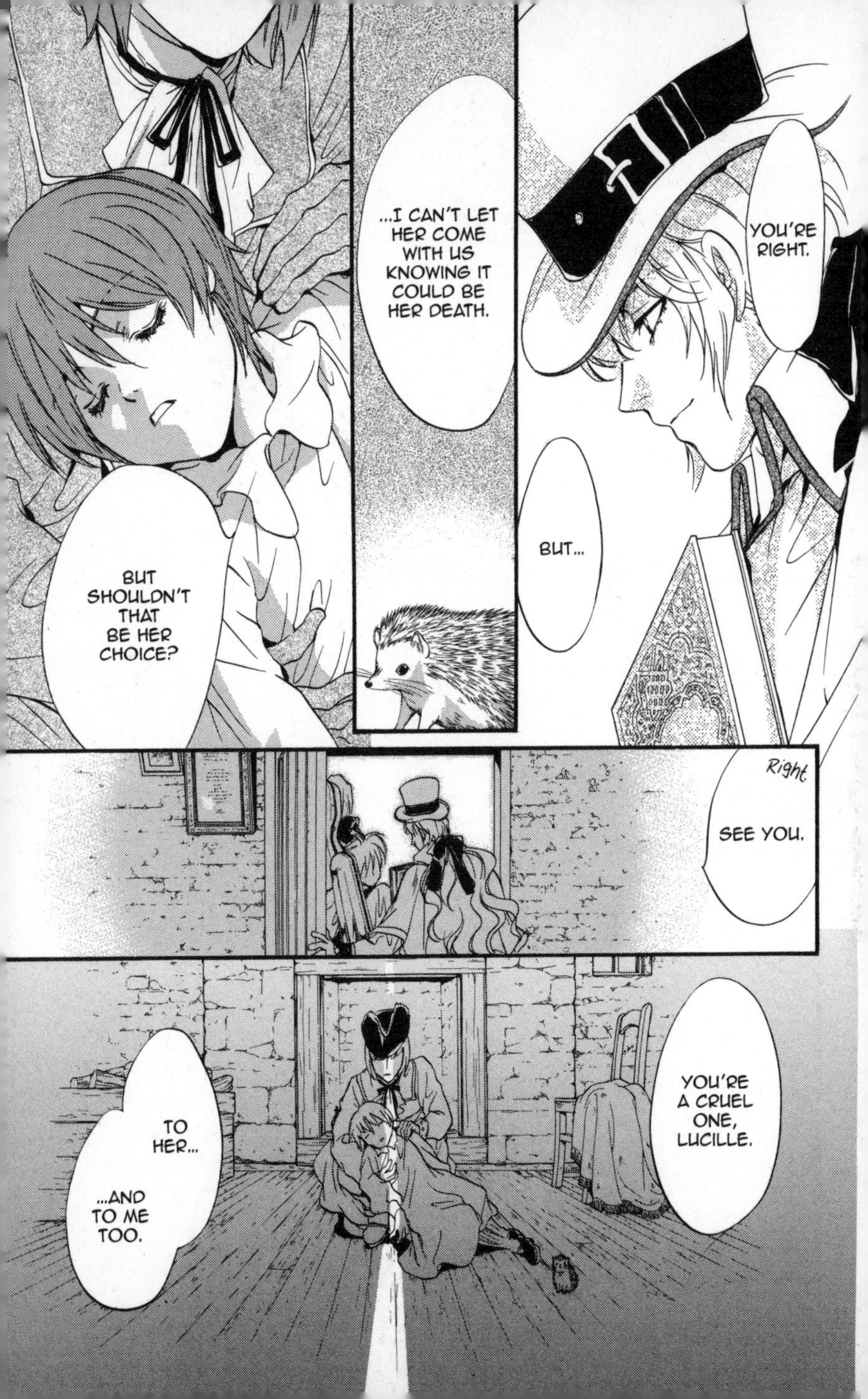
YOU'RE RIGHT.
BUT...
...I CAN'T LET HER COME WITH US KNOWING IT COULD BE HER DEATH.
BUT SHOULDN'T THAT BE HER CHOICE?
Right.
SEE YOU.
YOU'RE A CRUEL ONE, LUCILLE.
TO HER...
...AND TO ME TOO.

DON'T GO... NO!

LUCILLE!

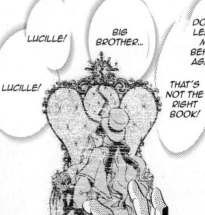

LUCILLE!

LUCILLE!

BIG BROTHER...

DON'T LEAVE ME BEHIND AGAIN!

THAT'S NOT THE RIGHT BOOK!

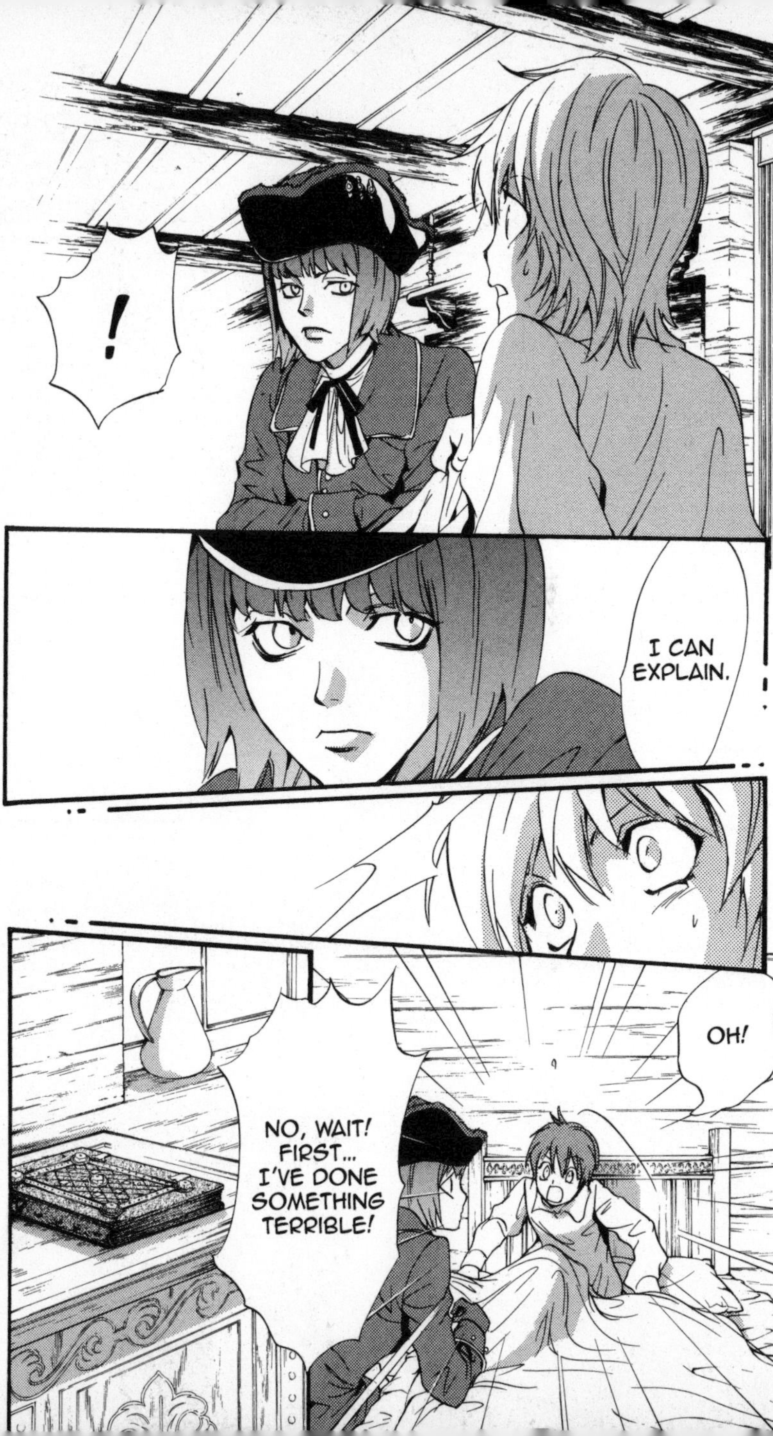
!
I CAN EXPLAIN.
OH!
NO, WAIT! FIRST... I'VE DONE SOMETHING TERRIBLE!

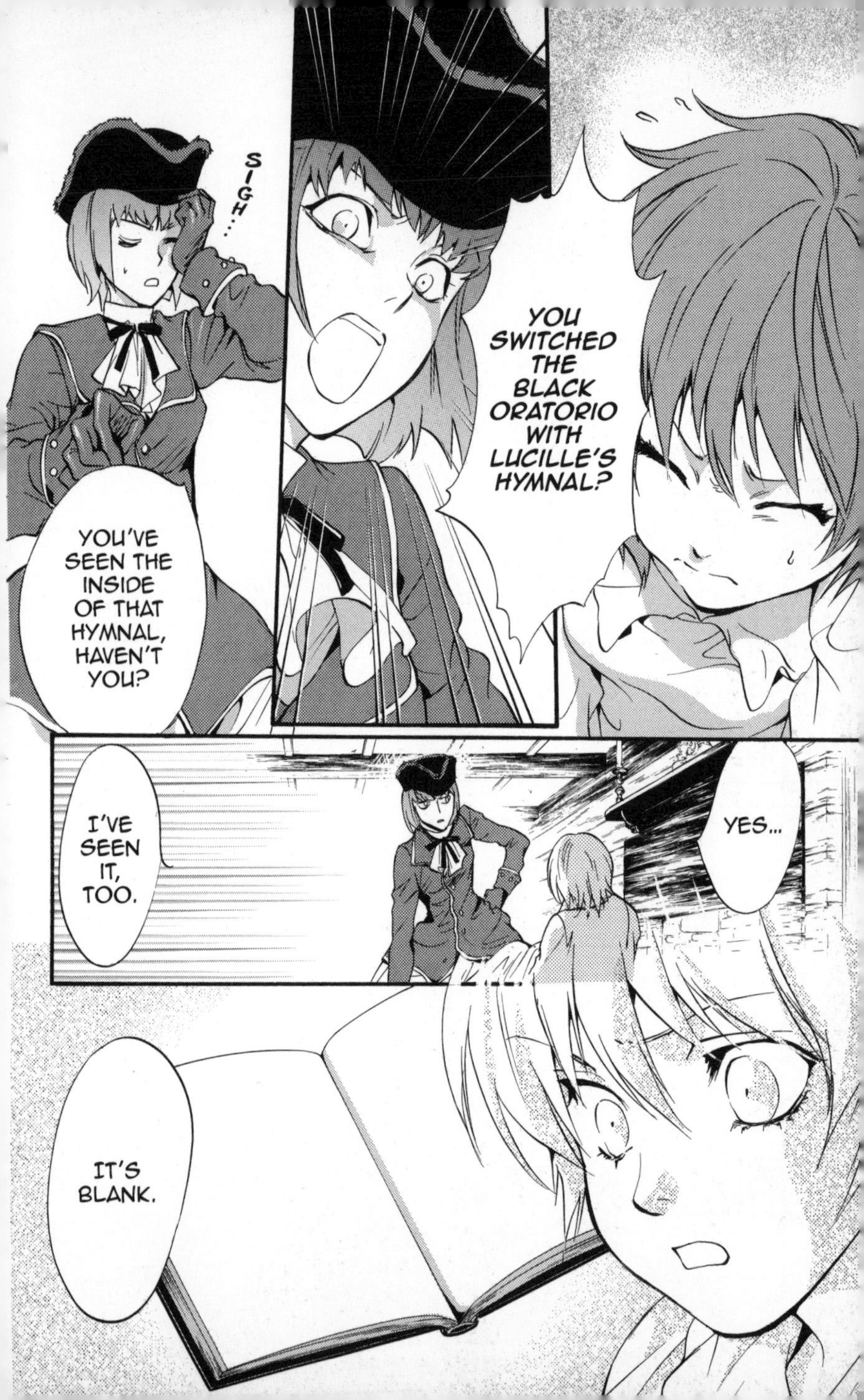
YOU SWITCHED THE BLACK ORATORIO WITH LUCILLE'S HYMNAL?
SIGH...
YOU'VE SEEN THE INSIDE OF THAT HYMNAL, HAVEN'T YOU?
YES...
I'VE SEEN IT, TOO.
IT'S BLANK.

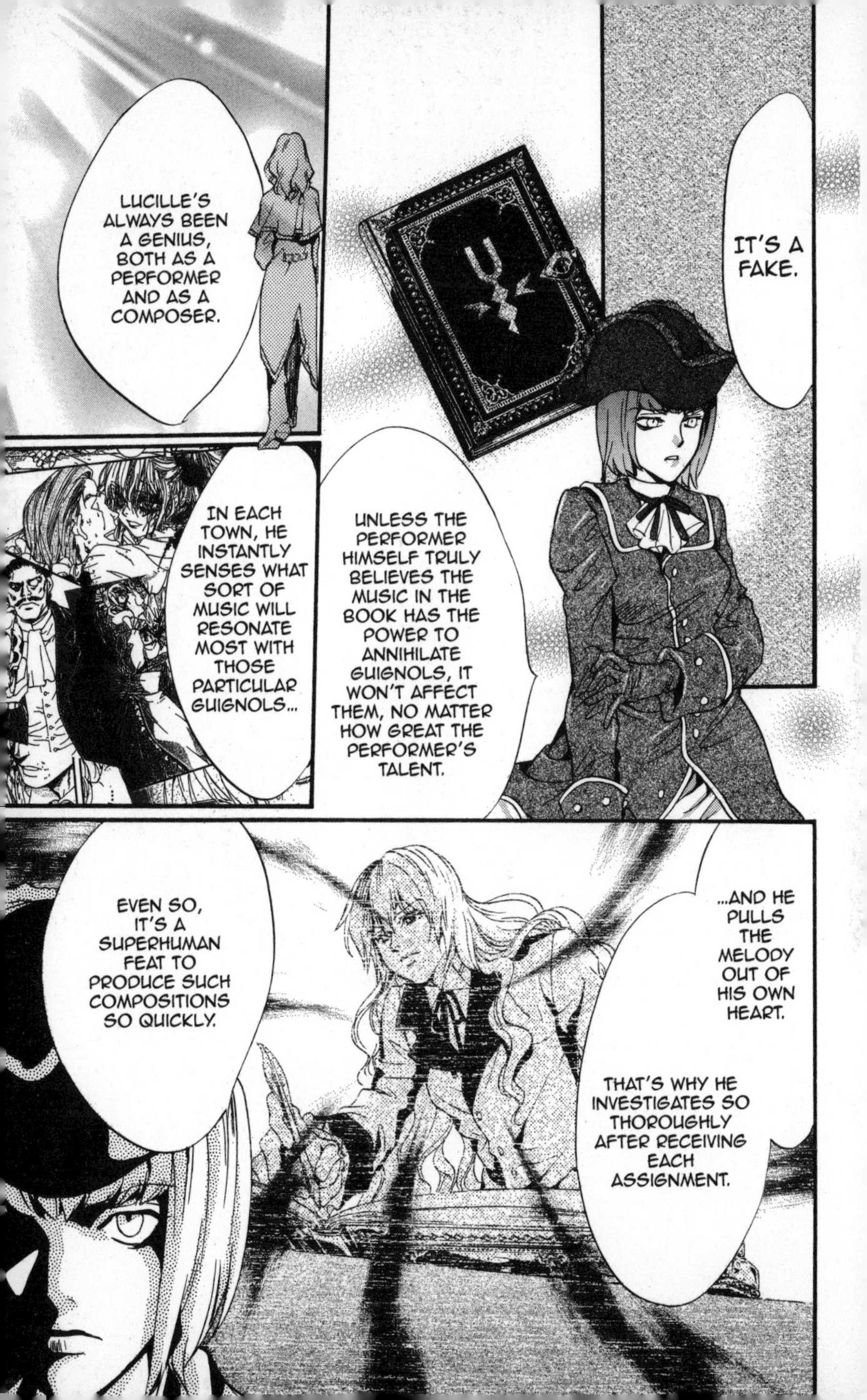
IT'S A FAKE.
UNLESS THE PERFORMER HIMSELF TRULY BELIEVES THE MUSIC IN THE BOOK HAS THE POWER TO ANNIHILATE GUIGNOLS, IT WON'T AFFECT THEM, NO MATTER HOW GREAT THE PERFORMER'S TALENT.
LUCILLE'S ALWAYS BEEN A GENIUS, BOTH AS A PERFORMER AND AS A COMPOSER.
IN EACH TOWN, HE INSTANTLY SENSES WHAT SORT OF MUSIC WILL RESONATE MOST WITH THOSE PARTICULAR GUIGNOLS...
...AND HE PULLS THE MELODY OUT OF HIS OWN HEART.
THAT'S WHY HE INVESTIGATES SO THOROUGHLY AFTER RECEIVING EACH ASSIGNMENT.
EVEN SO, IT'S A SUPERHUMAN FEAT TO PRODUCE SUCH COMPOSITIONS SO QUICKLY.

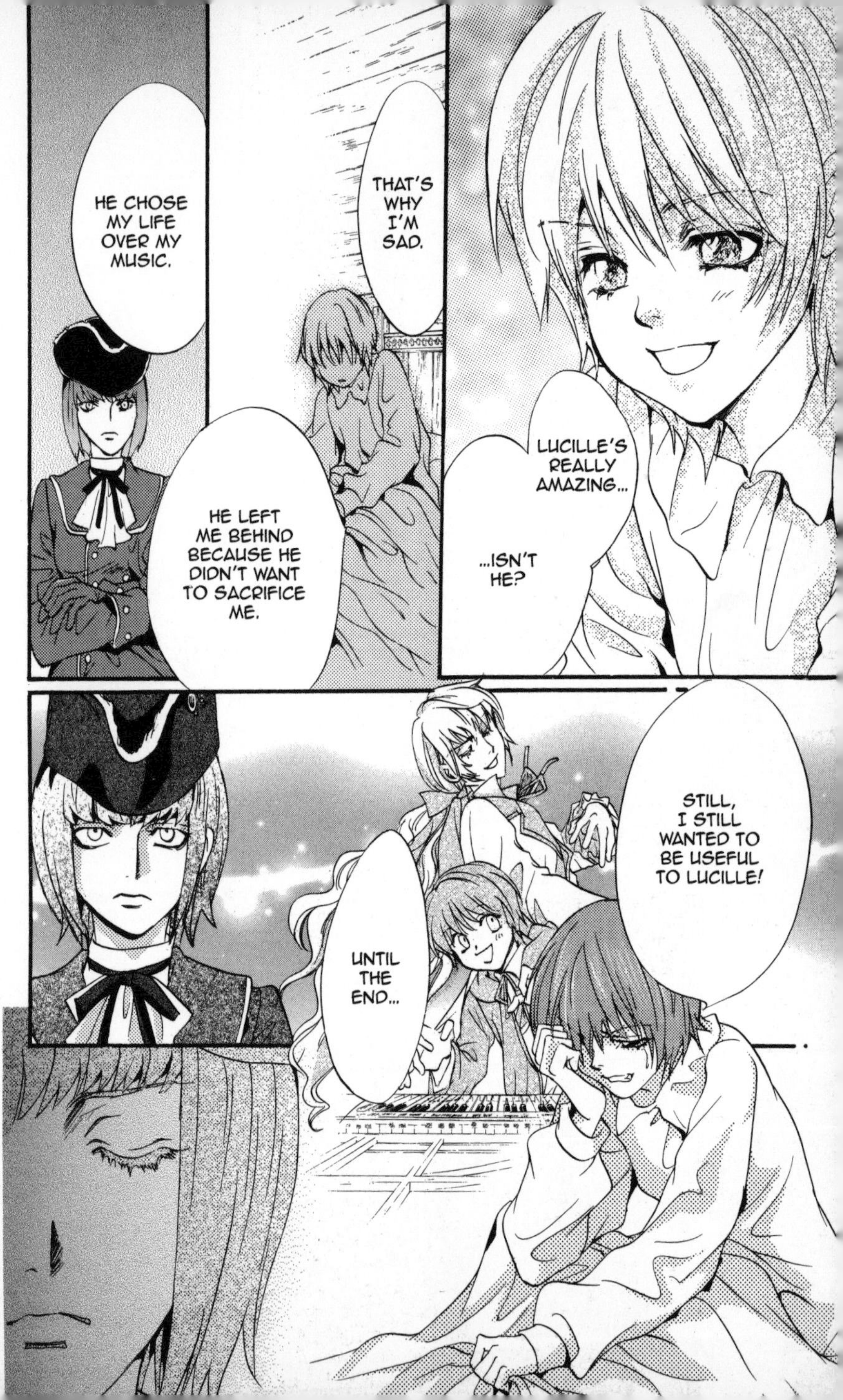
LUCILLE'S REALLY AMAZING...
...ISN'T HE?
THAT'S WHY I'M SAD.
HE LEFT ME BEHIND BECAUSE HE DIDN'T WANT TO SACRIFICE ME.
HE CHOSE MY LIFE OVER MY MUSIC.
STILL, I STILL WANTED TO BE USEFUL TO LUCILLE!
UNTIL THE END...

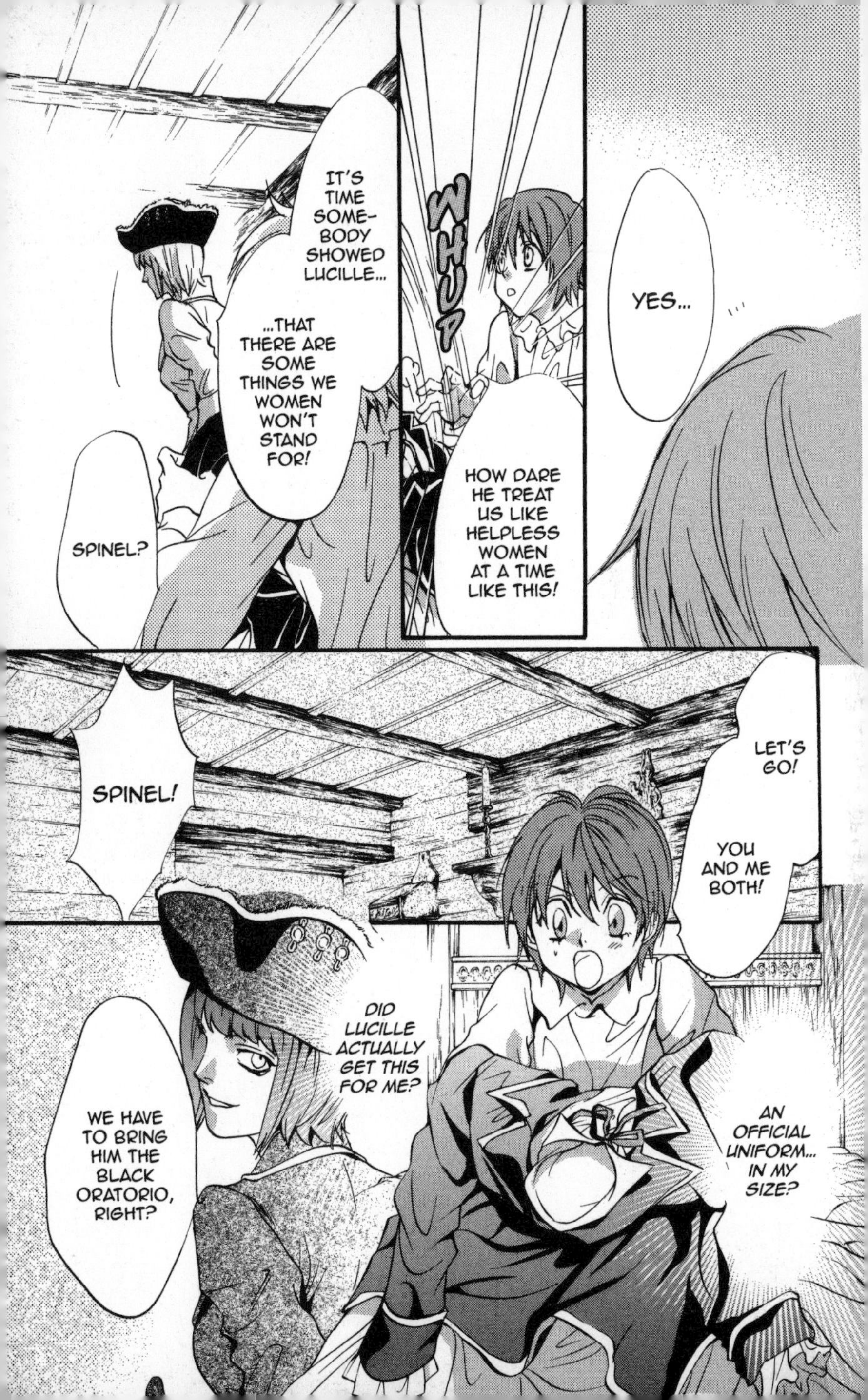
YES...
WHUP
HOW DARE HE TREAT US LIKE HELPLESS WOMEN AT A TIME LIKE THIS!
IT'S TIME SOMEBODY SHOWED LUCILLE...
...THAT THERE ARE SOME THINGS WE WOMEN WON'T STAND FOR!
SPINEL?
LET'S GO!
YOU AND ME BOTH!
SPINEL!
AN OFFICIAL UNIFORM... IN MY SIZE?
DID LUCILLE ACTUALLY GET THIS FOR ME?
WE HAVE TO BRING HIM THE BLACK ORATORIO, RIGHT?

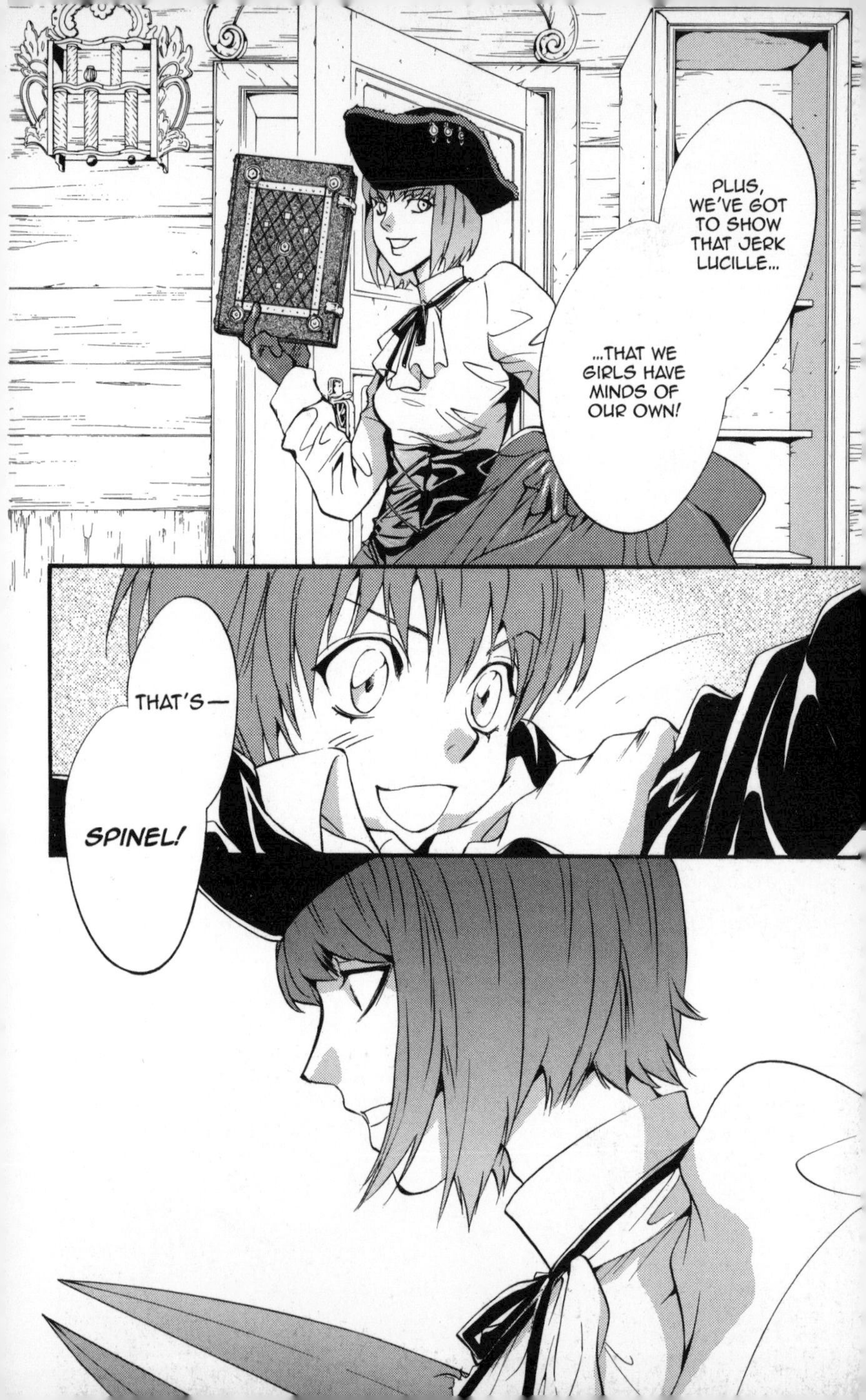
PLUS, WE'VE GOT TO SHOW THAT JERK LUCILLE...
...THAT WE GIRLS HAVE MINDS OF OUR OWN!
THAT'S—
SPINEL!

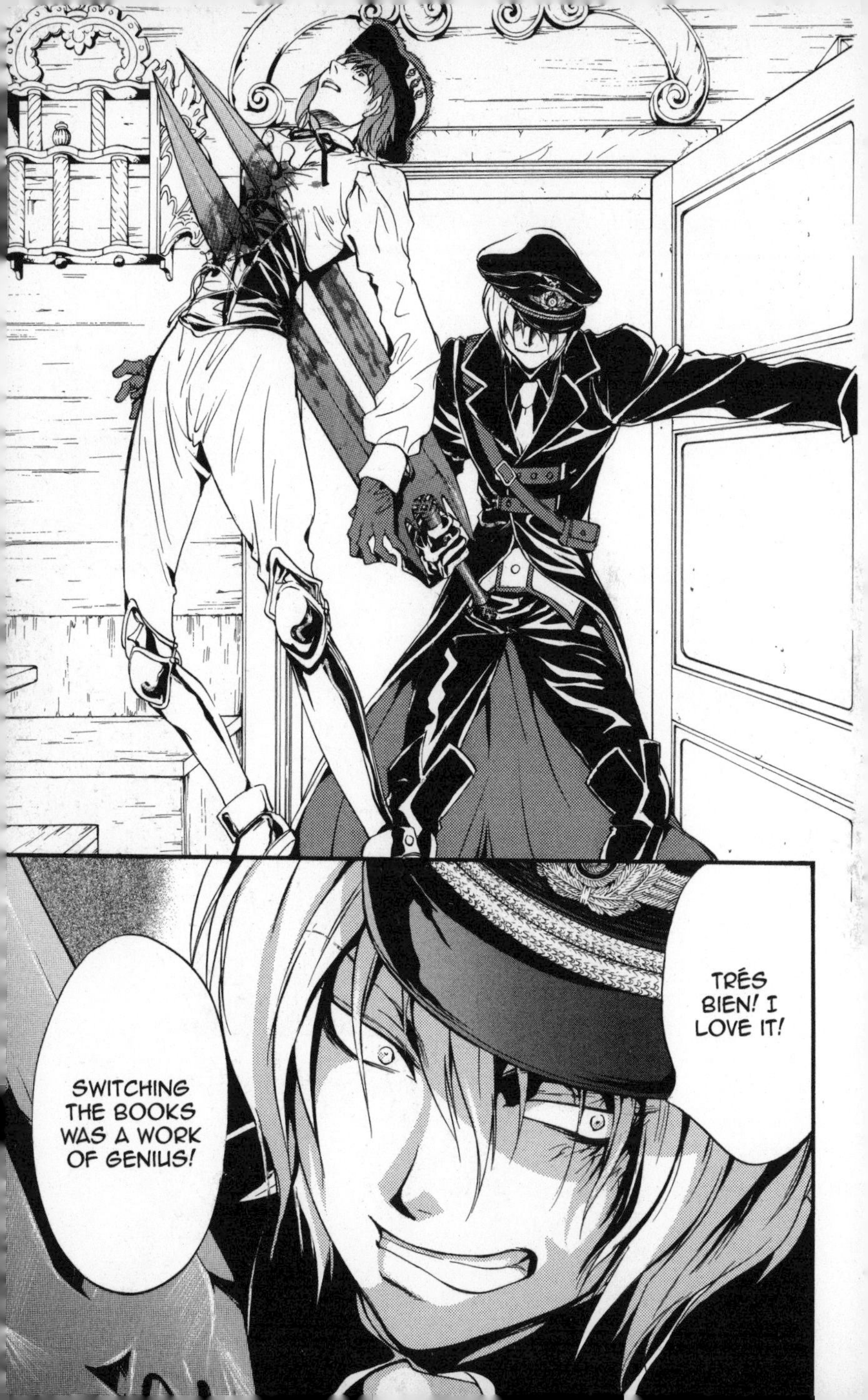
TRÉS BIEN! I LOVE IT!
SWITCHING THE BOOKS WAS A WORK OF GENIUS!

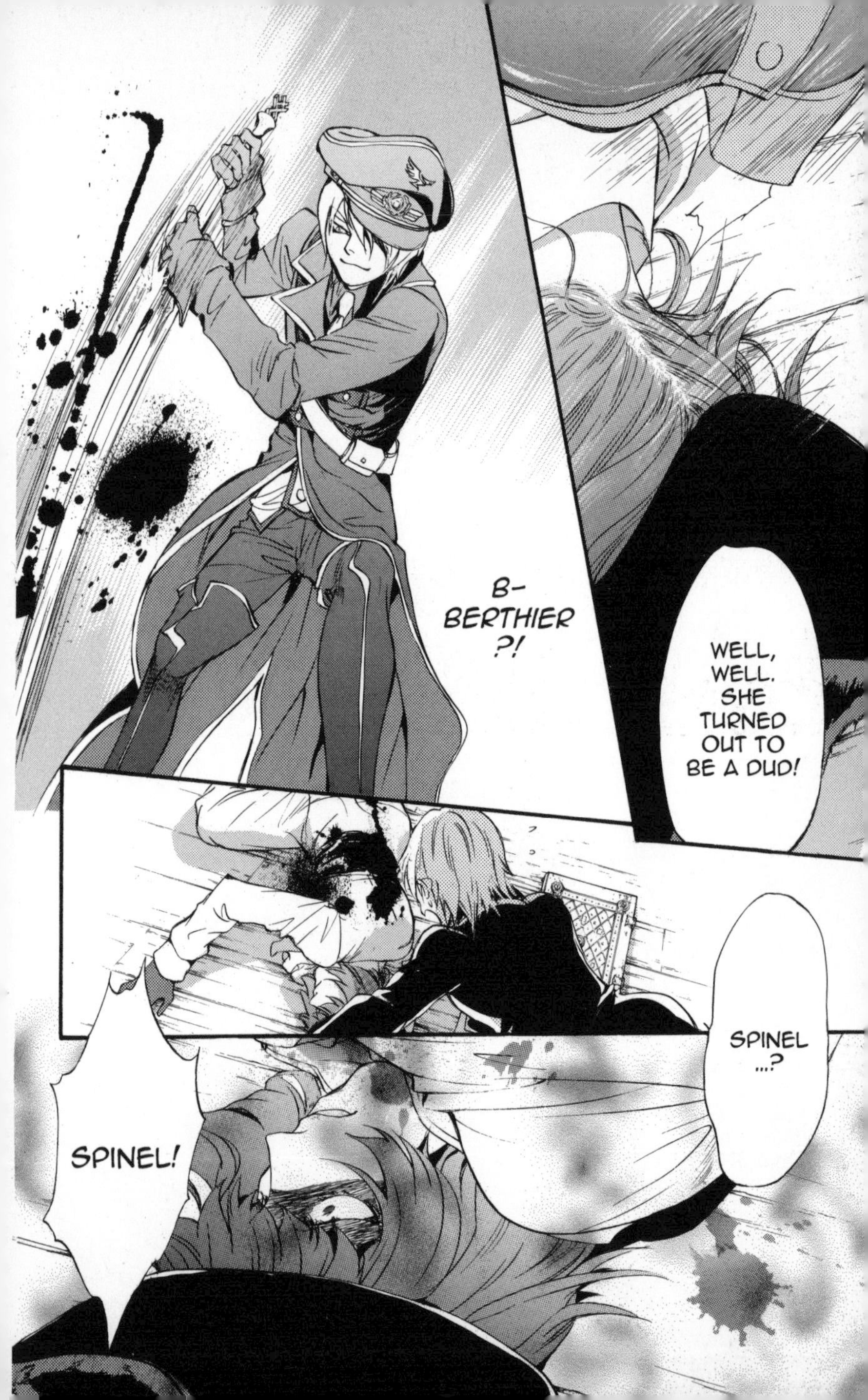
WELL, WELL. SHE TURNED OUT TO BE A DUD!
B-BERTHIER?!
SPINEL...?
SPINEL!

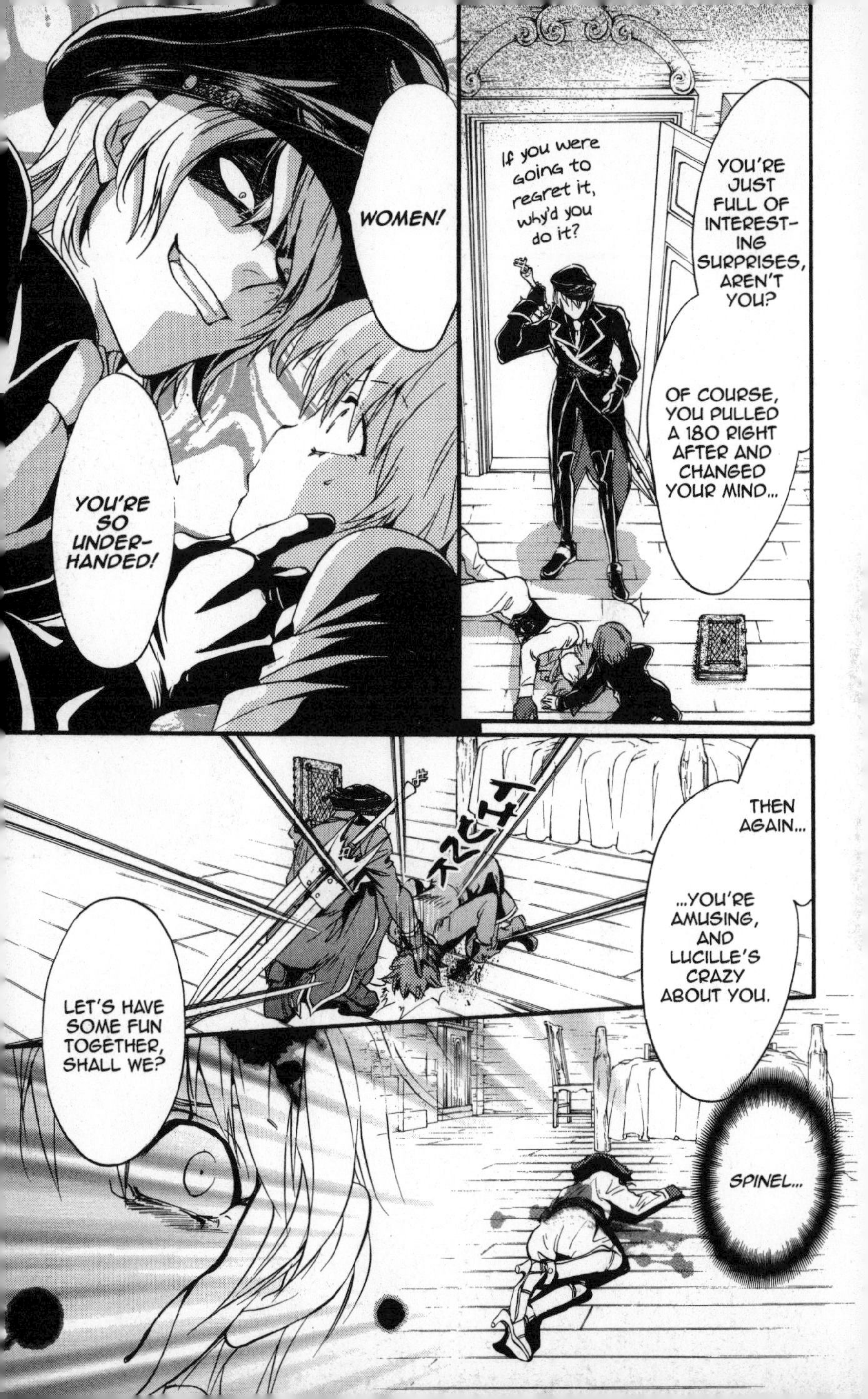
YOU'RE JUST FULL OF INTERESTING SURPRISES, AREN'T YOU?
If you were going to regret it, why'd you do it?
OF COURSE, YOU PULLED A 180 RIGHT AFTER AND CHANGED YOUR MIND...
WOMEN!
YOU'RE SO UNDERHANDED!
THEN AGAIN...
...YOU'RE AMUSING, AND LUCILLE'S CRAZY ABOUT YOU.
THUNK
LET'S HAVE SOME FUN TOGETHER, SHALL WE?
SPINEL...

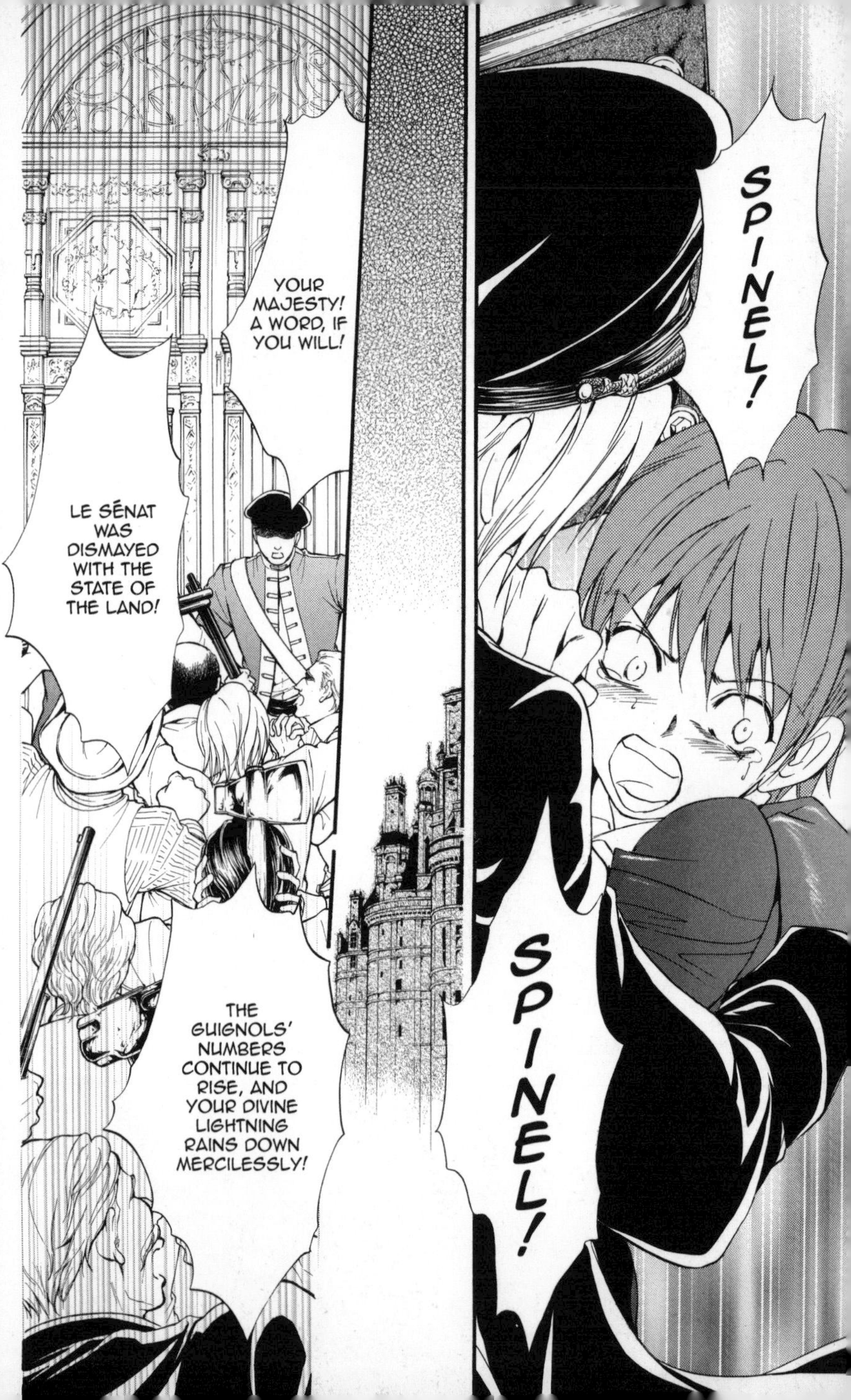
SPINEL!
SPINEL!
YOUR MAJESTY! A WORD, IF YOU WILL!
LE SÉNAT WAS DISMAYED WITH THE STATE OF THE LAND!
THE GUIGNOLS' NUMBERS CONTINUE TO RISE, AND YOUR DIVINE LIGHTNING RAINS DOWN MERCILESSLY!

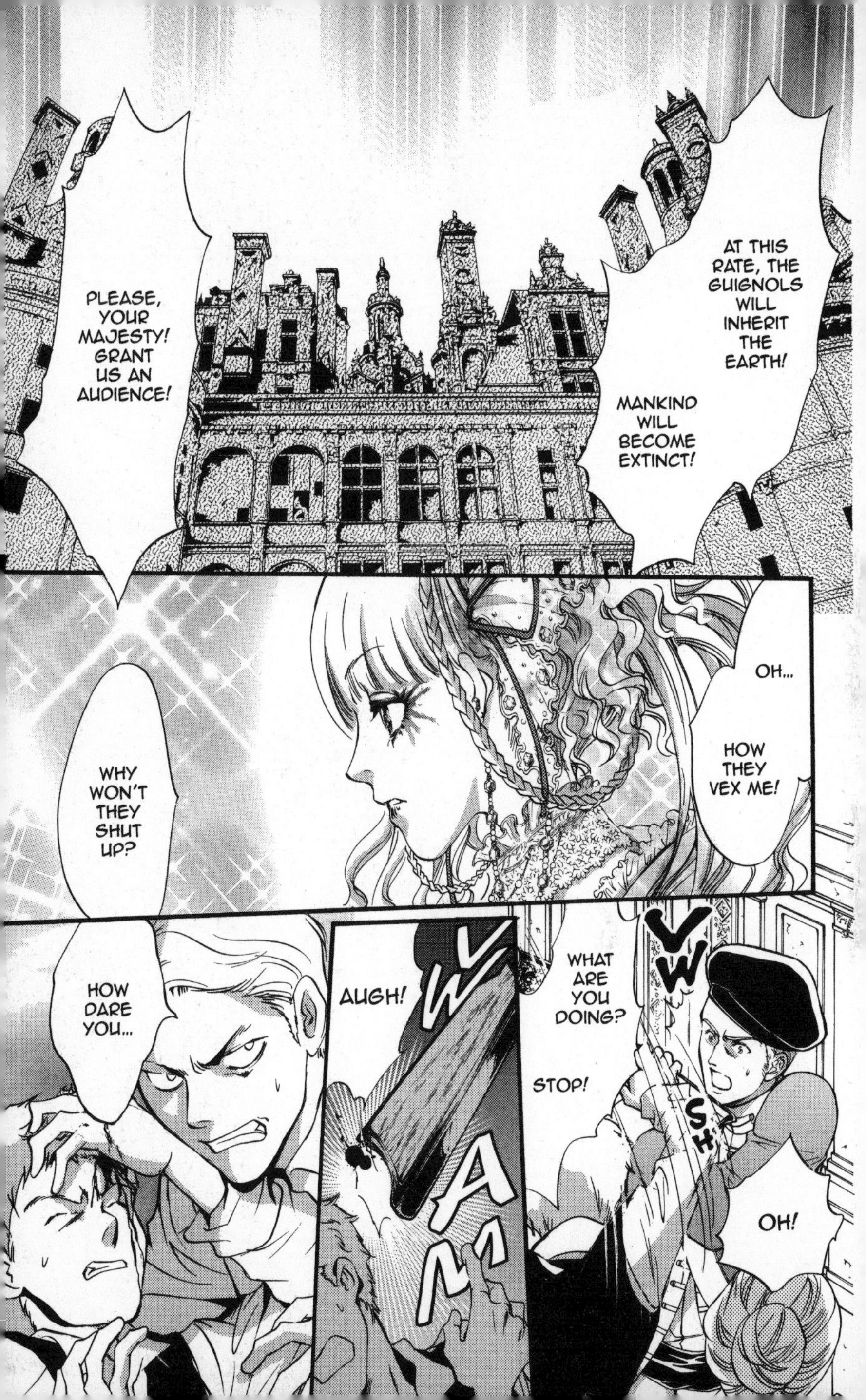
AT THIS RATE, THE GUIGNOLS WILL INHERIT THE EARTH!
MANKIND WILL BECOME EXTINCT!
PLEASE, YOUR MAJESTY! GRANT US AN AUDIENCE!
OH...
HOW THEY VEX ME!
WHY WON'T THEY SHUT UP?
VWSH
WHAT ARE YOU DOING?
STOP!
OH!
VWAM
AUGH!
HOW DARE YOU...

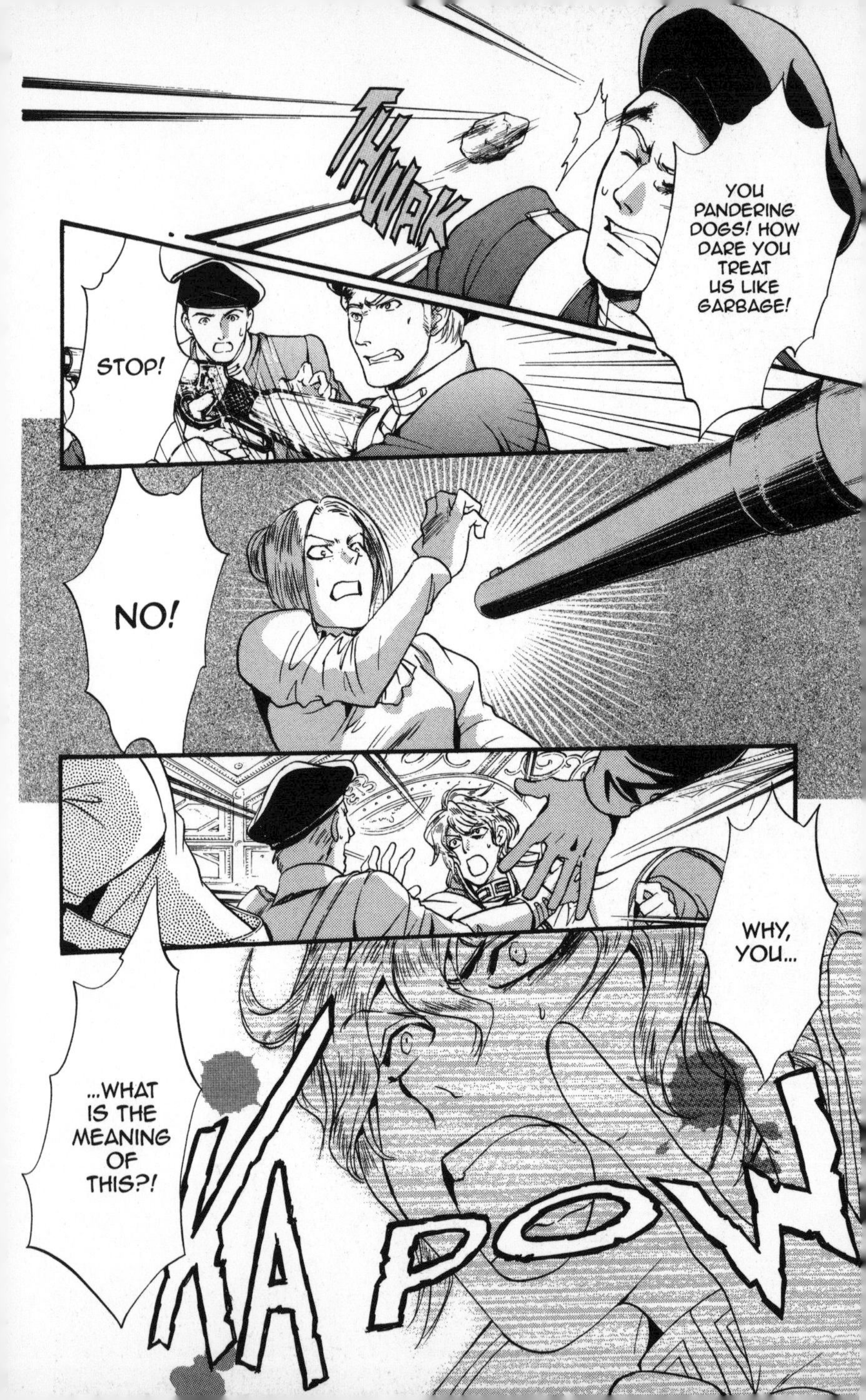
YOU PANDERING DOGS! HOW DARE YOU TREAT US LIKE GARBAGE!
THWAK
STOP!
NO!
WHY, YOU...
...WHAT IS THE MEANING OF THIS?!
KA POW

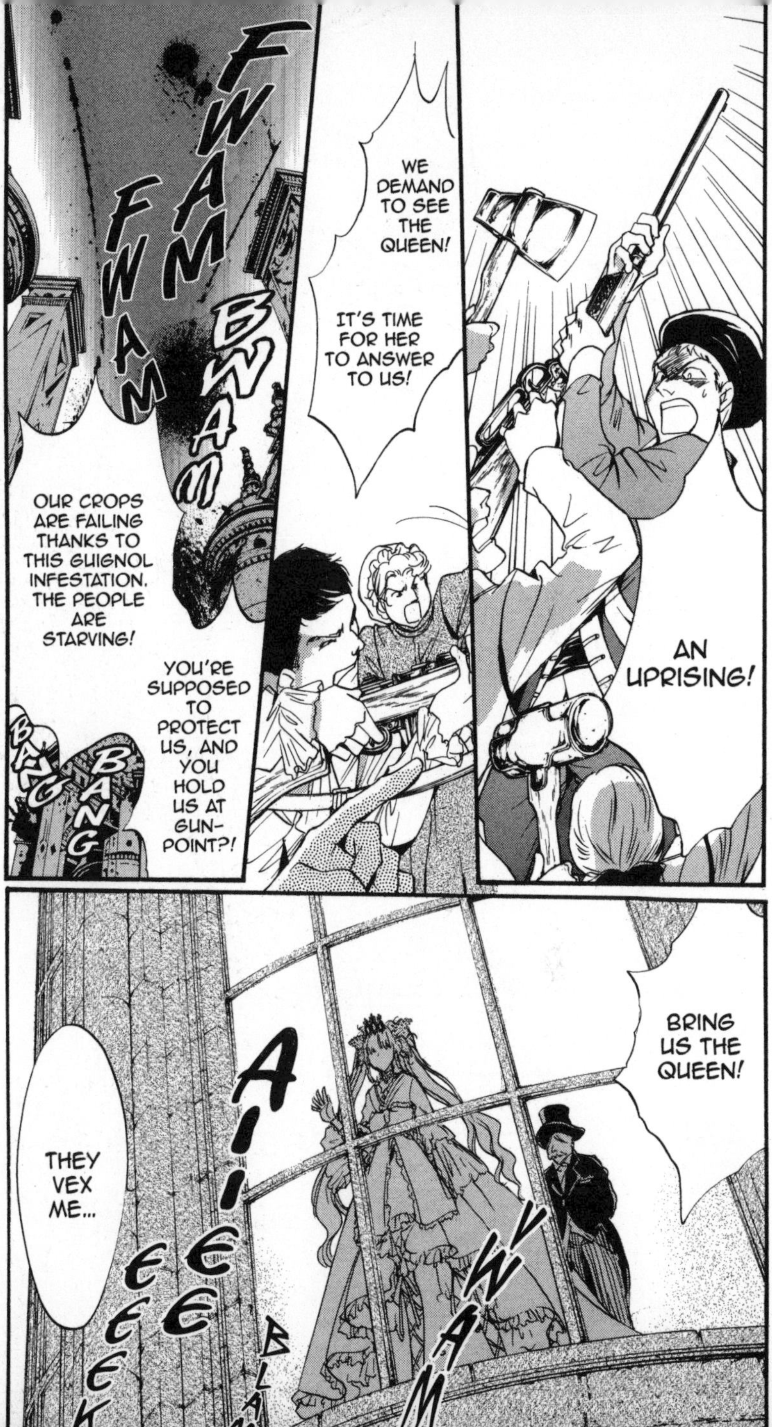
AN UPRISING!
WE DEMAND TO SEE THE QUEEN!
IT'S TIME FOR HER TO ANSWER TO US!
YOU'RE SUPPOSED TO PROTECT US, AND YOU HOLD US AT GUN-POINT?!
FWAM
FWAM
BWAM
OUR CROPS ARE FAILING THANKS TO THIS GUIGNOL INFESTATION. THE PEOPLE ARE STARVING!
BANG
BANG
BRING US THE QUEEN!
VWAM
BLAM
AIIEEEEEEK
THEY VEX ME...

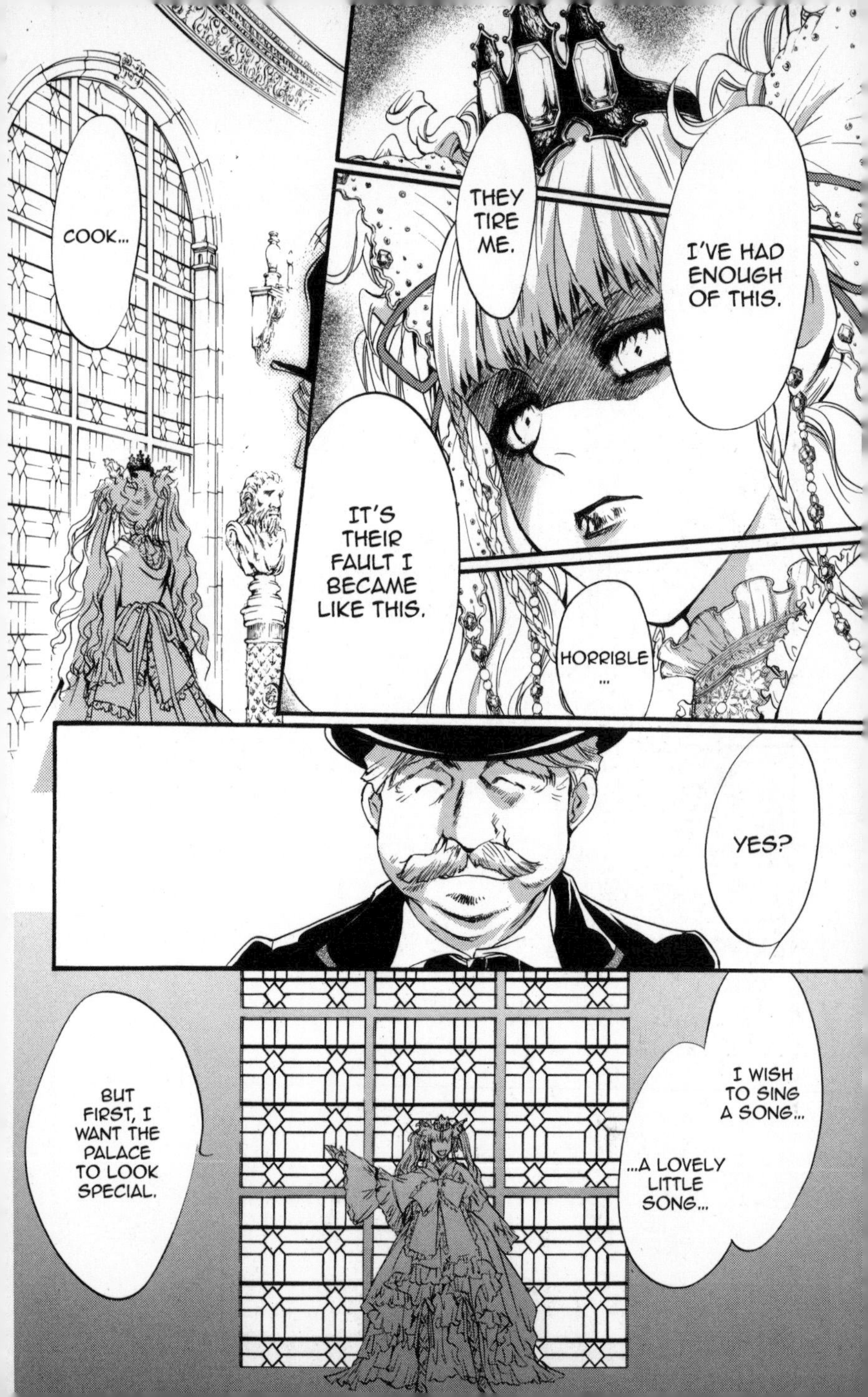
I'VE HAD ENOUGH OF THIS.
THEY TIRE ME.
IT'S THEIR FAULT I BECAME LIKE THIS.
HORRIBLE...
COOK...
YES?
I WISH TO SING A SONG...
...A LOVELY LITTLE SONG...
BUT FIRST, I WANT THE PALACE TO LOOK SPECIAL.

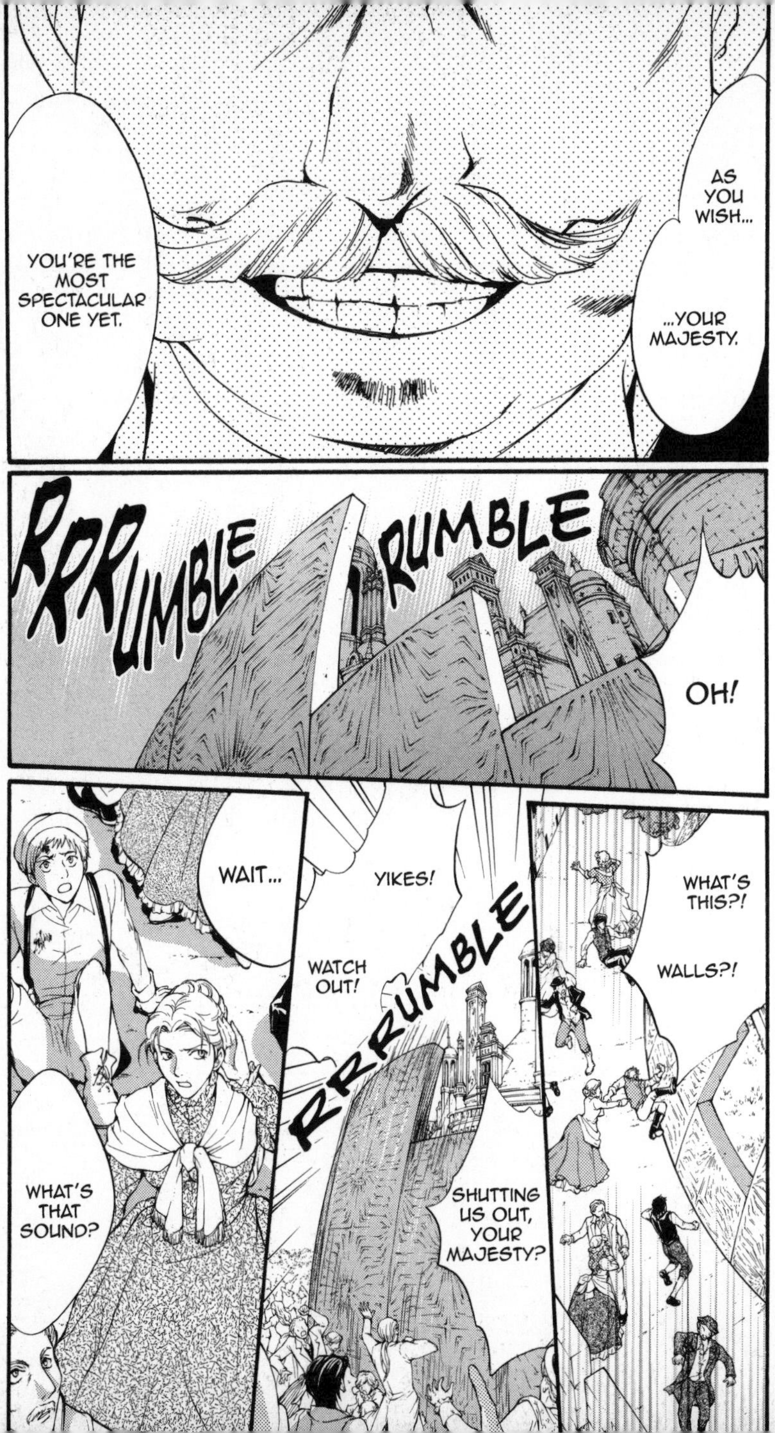
AS YOU WISH...
...YOUR MAJESTY.
YOU'RE THE MOST SPECTACULAR ONE YET.
RUMBLE
OH!
RRRUMBLE
WHAT'S THIS?!
WALLS?!
YIKES!
WATCH OUT!
RRRUMBLE
SHUTTING US OUT, YOUR MAJESTY?
WAIT...
WHAT'S THAT SOUND?

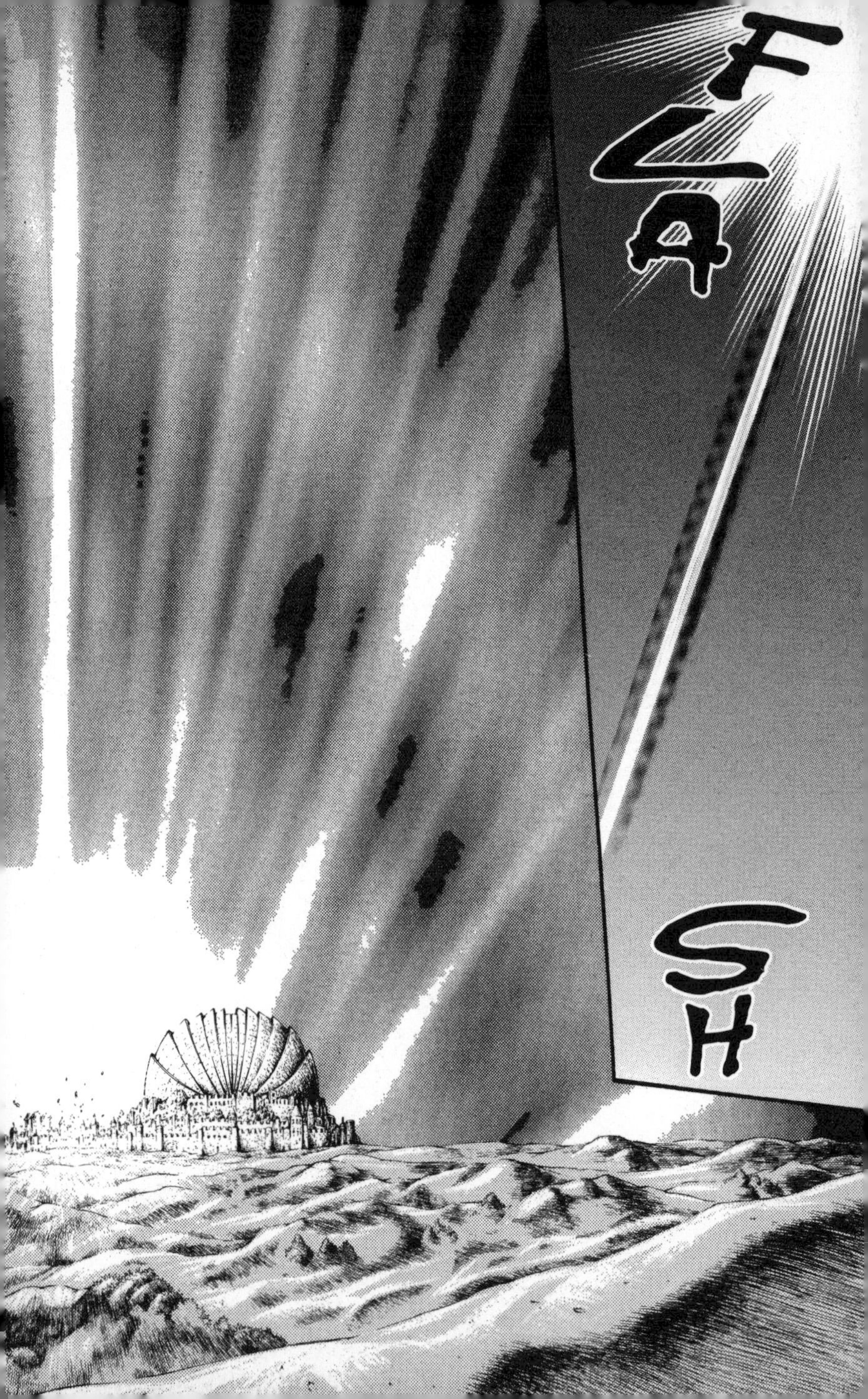
FLASH

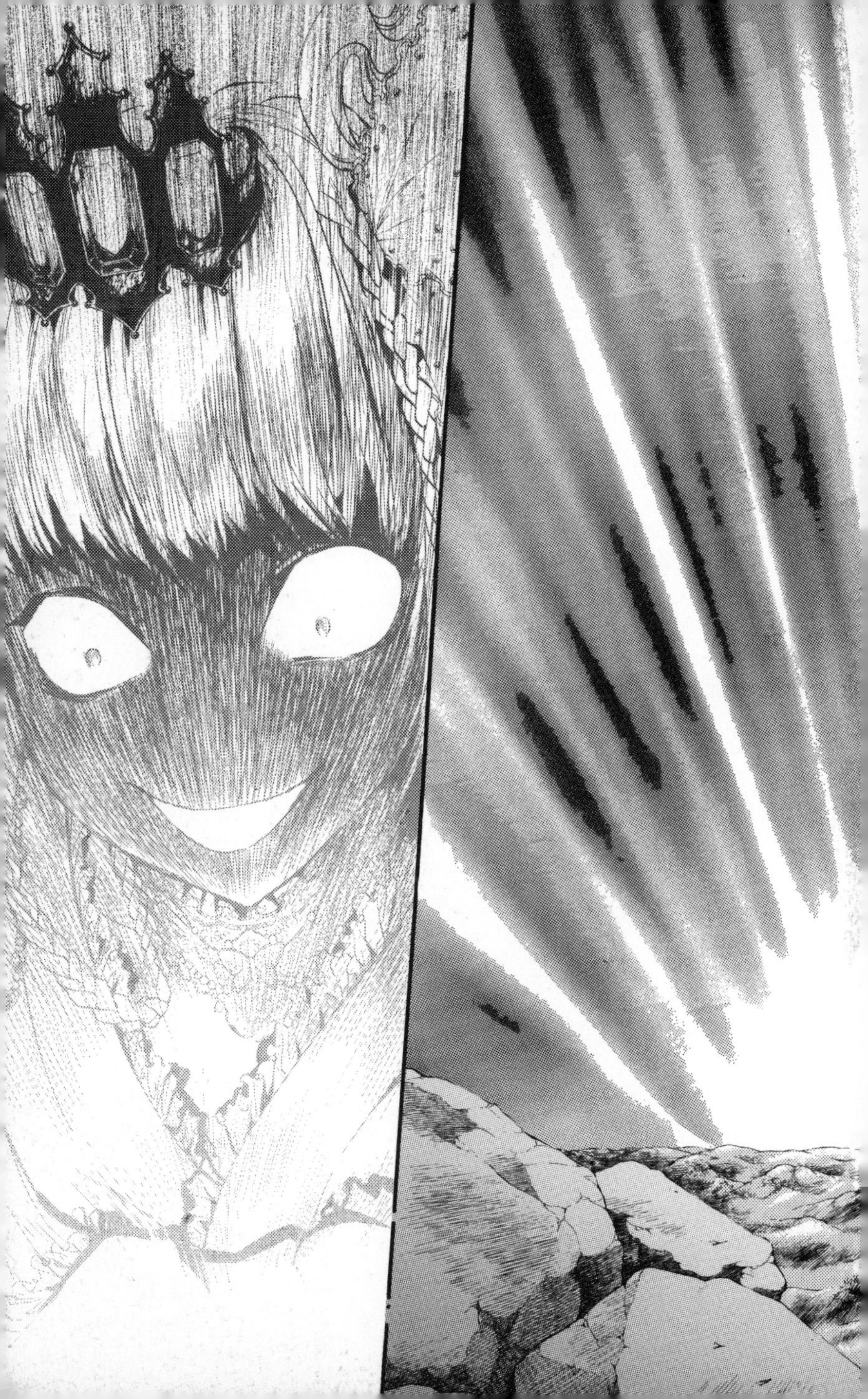

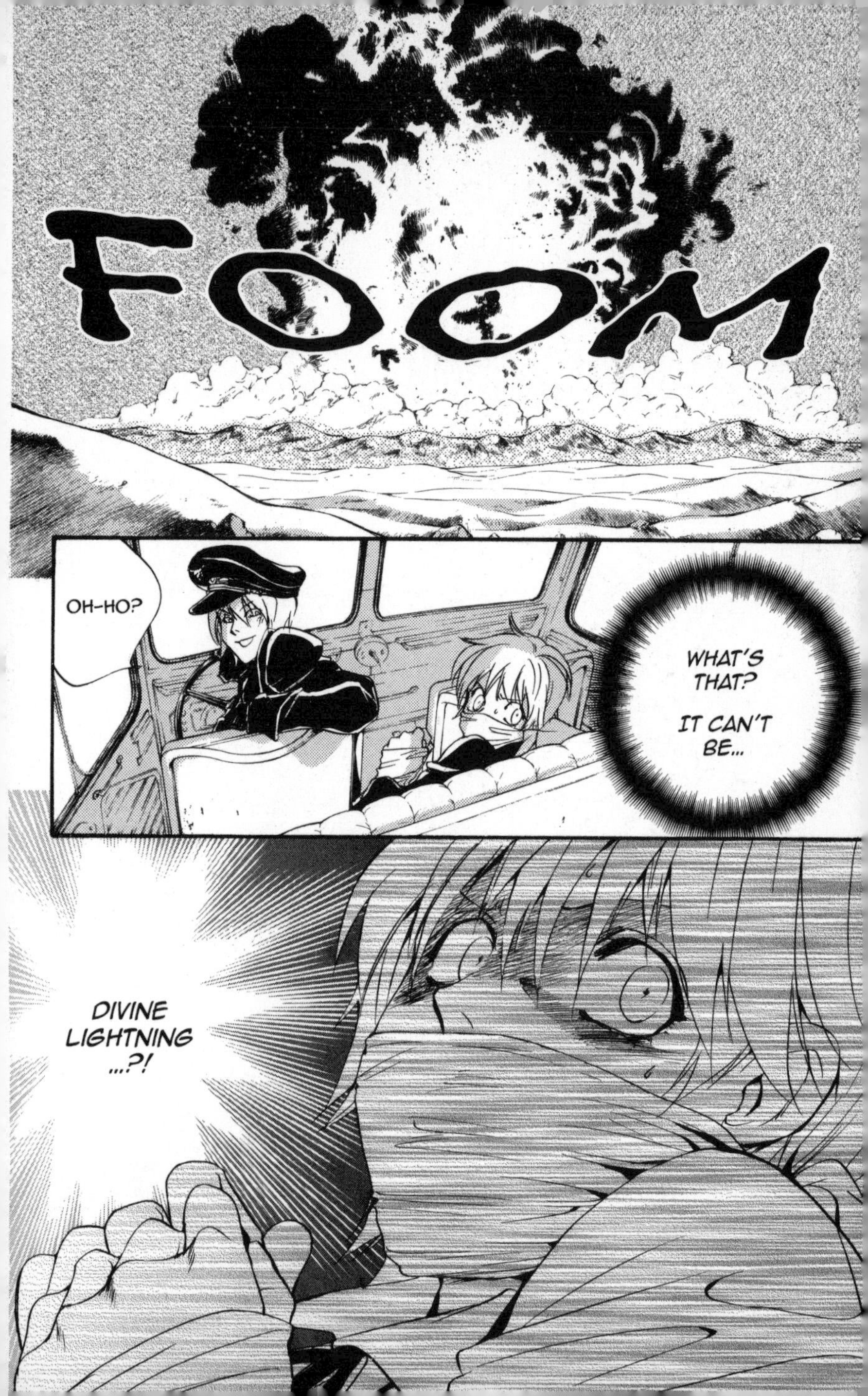
FOOM
WHAT'S THAT?
IT CAN'T BE...
OH-HO?
DIVINE LIGHTNING ...?!

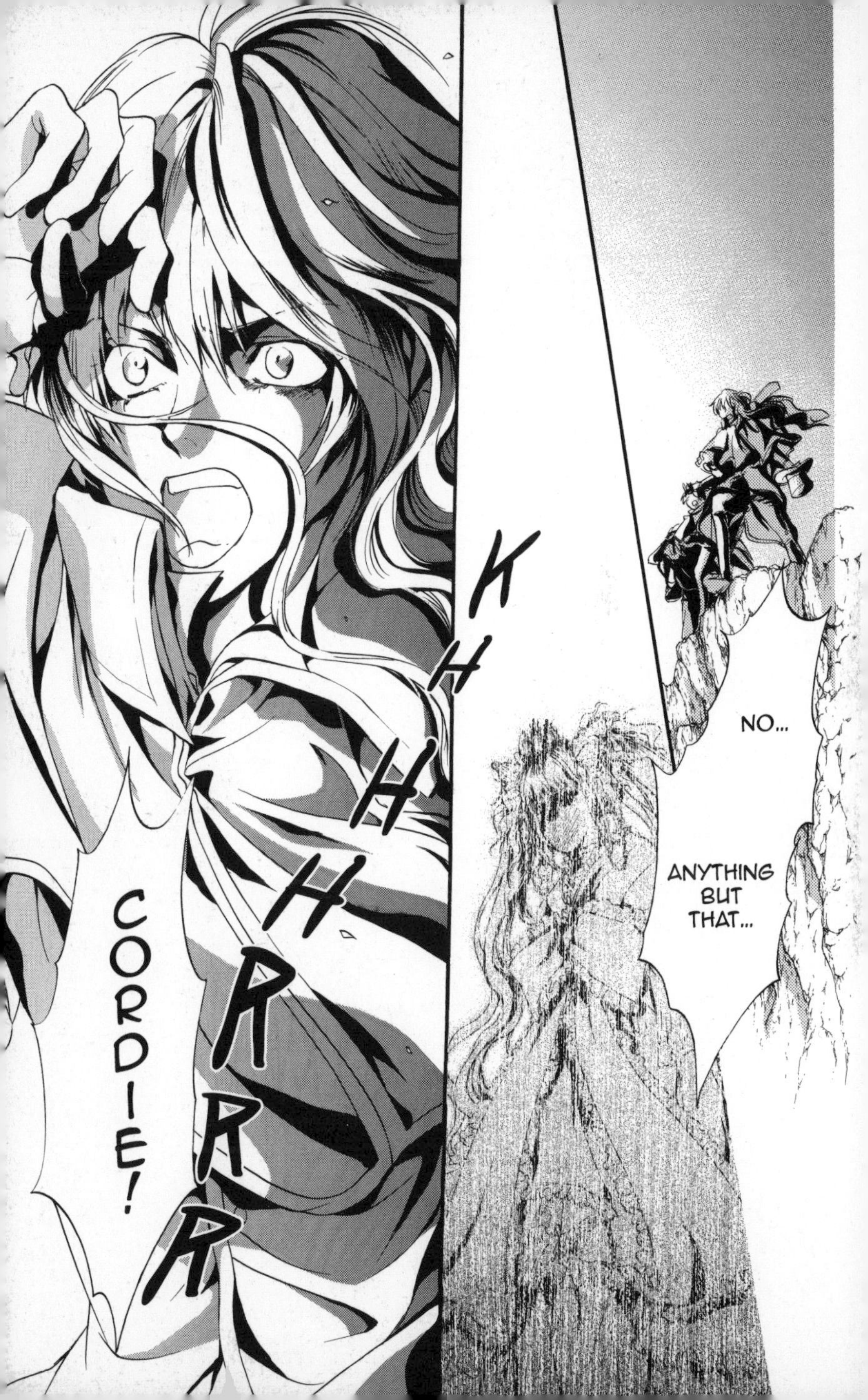
NO...
ANYTHING BUT THAT...
KHHHRRR
CORDIE!

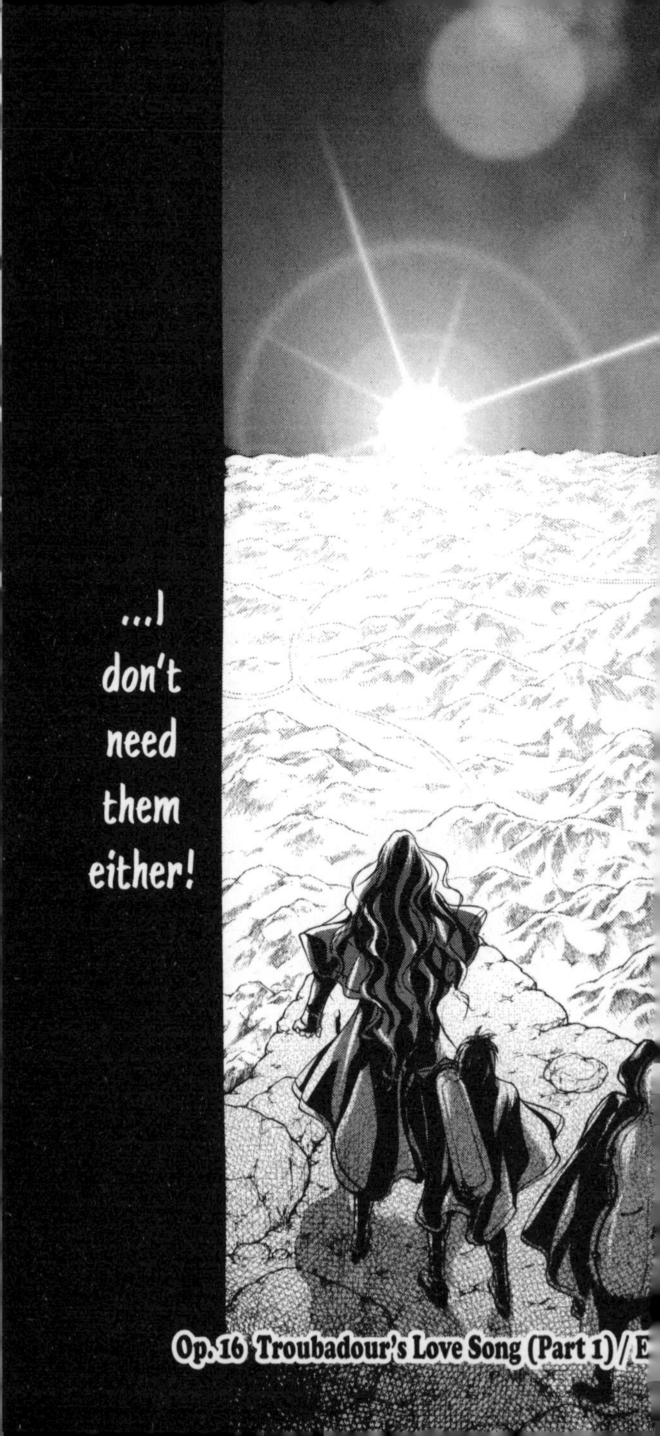
...I don't need them either!
Op. 16 Troubadour's Love Song (Part 1)/ E

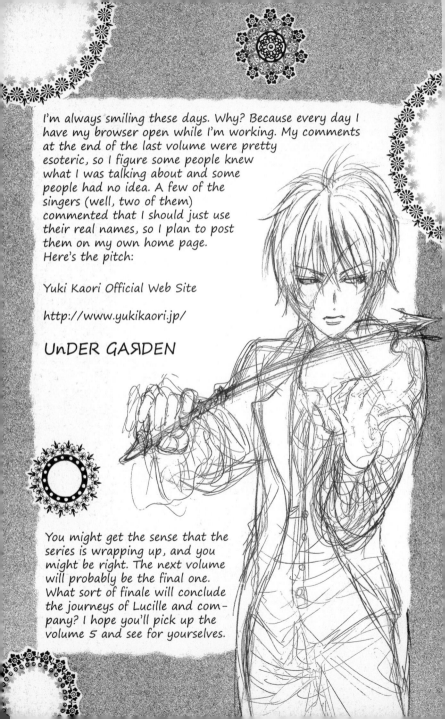

I'm always smiling these days. Why? Because every day I have my browser open while I'm working. My comments at the end of the last volume were pretty esoteric, so I figure some people knew what I was talking about and some people had no idea. A few of the singers (well, two of them) commented that I should just use their real names, so I plan to post them on my own home page. Here's the pitch:

Yuki Kaori Official Web Site

http://www.yukikaori.jp/

UnDER GARDEN

You might get the sense that the series is wrapping up, and you might be right. The next volume will probably be the final one. What sort of finale will conclude the journeys of Lucille and company? I hope you'll pick up the volume 5 and see for yourselves.

Creator:
Kaori Yuki

Date of Birth:
December 18

Blood Type:
B

Major Works:
Angel Sanctuary and *The Cain Saga*

 aori Yuki was born in Tokyo and started drawing at a very early age. Following her debut work, *Natsufuku no Erie* (Ellie in Summer Clothes), in the Japanese magazine *Bessatsu Hana to Yume*, she wrote a compelling series of short stories: *Zankoku na Douwatachi* (Cruel Fairy Tales), *Neji* (Screw) and *Sareki Ókoku* (Gravel Kingdom).

As proven by her best-selling series *Angel Sanctuary*, *Godchild* and *Fairy Cube*, her celebrated body of work has etched an indelible mark on the Gothic comics genre. She likes mysteries and British films and is a fan of the movie *Dead Poets Society* and the show *Twin Peaks*.

GRAND GUIGNOL ORCHESTRA
Vol. 4
Shojo Beat Edition

STORY AND ART BY KAORI YUKI

Translation **Camellia Nieh**
Touch-up Art & Lettering **Eric Erbes**
Design **Fawn Lau**
Editor **Pancha Diaz**

GUIGNOL KYUTEI GAKUDAN by Kaori Yuki
© Kaori Yuki 2010
All rights reserved.
First published in Japan in 2010 by HAKUSENSHA, Inc., Tokyo.
English language translation rights arranged with HAKUSENSHA, Inc., Tokyo.

The rights of the author(s) of the work(s) in this publication to be so identified
have been asserted in accordance with the Copyright, Designs and Patents Act 1988.
A CIP catalogue record for this book is available from the British Library.

Printed in the U.S.A.

Published by VIZ Media, LLC
P.O. Box 77010
San Francisco, CA 94107

10 9 8 7 6 5 4 3 2 1
First printing, September 2011

www.viz.com

www.shojobeat.com

Love Kaori Yuki?

Read the rest of VIZ Media's Kaori Yuki collection!

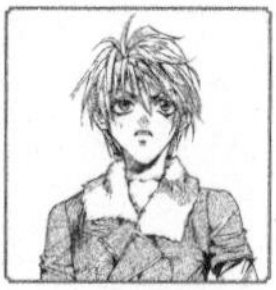

Angel Sanctuary • Rated T+ for Older Teen • 20 Volumes

The angel Alexiel loved God, but she rebelled against Heaven. As punishment, she is sent to Earth to live an endless series of tragic lives. She now inhabits the body of Setsuna Mudo, a troubled teen wrought with forbidden love.

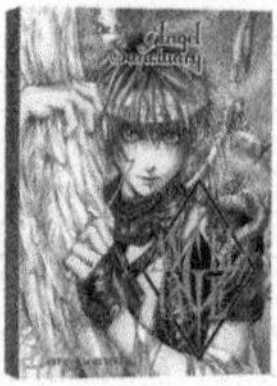
Angel Sanctuary

The Art of Angel Sanctuary: Angel Cage

The Art of Angel Sanctuary 2: Lost Angel

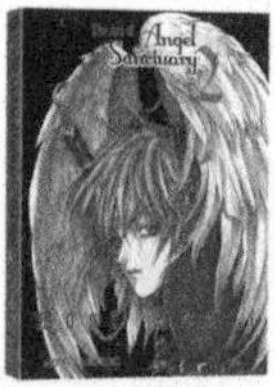
Angel Sanctuary

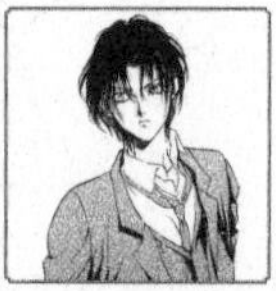

The Cain Saga • Rated M for Mature Readers • 5 Volumes

The prequel to the *Godchild* series, *The Cain Saga* follows the young Cain as he attempts to unravel the secrets of his birth. Delve into the tortured past of Earl Cain C. Hargreaves! Plus bonus short stories in each volume!

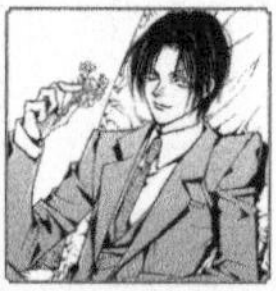

Godchild • Rated T+ for Older Teen • 8 Volumes

In 19th century London, dashing young nobleman Earl Cain Hargreaves weaves his way through the shadowy cobblestone streets that hide the dark secrets of aristocratic society. His mission is to solve the mystery of his shrouded lineage.

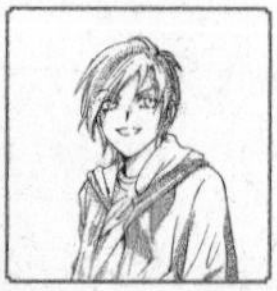

Fairy Cube • Rated T+ for Older Teen • 3 Volumes

Ian and Rin used to just *see* spirits. Now Ian *is* one. Using the Fairy Cube, Ian must figure out how to stop the lizard-spirit Tokage from taking over his life and destroying any chance he has of resurrection.

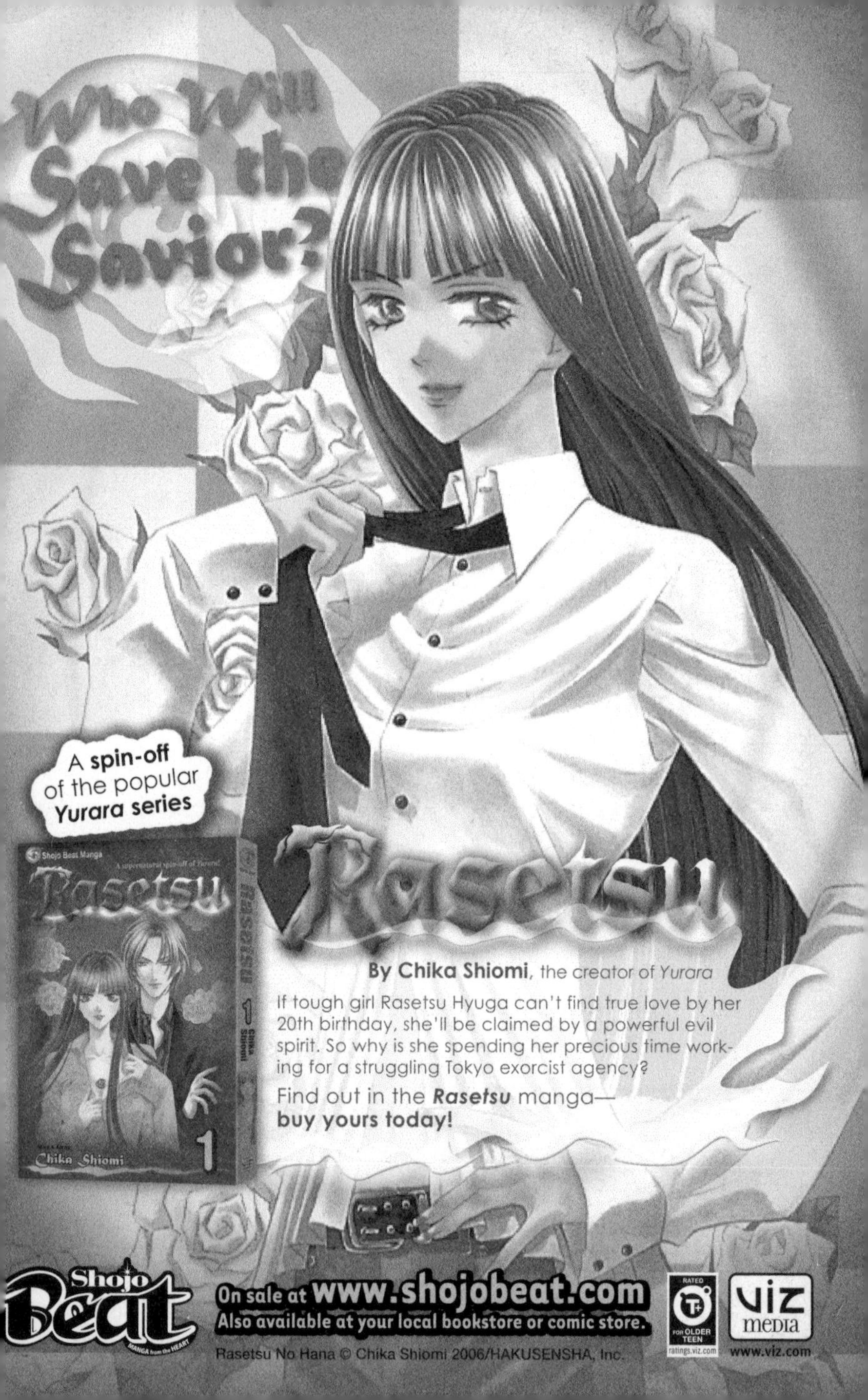
Who Will Save the Savior?
A spin-off of the popular Yurara series
Shojo Beat Manga
A supernatural spin-off of Yurara!
Rasetsu
1
Chika Shiomi
Rasetsu
By Chika Shiomi, the creator of Yurara
If tough girl Rasetsu Hyuga can't find true love by her 20th birthday, she'll be claimed by a powerful evil spirit. So why is she spending her precious time working for a struggling Tokyo exorcist agency?
Find out in the Rasetsu manga—buy yours today!
Shojo Beat
MANGA from the HEART
On sale at www.shojobeat.com
Also available at your local bookstore or comic store.
RATED T+ FOR OLDER TEEN
ratings.viz.com
VIZ media
www.viz.com
Rasetsu No Hana © Chika Shiomi 2006/HAKUSENSHA, Inc.

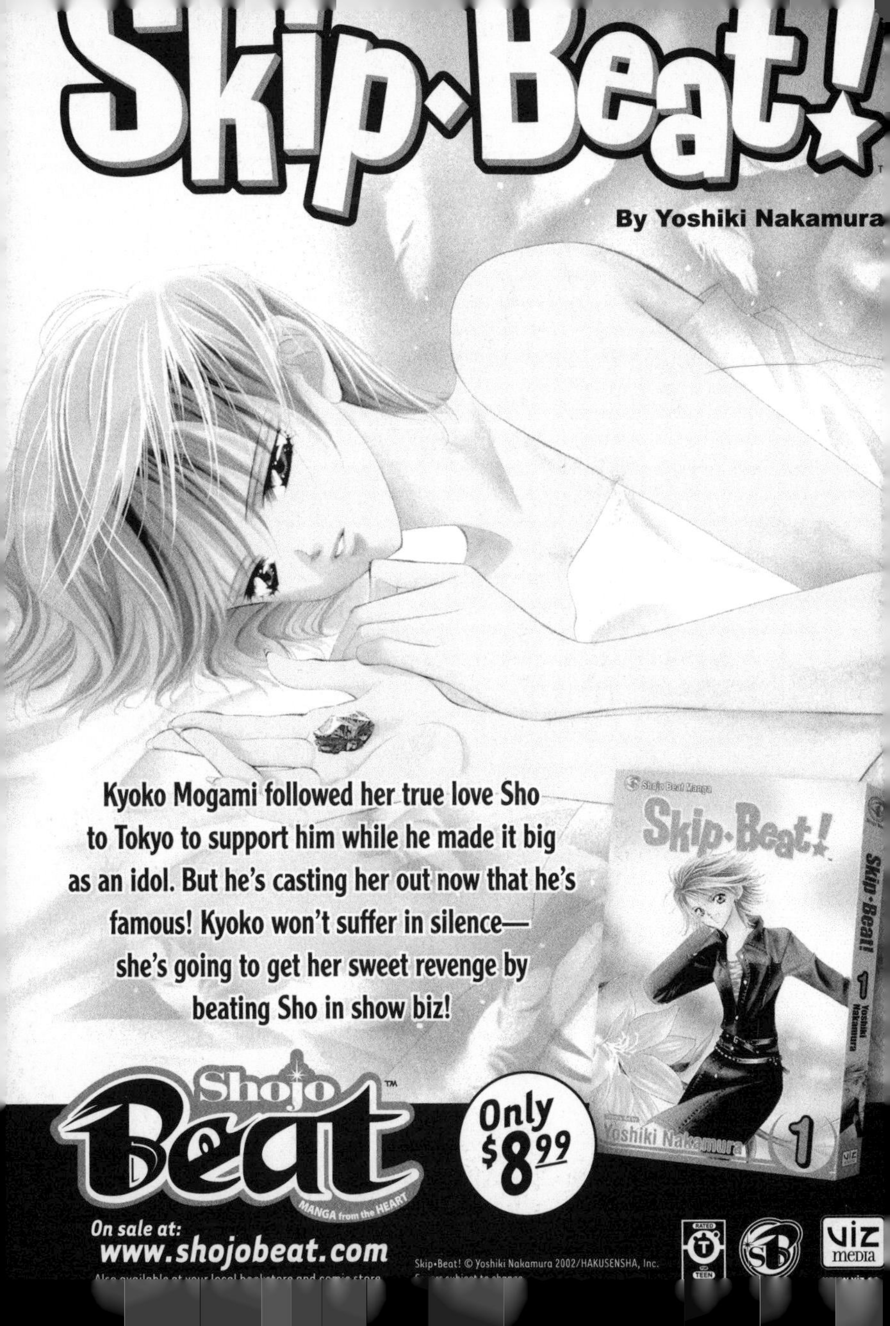
Skip•Beat!
By Yoshiki Nakamura
Kyoko Mogami followed her true love Sho to Tokyo to support him while he made it big as an idol. But he's casting her out now that he's famous! Kyoko won't suffer in silence—she's going to get her sweet revenge by beating Sho in show biz!
Shojo Beat Manga
Skip•Beat!
Skip•Beat! 1 Yoshiki Nakamura
Yoshiki Nakamura
1
Shojo Beat
MANGA from the HEART
Only $8.99
On sale at:
www.shojobeat.com
Skip•Beat! © Yoshiki Nakamura 2002/HAKUSENSHA, Inc.
RATED T TEEN
viz media

The secret the Day Class at Cross Academy doesn't know:
the Night Class is full of **vampires!**

VAMPIRE KNIGHT

Story & Art by **Matsuri Hino**
Creator of *Captive Hearts* and *MeruPuri*

Read where it
all began in the
manga

Get the Official Fanbook
with character sketches,
storyboards, student ID
card, color pages and
exclusive creator interview

Own original
and uncut
episodes on DVD

Get the complete collection at **store.viz.com**
Also available at your local bookstore or comic store.

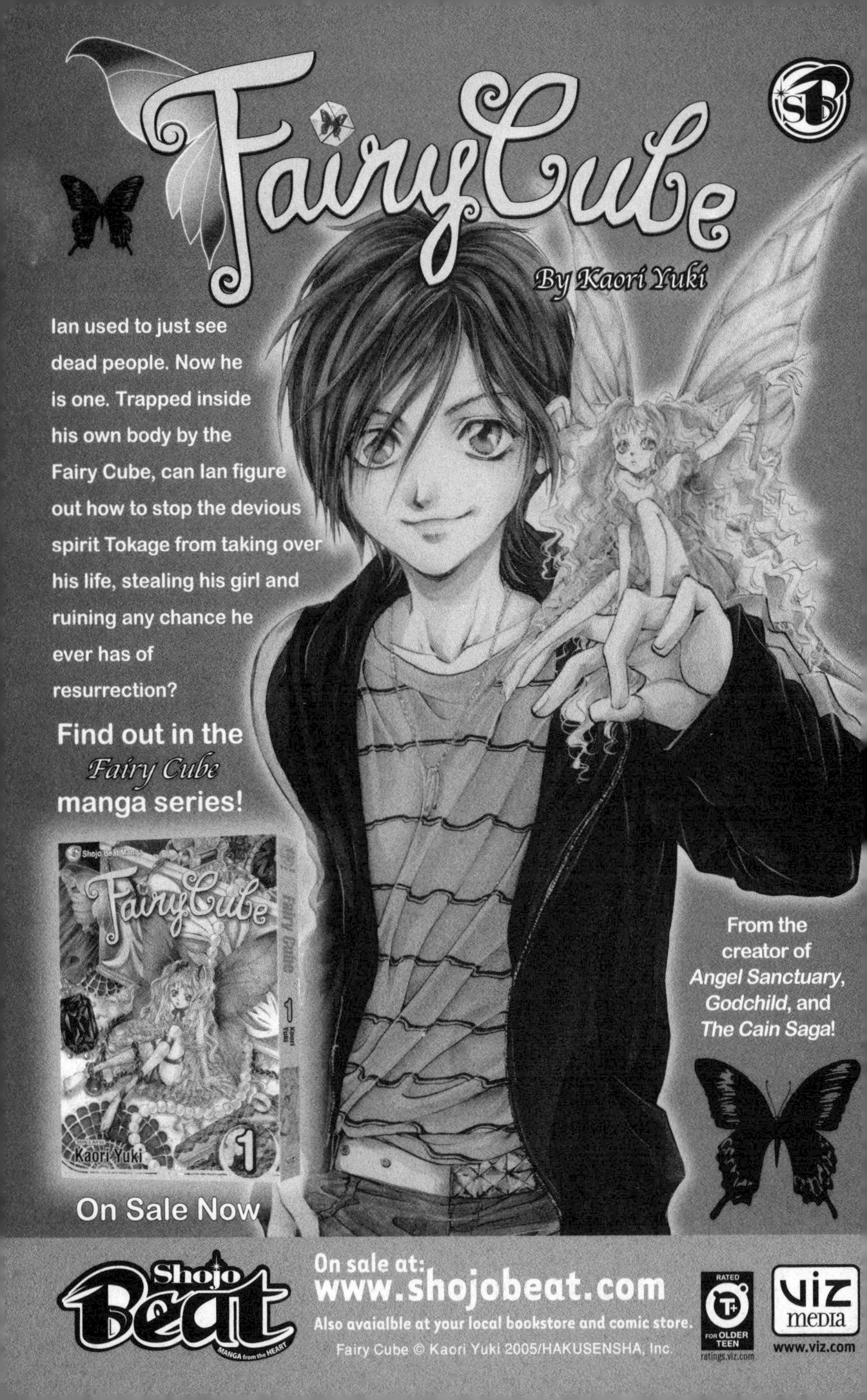

Fairy Cube
By Kaori Yuki
Ian used to just see dead people. Now he is one. Trapped inside his own body by the Fairy Cube, can Ian figure out how to stop the devious spirit Tokage from taking over his life, stealing his girl and ruining any chance he ever has of resurrection?
Find out in the Fairy Cube manga series!
Shojo Beat Manga
Fairy Cube
1
Kaori Yuki
On Sale Now
From the creator of Angel Sanctuary, Godchild, and The Cain Saga!
Shojo Beat
MANGA from the HEART
On sale at:
www.shojobeat.com
Also avaialble at your local bookstore and comic store.
Fairy Cube © Kaori Yuki 2005/HAKUSENSHA, Inc.
RATED
T+
FOR OLDER TEEN
ratings.viz.com
VIZ media
www.viz.com